And it all ended
with #TrueLove

T0692729

MEDIA

NEW YORK TIMES BESTSELLING AUTHOR

JA HUSS

By JA Huss

Edited by RJ Locksley
Copyright © 2017 by J. A. Huss
All rights reserved.
ISBN- 978-1-936413-86-7

SOCIAL MEDIA SERIES BOOK FOUR

STATUS

NEW YORK TIMES BESTSELLING AUTHOR

JA HUSS

Chapter One - Grace

#NotTheGirlWithTheWorldsBiggestProblems

KRISTI AND I drive in silence for almost thirty minutes. We're going east, I know that much, because the sun is glaring ahead of us and my sunglasses are missing from my little purse. I prop my head on my hand and lean into the window, the air-conditioning blaring into my face, which in combination with the sun forces me to close my eyes.

What did we do last night? Asher was so convinced that I talked. But I never talk. Why would I say those things to him? I do remember some things, I wasn't being entirely truthful with him. But he shocked me. How did he find out about my parents? How did all these people suddenly figure out who I am?

OK, Grace. Think hard. Did you tell him things? What happened after you went upstairs?

I remember the rug. God, I love that rug. And the pink champagne. That was delicious. We did have sex. And it was… my face heats up. It was spectacular, as usual. If there's one thing Vaughn Asher knows, it's his way around a woman's body. He knows all the sweet spots.

Sweets. He called me that all night. I remember that too. He said… *I'll be yours if you'll be mine.*

And I said…

Kristi sniffs back a sob and I open my eyes to look over at her. She has not spoken a word since we got on the freeway and right now she's deep in thought, chewing on her thumbnail.

I wonder if she's worried about ruining her manicure for the wedding. She can't really be thinking of ditching Johnny Blazen. Can she? Is this all my fault? For projecting my insecurities about Vaughn onto her situation? God, I am a horrible person. Because she probably does love that guy and I'm using her right now because she's helping me escape from Vaughn and the media.

That whole thing hits me hard and I just close my eyes again and shake my head. All these years I've been left alone. No one knew Bebe's mother was my lawyer during my trial because she practices law under her maiden name. And I don't know if people just couldn't stomach my reality, so they blocked it out, or if they just wanted to believe the fairytale ending. That my life went back to normal and I got the happily ever after. Either way, they lost interest in me. And even though it took many years of support from a small group of people who helped me through that time in my life, I did, in fact, recover.

Time is my friend. The more time between then and now, the better I get. I'm not broken any more. I'm really not.

"Do you think I'm crazy?" Kristi asks.

I look over at her again. She's tapping her fingernail on the steering wheel now, looking like a mess. The car is her wedding present from Johnny. A replacement for the 2008 model she's been driving in Denver. "I think it's cold feet, Kristi. I'm a complete fuckup. You should not listen to a damn word I say. I was reeling from that whole pregnancy thing with Vaughn." Just saying his name is enough to make my heart ache. I don't say any more and Kristi drops it as well.

I like the silence.

She turns the Mercedes into a driveway with one of those rustic entry arches cattle ranches have. *Red Desert Resort*, the sign hanging from the arch states.

"What's this place?" I ask, sitting up a little straighter.

Kristi looks over at me, her eyes red and teary. "My childhood home."

"Oh, you have family here? I didn't know that. Why didn't they come to the rehearsal dinner last night?"

She sucks in a sob and then places a hand over her chest to steady herself. "Because they hate me."

I just stare at her, trying to process her words. And I realize I know absolutely nothing about this woman. Aside from her being the almost-future Mrs. Blazen, I've not gathered any facts about her. I'm a terrible friend. "Should we go somewhere else?"

She ignores my question. Or maybe she just can't answer it right now. Silence is your friend when you're keeping secrets. So she just keeps driving. The road curves around and then we are at a guard house with a stop gate. Kristi pulls up to the guard and buzzes her window down with one hand while shuffling though a purse resting on the center console with the other. She finds her wallet and flips it open

"Can I help you, ma'am? The resort is closed right now, we're not accepting guests."

Kristi says nothing to him, just hands him her driver's license.

He takes it, studies it, and then looks at Kristi like he's trying to make a decision. "They're not here," he finally says. "They're on vacation."

Kristi straightens her shoulders and tips her chin up, steeling herself to be brave. "I'm not here to see *them*. Now open the fucking gate."

"Yes, ma'am." He retreats back into the guard house. The barrier lifts and our way forward opens up. Kristi buzzes her window up and drives off.

"What was that all about?" I ask. "You really grew up here?"

"Yes. My grandparents owned it, then when they died five years ago, the ownership was split up between me, my brother, and my parents." She looks over at me. "My partial ownership is the only reason I'm allowed to be here right now. I'm what you call the black sheep."

I have to admit, that surprises me. Perfect Kristi is the black sheep? "How? Why?"

She shakes her head. "It's a long story. I wanted my wedding to be in Vegas on the off-chance my parents would actually show up, but"—she looks over at me—"I guess that was a huge fail, right?"

I slump back into my seat. Her disappointment fills me up and makes me weary. I'm not the only one with problems. I sometimes forget that fact. This is how I get when I'm Daisy instead of Grace. I start thinking that I own the title of Girl with the World's Biggest Problems.

That's why I changed my name and started a new life. Daisy is a victim. Daisy is weak, and sick, and pathetic. Grace is graceful. Grace is strong, and determined, and brave. I've tried so hard to put my past away. Just lock it up and forget about it. Be the new girl. Be Grace.

But this today... I just don't know what it might mean. Will I ever be able to go back to being just Grace? Will I have to be Daisy again? Will I be some very fucked-up version of both of them?

I just don't know.

The road winds a little and there are thick patches of juniper and spruce trees, so when we finally round a corner and the resort comes into view, I'm breathless. I drop the pity party and take it all in. "Wow. It's stunning." There's a huge lake, man-made obviously, surrounded by a scattering of bungalows. The main building is a Santa Fe-style adobe, with a large terrace filled with empty tables. A café, I realize.

We pull up to the valet area, but no one comes to take our car. Kristi shuts the engine down and we just sit for a moment. "I knew they would be gone, I guess. What did I expect?" She looks over at me and a tear slips down her cheek. "They close the place down every year at this time so they can travel. So I planned the wedding during vacation and sent the invitation. Hoping, ya know?"

I nod. Because I get it. I get that desperation, that one last grab for love and acceptance. I had friends and relatives back in my hometown, but half of them thought I was guilty at first. And I can't live with people who think I could've done what I was accused of. The other half kept pestering me for 'my story'. They wanted me to talk to the media. Get paid for interviews. Write a book about my experience.

Use me. They wanted to use me. So I pulled back, severed all ties, and boxed that life up and packed it away. And ever since then I've had this wall around me. Oh, it's transparent, people get in, but there's a limit as to how close. Even Bebe. When I think about it, I'm a little bit ashamed that I never told her everything. I know she'd be there for me. But when you're safe, why invite the danger in?

I guess I can relate to Vaughn in that respect. He has his own wall. No authentic relationships. And if I had been honest with him about… well, pretty much anything… then he'd have bounced that question right back to me.

Because all my relationships are fake too.

The temperature in the car is rising fast, and the rush of hot wind as Kristi opens her door draws me back to my reality. We're on the run and now we're stopped. Decisions have to be made. "So what are we doing here, Kristi? Do you have keys to get in?"

She's wringing her hands in her lap with worry. "My brother is here. He was going to come to the wedding, but I called him last night and talked to him for a long time and he…"

I suddenly have a vision of Vaughn and his sister on her wedding night. How she went to him to confide her fears. How he was afraid of influencing her. "What did he say?" I ask. I need to know. I need to know this so badly because it's just not fair that I don't have a big brother to call for help. "What did he tell you?"

"He told me to come home and he'd make it all better." And then Kristi looks past me and a sob escapes. I turn to find what's grabbed her attention, and there he is. Her brother. Standing there in the huge doorway that leads into the lobby.

He smiles at her and she's out of the car so fast, running into his arms, I am left confused and feeling out of place. I'm spying on that private moment again. The one where people have actual blood relatives who love them. The one where little sisters get to run to big brothers and get everything they need in a hug. The one I wish for so badly it makes my chest hurt.

Kristi's brother embraces her and all those saved-up sobs come pouring out.

I get out of the car and wander up to them. He is whispering softly to Kristi now, telling her all the things a woman needs to hear after she runs out on her wedding day.

And then he notices me for the first time and gives me a smile as well. He's obviously older—the small lines around his eyes tell me that. And he's nice-looking. Rugged and rustic. Like he's lived on a desert ranch his whole life. He's wearing jeans, not shorts, which, when paired with the boots, makes him look a little bit cowboy. The white t-shirt is now stained with Kristi's make-up and he notices me staring at it and laughs. "You're ruining my shirt, Krissy! You didn't say you were bringing a friend. I'm Jack," he says, peeling an arm from around Kristi to extend it my way. "Jack Bolton."

Bolton. I never even bothered to press her for her last name. I shake his hand out of habit, but then my mouth goes dry and I'm not sure what to say back. I'm a whirling mess of guilt, regret, fear, and sorrow all twisted together right now.

"This is Grace, Jack. She's in the same situation as me."

I squint my eyes at her. "Not really." No matter what her secret is, she's so much better off than me. And maybe that's selfish to think my problems are more overwhelming. It probably is. But I'd give anything to be running away from a wedding right now instead of the past.

"The media is after her. And so is Vaughn Asher."

"Oh." Jack Bolton looks me up and down and nods slowly. "Well, that's quite a combination. Care to elaborate?"

I hesitate and he takes the hint.

"Never mind," he says. "Come on, let's go inside. Have you eaten?" he asks us as he leads Kristi inside, his protective arm still around her.

"No," Kristi answers.

I follow them, trailing behind like a lost puppy. I haven't felt this pathetic in years. A decade, in fact.

They stare at me with suspicion and questions... and blame. Aunt Rachel, who was always my favorite, narrows her eyes at me as I walk past and take a seat in the small living room. I fold my hands in my lap, pressing them together so hard they ache, and stare at them. Not daring to lift my head.

"What happened, Daisy?" they all ask. It's like, simultaneous. That demand comes out of their mouths in various forms and tones. But it all leads back to the same thing everyone has been hinting at since I came back.

What did you do to bring this tragedy upon our family?

Kristi, Jack, and I travel through the main lobby of the resort, which is decorated Santa Fe-style to match the desert exterior. My eyes are all over Jack Bolton and I am insanely jealous. I haven't thought about him in a long time, but I had a big brother once. I had a home, too. And parents.

I'm not talking. I decided that back in the hospital. I'm not talking. I'm not saying one word to these people. The nurses were nice but they started asking me questions that I not only didn't understand, but scared me to death. Sex, I knew they were asking me about sex. Did he touch me? What does that mean? Of course he touched me. Did I fight him? I don't understand that one either. Of course I fought him. Did he hurt me? That one I get, but that was after the other two. Maybe if they had started with did he hurt me, I'd have talked...

I want my mom and dad and brother so badly right now. I should call Bebe and my other parents, but I can't. I feel like it would be a monumental step backwards to run to them with this grief. After all they did for me—after all the time and effort and, yes, love, they poured into me to make me better—admitting I'm not OK, that I've been hiding behind a name, would be a slap in the face.

Kristi, Jack, and I arrive at the cafe before all those memories begin to surface and then I force myself to come out of the past—out of my nightmare—and try my best to live in my prefabricated fantasy.

I desperately need that fantasy life. Reality is really not my thing. Because my reality is… my entire family is dead. And now that I think about it, I remember something Vaughn Asher asked me last night. *Isn't it better to live?*

But when you are the reason your whole family is dead… then no. No, it's not better to live. How do I live with the guilt of knowing I'm the reason they were murdered?

Chapter Two - Vaughn

#ThingsYouCantUnknow

"TALK TO me, Ray. How is no one tracking that car? How is the paparazzi not tracking that car?"

"They gave them the slip on the Strip, V. That crazy football wife bossed her way through traffic and made a turn. Then they just lost them."

"Is that a rental car? Did someone get plates?"

"I don't think it's a rental car, it's got a temporary plate taped to the back window. But the tint is so dark, no one could read them. I put a call into Johnny Blazen, but he hasn't gotten back to me."

Fuck. I scrub a hand down my face and just stand in the middle of my hotel bedroom. "We need to find Grace, Ray. Before the media does. I don't think they know any more than they are reporting at this point, but Conner said that there's more to her story and whatever that *more* is, I don't want Grace to see it on TV before we find her."

"I understand, boss." Ray says that in his I'm-here-to-fix-things voice. "No matter who that car belongs to, it has to have GPS and is probably linked to a private security system that can access the location of the vehicle. So I'll keep trying Blazen and see if we can't figure out which room is his from hotel sources."

"OK, thanks." I end the call and walk over to the bed and sit down.

My bare feet can't help but appreciate the soft sheepskin rug and that makes me smile. Grace brought it in here last night so that the first thing she would feel when she got up to start her day was the soft fur. I lean over and pick up the empty champagne bottle. We did drink a lot of champagne last night.

Does she really not remember?

God, that kills me. I mean, I knew we were both pretty drunk by that point, but hell, I had no idea she was *that* drunk. I'd never do that against her will. That's just wrong.

And if she really doesn't remember, there's a chance she could remember at any moment. What if something jogs her memory and we're not together to discuss it?

Ah, fuck. I grab my hair with both fists. "Fuck! Why does this have to happen now? Of all times?"

I turn on the TV and flip on the cable news. Midday news is mostly gossip and right now the Bellagio, Grace Kinsella, Vaughn Asher, Johnny Blazen, and Kristi the Fiancée are the only things people are talking about.

And then the picture of Daisy Bryndle goes up. Grace, age thirteen. The murder scene at her home, a farmhouse out in the middle of nowhere. The missing child reports that went out all over the country as they searched for her. Both as a suspect in the murder of her family and as a missing child.

So confused were authorities on how to process the scene in a way that made sense, Grace was even on the FBI's Most Wanted List. It was removed less than forty-eight hours after issue, but that's not the point. A thirteen-year-old girl was on the FBI Most Wanted List. But they had to put someone on the list, I guess. They had no suspects other than Grace, even though it was highly unlikely that she would've been able to commit these murders alone.

The screen flashes to our fight outside the hotel. She's crazed, I can tell. Her eyes are wild and they are darting all over the place. Trying to take in the scene. Trying to come to terms with the fact that the life she built, no matter how fake and fabricated, is over.

I want to stop watching as the scene repeats over and over, but I can't. I just want to see her face. I just want to be able to see her face and I don't have any pictures of her.

Wait. I reach for my phone on the nightstand and pull up my videos.

I smile big as I press play. It's of the two of us arguing on the beach that first night we met. It's only like a fifteen-second video, but I play it over and over. Because even though she's mad, she's not sad. She's not scared. She's vibrant and alive. She's full of fight and demands.

That footage they are running outside the Bellagio, that's not Grace at all.

That's Daisy Bryndle.

Scared, defeated, lost Daisy Bryndle.

The door chimes and I walk out to the foyer and open it up. "Felicity, thank God." She comes in without saying a word and takes a seat on the couch. She pulls out her laptop and sets it on the coffee table.

"Conner is on his way. He's getting things set up for the Tray thing."

"Did he tell you what happened to Grace?"

"Not all of it, he says some of it he needs to tell you in person. And I'd just like to caution you, V. Make sure this is how you want to find out about it. Because once you know, you can't unknow. Things can't be unknown, you understand?"

"I need to know," I say quickly. "I need to know now."

"Why?" Felicity asks, with an edge to her question. "Why do you need to know? Because if this will change your opinion about her, then I'd advise you to drop it. And drop *her* while you're at it. Because this girl, Vaughn, she needs a win right now. She really needs a win. She needs someone who will stand by her, because this shit is about to get…" Felicity pauses, her eyes searching mine.

"What? It's about to get what?"

"Disgusting. Revolting. Nauseating. Repulsive. It's about to stop being about who murdered her family and start being about something else entirely. Something much, much worse."

I sit on the couch opposite Felicity and stare at her. "You of all people, Felicity, should know me better."

She nods and swallows hard. "I know, V. I do know you better, but I just need to make sure. Because Grace is gonna need you. She's gonna need you like I needed you. And she's never gonna admit that, ya know?"

"Like you never wanted to admit that, either."

Felicity nods. "Yeah. Because this shit is private. And I don't really want to show you, but I have always known you to be a good man, Vaughn. I know you have a shitty reputation and I also know you've earned it. But those people who see that side of you, they are the outsiders. Us insiders know that there's a big difference between the man and the actor."

"Felicity, I promise you. I have no intention of walking away because of what I find out. I promise you."

She lets out a long breath and then she pulls up a file. A police report. "This is her criminal file. All public record stuff, sealed, of course, since she asked the court to do that on her eighteenth birthday. Police report, pictures of the crime scene, which I am telling you now, you do not want to see." Felicity stares hard at me. "The perp used a knife. Enough said. And all kinds of other procedural things that go into a criminal file. This was not hard to get, but there's something else mentioned in this file that's not accessible. Her health records. I can't get those, Vaughn. I can't. I mean, I *could*, but I'd probably go to prison. Besides, it's one thing to go looking at her prescriptions at the drug store to see if she's on the pill. Yeah, I'm a cunt for doing that for you. But it's baby shit compared to what might be in those hidden records from her teens."

The blood leaves my face. My hands go cold, my legs start to shake, and my heart speeds up. "What happened?"

"She was not the murderer. The lawyer convinced the FBI somehow. Got Daisy to make one statement. Only one. These were the only words she gave to authorities. Ever. And she said…" Felicity pulls up another page on the computer. Another procedural form with the title *Witness Statement* at the top. She zooms in to find a signature at the bottom. Daisy Bryndle.

And then she scrolls up to the portion where the witness gets to write down what they saw. There's only one sentence and it says, 'I was abducted.'

I realize I'm holding my breath and when I read that sentence, it all comes rushing out. "How long was she missing?" I ask.

"Eight months."

I have to sit down. "And what happened to her during that time?"

"They have no idea."

I have to take deep breaths. "Where is the guy who took her?"

"They have no idea."

I stand back up. "So he's still out there?"

Felicity shrugs her shoulders. "I have no idea. These are things Grace never told anyone, as far as I can see. There are no statements. There's a mention of psychiatric appointments, but that's it. Just a mention. All those health records are locked away with whoever was treating her at the time."

"Is there a mention of the doctor's name?" I ask.

"Redacted in all documents."

"Well, if we can't get it, chances are no one can. So that's good, right?"

Felicity shrugs again. "For Grace's sake, V, let's hope so."

Chapter Three - Vaughn

#ThingsYouCantUnknowTakeTwo

I WANT to make a drink. Hell, I want to just sit down and get drunk, if I'm really being honest. But I can't. Grace needs me. So I sit on the couch and stare out the floor-to-ceiling windows that look out onto the Bellagio fountain lake and wait for Conner.

I'm impatient and my leg has been bouncing since Felicity stopped talking. She's been on the phone ever since, getting me things. Ordering room service, even though I'm not hungry. Calling Conner to coordinate the money drop to Tray, even though I should be doing that myself. And biting her nails.

It's been almost two hours since she came in and threw my whole world out of orbit. "Is she really in danger?" I ask Felicity as she ends another call and sits down next to me. "Because if so, Conner is taking way too long."

"Well, he got a hold of Johnny Blazen, who confirmed that the white Mercedes was a gift for his wife-to-be. The car is in her name and since they're not married yet, he has no access to the GPS location services. He's working his celebrity magic, Conner said, but it might take a few more hours to get that info. He's got a team of lawyers on it, so we just have to hold tight and hope that Kristi woman knows what the hell she's doing."

The door chimes and I jump up and cross the room in a few paces. I open the door and Conner is staring at me with a very serious face. "I've got the money."

"How much did he want?"

"Ten million."

Huh. I wave Conner in and close the door. "It's almost not fair, is it?"

"What's not fair?" Conner asks.

"It's like cheating luck."

He just shoots me a confused look.

"I won ten million dollars last night in punto banco."

"Well, dude," Conner replies, "if it makes you feel any better, luck is about to kick your ass. So I wouldn't be too guilt-ridden about your apparent win just yet. Think of it as a good omen instead." He walks into the living room and looks over at Felicity, who says nothing to him—there is no love lost between those two—and then takes a seat on the couch.

"Vaughn." Felicity breaks our uneasy silence and stands up to block me from taking a seat across from Conner. "Before you let him tell you anything else, you had better be sure you want to go behind her back like this. Because Grace strikes me as a grudge-holder. She didn't want you to know about her past for a reason. You should respect that."

"Her life is in danger, Felicity," Conner barks at her. "This is not a time for sappy bullshit like respecting her privacy."

Felicity throws up her hands. "I'm just telling you from a woman's point of view. If you take this secret from her, she might not forgive you."

I look over at Conner and he's frowning. "I'm just gonna take your choice away, Vaughn, OK? Make it easy on you. They think—"

But I put up a hand and he stops. "No," I say. "Felicity is right. I know enough. I know enough to realize I need to find her and keep her safe. That's all I need right now. I want to hear the story from her, and only when she's ready to tell it. Just tell me one thing. Is she in danger?"

"She could be, Vaughn. I don't know for sure. But all this media attention is not good. It's an invitation. They never caught the guy. And I'm not saying he's still got tabs on her, but he could have."

"OK, then let's get this Tray stuff started and then hopefully Blazen will have the car security hand over her location. What are we even doing? What did Tray actually say?"

"That guy is a scumbag," Felicity says.

Conner shoots her a look and she shuts up. He gets up and paces over to the window to look out. "He was collaborating with the media the entire time, Vaughn. In addition to suddenly being the only guy with info on your

Grace, he also has video of Sam." Conner gives me a sidelong glance. "Incriminating video."

"She told me she was a virgin."

"Not sex tapes, you idiot. That…" He looks over at Felicity and I can practically read his mind and shake my head at him. "That other stuff."

I shake my head again. "She doesn't do that anymore."

"She does, V. She does. And he's got her on tape. And as horrible as it would be for her secret to get out, who really gives a fuck? Right? The world is not going to care. But Sam won't be able to see it that way. She will not handle this well."

I sigh. My poor sister has been afflicted with worry since she was small. She's fragile and vulnerable. I thought I was doing the right thing when I got her away from Tray, but maybe that was the worst possible solution? Maybe I made things worse? Made Tray more vengeful and angry? "Did you know that her disorder was manifesting before Tray did?" My words are accusatory, but I don't care because he's nodding his head yes. "Why the fuck didn't you say anything to me?"

"I only suspected," he clarifies. "I saw her do something strange last Christmas. Right after she and Tray started dating. But none of that matters. What matters is that we pay this asshole and get those videos back and figure out what he knows about Grace."

"What if he keeps copies of Sam?" Felicity asks, still chewing on her fingernails.

Conner shoots her a sneer. "We're gonna get the copies, kid. Don't you worry about that."

Felicity stiffens, but says nothing back. She's an expert at quitting while she's ahead.

"So how did he get all this info on Grace?" I ask.

"Your guess is as good as mine."

"Well, the obvious guess is also the most dangerous," Felicity says. "What if that person who abducted her and never got caught somehow got to Tray?"

"But why? And how would Tray know that Grace would be part of this deal? It just exploded on the media today. Meeting Grace on the island was a fluke. It wasn't something you could predict."

We stare at each other, unwilling to consider the alternative. That everything about Grace was a setup to get the two of us together. To put this all in front of the world again. To maybe... make another spectacle when she disappeared a second time. "Jesus Christ. We need to shake the fuck out of Tray." I stand up and start towards the door, but Conner is in front of me, pushing me back to the living room.

"Calm down, Vaughn. We have to think this through. We've only got one chance to set it right. And we're not even sure that the guy from her teens is even involved. It could be that Tray is an expert dickhead."

Not likely.

Not fucking likely.

But that's what we go with to ease our minds and keep ourselves on track because that's all we can do right now. To put a voice to the most likely situation is a sure way to invite it to happen. I don't know what really happened to Grace during those eight months she was missing with an abductor. And maybe I never need to know. If that's what she decides, OK. I'll respect that. But the media… the media does not respect boundaries. There will be no reprieve from them.

Chapter Four - Grace

#ThisIsHowYouMakeAnEntrance

THE FAMILY resort is spectacular, even though the three of us are by ourselves and the only food Kristi's brother Jack is capable of offering is a few frozen dinners.

Kristi and I scarf them down like we are starving. She's pregnant, so she's always eating, and I don't even remember the last time I ate—literally, I have no recollection of that dinner with Vaughn last night—so my mind doesn't even count it as eating.

Jack fills Kristi in on various resort news while we eat. They built a new barn. They added a new hiking package to the list of services. They hired a spa director who only speaks Swedish. And then he must run out of small talk, because he folds his hands, steeples two fingers against his chin, and just outright asks about the elephant in the room.

"So, you wanna tell me how you got into all this trouble or not?"

"Will you listen and not judge me?" Kristi asks, the tears threatening to roll down her cheeks.

"I've never judged you, sis. You know that."

"You took their side."

"You stole half a million dollars, for fuck's sake!"

"It was *my* money!"

Holy shit. I have no idea what's going on. "Maybe I should just excuse myself so you two can talk."

"No, Grace," Kristi pleads as she grabs my wrist. "Please don't leave me alone."

I settle back into my chair and nod. She's been a good friend to me. Being here for her confession is the least I can do for her.

"I had a gambling problem," she says to me and not her brother. So I guess this is not news to him. "I had a big debt. I own one fourth of this resort." This she does direct to her brother.

"Yeah, but just because the bank account says there's money in there doesn't give you a right to take it, Kristi. It's called embezzlement. We could've pressed charges."

"It was still my *share*, Jack." She turns her attention to me. "It was my money. They wanted me to reinvest it and I said no." Again, her attention goes to Jack and then back to me. "I just needed to start again. I needed to wipe my debt, Grace. And leave Nevada to get away from my temptations."

"But your wedding!" I exclaim.

"I know," she says. "It was a big risk, and if I'm honest, that's probably why I'm so freaked out about everything. I wanted my parents to come to my wedding. I wanted them to forgive me and tell me I'm still their daughter. I do have a problem with gambling. So after I paid off my debt I left and moved to Denver and got a job as a makeup artist at the local TV station. Taking that money and giving myself a second chance was the best thing that ever happened to me because…" She looks over at her brother for this part. "Because that job led me to Johnny." She swallows hard. "His wife, actually. I met her first and she had a proposition for me—"

"Oh, fuck," her brother says, standing up. "Please tell me you're not involved in some underground *Fifty Shades* of kinky fuckery."

My eyes go wide and I look away.

"Of course not, you asshole. It's just—" She looks at me, then her brother and then back to me. "Grace, it's just his wife, she… she couldn't conceive. So they asked me to be their surrogate, and I agreed. They gave me that house in Park Hill. They set me up with health insurance. They paid me a lot of money. But then… after the pregnancy was confirmed, Mrs. Blazen changed her mind. She said I had to get an abortion. She couldn't raise another woman's child and pretend it was her own."

"Oh, shit."

"I refused, obviously. And Johnny refused as well. And that's why they got divorced. I never slept with him. I've been trying to tell you for weeks, but the NDA was technically still in place, and I wasn't allowed to talk about it."

"They were gonna hide it? Fake everyone out and pretend Mrs. Blazen was the birth mother?"

Kristi nods and then looks over at her brother. "She didn't want anyone to know it wasn't her child. She didn't want anyone to know I was the real mother. And now she doesn't want anyone to know what a heartless cunt she is after I said no to the abortion. And Johnny has been so great about the whole thing. He said… he said he wanted to give parenting a try. Together, you know? And God, he's so handsome. And sweet, Grace. He's so perfect. That's why I got so mad at you last night."

I am a grade-A asshole. I feel so fucking stupid right now—even worse than I did earlier. Her relationship with Johnny Blazen really is a fantasy. It's beautiful and filled with trust and love. And I am just some jealous bitch who can't even keep a man, so I had to fuck it up for her by filling her head with stupidity. "I'm so sorry for telling you all those terrible things last night, Kristi."

She gives me a sad smile. "It's OK, Grace. I needed this time, I think. I just needed to take a step back from the situation and tell someone about it. That NDA was killing me. And now that I've said it out loud, I can start to make sense of my feelings. Do I really love him? I don't know. Maybe I only love the baby?"

"But obviously he loves the baby too or he wouldn't be going through all this."

"True," she says, her head bowed as she stares down at her stomach. "I just don't want the baby to be the only reason, you know?" She looks up at me and I do know.

Because that's exactly how I feel about Vaughn. I don't want him to want me just because we have this stupid arrangement where I let him dominate me sexually. "I want Johnny to love me for *me*."

"Why don't you just ask him?"

We both look over at Jack.

"I mean, it's not a fucking puzzle. OK? You take the guy aside and tell him what you just told us and see what he says. If he doesn't give you the answer you're looking for, well—" Jack throws up his hands. "Ditch him. Life's too short to settle for less than love, Krissy."

"But what if he doesn't love me and only wants the baby?"

"Then it's better to know. So you can move on. Get the custody worked out and find a guy who does love you."

Kristi wipes her tears and nods. "I'm sorry, Jack. I truly am sorry that I put myself first when I took that money out of the accounts. But I'm not that person anymore. I want to be this person now. And I want you guys to be a part of it."

Jack gets up and walks around the table to his sister. He pulls her to her feet and gives her a big brotherly hug. "Mom and Dad are in France, so they can't be here even if they wanted to. But if you decide to get married, Kris, I'll be there."

Kristi sobs, but she's cradled in his protective embrace. "I need some time to think. And then maybe I'll call Johnny tomorrow and talk things through with him."

I watch them as they put their broken relationship back together and wish, more than anything, that I could do the same for mine. But my family is gone and no amount of making good will ever bring them back.

Kristi gets up and excuses herself to the restroom and that leaves me alone with Jack. He's staring at me and I'm not sure what to do. "Um, sorry for barging in on your family time."

"So what's your story?" he asks. "You look worse than her." He jacks his thumb towards the restrooms on the other side of the empty cafe.

I scan the room and find a large TV mounted on a wall. "If you turn that one to the *Buzz Hollywood* channel, you'll see."

He raises one eyebrow at me. "*Buzz Hollywood*? Really? You're some bigshot actor in a bit of Vegas double?"

I laugh, but it's not funny. "No. I'm—well, I was—sorta dating…" I sigh. There's just no good way to explain this to a stranger. "Just turn the TV on."

"OK," he says as he gets up and walks behind the counter. A few seconds later the TV comes to life and he does a search for *Buzz Hollywood*. As soon as the channel comes up, there's my face. Up on the airwaves for everyone to see.

"Grace!" the voice yells on the TV. Then it shows me making a mad dash to Kristi's waiting Mercedes.

I sit in silence as the whole scene unfolds for Jack. After a few minutes he's got the gist of it and mutes the sound. "Well, that sucks."

I nod. "Yeah."

Kristi is back from the restroom now and she reaches over and squeezes my arm in support.

"You wanna tell us what happened?" Jack asks.

I swallow hard. "I met Vaughn Asher on Saint Thomas and he—"

"No," Jack interrupts. "Fuck Asher. What happened to you back *then?* That's what they're interested in. Not that actor. I remember that story. *Your* story," he corrects. "I remember you going missing. I remember thinking, fuck, she's probably dead by now. And I remember you coming back. The whole country was stunned. I was working in here that day, actually, and the whole place went silent. People were crying. And then they charged you with murder."

My throat is closing up and suddenly I can't swallow. My face becomes hot and prickly and the tears spring forth. They are running down my face before I can even blink. And the funny part—the thing that always gets me, makes me sadder than anything else—is hearing how people felt when they found out I was alive.

I don't know why that makes me so damn sad, but it's like a moment in their lives. My moment is their moment. And it's something people remember. All the people who knew the old me told me about their moment.

I was in the icecream store, buying a cone for my kids, the booking officer said as she fingerprinted me when I was charged with the murders. *And we sat in that icecream shop all afternoon with the rest of the customers, just watching the story unfold.*

Her day stood still.

I was at work and heard it on the radio, the receptionist at my psychiatrist's office said. *And then we turned on the break room TV and no one worked the rest of the day. Even the patients watched.*

When I came back, I stopped people's lives, that's how traumatic it was for them.

Now just imagine how traumatic it was for me.

"Oh my God, Grace. That was you?" Kristi scoots her chair closer to me and puts her arm around me.

I say nothing. Not even a nod.

"And then"—Jack picks right back up with his recollection, and my heart is beating so fast I think I might pass out—"you disappeared again. Just poof. They refused to answer any questions, just said the charges were dropped and that was the end of it. Daisy Bryndle disappeared off the face of the earth."

We sit in silence as I struggle to put Daisy away. It takes me a couple minutes of long, deep draws of air to calm myself. "I was adopted," I finally croak out. "A family adopted me." Jack just stares, like I'm going to elaborate, but I've been living with this secret for ten years. If he thinks this one conversation is enough to make me give it up, he's out of his mind.

He finally nods and accepts the fact that he won't be the first person to hear my story. "So what are you two gonna do?"

I shrug.

"We're gonna go sit at the pool and relax," Kristi says. "Sound good, Grace?"

I can't reply because there's a huge rock in my throat. It's stuck there, just waiting for me to say something so it can unleash all the pent-up sadness and fear.

So I just say nothing.

I don't care what we do now. As long as it doesn't involve talking about my past, I'm up for it.

Chapter Five - Vaughn

#ThingsYouCantUnknowTakeThree

CONNER'S PHONE rings and he looks over at me. "It's Tray." I nod at him and he accepts the call. "Yeah," he says, looking at me. Then he nods. I look over at Felicity and she's biting her nails. She gives me a tenuous smile. "Got it." And the call ends. "He's in a room down the hall."

"Well." I let out a sarcastic laugh. "How convenient. Doesn't he just think of everything?"

"We ready?" Conner asks, ignoring my statement.

I look over at Felicity and she shrugs. "Good luck."

"Thanks."

Conner and I exit the room. He checks the plaques on the wall that tell us where to go to find the room Tray is waiting in, and then we take a left and walk around the corner.

"Remind me why this is a good idea?"

"Vaughn, are you in or not? We've got ten seconds to decide. He's got video of Sam. Do you really want that shit on YouTube tonight?"

I stop walking and grab his arm to make him stop with me. "Is it bad? That Sam stuff? I mean, what are we talking about here?"

"It was last Christmas, just after they met."

"Did you ask her about it?"

Conner laughs. "Are you crazy? That's enough to set her off right there. But I've spent a lot of time with her over the past few months. She seemed fine to me. And she came and stayed with me a few days up in Santa Barbara before the wedding. She was great. So I'm thinking it was a one-time thing. Maybe even related to Tray, ya know? We need to just get rid of this guy."

"But Grace? What about that?"

"If he really knows something, then I've got a plan. Just trust me, bro. This is my area of expertise. You handle the media, I'll handle this."

I nod and let out a long breath. "OK, let's do this then."

"At the very least, V, it buys us some much needed information."

We continue walking and a few seconds later we round another corner and we're face to face with the door. Conner looks over at me as he knocks.

It opens to a goon pointing a gun at my head. "Come in," he barks in a low voice.

What choice do we have? We enter the room and find ourselves in a suite larger than the one I'm booked in.

I spot Tray sitting at the bar on the other end of the room. He looks like fucking shit.

"Do you have information for me?" Conner asks.

I say nothing. I might be tempted to choke this asshole out, and that would definitely be a bad idea since he's got a bodyguard.

Tray points to a computer sitting on the other end of the bar. "It's on the flash drive. Watch it."

Conner walks over to the computer and fucks with it for a second and then a video pops up. The sound is low, but I can still hear the hitches and stuttering in Sam's voice. It's Christmas—I know this because she's sitting in her old room at the parents' house and her bed is filled with wrapping paper and boxes. Sam always sleeps over at the parents' house on Christmas Eve and she brings all her gifts with her to wrap them. It's a tradition she's had since her first year in college.

"My name is Samantha Asher and I—" She stops and looks up at the person holding the camera. "I don't want to do this," she says, on the verge of tears. Her face is all red and her eyes are filling up. She's definitely not in control.

"Go ahead, baby," Tray says back. "The world wants to know the real you."

"I don't want the world to know me this way. I've done everything I can to stop the world from knowing me this way."

"Turn it off," I say, walking over to the computer. I slap the laptop closed and whirl around to face Tray. "You know what, asshole? You are the lowest piece of shit I've encountered in a very long time. I'm not paying a fucking dime for that. You set her up. You encouraged her, didn't you? You pretended to love her this whole time so you could sell her out in the end. I'm not paying you a fucking dime. And just so we're clear, that money means nothing to me. Nothing. I have more money than I need. Ten million dollars is nothing. I won that much last night in an impromptu game of baccarat. But you. Will never. Get a fucking cent from me. Publish this, Tray. I fucking dare you. I will take Samantha's hand and lead her through this with her head up. Her secret will be out and she will finally, *finally* be able to come to terms with that part of herself." I look over at Conner and he's just staring at me. "Conner, we're not paying him for this shit."

Conner lets out a long breath. I know I just fucked up his plan, whatever it was, but I don't care. I refuse to play along with this bullshit. "OK," he finally says.

"Vaughn," Tray says from his perch on the barstool a few feet away. "Whatever you think, I did that for her own good. She confided in me, and no matter what you think is happening here, you're wrong. I thought she could handle it, and she did pretty well, but she cracked at the end and lost control. So I stopped. If you watch the whole video, you'll see. I did that to help her."

"And you're here asking for ten million dollars because you love her?"

"No." He stands up from the bar and I realize something isn't right. His clothes are all rumpled and there's a rip, like someone took a razor and sliced the front of his white dress shirt. His jacket pocket is hanging by a thread, and his tie is too loose. "No, I just needed to get you here. I just needed you to come hear me out. It's not for me, OK? I don't want your money. I want your sister. But she walked out and I was trying to process what was happening with"—he waves a hand at the computer—"this fucking bullshit."

Conner seethes next to me. "Why the fuck are we here, Tray?"

Tray looks right at me. And this, for some reason, scares me. "Grace," Tray says, his eyes never leaving mine.

"What?" I growl at him. I'm so fucking close to beating the shit out of this guy. The only thing that holds me back is the knowledge that he wants me to do that. He wants me to do that so he can sue me and drag my name through the tabloids. "How the fuck would you know anything, asshole? The whole thing is sealed up."

"I don't need records, Vaughn. I got a phone call back on Saint Thomas. That morning Sam left, in fact. I got a call and that's why I was out drinking. He threatened me, you guys. He threatened to kill Sam if I refused to help him. And somehow he got this video. That's not my account on YouTube, OK?" Tray says it like he's pleading with us to believe him. "That's his account. The video is private right now, but at six tonight, he's making it public. He said that's my payment for being perfect and privileged. Everyone needs to pay, and I'm no different. That's what he said. So no matter what, that video of Sam is going to be all over the internet tonight."

"That makes no sense," Conner says. "Why release the video if he gets what he wants? That's not how guys like this work."

"He's crazy, Conner. He said girls are weak and can't face reality without the guidance of a man. He said he liked me because I got Sam to make that video, but that I was a coward for not publishing it and making her face her fear. So he was going to take away my options. My decision, he said that specifically. He was going to take away my decisions and force me to behave like a man."

All I can think of is Grace. Is this why she prefers her fantasy life? Did this sick fuck mess with her brain? Confuse her and force her to believe that she was incapable of living in reality?

"And then," Tray continues, "I got a visit a few days ago and that computer was dropped off. Open the computer back up, Conner. There's a minimized window. Bring it up and watch."

Conner defers to me and I nod. "Do it." We might as well understand what's happening and if we walk out and refuse to watch, we'll be in the dark.

The video starts out with just a black screen but it's jarring and shaky and there's sound, but it's not clear. Muffled voices and maybe crying.

My stomach lurches inside me because I recognize that voice.

Teenage Grace.

The camera angle changes and then she comes into view. She's bound and gagged, lying on her side in a dark corner of a filthy room. Her eyes are wide with fear and her nightgown is tattered and dirty. She squirms as the camera approaches her—

Conner reaches out and flips the computer closed this time. "Enough."

"He says he taped her. He says he has days, weeks, months' worth of video of her, Asher. And he's left her alone all these years because she never told anyone and she never got attached. But apparently that's changed. He said he's been watching and to tell you, 'She's mine.'"

I just stare at Tray. If he's trying to throw my whole world off its axis, mission accomplished.

Tray meets my stare and holds out a piece of paper with a trembling hand. "This is an account number where you need to transfer the money, Asher. It's not for me, it's for him. I'm just the messenger. My job is to deliver the message and he won't hurt Sam."

Conner and I look over at each other.

"And now I've done that. So make the transfer because I believe him. I think he really will kill Sam if you don't. Or even worse, I think he might *take* Sam if you don't."

I give Conner a nod and he walks towards Tray and takes the paper from his outstretched hand. Then he pulls out his phone and texts the bank in Switzerland.

I stare at the computer, wondering if I should watch more of the video. Wondering if I can actually stomach more of the video. And knowing I have no choice in this matter. If I want to save Grace, I need as many facts as I can get. She might hate me for inserting myself into her life, but that's a chance I'll have to take. It's more important that she's safe.

"Done," Conner says as he reads an incoming message.

Tray straightens his ripped and rumpled jacket, lets out a long breath, and heads for the door, giving his bodyguard a nod as he passes.

"Wait." I snap out of my stupor before Tray makes it to the door. "When you talked to him… what did that sick fuck say he wanted?"

"Grace," Tray calls out, his back to me as he walks away. "He says he wants Grace." And then he stops and turns his head slightly so I can see his profile. "And he said he's coming to get her and there's nothing you can do to stop him, so be ready."

They walk out and the door closes behind him.

"Come on," Conner says. "Let's get the fuck out of here. Everything is about to explode and we need to get ahead of it."

"How, Conner? How the fuck are we gonna get ahead of this?"

"I'm calling Dad and the PR people. We need to have a solid plan for dealing with Sam and that video. It's not the end of the world, V. You and I both know her bottling all that up inside is not good for her. We will walk her through it and she will come out the other end better than ever."

I nod, and I do believe that. But believing you should do something and actually doing it are not the same thing.

"I'll take care of Sam, see what kind of info I can pull off this computer. You take care of Johnny Blazen and ask him what he needs to get that car location info. Maybe we need to pay off a judge or something. I don't know. We need that info. Because that video of Grace, V, that was some sick fucking shit. And even though I sorta knew that's what happened, it shocked the shit out of me. I never imagined he could've filmed her."

I scrub my hands down my face and let out an exhausted sigh. How did my life go from dreams to nightmares in one twenty-four-hour period?

"Just go find that Johnny Blazen and get Grace back, OK? I'll take Felicity with me and we'll go work on the computer."

Just hearing Felicity's name snaps me back. "I don't want her involved, Conner. I don't want her hurt. She can't be a part of this."

"Fuck that, V. That girl is gold when it comes to hacking. We need her." Conner grabs the laptop and tucks it under his arm and walks towards the door. "She's gonna tear this computer apart and figure out if there's anything we can use on here. And then she's gonna set Sam up with a YouTube channel and have her make another video. One that shows a very composed and self-assured Samantha Asher talking candidly about her disorder."

All the people I care about are suddenly a part of this fucked-up mess. Is this my fault? Did I invite all this hatred? Am I the reason why Grace's abductor has resurfaced after ten years? Am I the root of all the pain and humiliation that is about to be unleashed?

"Vaughn!" Conner yells from the door. "Pull it together and go find that quarterback!"

I nod and follow him out. We walk back to my suite without words and before we even reach the door, Felicity is opening it for us. She scans our faces and frowns. "Oh, shit. Please tell me something good."

I shake my head at her. "It's worse than we imagined. I hate to ask you—"

"Vaughn, you know whatever you need, whenever you need it, right? I'll do anything to help."

Conner and I walk through the door and she shuts it behind us. I pull her close for a hug. "Go with Conner and help him. We've got a computer for you to look at. I'm just so glad you're part of my life. Do you know that?"

"I know, V," she says in a soft voice. "I'm the luckiest girl alive and it's all because of you. I'd do anything to make you happy."

I come from a level of privilege few can comprehend. I have a loving family and I've never wanted for anything in my life. And yet the day this kid hacked her way into my life I realized how much I was missing. I feel the same about Grace. I never knew how sad my intimate relationships were until I saw what they could be.

I can't lose Grace. Not only that, I feel like it's my life's purpose to keep her safe and I'm going to do everything in my power to make sure that happens.

I watch Felicity and Conner leave, closing the door quietly behind them. And then I go back to the living room and call the concierge desk. "This is Vaughn Asher," I tell the woman on the other end of the line. "I need Carl up here immediately."

No time to dwell on consequences if we don't succeed. There will be plenty of time for that if we fail. Right now, finding out where Grace went is the only thing that matters. And my best chance of doing that is making nice with a certain football player.

Chapter Five - Grace

#CallMeDontCallMe

IT TURNS out the past is a lot more difficult to avoid when it's all around you. We look at the TV, and there I am. We check the internet, and once again, I'm the star of the day. They are talking about me everywhere. My face, my poor teenage face, is plastered all over the airwaves. Bebe is texting me. Her parents—my parents—are texting me. And even though I really need to call them back, I just can't do it. They will want to whisk me away to a safe place. And I've been there, done that. I spent almost a year tucked away in a safe place after I came home and I can't go backwards. I can't.

News organizations are calling as well. I know what that means. They want interviews. They wanted interviews back when I was fourteen too, but they never got one then and they're not getting one now.

The Big Guys are calling, hell, even the Little Ladies are calling. Although that might be about Kristi's fucked-up wedding. I'm not one hundred percent sure about that.

Probably not though. That's probably about my past as well.

But the one thing that surprises me the most is that Vaughn does not call.

Why?

Is he so disgusted about what happened in my past? He said we had a good time last night. And I honestly wish I could remember. I do remember the gambling. I remember him being there. I remember being so angry. And I know I walked out and then there's a gap before we were in a restaurant together. He talked about... I don't remember exactly. But I think it was personal stuff. I can remember being ashamed because he was weaseling his way back into my fairytale and I was giving in.

God, everything about my life since Asher came into it has been a mess. I'm a mess. This guy is not good for me.

So why do I care so much that he hasn't called?

Maybe he figures I won't answer?

He's right, if that's what he's thinking. I won't answer. I'm paranoid since my phone went missing and then reappeared the next day a few weeks back. Maybe someone hacked into my phone somehow? I don't know how wiretapping works, I could be tapped, right? Who knows who could be listening on the other end.

But still, there is this emptiness inside me that craves to hear his voice. I take a deep breath and stare at my phone as it buzzes its way across the glass table. I could call him.

Jesus, Grace. Make up your stupid mind.

Right. I'm not calling him. There's too much happening right now. The last thing I need is him making things more complicated.

"Earth to Grace?"

"What?" I look over at Kristi and her brother. They are staring at me. "What?" I repeat.

"Your phone?" Kristi says as she points to the buzzing tech on the table next to me. "It's driving me nuts. Just answer it."

I pick up the phone and check the number. "It's Vaughn." I smile before I can stop myself.

"Just answer it," Jack says. "It's obvious you want to talk to him."

I shake my head no. "I can't talk to him right now, you guys. He's going to want answers. You don't know him. He compels me to do things I shouldn't. He makes me impulsive. He's demanding, and bossy, and—"

"And on the TV right now," Jack says, pointing to the flatscreen over the bar on the other side of the pool. "Look!"

I do look. I can't help myself. I even get up and walk over there so I can hear.

"Shit," Kristi says as she joins me. "And there's Johnny."

"Please," Vaughn says to the camera. "We need your help. Grace Kinsella and Kristi Bolton were chased off the premises this morning by the paparazzi. We need your help to find them. Grace is my girlfriend and by now you already know about her past. She is Daisy Bryndle. Her story was never told, and I'm not going to be the one to tell it now, I don't even know most of it. But I do know that she could be in danger. The psycho who killed her parents has resurfaced. In addition to that, my friend Johnny Blazen is also worried about his fiancée, Kristi Bolton. She's six months pregnant and they are due to get married this evening. We need your help. We need to find these two women and get them to a safe place. Please, if you have any information, call the number on the screen."

"Do you think it's true, Grace?"

I have to lean over and place my hands on the table to steady myself. Back? He's back? Could it really be true? My mind is just spinning out of control right now. The TV switches to the scene at the hotel where I escaped with Kristi. I walk back over to my lounge chair with wobbly legs and take a seat.

"I think you should call him," Jack says. "Seriously, if there's some guy after you, you need to be protected. This resort is huge, you're not safe here. We have guards at the gate, but everyone else is gone on vacation. No one will be around for weeks."

"Jack," Kristi says in a stern voice I'm not used to hearing from her. "We're not ready, OK? We're sorting through things. And if we go back now, we'll be pressured into making decisions. And we don't feel like making any decisions right now. Right, Grace?"

I nod. "I can't. Not yet. I need to process this. And Kristi, I know I'm totally in debt to you right now, but can I borrow some clothes? Even if I need to buy them from your gift shop or something? And take a shower?"

She gives me her best pouty face and takes both my hands in hers. "Yeah, I'll take you up to one of the rooms. Come on."

I grab my purse and my phone and follow her into back into the resort. I catch a glimpse of myself in the gift shop window and cringe. I look like hell.

"Come on, we can raid the shops. We'll pay them back another day. Perks of being twenty-five percent owner."

I pick out shorts, tank top, some underwear that is not tighty-whities, and she gets the same, but in a size that can accommodate her belly. Jack delivers two room keys to us and then we take the elevators up two floors, which is the top floor here, and she directs me to a room. "I'll be across the hall if you need anything, OK?"

I take a deep breath and let it out. "Thank you. So fucking much. I'm so sorry I ruined your wedding. I hope you'll forgive me and if you want, I will totally tell Johnny it was all my fault."

She shakes her head at me. "No, Grace. It wasn't you, really. I needed this time to get my head straight. If he loves me, this will not stop him. It's just a bump, that's all. Just a little bump in the road. I don't need a man who will run away at the first sign of trouble, ya know? I need one who will stick."

Hmmm. This really makes me think hard. We ran off today, right? So technically, aren't we the ones who walked out at the hint of a bump in the road? I admit, my problems are pretty unique. But Vaughn was trying to help me and I pushed him away.

Why do I do that?

Pfft. OK, stupid question, Grace.

Kristi turns to go into her room and I go into mine. It's a beautiful suite. A living room with a mountain view, and two bedrooms flanking the large living space. I head straight to the shower, and even though the soaking tub is totally calling my name, it's all I can do to manage to stand up in the shower without passing out from exhaustion.

Kristi's words are echoing in my mind. She wants someone who will stick. We all want someone who will stick. But what do I do at the first sign of trouble? I come loose. I take off. I run. I get the fuck out of Dodge and hit the road.

I can't help it either. I really can't. I'm not good at confrontation. I have been fighting with Vaughn since the moment we met. Literally, the moment we met in that bar and he was bossing me into that key lime pie martini. And that is so not like me. I've been the yes girl for so long, switching to the no girl just throws me all off balance.

Why does he bring that out in me? He must hate me. I'm not sticky at all. He deserves sticky too. And maybe it's just my overactive imagination, but I think he was trying to tell me something important about this last night.

Goddammit, why can't I remember what happened? And why would he ever want me? I'm so fucked up.

I wash myself quickly and then slip on my new clothes and lie down on the bed. The air-conditioning is cold, so after a few minutes I slip under the covers and my eyes get heavy.

The stench of urine and feces is all around me. No, *my mind says.* No, Daisy. That stench isn't around you. It *is* you.

I gasp as the footsteps approach the closet door. I'm bound and gagged, but not blindfolded. He always wants me to see him coming. I lie on my side, my cheek pressed up against the nasty carpet, and I can see his boots through the crack under the door. He stops outside my closet and then the chain rattles as he unlocks it.

The door swings open and even though I've been staring out that crack for hours, trying to get my eyes ready for the blast of light that always blinds me when he opens the door, I'm blinded.

I have to close them, and he hates that, so he kicks me in the ribs. I moan, because he always kicks me in the same place and they are broken, I know it.

He leans down, right into my face, and when he talks, I piss myself. "Daisy. Are you ready to learn how to behave like a lady, my girl?"

He wears a mask so I can't recognize his face, but I will always be able to recognize his voice. I will never forget his voice.

I wake up screaming and then hands are on me, and I'm struggling to get away. He's back! He's found me! He saw me on TV and he's back!

"Grace!" Vaughn says as he pulls me close. "Please, Grace. Calm down. It's OK, I'm here. I'm here."

I start to cry. Just straight up bawling and wailing as he holds me. I tremble and shake, but his soft words make their way to me though all that. "Shhh," Vaughn says. "He can't get you, Grace. He can't get you. I will never let him get you."

Chapter Six - Vaughn

#IWannaBeThePrince

SHE TREMBLES in my arms and I hold her tighter. "I'm here," I tell her softly. "That was just a bad dream."

She shakes her head in my arms. "I wish. I wish it was just a bad dream. But it's not. That nightmare was my reality for eight months. You don't understand, you don't know—"

"I don't, you're right. But that's over now. You're here, with me." I smile down at her and all the pent-up tension in my body evaporates.

She pushes me away. I give her some space, but I'm not about to let her go. "How did you find me?"

"Kristi's brother called the hotline and we came right away."

"We?"

"Johnny is talking to Kristi right now."

Grace stops struggling and relaxes at the mention of her friend. She needs a friend right now and that's exactly what I plan to be.

"Are you still mad at me?" My heart is beating so fast and my leg is bouncing as I wait for her response.

"Do I have a reason to be mad at you?" Her head tilts up and she finally looks me in the eyes. "I don't think I do."

I give her a weak smile, but she doesn't know what I did yet. I might've fucked up royally. She might not forgive me once she finds out. "I'm not sure why you and I argue so much, but Grace, if you will just give me a second chance, you'll see we can be good together. I can give you what you need."

She stares at me. Silent.

"What do you need?" I ask.

"I don't know."

"Freedom? Equality? Bossing power?" She smiles at that and my body relaxes even more. "I get that you're assertive and used to being in control. Calling all the shots for yourself—"

"No, Vaughn. You're so wrong. That's not me at all. All this fighting we've been doing? That's so not me. I hate confrontation. I hate arguing. I never stand up for myself. I never make waves. I go along. I give in. I'm weak. I'm a…" She stops and I realize I'm holding my breath, hanging on her every word.

"You're what?" I prod.

"I'm a… victim."

"Oh, fuck." I hold her tight again, bringing her cheek right up against my chest. "You said that the first night we met and if I had known what happened to you, Grace, I swear, I wouldn't have been so callous with your emotions.

You're not a victim, you're not weak. You're a fucking fighter if I ever saw one. You are so strong, you have no idea."

"I'm not. I'm the weakest link. I'm the one who got them all killed. You don't know what happened, Vaughn. No one knows what happened."

Shit. I'm so confused as to how to proceed with her. Do I prod her for answers? Or do I leave it alone? She's held it in for ten years, is it just my movie-star ego talking when I think I might be the one she can finally confide in? "Do you want to tell me what happened?"

She's silent for a long time. I let her think. I don't push. I asked her the question, now she needs to figure out what her answer is. Finally, after what seems like minutes, she makes a decision. "I never told anyone because he said he would come back and kill me if I did."

"He can't get you, Grace." And even as the words come out of my mouth, I know this is a lie. He *can* get her. He's proved that today with the message he sent us via Tray. He's watching very closely. But if Grace won't open up and tell someone what's going on, then our chances of finding this sick fuck are gonna be slim. We need to put an end to him, once and for all. "I'm here, OK? I'm going to protect you. No matter what. I'm going to protect you."

She nestles herself deeper into my embrace, pressing her face to my chest. "I don't know who he is. He never took off his mask. Not once. Not once did he ever let me see his face."

"Did he rape you?" She says nothing and the rage is coursing through my veins when she gives her head a small shake. "No?" I ask, to clarify.

"No. He… he said he owned me."

"What?" My whole body goes still.

"He tried to convince me I was sold to him by my father and brother and the reason he had to kill them was because they went back on the deal. He said I needed to practice how to be a good wife and follow orders. He said I was his. He owned me…"

She keeps talking but I stop listening. I stop listening because those are words that came out of my mouth too. I wanted to possess her. I wanted to own her. I wanted… I want her to be *mine*.

What must she think of me? Does she imagine I'm like her abductor? "Oh my God, no wonder you hate me. I'm so sorry, Grace. I'm so sorry."

"I do not hate you, Vaughn. I swear, I know the difference between him and you. I don't see you like that at all. You're not him. I know that. You're not him. You're nothing like him. You're my fantasy—"

"Jesus, I'm an asshole. I'm your nightmare, not your fantasy, Grace. I'm everything that went wrong back when you were a girl. I swear"—I cup her face and make her look me in the eyes—"I swear, if I had known, I would've never—"

"Touched me?" she asks in her sweet voice. "You would've never touched me, would you?"

And I don't know what to say. I have asked every single sub I've ever had if they've been abused by a man. And the ones who answer truthfully and tell me yes, I get rid of them immediately. She's right. I would've never touched her if I had known. It would've scared the shit out of me. I want to lie to her, tell her that I would've been able to see past her answer, but I can't. I can't do that to her right now. She needs the truth, no matter what.

"I would not have gone any further with you, no."

She lets out a long breath of air. "I knew it. That's why I lied. I wanted you that night. Even though I was fighting you on everything, I wanted you." She lifts her heavy eyes up to meet mine. "I still want you. But I don't think we're ever going to be together."

"Why?" I interrupt her. "Why can't you see me as the perfect Vaughn Asher? I mean, I get it, Grace. I'm a huge asshole at times. I'm a dick. I'm a kinky, dominating control freak and that's the last thing you need. But I have another side to me too. I tried to show you last night, and I thought I did a pretty good job, but now you say you don't remember any of it. And I'm sorta stuck here, Grace. I'm stuck because we had the perfect night, sweets. We did. It was beautiful, and slow, and filled with moments."

"And I missed it, didn't I?"

"I—" But just as I'm about to tell her, there's a knock on the door.

"Grace?" Kristi asks from the other side. "Can I come in?"

"One second," she says back and then she pushes me away and we both sit up. "Are you going to stay?" she asks me with her sad blue eyes.

"I'm here and I'm not going anywhere."

She leans in and kisses me softly on the lips. It's just a quick kiss, one that you'd give someone who is familiar to you. A peck really. But I swear to God, that kiss means everything to me. It's like an invitation into her world. It's like forgiveness and promise all wrapped up together. It's like... a fresh start.

"I've been a bitch and I'm sorry."

"Grace, please. I can't have you apologizing right now. It will tear me up if I have to listen to you apologize. It's not your fault."

She gives me a solemn nod and then we get up. She smooths her t-shirt and squares her shoulders to prepare herself for the world once she answers the door.

Kristi is on the other side of the door looking sheepish. "Can I come in?"

"Of course."

"OK, ladies, I'm going to step outside and make a phone call while you chat." I give Grace's shoulder a squeeze of support and exit the room, walking far enough away so that my voice doesn't carry. I speed-dial Conner. "Anything?" I ask.

"No," he replies. "Not so far, anyway. But I'm not optimistic and neither is Felicity."

"So what's that mean? He's savvy in this computer stuff? Tray can plop a laptop down with a video for us to watch and we can't get any info off it?"

"Pretty much means we're dealing with someone smart and calculating."

"Which he obviously is. Grace just admitted two things to me. He wore a mask, so she has no idea what he looks like. And he did some kind of brainwashing on her, trying to make her believe she was sold to him by her father."

"What a sick fuck."

"Tell me about it."

"OK, well... we need more details. Do you think she'll tell you anything else?"

"I'm not prepared to ask her, Conner. Not yet. I think it's a bad idea to expect her to be forthcoming after all this time. She needs to make that decision herself. I'm not letting her out of my sight. We're flying home to LA tonight and I'm keeping her there until we know more."

"What if she refuses to stay with you? What then?"

"I'm already on it. Been on that for weeks in fact. She will either be with me or under constant surveillance."

"She's not going to like that."

"Maybe not, but she has no say. It's done. Call me if you find anything, otherwise I'll talk to you tomorrow." He says goodbye and I press end just as Grace and Kristi come out of the room all smiles and laughter.

Kristi is overflowing with excitement. "Johnny and I are going to get married today after all. Here!" she says.

"Kristi, that's wonderful. Congratulations."

Kristi looks up at me with surprise. I'm a little surprised myself. I have never talked to a friend of a girlfriend before. I mean, I really haven't had a girlfriend like Grace before. But I'm tired of being that man. I want to be the Vaughn Asher Grace saw me as before we met. I want real relationships and that starts with making real friends. "If you don't mind, I'll stay by Grace's side. I'm afraid I can't let her out of my sight until we know what's going on."

"Of course. And you don't need to change, Grace. Just hang out and relax. Your phone call to the hotel to get things moved over here worked like a charm. Thank you."

"God, I so don't deserve that. I'm the one who ruined your wedding in the first place."

"Grace, stop. You asked me all the right questions. Questions I never wanted to face. And in the end I thought them through and decided Johnny and I are good together. I love him. He loves me. And we're having a baby. So I really owe you a debt."

They have a little personal girl moment and I walk back into the room and start collecting Grace's things. There's a plastic bag in the closet, so I stuff her blue dress from last night in there and twist up the ends. By that time Kristi is gone and Grace is sitting on the bed.

"Are you OK?"

"Are you going to tell me what's going on?" she asks. "About the moments we had last night? Because I'd really like to hear about them."

I pull her up off the bed and hug her close. "I'll tell you, but under one condition."

"What?" she asks, warily.

"You come spend the night at my house in LA tonight."

She raises her eyebrows at me. "You're serious?"

"Totally serious." I'm not sure if she wants to argue with me about this or not, but I'm not ready to give in. So I give her more. "Grace, I've never had a woman at my house. Felicity and I bought this house together after I adopted her, and I told myself then and there, no women. But you're different. I want you to be the first woman to come to my house and I want you to spend the night."

"Won't Felicity be mad?"

"No, sweets. She understands how I feel about you, even if you don't just yet. I know that last night we were playing a little game with the word *like*, but I don't just like you, Grace. I'm falling in love with you. I am, I can't help it. I'm falling in love with you and I need you to just stop blocking me and keep an open mind."

She considers this for a moment. "If I come spend the night at your house, can we have those conversations all over again? So I don't feel like I missed out on the best night of my life?"

I laugh at her. God, this girl. She does it for me. I want to make her world perfect. I want to keep her happy. I want to give her that fairytale and I want to be her prince. "We can have a total repeat, Grace. As many times as you need to hear what I had to say, I will tell you. Last night wasn't perfect. We were fighting and I was so worried about losing you. So worried that you'd walk out on me again… well, I rushed it, I think. I won't rush it tonight, I swear."

"OK," she whispers out on the slightest breath of air. "OK, I'll keep an open mind." She wraps her arms around my neck and then leans up on her tiptoes so she can plant another one of those sweet kisses on my lips.

I smile all the way through it.

Chapter Seven - Grace

#IReallyDoNeedAPrince

I STAY out of the way for the wedding. I feel awkward and a bit of a failure, if I'm being honest. The wedding I planned for Kristi is about as far from this low-key event as you can get. The Blazen family is transported over to the resort and I help Kristi's brother set up chairs and direct the caterers and florist. By the time we're ready for the ceremony, it's almost ten PM. But one look at Kristi and Johnny, and I can tell they do not care what time it is. They *are* in love. Kristi's meltdown is history, and Johnny places a hand over her belly as he says his vows.

Vaughn and I stay until the reception starts and then we slip away quietly. He's clearly anxious about something, and for a while I thought it was just the stress of the day. Because really—what a day. But I think it's about more than that. It's the media, sure. It's the attention. And yes, that scares me too. But there's something else going on with him that I just can't put my finger on.

We have one of the limo drivers take us to the small-jet airport in Vegas, and we spend the entire flight lounging against each other, watching a movie. Like this is just another day for us. Like we always take private jets home from midnight weddings in Vegas. And don't even get me started on how my life went from completely ordinary to being Vaughn Asher's girlfriend. Because that's how he's treating me now. Not like his plaything or his submissive. But his girlfriend.

And the scariest thing is, it feels very... normal.

I don't do normal, so the whole time we're in the jet I've got this little nagging feeling in the back of my head. Just picking away at me. Normal implies that my future is not dictated by my past. But it is.

We didn't turn the news on all evening, so I have to use my imagination about what they've been saying about me. But Vaughn has this little crease in his forehead from the narrowing of his eyes.

He insisted earlier that my long-ago abductor couldn't find me and he'll never get me again. So why would he say that if he wasn't worried about it?

I know better anyway. I lived with that sicko for eight months. I am quite possibly the only person who knows exactly what he *is* capable of.

"What are you thinking about?" Vaughn asks as we pull up to a large home somewhere in the movie-star neighborhoods of Los Angeles. I am not familiar with LA at all, so even though I know his home address from my stalking, I have no idea what the neighborhood is actually called. It's hilly, and pretty, and I can see the lights of LA off in the distance, shimmering the way they do on a hot night. It's hot tonight, a lot hotter than it is in Colorado in late September, and we have the air-conditioning on. It segregates me from the outside world, muffles the noise of traffic and activity.

"Nothing," I say. I would be so lost in this city if Vaughn wasn't here. That makes my heart flutter with suspicion and fear for a second, but a calming hand on my leg as we pull into the attached garage of a modern mid-century rambler brings me back from a panic attack.

That worries me a little. The fact that I still freak out if I'm not sure where I am. It's like nothing ever got better.

After I came home I was unable to talk. Not just unwilling, I was that too. But unable. Too many months of forced silence. I was re-educated, they said. I looked that word up and it scared the shit out of me because it came with other words attached to it. Thought-reform and compliance and persuasion. How did one man turn me into something I wasn't over just a few months?

I don't know. I didn't understand what happened to me back then and I don't understand it now. And even though it looks like everything is fine, my sudden paranoia betrays the things I'm hiding inside.

Vaughn turns the ignition off and we sit in silence for a second. "You ready to see my awesome bachelor pad?" he asks with a wide grin.

I nod. "Ready as I'll ever be."

We get out and walk to the door that connects to the house. He unlocks it and an alarm beeps until he keys in a code to make it stop. "After I adopted Felicity, we bought this house for just us. And we had a deal about dates. Because you know, she's not my kid. She makes that clear every chance she gets. But I'm protective of her. She's sort of a cross between a best friend, a daughter, and a sister. So I told the designer to make it feel... like a home." He looks down at me with a smile as we enter the main room and I have to admit, this is not what I was expecting Vaughn Asher's house to look like.

The couches are black leather, that's totally him. And there's a huge TV on the wall. That's him too. But there are dishes on the coffee table. Coffee mugs on the kitchen bar. The bar stools have jackets and sweatshirts hanging off them. And it's not exactly a *mess*. It's just... lived in. Comfortable.

"It's weird, huh?" he asks me. I give him a quizzical look complete with a raised eyebrow. "Adopting a sixteen-year-old girl when you're only twenty-six. I get it, most people don't do that. But... she really needed me, Grace." He draws in a long breath. "And I needed her too. She's the only thing that made me good for a while there."

I take his hand and give it a squeeze. "Why are you trying to justify it, Vaughn? I think it's awesome. I was adopted at fifteen, so I can appreciate how much you probably changed her life."

"Bebe?" he asks me. I nod. "Her mother was your lawyer?"

I nod again, but my heart is starting to beat very fast. "How much do you know?"

"Not nearly enough," he says as he tenderly glides his knuckles down my cheek and then leans in for a small kiss. "I know you were abducted. Felicity is my partner in crime too. She's a genius hacker and she pulled the police reports."

I stare at him for a moment. Should I be mad about that? It would be very easy to be mad. Call it an invasion of privacy, or hell, call it what it is... illegal. Anger is the expected emotion when you find out your boyfriend is spying on your past. I should start a fight to push him away.

But I don't want to. I don't feel like being mad. And as much as I really *don't* want to talk about it, I figure it's probably better to just get some of it out of the way early. Put a stop to it, right? That's what I do when people ask about my childhood. Not the real one. Not the one where my family is murdered and I'm kidnapped by a sick freak and held captive for months.

No. That one is buried.

I tell them that fake story about living in Highlands in Denver. I tell them my parents died of carbon monoxide poisoning. I never admit to a brother at all. I tell them I was homeschooled, which is not even a complete lie.

I've only told Vaughn part of this lie, so I don't have much explaining to do. That's a nice perk. It's too late to tell him that other story anyway. Obviously I didn't grow up in Highlands and he surely knows this by now if this Felicity girl has been poking around enough to get police reports. So I feed him some truth to make the questions stop.

"I was taken," I say as I look up at him. And even though I know he knows this, his face falls. His whole expression changes. This is the part I hate the most. When I see that sadness in the eyes of people who love me. I can't take it. It breaks down my walls and makes me sad and depressed. In that one look I see all the questions running through his mind, so I address the most obvious one first. "I was not molested or abused sexually. Ever."

He gives me a small smile as if to say, *Thank God.*

"But I was not treated well either. And even though you think you want to know what happened—everyone thinks they want to know what happened—you don't, Vaughn." My chin starts to quiver and I hate myself for letting that freak of a monster make me cry ten years later.

Vaughn reaches out but I pull back and see the hurt on his face. I put a hand up and shake my head for a second. "Please, don't feed it. Don't feed those feelings. Don't feel sorry for me. Don't say, *I can't imagine…* because it gives him power over me. And I don't want him to have that power."

He stares at me, his eyes searching for more. But then he nods and says, "OK."

I walk to the window and look out onto his back yard to distance myself from the feelings this conversation evokes in me. We are up in the hills, looking down on the city. "It's beautiful," I say, not really meaning to change the subject, but OK with the fact that I did. "Your pool looks amazing." The underwater lights must be blue, because the color of the water is pure turquoise. "It reminds me of the water around Saint Thomas."

Vaughn comes up behind me and slips his arms around my waist. "Wanna go outside and look around? In here it's pretty nondescript. Homey and comfortable. But outside is where all the movie star in me comes out."

I laugh, I can't help myself. "Is that right?"

"Come on," he says. "I'll show you." He slides the doors open, and then he folds them away, making the house merge with the outdoor patio.

"Wow," I say, amazed at the folding glass wall. "I've never seen that in real life before." I look between the living room and the pool area and yes, that is very movie star.

He takes my hand and leads me over to the water, and then he kicks off his shoes and steps into the beach entry pool. I do the same and follow him in. The water is surprisingly warm as it folds over my feet in little lapping waves. "There's a current in here?"

"I own five lots on this street," he says, pointing over to a thicket of lush greenery on either side of the pool. "Two on either side of my house." His smile is surprisingly boyish and it charms me for a moment. "And the only reason I needed to take up so much prime LA real estate was so I could build my own lazy river. I fucking love those things."

I laugh. I can't help it. "Do I get a VIP invitation?"

"Baby," he whispers as he leans down. "You are the new owner as far as I'm concerned. You can do whatever you want on this lazy river."

"Is it too late to take a spin?"

"Never. We're open twenty-four seven, sweets." And then he leads me off to the side of the main pool, between two palm trees that are acting like a gateway to another world.

"Do we want separate rafts?" he asks with a wink. "Or should we float together?"

"Together, of course."

He walks over to a storage shed and opens the door, rummages inside for a few moments, then comes out with an inflatable raft that will indeed fit two, but only if they are sitting very close together. I eyeball it with suspicion but he just grins.

"I don't have a suit," I say, my words sounding a little breathless.

He whips his shirt over his head and throws it on the ground. "Me either." And then he unbuttons his jeans.

My eyes track every movement as he pulls his zipper down and then stops. I look up at his face.

"Does this make you uncomfortable?"

Fuck, no, I want to say. *Unleash that baby.* Instead I whip my shirt over my head and send him a smile. "Bra on or off for a midnight float down the movie-star river?"

"Mmmmm," he says. "Hard one." And then he gives his jeans the slightest tug and they fall to the ground. He's commando and not completely hard, but my heated stare makes up for that and his cock springs to life.

I reach behind me and unsnap my bra, letting it hang loose for a moment before slipping my arms out. My nipples perk up and my breasts are instantly firm and taut. I move to my shorts, and after a few deft tugs, which Vaughn watches just as I watched him, I wiggle them over my hips and they fall to the ground.

We step away from the clothes at the same time. He holds his hand out to me and I take it, letting him draw me close to him.

My whole body is humming, but my pussy is throbbing like crazy.

I want him.

I want him in the worst way. I think we had sex last night, but I don't remember it. So in my mind, it's been weeks and I'm so ready for him.

"Grace," he says as he leans down to kiss my neck. "I want you right now. No one can see us through the thick foliage, but if you prefer, we can go inside. Go up to bed."

"Are you kidding me? And miss out fucking you on the Vaughn Asher River?"

He chuckles and his hand dips between my legs.

I'm so horny, I'm not surprised when he finds me slick and ready before we even get started. He inserts one finger inside me and my whole body trembles. "That feels so good."

"I want to be inside you so fucking bad right now, Grace."

I feel the same way. I don't want to mess with foreplay at all. I want his hard cock buried within me. I want him to fill me up and make me whole. Put me back together and take all the pain away. It's stupid to think a good hard fuck can do that, but it can.

As if reading my mind, he reaches around and cups my ass, then lifts me up. His hard length rubs the wet lips of my pussy as he positions me. And then he walks over to the side of the small building, pressing my back against the hard stone.

"One hard fast fuck. And then we can relax on the river."

"Yes," I breathe into his ear. "Fuck me hard, Vaughn. Ple—"

His cock enters me, sliding past my folds, stretching me, bumping up against my clit, and rubbing my g-spot all at the same time. My head rolls back, my eyes close, and my mouth opens to release a moan as the walls of my pussy stretch and he buries himself deep inside.

He pauses. Just for a moment. And in that moment I realize something—fuck that fantasy. Because my reality rocks.

He pounds into me the moment that realization hits. Vigorously pumping and thrusting. His hands grip my ass cheeks, spreading them wide. A fingertip slips alongside my bud, dragging the wetness we are creating along with it, and a second later, it's inside me as well.

I push my ass back into the pressure, begging him for more with my actions.

"I want your ass, Grace. I want to fuck your ass so bad. But my fairytale cock is currently enchanted by your princess pussy."

I laugh as I continue to move against him.

"I am your fucking prince, Grace. Do you understand me? I'm the prince you've been looking for. Say it, Grace."

"You're my prince, Vaughn." I laugh a little.

"Damn right." He grinds his hips, hitting my clit in just the right way, and it's over.

My prince makes me see fairy dust.

He bucks against me at the same time, spilling inside me, his head falling back and his jaw tight as I clench my pussy around his pulsating shaft.

"Fuck," he says. "Fuck, fuck, fuck." I tighten around him again, making him let out a long moan as he grips my ass tightly, riding out the wave of pleasure.

My heart is beating so fast I think it might explode out of my chest. I place my hand over his heart to calm myself—to reassure myself that he feels this way too. And he does. His rhythm is quick and pounding. One hand goes behind his neck and the other grips his thick hard biceps. It trembles beneath my touch and I rest my cheek against his shoulder. "Don't let me go."

"I'll never let you go. Ever." After a few moments he relaxes, setting me down slowly until my feet touch the smooth concrete. "I need this every day for the rest of my life. I will never let you go."

He spins me around so my back is pressed into his chest, his arms crossing over my heaving breasts as I try my best to catch my breath. "You're mine," he growls in my ear. "You're never getting away again. I won't let you get away again. So please, Grace. Please don't try."

"I cannot imagine anything that would make me want to give you up either, so don't worry."

He sighs. And it's long and laced with relief. "Thank you."

"What for?" I ask, leaning my head back into his chest. I'm so tired, all I want is to get on that raft and drape my arm across his chest and sleep as I float down River Asher. "I should be thanking you. For sticking it out and not letting me push you away."

"I was an asshole. I get it. I told you this last night, but I'd like to say it all again, if that's OK. Because you don't remember much, do you?"

I pull away and turn around so I can look up at his face. "No. But… I feel different. Like our relationship has changed. And instead of fighting it off, I'm just gonna go with the flow." I point to the water. "And I'd like to go with that flow."

He picks up the raft and walks down the sloped edge of the river's entrance and places the raft on the water. He holds out his hand, beckoning me. "Come on. I've never floated on this river with a woman before. Let's make memories."

Wow. Maybe he really is my prince? I walk forward and take his hand. He gives it a squeeze before letting go so we can climb on the raft. When he's settled, he opens his arms, inviting me to join him.

I climb on and settle against his chest. My body instantly stills. Relaxes, sinks into him, trying to become one. The stress of the day seeps out of my weary muscles. The reality slips a little. And even though I'm ready to embrace it, what's one more night of denial? That's the thing about reality. It's always there waiting for you. "This is perfect."

"Yeah," he says back, his voice rumbling up against my ear. "I like the lazy river because you don't have to think.

You just plop yourself on here and forget. You can forget everything and just exist. And this one was perfectly made. The trees are placed so that you float in and out of the sun every few minutes. It's almost impossible to burn because the light is so fleeting."

My eyes are already closed. His voice is so soothing. "Tell me more, Vaughn. I just want to listen tonight."

His chest rises and my head rises with it as he considers my request. "Once upon a time," he finally says a few moments later, "in a land far, far away... there was a princess. And she was strong and brave and didn't need a prince to save her..."

I listen to every word. I hang on every word. Because this man is the one I dreamed about. This man is the one who comes galloping up on the white horse and sets everything back in place.

"I do need a prince," I interrupt. "I really do. Maybe I don't need saving, but I like the thought of being saved all the same."

Vaughn Asher hugs me close as we float down his lazy river. He lightly strokes a fingertip up and down my arm as he talks. He twines his leg with mine and swipes an errant lock of hair from my eyes. Never pausing his tales of life in the Land of Happily Ever After.

Tonight that place doesn't seem so far away.

Right now that place is all around me.

I'm there.

Chapter Eight - Grace

#UseYourMasterVoice

"GRACE?" VAUGHN whispers in my ear. "Wake up, sweets. I have to go to my parents' house this morning and I want you to come with me."

I roll over in bed, trying to drag myself out of the best sleep I've had... like ever. But his strong arms pull me close and he tucks me under his chin. "Don't go away," he rumbles.

"I'm not, I just wanted to look at you."

"Mmmm. We're gonna take a shower and you can look at me all you want. Then we're gonna get dressed—I have clothes for you, don't bother asking—and then we're going to my parents' house. I didn't have a chance to tell you, but Samantha left her husband."

"What?" That wakes me up.

"Yeah, she called me upset and said she couldn't stand the thought of sleeping with the guy, so I had her come home. But—"

He pauses and this is how I know the 'but' is a big deal. "But what?"

"But Tray—that's her husband—made an embarrassing video of her and we think it's best if she just addresses it before it gets too complicated."

"Oh. Wow. I'm so sorry."

"Don't be. This will be good for her. So we gotta get up, OK?"

He loosens his grip on me and I roll over so I can see him. God. Damn. He is so fucking gorgeous.

He smiles and his eyes light up. A hint of a chin dimple appears that I've never seen before. I reach up to touch it. "I never knew you had a chin dimple."

"No? Well, my number one stalker is seriously slacking. You should be ashamed."

"Seriously, how did I miss that? It's adorable." But just then it fades away. "Hey, it's gone."

"It's only there when I'm smiling a certain way." And then he grins and sure enough, the little cleft is back. "I have to be really smiling, you know. It's my shit-eating-grin smile. And I never use it, or they Photoshop it out. It makes me look too soft for the action roles, they tell me."

"They are stupid," I say as I lean my mouth up to touch his. Our lips connect and electricity shoots though my whole body. God, I want him like now. He draws me closer and presses his hard cock against my leg. "Do we have time?"

"I don't even think that question deserves an answer. But if you need one"—he flips me on top of him and hikes my ass up so my pussy is right over his hips—"this is your answer."

"Oh, fucking Vaughn Asher in a bed is my new number one request."

His smile drops and the dimple disappears again. "We already did it in a bed. That night you got too drunk to remember what happened."

I lift my hips up and slide my hands between my legs, guiding his thick cock into my entrance. I watch his face the whole time. He watches mine back. I ease down on him and let out a gasp as he stretches me. He grabs my ass and pushes down, completely filling me up.

"Your pussy is so wet for me, Grace."

My hair falls over my shoulders and hangs down, draping across his chest. He reaches up with one hand and then palms my throat. I stop my slow rocking for a moment, taken by surprise.

He waits to see if I'll object. But I'm not about to object. We are so far from those two people who bickered on the beach about limits. So very, very, far.

I swallow hard and his palm is tight enough against my throat that I know he feels it. This makes me start my motions again. I slide forward, lifting up a little, and then drag my clit across the flat plane of his lower abdomen.

He tightens his grip, watching me. His eyes are attentive and not at all consumed with lust like mine must surely appear.

I repeat my motions, more forcefully this time. His other hand reaches between my legs and then his finger is pressed against my asshole.

I groan as he slips his thumb up against my pussy, sliding it in alongside his dick, and then uses that slickness to lubricate my ass.

My body wants to collapse against his chest, but his palm on my throat keeps me erect. I rock harder, lifting my hips high so his cock almost fully withdraws, and then slamming down onto of him.

His jaw clenches each time. "Fuck," he growls. "I want to flip you over and fuck your ass so bad."

"Let me get off and then you can."

In one swift second I'm face down on the bed, his hands holding my hips in place and his cock pressing up against my asshole.

"Don't boss me, baby. I'll take that ass any time I want."

Oh, shit, as much as this should piss me off, it doesn't. It turns me on so fucking bad. "Sorry, Master," I say, turning my head to see what he thinks of that.

He leans down on me, his muscular chest, hard and corded, pressing against my chest until almost his full weight is on me. "Mmmm, that shit still turns me on, Grace, but it's just a game. Don't take it too seriously."

"Yes, Master," I say back with a giggle.

He presses the head of his cock against my puckered entrance and I squirm, but his palm is back on my throat, keeping me close. "If I had lube here, I'd use it. But I don't, baby. Do you still want me to take you from behind?"

"Go slow," I whisper.

"I will, sweets." His fingers drag my wetness up to my ass to get it nice and slick for his cock. "I want all the moments we have together to last and last." He presses the head of his dick against my opening and I gasp and pull away a little. "I want the perfect moments to drag on forever." He brings his fingers to my mouth and slides them inside, pressing down a little on my tongue. "Get them nice and wet for me baby." I let my saliva pool inside my mouth and then he swipes it out, dragging a sticky strand past my lips. It's cool when it touches my ass, but that sensation is replaced by his thick cock as it enters.

I moan through the pain and discomfort for the first few seconds of penetration, recalling that he prepared me for this the last time. But then his dick gets past some critical point and it slips in easily.

"Fuck, you are so tight, Grace. I love this, I love fucking your ass. I love the way you clench around me"—he slips his fingers between my legs to play with my clit—"when I do this."

"Ohh," I moan out as he flicks the sensitive folds with his finger. And then he withdraws his cock, leaving me wanting so badly. "Don't stop," I plead. "Please, more," I groan.

He lifts my hips up. "On your knees, Grace," he says in his Master voice. "Get on your knees."

I don't have to do much, just prop myself up mostly, because his strong hands lift up my hips and that's all it takes. He reenters my ass—this time it slips in easily—and pounds me from behind. I forget that a few moments ago I was lamenting the withdrawal of his fingers, because his balls slap against my clit with each forceful entry.

"Yes," he says, laying his chest over my back. Covering me completely. Dominating me completely. His dick far up inside me. "Come for me, sweets," he says in a low whisper. "Come for me. Squeeze my cock." And then his mouth is on my shoulder, biting, a sting that drives me wild, because his hand is between my legs, teasing my pussy.

I feel my orgasm building. His fingers increase their motion, and then his teeth find my earlobe and it's over for me. He's biting, his dick is in my ass, and then he places his fingers, still wet from my own juices, against my lips. My mouth opens and I suck off his hand as I explode.

My body shudders. The muscles in my legs are trembling so bad, I want to collapse back onto the bed, but his hand is still covering my pussy, holding me up as he continues to thrust.

And I'm barely done when he withdraws and flips me over again.

I'm jelly now. Pliable. Malleable. Satiated, still reeling from my release.

He points his dick at my face and when I look up at him, he's asking.

I open my mouth, my heart beating fast from the orgasm and the fear.

He releases the dimple just in time for me to catch it before hot semen spills on my cheek, not quite making my mouth, and his head falls back with a long groan.

It takes several moments for him to compose himself and then he falls down onto the bed and wraps me up in his arms.

"I love you."

What?

"I love you, Grace. I love you. I don't even care if that freaks you out or whatever. It's real. And I'm saying it. You don't have to say it back. But I love you and you're mine."

Chapter Nine - Vaughn

#SheDidntSayItBack

SHE DIDN'T say it back.

I am a complete loser for telling her I love her. I've known this woman for a few weeks and I'm caught in this unwinnable situation, and even though I know this shit is getting complicated, I can't stop feeling this way.

I fucking love this girl. She's beautiful, and funny, and smart, and honest. And even though she thinks she wants things from me, she doesn't. She has zero expectations.

It's just... I'm afraid the reason why she has zero expectations is because she doesn't feel she can count on me. And that sucks. I feel like such a failure.

"Wow, is this your parents' house?"

I look over at Grace as we pull up to the gate house. "Like it?" She cranes her neck, trying to get a better view. You can see the house from the gate, but only a little portion of it.

The guards wave me through and we cruise up the driveway and park in front of the fountain.

"Wow," Grace says as I pull the e-brake on the 911. Grace lets out a long whistle. My house is Hollywood Hills nice. But my parents' house is Beverly Hills royalty nice.

"Stay put, please," I say as she unbuckles her seatbelt. "I open doors," I explain when she shoots me a puzzled look. She smiles big at that and I catch her biting her lip as I get out.

I go around to her side and open the door. One long tanned leg steps out and I'm fixated on her pretty peach toenail polish. I smile at her as I help her out of the low-riding sports car.

"Thank you," she says with a hint of shyness.

I put my arm around her shoulder. "You're welcome." I point to a white van with a satellite dish parked at the side of the house. "The media is here, Grace. But they have strict instructions not to approach you. So don't be worried."

"Oh," she says as we stop in front of the large white double door that stands ten feet high. The house is what I'd call ornate. Very reminiscent of Old World royal families. I hate it, but it is what it is. The door is covered in fancy scrollwork and there is no door handle, but it opens up almost immediately.

"Welcome home, Vaughn," my mother says. She leans in for a kiss and then directs a beaming smile at Grace. "It's lovely to see you again, Grace. Please come in."

"Thank you," Grace replies in a soft voice. One that tells me she's not sure what to do and my mother is making her nervous.

But my mother always greets me at the door. I could just pull around back and go in myself, but we've been doing this welcome-home thing for almost a decade. It's a tradition for me. Not one I want to break. I have very few normal traditions in my life and this is one of them.

"The crew is set up in the atrium, Vaughn. Conner is finally back from his trip, so he's here."

Yeah, Conner's trip was really a cover for the new business he's been trying to set up for the past six months. But my parents don't know anything about that yet and that's how it's going to stay. One thing at time.

"Great, is Felicity here yet?"

"Yes, she stayed the night. She said"—my mother chuckles—"she went home last night and you had broken the no-date rule, so she left."

"Oh, no," Grace says, her face stricken with panic.

"Felicity is just dramatic, Grace. Don't let her guilt you. Is she with Conner, Mom?"

"Yes, they're both in the pool house. Why don't I give Grace the tour and you can go talk to your brother. He's anxious about something and he's been asking for you constantly."

Grace bubbles her approval for a tour and so I kiss her on the cheek and leave her with my mother. I need to speak with Conner before this interview starts. I need to know what the fuck he and Felicity have found out about her abductor.

I walk through the house, exit into the back yard, and then make my way past the gardens to the pool area. The pool house is actually a two-bedroom apartment that I used to live in back when I was a teenager. Now it's basically just used for storage, though it's still a nicely equipped apartment.

I grab the handle on the door and twist, but it's locked. "Hey." I pound on it. "Open the fucking door, asshole."

I'm still pounding when it opens and Conner stares at me, blinking back the sunshine, shirtless and looking like he just rolled out of bed. I push past him and find Felicity making coffee in the little kitchenette.

"'Bout time," she says, annoyed.

I study her. Then I look back at Conner, who is pulling a shirt over his head. I look back at Felicity and she's already forgotten I'm here.

"OK," I say, a little miffed at finding them in here together. Alone. "What's the deal?"

"I got nothing," Conner says as he takes a cup out of the dishwasher and pours himself some coffee while the pot is still brewing. The drips hiss on the hot plate until he returns the carafe and then it sizzles instead. "I've looked through every file they have, even Felicity looked. She didn't find anything either. No one has any idea who this guy is. Grace never gave a statement beyond that one sentence. So if anyone knows, it's her."

"I don't think she's talking."

"No shit, asshole," Conner says as he pulls out a smoke and lights up. I grab his cigarette and plop it into a water-filled glass in the sink. He just shrugs and pulls out another one. I let him win that battle. I have better things to do than police my little brother's smoking habits.

"And I don't want her talking either. She's not ready."

"It's been ten years. This guy made a direct threat, Vaughn. I think if we tell her that, she'll get ready real fast."

I consider this for a moment. He might be right. She held herself together very well when she told me about it last night. But then again… "No," I say, coming back to my senses. "Let's just get through this interview with Sam and take it from there. Agreed?"

He takes a long swallow of coffee and says nothing. But I'm running this show and his silence is the same thing as an agreement, even if it's a contested one.

"Let's go then. I'm sure they're ready for Sam and I just want to get this over with. Did you prep her on what to say?"

"No," Conner says as the three of us walk out the door together and cross the lawn. "I went up there to do that a few hours ago, but she said she had it all planned out. I figure this is her deal, right? She should get to explain it any way she wants."

"I hope to God we're not making a mistake."

"I hacked into *Buzz Hollywood*'s email this morning," Conner says. "And the video is already there. They're prepping it for an internet exclusive this afternoon. We've got our own cameras set up in the room, secretly, of course. And we'll be taping the interview as well. We'll release it before the *Grapevine Hollywood* reporter leaves the premises."

"*Grapevine*? Fuck, I hate those assholes."

"Well, they just hired a new reporter who went to school with Sam and since this is her thing, she got to choose the reporter she wanted to talk to."

Fair enough, I guess.

We step inside the atrium and I almost have a heart attack when I see the interview has already started.

Only it's not Sam in the hot seat getting grilled.

It's Grace.

Chapter Ten - Grace

#BadAssPrincess

"WHAT HAPPENED to you, Miss—do you like to be called Kinsella? Or Bryndle?"

"Daisy Bryndle no longer exists," I tell the reporter calmly. "That name has been erased from my life. I am Grace now. Please call me Grace."

"OK, good to know, Miss Kinsella, errr… Grace. Can you tell us where you were for those eight months you were missing?"

I shake my head. "No, I can't."

"You can't?" the reporter prods. "Or you won't?"

"Can't. I was never allowed out of the house."

"What about when you escaped? Didn't you know where you were at that point?"

"I didn't…" I swallow hard and take a cleansing breath. "I didn't escape. I was… let go."

The reporter just stares at me and I get uneasy. Maybe this was a mistake? Sam seemed so confident when we were talking up in her room a few moments ago. She said she needed to tell her secret because it would set her free. Allow her to move past it and take away the power these reporters had over her.

I agreed with her. I still agree with her.

But this is hard. It's a lot harder to talk about than I thought. But it's too late now. I started this. They'd air this unfinished if I get up and walk out, so I might as well get on with it.

Just then the door opens and Vaughn walks through with Conner and Felicity. He's about to burst through the wall of media people and put an end to this, but I put up a hand and shake my head. He stops.

I clear my throat. "I didn't escape. I was let go." I wait a beat to find the right words. "I was let go because... well, I'm not sure, really. I think he got a call. A job offer, actually. I heard him talking on the phone one night and it was about a job. But it sounded like he had to move someplace far. Pick up and go, he said. I'm pretty sure. So he had three choices. He could take me with him, and clearly he was not going to do that. He could let me go, and that didn't seem to be an option either. Or he could kill me."

I stare at her, and then my gaze pans the room. No one makes a sound. No one moves. They are riveted.

I take another deep breath and continue. "I figured I'd be dead that night because I knew he was leaving in the morning. So I just... gave up."

"What's that mean, Grace? What did it mean for you to give up?"

"I just accepted it. And when he came to my door, I told him as soon as he opened it, 'If you just let me die peacefully—drug me,' I remember requesting—'if you just drug me so I go easy, I'll forgive you for everything.' I figured that's the only weapon I had in my arsenal, you understand?" I wait for her nod, but it never comes. She does not understand. No one will understand.

Grace, the terrified teenager named Daisy says in my head. *Make them understand.*

"He was... is... not well. But even though he really messed with my head, he never touched me sexually. And he could've. At any time, he could've. So I spent a lot of time thinking about this. Why didn't he do that? What did he really want? And I came to the conclusion that he wanted me to *want* him. So if I told him he was forgiven, maybe he'd see that as a fair trade to let me die in peace."

"But he didn't kill you."

"Obviously."

"So your words touched him?"

"I suppose. He did drug me, but not enough to kill me. At least not quickly. He dropped me off on the front lawn of a small-town hospital in Nebraska."

"Is that where he was keeping you? In Nebraska?"

I shrug my shoulders. "I have no idea."

"Could you pick him out of a lineup if you wanted to try and put him away? Make him pay for what he did to you?"

I shake my head no. "He wore a mask the entire time we were in the same room."

"What kind of mask?"

95

"It was one of those lifelike ones. Like they make of presidents and stuff. Only this was not a famous person. It was…" I clear my throat and swallow hard. "He was wearing a mask of a boy. A boy I knew from summer camp." I add in a whisper.

Everyone is silent again as they all think about this.

"That's creepy," the reporter finally says. "Did you tell anyone about this mask?"

I shake my head. "I never told anyone anything."

"Why?"

"Why do you think? I'm sure you can figure that one out."

Sam scoots in close to me and puts her arm around my shoulder. She rests her head against mine, like she's my very best friend in the world. I think Bebe will hate me when she sees this. I never told her. I never told anyone. And now this family I barely know and this reporter who has no connection to me at all, they are the first to hear it.

"What were your days like?" the reporter asks to keep the flow of the interview going.

But I'm done talking. I don't even bother to say that, either. I just stop.

"I feel so stupid," Sam says. "I called this interview so I could tell the world about a secret I was hiding. But now that I've heard Grace's story, I realize I have no idea what it means to suffer true, deep, emotional pain. I'm so sorry, Grace."

I nod and then unhook the little microphone from my shirt and hand it to the stunned reporter. She's probably wondering what just happened. A moment later, Vaughn is there, leading me out of the room. We keep walking, right to the car. He opens my door and places me inside, drawing the seatbelt tightly across my chest before closing the door and walking around to his side.

When he gets in, he lets out a long exhale and starts the engine. "I don't know what to say. I shouldn't have left you alone in there. I'm sorry if you feel ambushed."

"I don't," I say back, gently placing my hand over his on the gearshift. "I was talking to your sister, and she asked me if I ever felt like a victim."

Vaughn looks over at me quickly.

"Because she said she feels like a victim. But I told her no. Because even though I do feel like a victim, I have had all the proper answers fed to me while I was in *recovery*. I lied. I do feel like a victim. Well…" I stop for a moment so I can try and make sense of it. "Daisy Bryndle was a victim. But Grace Kinsella did a pretty good job at keeping that useless emotion at bay with her fantasy world."

He places his hand on my leg. "Is that why you were on Twitter? To live in a world where you had all the power?"

I can't look at him. I'm embarrassed to admit I've been running from my weakness. Covering it up with a rich, online fantasy world.

"I love you, Grace."

I look up at the real Vaughn Asher and force the tears back. "Why?"

"You're my fantasy girl," he says softly. "All the best fairytale princesses have the most horrific pasts. But they endure and persevere. And even though the fantasy dictates that the prince saves her, that's not how it really happens."

I gaze up at the man who wants to be my prince with longing and hope. "How does it really happen?"

A single finger tips my chin up so I have to look him straight in the eyes.

"Grace, the princess always survives, and she does that all on her own. Never mind the rescue—the real challenge is surviving long enough for help to arrive. And all the fairytale princesses do that all on their own. You're not a victim, you're a survivor. And I get it. I understand what you meant back in Vegas when you said sometimes living is the worst possible thing that can happen. And you're right. Giving up is so much easier. But you never did give up. The fact that you're here—a strong-willed woman with a college degree and a life eked out from the debris of Daisy Bryndle—well, sweets, that's the opposite of victim. That's badass."

I giggle and shake my head.

"Bad. Ass. Princess. That's you, babe."

And then he starts the car, revs the engine, and we leave the castle.

Maybe a little sadder than when we came, but maybe a little stronger too.

Chapter Eleven - Vaughn

#Flashbacks

I LOSE track of time after that. I lose track of life after that. Her eyes, her words, her body… these are the only things I see, or hear, or feel for the next twenty-four hours. We drink, and eat, and fuck, and swim.

And this is all I care about. I blow off phone calls. I blow off a Friday afternoon meeting about *IM2* marketing. I don't return messages. Hell, I don't even check messages. My life is a whirlwind called Grace.

And the next day, when I wake up and she's all pressed up against me, comfortable, safe, and still asleep… I know I can't keep hiding it from her.

I need to come clean.

I do. I know this. Every day I wait to tell her, it compounds the repercussions. But I'm not ready to end this… this… whatever it is. This perfect weekend. This chance she represents. I don't want her to know I'm a sneaky asshole, even though she probably already knows that. I'm getting the impression that I've erased some of my bad behavior on Saint Thomas and I really don't want to fuck that up.

She rolls over and turns her back to me in bed. I take this as a sign. I'm a superstitious actor, I look for signs. And this qualifies. I can't tell her yet. Tomorrow. When I take her home. I'll tell her before I leave. For sure. She turns back and her hand slides up and down my abs.

"You've got my attention, Mrs. Invisible Man."

"Mmmm. I need to go home."

'What?"

"I do, I have so much to do. Should I buy a ticket?"

"What?" I'm floored. Never in a million years did I think she'd want to go home today. "But it's Saturday."

"Yeah, I know. But I can't keep avoiding Bebe. She will want to talk about the interview."

They aired it last night. The video of Sam last Christmas was all over the place before dinner, but Sam handled it well. She was diagnosed with Tourette's Syndrome when she was nine and it devastated her. She had no control over the tics for years. Rapid blinking. Sucking in her breath. Not swearing, she had very few verbal issues. But it was enough to kill her self-esteem and give her a case of obsessive-compulsive disorder as well. She outgrew most of it, but when she gets stressed, she panics and they come back.

Tray was her first real relationship. I guess I shouldn't have been so surprised that she was a virgin. That must've been enough to bring back her condition.

That interview was a major step forward for her. It's time and she knows that.

"What's wrong?" Grace asks, lifting her head up off my chest so she can see my face.

"Just… Samantha. She's been doing so well for so many years. I really thought it was over."

"She was very strong and determined in her interview."

She was. I feel very proud of my little sister right now. And no one gave a shit about that video of her. The whole country is talking about Grace. "I know she was exceptionally strong and it went better than I ever imagined. But I worry about her. And you," I add. Because I'm far more worried about Grace than Sam. "Bebe is your best friend," I tell her, bringing us back to the topic of her leaving. "You can call her on the phone and go home tomorrow, no big deal."

"Yeah, but I don't want to turn into one of those girls who drops her BFFs for a guy. Even if said guy is a famous movie-star. Tonight is Dirty Heaven and I've been absent so much lately. I don't feel connected. I feel… sort of… adrift."

"You're having social media withdrawal?"

"Mmmm," she says. Her hand dips down to my hard cock and I smile. She doesn't want to leave, she just feels obligated to spend time being herself. And that's not a hard wish to grant in our fairytale land.

"So play Dirty Heaven here."

"Here?" She looks around quickly. "Oh God, I'd be way too embarrassed."

"Why, because all your tweets are about me?"

"That, and if they know I'm with you, and they will, they will torment you relentlessly."

My hand slips up to her breast and I pinch her nipple. Not hard, but forcefully, making her squeal a little. "So let them. You can guard my honor."

That makes her snort. "I have to be honest, for the last three years my Dirty Heaven nights have been all about you. Now what do I tweet about?"

"Ah," I say as my hand dips down between her legs. "I see the problem. You don't want to make any promises you can't keep."

She giggles against my chest.

"Just call up Bebe, once we're finished fucking, of course, and chat with her all you want. Take selfies on the lazy river. Get drunk with her on the phone. Fucking Skype, for all I care. Spend the whole day with Bebe, but please, Grace. Do it from here. It's not time to go home yet." She's silent for a few moments and I have a little wave of panic. "Unless you really don't want to spend the weekend with me?"

"No," she says immediately. "That's not it at all."

I flip her over, straddle her ass, my hard cock pressed against the slit of her pussy, and I lean into her neck and give her a small bite that makes her buck underneath me. "Then it's settled. You stay here. I fuck you until you're sore. Then I'll share you with Bebe and the rest of the Filthy Blue Birds." She turns her head and I immediately go in for a kiss. "Is that a deal, sweets?"

"I don't have any clothes. You only got me that one outfit for yesterday."

"Oh, I forgot to tell you. This is a clothes-free zone. You have to be naked. Sorry, that's just how it is."

"Since when?" she squeals. "What about Felicity?"

"Yeah, well, she's staying at the parents' pool house with Conner, I think."

"Are they dating?"

"Fuck, no!" I say a little too quickly. "Fuck. No. They're working on a project for me. Together. That's all. Now let's get back to our little deal where I get to fuck you sore today."

Even though her head is tilted to the side and her long blonde hair is spilling over, practically covering it, I see her smile.

"You're mine," I growl into her ear. "Say it," I insist.

All her pretenses are over. All the feigned indifference is gone now. She turns towards me so I can see her smile full on. "I'm all yours."

I lean down and touch my lips to hers, just the slightest touch. "Forever. Say it. Even if it's an abstract concept. It's the right thing to say right now and I need to hear it."

She bites her lip and my heart is pounding inside my chest with doubts. These doubts double the longer she hesitates. Because I've never felt afraid that a woman would reject me and I am, in this moment, very, very afraid. My heart is responding with desperation. "Say it," I urge again.

"Forever." The word comes out like a sigh. Or a whisper.

I hug her close and lean into her ear. "Thank you."

WE FUCK wildly for hours. We stay naked the entire day and it's well into the fading light of late afternoon before we drag ourselves up and start to think about food. Well, I think about food. Grace is on my laptop, logged in with her Twitter friends while simultaneously chatting with Bebe on my phone. I'm thrilled that she ignored Bebe all day in favor of sex with me, but Bebe is the best friend. Her acceptance is critical and tonight is the first step in gaining that stamp of approval.

I shut down the grill and take the plate of burgers over to the outdoor kitchen. She likes American cheese, pickles, ketchup, mustard, and pepper. I asked her before she got distracted by the phone. I want this evening to be seamless and knowing what she likes is part of that.

I set her plate down on the small table next to her lounge chair and she smiles up and mouths thank you as Bebe continues to talk on the other end of the line.

I go inside and grab Felicity's kitchen laptop and take it back outside with me. Then I settle in the lounge chair next to Grace and open up my own Twitter account and navigate to the Dirty Heaven list while I chew on my dinner. I snap a picture of Grace with my laptop camera. She's got a towel wrapped around her because she was chilled after our last swim, so she's not naked.

MovieStar @VaughnAsher
@FilthyBlueBird You look #Fuckable…

Her laptop pings a new interaction and I take a big bite of burger and chew as she reads it. The look on her face… priceless. "Oh yeah, baby. Game. On. Tonight." She rolls her eyes and tries to continue her conversation with Bebe, but even I can hear the screaming coming from the phone as my tweet filters out to the world.

MovieStar @VaughnAsher
@FilthyBlueBird #DirtyHeaven is mine tonight.

The ping. The smile. The feigned indifference. She hangs up the phone. A few seconds of furious keystrokes and…

Grace @FilthyBlueBird
@VaughnAsher I own #DirtyHeaven, bitch. *#VaughnAsherIsMyBitch*

I laugh out loud. She chews her burger, as she positions the laptop so I can't see her screen.

MovieStar @VaughnAsher
@FilthyBlueBird #FlashbackTime Get ready.

I navigate to Felicity's Twitter list of @FilthyBlueBird. It has all of Grace's tweets. After Grace made her big escape from Saint Thomas and left me searching the airport like a maniac trying to make sure she wasn't just hiding from me, Felicity figured out who she was on Twitter and started compiling. She even copied them into dummy accounts in anticipation of a possible full account deletion.

I admit, after I realized Grace was not in fact waiting for me to pick her up from departures, I went through her entire timeline. From. Day. One.

I chuckle and look up at Grace. She's got one of those *oh shit* looks on her face. "Remember when you wrote this…?" I press the retweet button and shoot her a wide grin.

Her laptop bloops and she looks down. I look down too, so we can read it together.

Grace @FilthyBlueBird
Come here and take off my lip gloss @VaughnAsher #OnMyKneesWaiting

She looks up, biting said lip, and I quickly press send on my reply tweet.

MovieStar @VaughnAsher
@FilthyBlueBird #Flashback to last night. Oh, you weren't wearing lip gloss. But you are now. #GetOnYourKneesAndWait

She chuckles and smirks as her fingers fly across the keys.

Grace @FilthyBlueBird
@VaughnAsher - Dabbing lips with a napkin. #ThatAllYouGot?

I choose my next favorite tweet of hers and press the retweet symbol.

Grace @FilthyBlueBird

I love Shark Week. And I'm convinced #Megalodon is actually @VaughnAsher penis #hidingInHisPants #NotTheOcean

She covers her face for that one and I use her recovery time to type my response.

MovieStar @VaughnAsher

@FilthyBlueBird Right now. #Megalodon #ReadyAndWaiting for a secret rendezvous. Come on in, the #WaterIsFine

She types out a hasty response.

Grace @FilthyBlueBird

@VaughnAsher - Waiting for a proper invitation #BegForItMaster

MovieStar @VaughnAsher

@FilthyBlueBird My command is your proper invitation #ThoseWhoFollowOrders get rewarded. #MastersDontBeg

"Grace, my sweets. I always win. Why must you fight me? Come on, come sit with me. We can dirty-tweet together, have a melding of the mind. And body." I wink at her.

She shakes her head and starts typing again, then chews her thumbnail as she deletes, types, deletes again. After several minutes of this, she looks up and swipes her tongue across her perfect lips, pressing a button on her keypad with a flourish.

Grace @FilthyBlueBird

@VaughnAsher #CommandMe and I'll comply. #AskMe and I'll give in. #LetMeChoose and I'll #BeYours Which do you want more?

When I look over at her, she's twisting her hair, her eyes are wide and expectant, and her breathing is faster than it was. She's nervous. "Is there any doubt in your mind which one I want more?"

She points to the computer in my lap. "Tell them, not me."

"You need reassurances?" She nods but lets the question hang there. "You want a public declaration, just like I wanted a public submission?"

She nods again. "I don't want to be your secret."

"You're not a secret. We're tweeting as ourselves. Everyone can see it."

"I don't want to be your servant, either."

"It's a joke, sweets. Since when do you take it so seriously, anyway? You never took it seriously on the island. And you have to admit, I've been so much better since we came back to our real lives. I'll stop with the jokes if you want, but that's all it was. Am I calling you girl? Are you calling me Master? No. We're in a different phase now, can't you tell?"

"I…" She exhales and closes the laptop. "I'm not sure. I'm not sure what I'm doing. I need to go home. I'm really confused, to be honest. I mean, so much is going on outside this sanctuary. I'm worried about the fallout. I'm worried about my job. I'm worried about... you. And me. And I have to admit, you're so much closer to the dream guy I envisioned now, it scares me."

"Why?" I laugh, but I don't mean it as a joke. I just don't understand where she's coming from.

"God, are you really that oblivious? Do I really need to spell out having your parents murdered, your life ripped apart, and the feelings that leaves behind?"

I close my laptop too, then put it aside. I stand up and scoot over to her lounge, moving her over and wrapping her up in my arms all in the same gesture. I place her on top of me, her head leaning on my chest. "I didn't mean it that way, Grace. At all. I was just playing with you."

"I know, but I have a hard time understanding when the game stops."

"The game is over. I won. You're mine."

"That's caveman talk, Asher."

"Yeah. But it's true. And it's simple. I don't think it requires explaining. But if you need it explained, Grace, I'm in love. I love you. It's not even difficult for me to say, it's easy. And if you need me to go online right now and say it in a tweet, fuck yeah. I'll do it."

"No, that's not what I meant. Not really. You say I'm yours, but I don't *feel* like yours."

"Aww." I squeeze her a little tighter because my heart hurts a little with her admission. "I'm gonna have to make you feel like mine, then?"

"Yeah," she says in a pouty voice.

"Mmmmm, that I can totally do. Should we go out tonight? It's not a good idea. The paparazzi will be on you for a while and I'll probably end up in a fight if they get too close. But I'm happy to take you out."

She thinks about this for a while and I let her take her time, just stroking her hair and relaxing. Enjoying what we have.

"It really doesn't scare you?"

"What, sweets?"

"Losing."

I huff out some air though my nose. "What should I be afraid of losing?"

"Me," she says with an incredulous tone.

Chapter Twelve - Grace

#AlwaysWantedToBeCharmed

CAN HIS life really have been so charmed? That he has no fear of losing anything? God, what would that be like? "I don't think I understand you, Asher."

"Asher?" he asks, sitting up a little straighter so he can look at me. But I turn my head so he can't. "Why the hell are you calling me Asher now? What did I do?"

"I just can't relate. And even though I shouldn't hold it against you, I do. I'm fucking pissed that my life is so fucked up and yours is so perfect."

"Perfect?" He laughs. I can feel it through his chest. "You know, my whole life people have thought that about me. I've heard it so many times I stopped listening. But coming from you, shit. That kinda hurts."

I scrunch up my face in confusion, but I stay still. I know it's wrong to assume his life is perfect, but from my perspective, it is. There's just no comparison.

"You want to know my demons, Grace? Do you need to know my secrets to be able to accept that I'm capable of understanding what you feel? What do you need?"

Do I? Do I need for him to be damaged for me to accept this… whatever this is? And if I do, what does that say about me? That I can only relate to the lost and the tragic?

"Because if that's what you need, then fine. I have never really articulated it in words before. I've never had to," he says in a whisper as he gives me a squeeze. "No one ever wanted me to justify my personal trauma to prove that I can understand them. But I will."

"Wait." I stop him with a hand on his chest. I push myself up so I can look him in the eye. "If this is really fucked up of me, then no."

"Grace, why does it matter if it's fucked up? Why do you care what I think of your request?"

"Because I don't want you to think I'm…" I let out a long sigh. "That he… ruined me. That I'm damaged and dirty and unlovable."

"Do you think he ruined you? Do you feel damaged and unloved?"

"Yes." I exhale and then immediately take a huge gulp of air. "Yes, I think all that stuff."

"Then why do you want to hide that?"

"Because…"

"Because you think I won't love you?"

"How can you?"

His brows knit together, his confusion so real, painted so clearly on his face, it sets me back a second. "Jesus, I'm not that shallow, Grace. I *am* a human being."

"I didn't mean it—"

"No," he says, cutting me off harshly. "Enough with the didn't mean it bullshit. OK?" his eyes dart back and forth as he searches for my intentions.

What are my intentions? "I just…" I have to swallow hard and look away. "I just… need reassurances."

He shakes his head. "Try again, sweets. I'm not interested in lies, and maybe you're not lying to me, but you're lying to yourself. And if we're in a relationship, that's the same thing."

God, now look what I've done. He wants me to face things I've pushed away for a decade, and he wants me to do it now. What if he leaves if I can't do it? What if he walks away?

"Did you have a therapist after you came back?"

"Of course. I still have one."

"So their plan was to let you deny things? Because that's a new one for me. I think everyone in Hollywood has at least two therapists on the payroll at all times. It's just something you do. So I've had my share of therapy, and none of them ever let me lie to myself."

"What is it you think I'm lying about?" God, he's so confusing. Is this about me or him? Or the way I feel about him? Or the way I feel about myself? I don't get it.

"What really happened to you?"

I shake my head. "I'm not talking about it."

"Why?"

"Why?" I laugh. "I'm pretty sure you can figure that out."

"OK, I'll figure it out for you then. Because you're in denial."

"Believe me, Asher, I'm not in denial."

"And we're back to Asher again, are we?"

"Jesus, what the hell do you want from me? You want me to tell you what those eight months were like? Why?" I sit all the way up, between his legs, and rest back on my butt with my legs underneath me. "Why would you want to hear that? Why would you want me to say it?"

He reaches up and strokes my cheek. "I don't want to know that shit, Grace. I don't want to know any of it. You're crazy if you think I want to hear you talk about it. I don't. But you are mixing up my intentions with that experience. You're not looking forward. You're stuck in the past."

I get up off the lounge chair and walk away.

"Where are you going?" he calls out after me.

"Home."

He's up next to me, grabbing me by the upper arm and turning me around. "Grace, running away only makes it worse. Just spit the words out."

"What fucking words?" I shout.

He cups his hands around my face and leans in for a kiss. It's soft and sweet. So small, yet so meaningful. "How did you get away, Grace?"

"You heard this part. He dropped me off at a hospital in Nebraska."

Vaughn lets out a long breath and pulls me into a hug. "I think—and maybe I'm wrong, because I don't know what happened to you while you were with him—but it must've really messed with your head to be so... *coveted* for so many months and then to just be dropped off like that."

I push him away. "Are you saying I'm fucked up because he let me go? Oh my God!"

Vaughn holds me tight. "It's psychology, Grace. It's a mind fuck, right?"

I push back again, but his arms are all the way around me now. "That's not what it is. I was grateful he let me go. I thought he was going to kill me."

"OK. You know better than me, sweets. You were there, I wasn't. So you know the truth."

But I know what Vaughn's saying underneath those words. He's saying I know the truth, but I won't accept it.

"Wanna finish Dirty Heaven?" He changes the subject. "Or go out to eat? Or make a sex tape?"

I allow myself to chuckle at that.

"I can think of so many, many ways to let the world know you're mine, Miss Kinsella. These are but three options for tonight. And you're not going home tonight, that's for sure. Tomorrow. I have lots of plans for tomorrow in Denver."

I melt into his embrace and try not to cry. He can sense my shift and my sadness, because he strokes my head and continues to talk.

"I have so many surprises for you in Denver."

The soothing rumble of his voice vibrating up from his chest makes my body feel pliant and supple. "I want to go to bed," I decide. "And watch movies."

"I have a DVD of *IM2*. It's in my contract so I can have private screenings. Wanna watch me be a super anti-hero who doesn't save the world but leaves it a better place?"

"Oh my God! Do you die?" I'm appalled.

"Hmmm, you think I'll spoil the ending for you? Pffft. You're cray-cray."

I laugh. "Yes, I definitely want to watch *IM2*." I pull away so I can look up at his face. "I loved that first movie because you were so unexpected. Did you ever read the book?"

"Of course."

"He's not really a good guy, is he?"

"No, he's not. That's why I wanted to be him. Even with the occasional rumor, people saw me as bright and clean and perfect before I did that movie. And now they see me as him."

"And you like that?"

"Yeah, because he's damaged, Grace. And so am I. We all are. People relate to that, there's nothing wrong with it. It's just... human nature."

I know Vaughn's really talking about me, but I don't care. I'm done talking about me for now and he's gonna let it go, and for that I'm grateful. But I don't want him to think that all that serious talk was a waste, either. I want him to know that I'm listening. "I don't need a public declaration, Vaughn."

"Yes, you do, Grace. But we have time for that. Believe me, life will be filled with public moments tomorrow. Let's enjoy the private ones we have left tonight."

I couldn't agree more. So I let him lead me into his not-so-movie-star house. We walk through the halls and end up in a home theater, but not the kind with oversized leather chairs set up stadium-seating style. There's a huge sectional sofa in the shape of a square. It's not leather, either. It's something soft and plush. And there's pillows and blankets.

"Have I mentioned I love to watch movies?" he asks me, pointing to the couch. "Climb in, Grace," he commands. I crawl on the couch and settle against the back. He disappears for a second, then returns just as the movie begins to display on the white screen in front of us.

"It's huge. I've never seen a projection screen so big in a house before."

He shoots me a smirk. "Size always matters." And then he bounces on the couch next to me. The room is filled with the surround-sound experience and I'm swept into the world of the Invisible Man.

But Vaughn twines his fingers with mine. He pulls me so close, I'm part of him. He wraps me up and whispers his lines in my ear.

The man next to me turns into the man on the screen. Vaughn Asher might not be a prince to the outside world, but in here, he's my hero. It's something very private, I think. To watch him *be* his art. To be pulled into his experience. To have him perform this movie just for me.

And even though I told him I needed the declaration to be public, I was wrong.

The only people who matter in this relationship are right here in this room.

Chapter Thirteen - Grace

#ThereIsAlwaysTimeForPussy

THE FLIGHT back to Denver is too short and when we land at Centennial Airport, it hits me that my fantasy weekend is over. This is so much worse than coming home from Saint Thomas. Back then, I was pretty sure I would never see Vaughn Asher again. But now I'm having a hard time coming to terms with the fact that I don't want him to leave.

I hate the clinginess. I've never liked getting to attached to men and even though I really, really, really like Vaughn, I still hate that feeling. I know that the minute he leaves I'll be thinking about when I can see him next. I'll be checking my phone for texts, or Twitter for a chance at some sexy banter.

There's a limo waiting for us, so the ride back to my neighborhood is filled with chitchat, phone calls for Vaughn, and in my case, an explosion of regret.

I regret not being more honest with him. For not being more adventurous with him last night. When *IM2* was over we watched another movie and I fell asleep. *We* fell asleep. Right there on the movie couch. And that's where we stayed all night. No goodbye sex. No proclamations of... whatever. No see-you-next-time plans.

So regrets. Lots of them, actually.

I look up at Vaughn and he's watching me intently as he talks on the phone about a meeting he has later today. It's Sunday, but his next project is directing the *IM* spin-off and from what I can gather, it's a seven-days-a-week kind of thing. *What's wrong?* he mouths.

I smile and shake my head. And then I look out the window. We're just getting off the freeway near the Pepsi Center and heading towards LoDo where I live. The limo is not long, thank God, because as soon as we turn onto Wazee Street, things close in and the streets get narrow. My building is just shy of the 16th Street Mall, and there is no parking out front. I'm just about to tell the driver he might want to swing into the alley, but he's a step ahead of me. He maneuvers the limo past cars and finally pulls into the small lot that belongs to my building. My car is right where I left it.

As soon as we stop Vaughn is off the phone. "OK, ready?" he asks, taking my hand.

"For?"

The door opens from the outside and Vaughn tugs on my hand as he exits the car, pulling me along with him. I step out into the familiar lot and blink back the bright sunshine. Somewhere church bells are ringing. "I feel like I've been gone forever."

Vaughn just smiles wide as he leads me up to the back door.

"Shit," I say. "I don't even know where my key is. I think I left it back in Vegas!"

"I had your stuff packed up from your room, Grace. It's upstairs. But you won't need it."

"I need it to get in the building!" But as soon as the words come out, Vaughn jingles a keychain at me. "You have a key to my building?"

He shakes his head and inserts the key in the lock. "You mean"—he pushes the door open and I step inside, confused—"*my* building?"

"What. The. Fuck?"

"Grace, language, please."

But I just swat his arm off me as I try to take in what I'm seeing. "Where am I?"

He chuckles. "Your building."

"No," I say back. "My building doesn't have a doorman and a security lobby."

"It does now. Grace," he says, leading me over to the man at the desk that wasn't there last week, "this is Bigmy. Leo Bigmy. He's in charge of building security."

Mr. Bigmy has one of those describing names. He's a very big man who looks more like a bouncer than a doorman. He's wearing a dark suit that fits him nicely, but it can't hide the muscles underneath. "My pleasure to meet you," he says in a thick Eastern European accent, "Mrs. Asher."

"It's Kinsella. And you can call me Grace." I look up at Vaughn, questions all over my face, because he just starts explaining as he leads me to the stairs.

"Bigmy is new. A local, incorruptible, at least for the right price. And my price was right, wasn't it, Bigmy?'

"Yes, sir. No one gets in the door without an access card."

And then Vaughn produces said access card and places it in my hand. "That's yours. It's the only way to enter the building. You have to key in a code as well. Two-step security."

I look around for a second. My lobby has been transformed. In addition to the desk, there's a new hardwood floor, new drapes on the two windows that face the street, a fire in the fireplace that used to look like it hadn't been lit in a hundred years, and a cozy seating area in front of the flickering flames. "I don't understand."

"I bought the building, Grace. The day I had to cancel our first Twitter date. I'm sorry for that, by the way. Conner gave me a heads-up on the reporters lurking around Sam and I took it one step further and included you in my heightened security."

"You bought this building?" It's sort of blowing my mind.

"And upgraded your security. And your apartment, as well. That asshole across the hall, gone."

"Gone?" I'm still staring at the lobby, but he's leading me to the stairs now.

"I wanted to put in an elevator, but these old buildings. Too many permits. I had to grease a lot of palms to get this done while you were out of town as it is. Maybe later we can put in an elevator?"

"Later?"

We walk up the stairs and he continues talking. "Whole new apartment, Grace. Everything new, but of course I kept all your old stuff too. The decorator said you have nice taste, she…"

I stop listening because I'm just too stunned to understand what's happening. When we get to my floor I don't even know where I am. There used to be a small hallway here. That same hallway where I gave Vaughn a blow job in front of the neighbor. But now it's gone. In its place is a door.

"Here's your new apartment."

Vaughn punches in a security code and the door beeps. There's a man standing off to the side looking a little too much like a Secret Service guy with his wrist microphone and dark sunglasses.

The door opens and the sunshine floods my face, making me cover my eyes from the glare. I step inside and move away from the sun.

My apartment is huge. As it should be when one knocks down walls and combines two places into one. "I have this whole floor?" There were only two apartments up here to begin with, and now there is only one. "Laundry room?"

"Oh," Vaughn says, pointing down the hall. "Inside now. I can't stand the thought of you having to leave the apartment to do laundry. That's a security risk I won't have."

I walk forward and my fingertips trace down the smooth silver granite countertops of my brand new kitchen. The cabinets are black and the appliances are stainless. There are so many details I love about this kitchen, I can barely take them all in.

I look over at the new living room. It's decorated in neutral grays with pink accents. It softens the modern colors in the kitchen and makes it much more feminine.

"Well." I take a big long breath and let it out. "I'm not sure what to say."

And that's when I see the cat. Sitting on the windowsill, licking its paw so it can clean its face.

"You said you loved cats, remember? Back on the beach in Saint Thomas? But the building had a no-pets policy."

I squint my eyes. Did I say that? How does he remember all that stuff?

"She's a shelter cat, Grace. Adoption is our thing, right?"

And then I smile. And relax a little. "It is, yes." I walk over to the cat. She's big and orange and has some subtle tiger-striping. She stops her cleaning to peer up at me, then promptly goes back to her business.

"They called her Layla, but you can name her whatever you want."

"Layla," I whisper. "I have my own cat." I turn around and look up at Vaughn. "Why did you do this?"

"I want to keep you safe and make you happy." It comes out so quickly, it has to be true.

I want to ask him so many more questions. Why? All of them are whys. Why me, mostly. What the hell does this guy see in me? I really don't get it. And it's not like I don't think I deserve a great man, or to be spoiled like this. And that's what this is, plain and simple. It's spoiling. That's not it. It's just... he could have anyone. And I'm such a pain in the ass. And I have so much baggage. And I'm not even nice, actually. I'm sorta mean to him.

"Don't overthink it, Grace. Just let it happen."

I walk over to the window, not the one framing the cat, and look out. This is the old neighbor's side of the building and he has a view. *I* have a view. And it's a cool one. Looking straight down onto Wazee. A mall bus rumbles down 16th Street and it begins to sink in.

Vaughn Asher built me a dream house in five days. Four, really, if you don't count today.

I turn back to him and smile. "I really... I have no words, Vaughn. Only thank you, but it seems so inadequate."

He simply shrugs and smiles. "Does it make you happy?"

I nod. "It does. But—"

"But? Oh, please don't be one of those women who can't accept a gift, Grace. Don't."

"No, that's not what I was going to say. Never mind. I love it." I walk towards him and he opens his arms and wraps them around me.

"Shall we christen the new bed?"

"Do you have time before your meeting in LA?"

"Sweets, there is always time for pussy."

Chapter Fourteen - Grace

#JustWhatTheFuck

VAUGHN GRABS me by the waist and jerks my hips forward until I slam against the hardness beneath his jeans. "I'd rather you stayed with me in LA, but I get it. I have to share you with your friends and family here. By the way," he says, cocking his head a little. "You've met mine, so when do I get to meet yours?"

His question catches me off guard and I find myself holding my breath. I don't have a good answer.

"Grace?"

"Sorry," I say, shaking my head a little. "I just…" I look up at his movie-star face. His perfectly chiseled jawline. His deep blue eyes. His hair is a little bit messy, just the way I like it. His smile is still large and genuine, but as the seconds tick off, it falters.

"Grace?"

"I just… I've never brought a man to meet my…" I shrug my shoulders a little. "I don't bring people to meet Mr. and Mrs. Chambers. I mean, I never have."

"You call your parents Mr. and Mrs. Chambers?"

I duck my head so I don't have to meet his gaze. "I just never knew what to call them. I called Bebe's mom Marjorie when she was my lawyer, but then…" Shit, why is this so hard?

"But then… you couldn't bring yourself to call them Mom and Dad once they adopted you?"

I nod.

"Felicity calls me Vaughn. Or V. I'm not her dad. But sometimes I feel like her dad."

I look back up at him and even though the smile is gone, he still looks… OK. Happy. "I don't call them Mr. and Mrs. Chambers to their face, obviously. Or in front of Bebe. I *do* call them Mom and Dad. To make them feel good. But it's never felt right for me. It feels fake. It's dishonest to tell strangers that they are my parents. They aren't. They didn't raise me, Vaughn. They saved me, yes. But they didn't raise me."

"Felicity said the same thing. She was not born to worthless people. She just… didn't win the family lottery like I did. That's what she told me when we discussed what she wanted to call me. Of course, I never expected her to call me her father. She just wanted me to know where she was coming from before I took financial responsibility for her."

I like hearing about Felicity. It makes Vaughn so much more real. And he's probably one of the few people I've met who might understand my feelings.

"Hey, wanna watch TV? Look at this baby." Vaughn points to the sixty-inch flatscreen on the wall. He leads me over to the new couch. It's light gray leather with pink pillows. Much nicer than the one I got from the thrift store that is nowhere to be found. Whoever did the design in here must have deduced correctly that it was trash, not treasure.

I sit down and the buttery leather almost makes me moan. "Don't you have to get back?"

"Sure, but the plane doesn't leave until I get there."

We kick our feet up on the coffee table and he pulls me into his chest as he flips the TV on. "ESPN or ESPN?" he asks.

I laugh. God, how weird to have a man in my house.

Shit, how weird to have this house.

"I'll take ESPN, thanks."

"Thought so. Now if I can find the damn channel. I think it's one forty-five." He flips through the channels, hunting for sports talk, and my face flies by.

"Go back. I saw me."

"Noooo. That's a bad idea, Kinsella. You learn to ignore that shit quick. Just pay no attention to it or it will drive you wild." He finds the sports channel and sets the remote down on his leg.

"But it said something about a wedding. It must be about Kristi and I want to see what she's saying."

"But it's football stuff, sweets," he says, pointing to the TV.

I grab the remote and start flipping channels. "It'll take like two minutes."

Kristi's face appears, smiling and happy. The camera pans down to her obvious baby bump.

"No questions," she says, placing a hand over the camera. But it's in a good-natured way. She's not running anymore, she's content. Johnny Blazen steps forward, the media darling personality taking over.

"He didn't tell me anything. I barely know the guy. Vaughn Asher was only interested in one thing when we were together last week, and that was making sure Grace was safe."

"Hey, he's talking about you." I look over at Vaughn and he's gone white. "What's going on?"

The reporter in the TV redirects my attention. Vaughn is reaching for the remote in my hands, but I jerk it away as I read the crawl at the bottom of the screen.

Vaughn Asher marries Daisy Bryndle in a three AM ceremony in Las Vegas last Thursday.

"What the hell?" I look over at Vaughn and he's staring at me.

His mouth is a tight line, his eyes pleading with me. "Just... change the channel and we can talk."

"What? Why are they saying we're married?"

Silence. Just more staring.

I bite my lip as I wait, but the seconds tick off and I can't be patient. "Please, for the love of God, tell me they're lying."

He says nothing, but his head shakes out a no.

"Vaughn, this isn't funny. There's no way we got married that night. I was passed out drunk."

His stupid head just continues to shake. "You weren't drunk, Grace."

"I was. I have no memory of any of it."

"You weren't drunk. And I've been trying to tell you—"

"You've been trying to *tell me*?" I stand up and he reaches for my arm. But I smack his hand off. "You were trying to tell me what?" I walk across the room and stand near the window where the cat is now curled up in a ball, fast asleep. "You did *not* marry me knowing full well that I never wanted to be married. You did not." He stands up and starts towards me, his arms reaching. But I put a hand up. "Stop. Don't. Tell me right now, what the hell happened that night?"

"Grace… you were so insecure. You were talking about your parents—"

"I never talk about my parents, Vaughn. And all that was before the media ambush. That's the only reason I talked about them this weekend, OK? So I know—"

"You *don't* know, Grace." His words come out stern and strong. They stop my outburst mid-sentence. "You don't know anything. Because you don't remember. I was there. That," he says, pointing to the TV, "proves everything I've been telling you."

"Telling me? You haven't told me anything, apparently."

"I've been telling you how I feel. And that wedding was proof. I married you. You," he stresses, "married me too. *We* got married."

"No. How could you? After everything I told you?"

"Everything what? I don't get your aversion to marriage. Haven't I proved I'm in this for real? What more do I have to do? I told you I love you."

"Oh my God. You told me that because you married me. You told me that so when I found out, I'd think it was real!"

"Grace! Listen to yourself. It's real. We're married. We signed the license. You," he stresses again. "signed the license."

But I'm not listening. My mind is reeling from this fact. I'm married.

No! I am *not* married. My mind says it over and over and over again. *I'm not married. I'm not married.*

"Grace." Vaughn grabs me by the shoulders so hard it hurts. I push him off and fall to the floor, my head spinning. "Grace? What's wrong?"

I crab-walk backwards across the floor as he moves closer. "Stay away from me!"

"Grace, please. Just… calm down and listen."

"No. Get out."

"What? No, I'm not getting out. That's bullshit. You're done running, baby. You're done running. We're talking this out like adults and you're going to tell me exactly what's going on."

"What's going on? You fucking married me!"

"I love you."

"You don't love me. You don't even know me!"

"Why are you freaking out? Just tell me."

"You know why." I stare at Vaughn, the tears burning the back of my eyes until they burst forth in long streams. Not drops. Streams. Rivers of tears run down my face. "He tried to convince me we were married. He brainwashed me. He had me so convinced I was his wife, I fucking *wept* for him on the front lawn of the hospital when he let me go!"

Chapter Fifteen - Vaughn

#TheCouchIsMyFriend

HER WORDS echo in my ears.

I was right. He fucked with her head and when he left her, she didn't know how to process it.

I take a deep breath and let it out slowly. "Grace, just relax. OK? We can get an annul—" I stop before the word finishes. But it's too late. She heard it and I can't take it back. "I don't mean that."

"You *do* mean that, Asher. You do mean that. Because now that you know how broken I am, you don't want to touch me."

I shake my head, force myself to stay calm. "That's not true. I want what's best for you."

She covers her ears like a child and shakes her head so hard her hair whips across her face. "Leave."

"Grace—"

"Leave!"

"I'm not leaving."

She stops her childish tantrum and says very clearly, "You *are* leaving. Get out!"

I weigh my options. I can stay and fight with her. Or I can go wait in the hallway for a little bit, give her a chance to calm down and keep an eye on her.

I opt for the hallway.

"OK, I'm gonna go out in the hallway. But I'm not leaving, do you understand? I'm not leaving. I'm gonna give you space to calm down and think this through, see that this is nothing like what happened to you as a child, and then I'm going to call you. Do you understand? We will talk about this. I refuse to go home until we talk about this." I start backing away from her, towards the door. "I'm gonna be right outside."

She shakes her head. "No. If you stay in this hallway, I will call the police. I'm not fucking around."

"I own this building, Grace."

"You do not own *me*, Asher." She says it with such venom I recoil.

"I know that, sweets. I do."

"Then leave. Respect me. For once. Respect me."

That hurts, I have to admit. I do respect her, but I've got no good excuse for why I didn't tell her what we did that night besides fear that she'd react badly. And why did I fear that?

Because I knew it was wrong when we did it. I knew.

And she knows I knew.

I give in and retreat. I walk to the door, open it, step through, and close it behind me. The chain lock engages and

I force myself to walk towards the stairs. I take them slowly, telling myself the whole way down to the lobby that once she cools off, we will talk about this and figure it out.

But until then, I walk over to the chair in front of the fireplace I had refurbished for the building lobby and take a seat. Until then, I will sit right here and wait.

Chapter Sixteen - Grace

#NotMyInvisibleMan

THE BUZZING of my phone wakes me. My eyes are so swollen from crying, I have a hard time opening them to see the screen.

Unknown number.

Vaughn.

Meet me on the roof.

Jesus, can't that guy take a hint? Why doesn't he ever give up?

Do I want him to give up? I ask myself honestly. Or is this whole freakout a test to see how committed he is? Isn't it a good thing that he's still hanging around? I know he was down in the lobby because there's reporters outside now. I was watching TV for hours as they set up camp in front of my building. If Vaughn hadn't put in the new security features, they'd probably be camped out in my hallway.

But the marriage...

Bebe called and I told her I can't talk about it yet. Not to her. I need to figure it out and I don't need all that old psycho-babble they used to feed me when I... came back.

I need to think about it in new terms. Vaughn was right. I was traumatized when I was let go. I'm not sure if any of my therapy sessions mentioned that or not. I refused to talk to any counselors. Just refused. I went for more than a year. Three times a week. And never once did I say a word.

So once I was adopted by the Chambers family, they let me decide if I wanted to continue wasting my days that way. And of course, I said no thank you.

Things got better after that. I got to recreate myself. I got to choose a new name.

In the hospital I was wild. And vulgar. And undignified. I lost myself in those eight months. So I chose Grace.

I wanted to remind myself to be graceful. To act with grace. To never, ever let that freak win. He made me into a primitive and weak mess. He made me uncivilized and rude. Withdrawn and silent.

I wanted to be Grace and so I became that girl. The yes girl. The girl who pleased people and fit in. I became... *social*. And perky and sweet and cute.

I chose Kinsella because Sophie Kinsella is my favorite author. I read every book of hers while I was locked up that year. She kept me going. She kept me alive. She made me laugh again. I wanted to be the girls in her books. I wanted to live those lives. I wanted to be anyone but me.

And so I am. I am a cliché of chick-lit females.

Are you coming? a second text asks me.

Am I coming?

What would those girls in the books do? That's how I've made my choices since I became Grace Kinsella. WWKGD? *What would Kinsella girls do?* Blow off the millionaire movie star one last time? Or admit they need him, and humbly ask for another chance?

I throw my covers off and pull on a pair of jeans and grab a hoodie. Kinsella girls don't wear hoodies to meet millionaires on the roof, but it's dark. So who cares?

I grab the keychain with my new house key off the foyer table and stick it in my jeans pocket, and then step out into the quiet hallway. I pull the door closed with a soft whoosh and listen for noise downstairs.

Nothing.

I take the stairs up to the roof and push through with the start of a smile on my face. I haven't been up here since that dinner we had all those weeks ago. The roof is dark, but the lights from the building across Wazee Street backlight the palm trees. I bet they are gonna die soon if they stay here. It will be cold and snowy before long. I look for Vaughn as the door closes behind me but there's no one.

"Vaughn?"

A foul-smelling cloth covers my mouth and I inhale before I realize what's happening.

My eyes look up and find his face.

No, not his face.

His mask.

This time not the boy from camp. This time he's the Invisible Man.

"You're mine," he says, the voice taking me back ten years. "I told you, Daisy. You're mine."

That's the last thing I hear as my world goes black.

Media by JA Huss

SOCIAL MEDIA SERIES BOOK FIVE

PROFILE

NEW YORK TIMES BESTSELLING AUTHOR

HUSS

Chapter Seventeen - Vaughn

#BlueberriesAren'tNews

LAUGHTER from a tenant and a sharp pain in my back pulls me out of my hazy slumber. Note to self—the lobby of Grace's building needs better furniture if I'm going to be sleeping on the couch every time she gets angry.

I chuckle a little at that. It should annoy me, but it doesn't. It makes me feel... part of something. Part of a relationship. And I am, right? We are married. We. Are. Married. And I know she's wary and I know she's unhappy about how it came about, but the fact is, she married me. She said, 'I do,' and signed her name on the license.

I realize now that we were both far too drunk. I mean, she has no memory, so yeah. I huff out a breath. She was definitely far too drunk to make that decision. But it's done. And I'm not interested in getting unmarried to Grace. In fact, I'm interested in doing it all over again, only this time making it a huge production. Hollywood style, maybe. Hundreds of guests. Lavish place settings and those little bags they give out filled with items you don't need but which have the bride and groom's name on them.

"Boss?"

I want a huge cake as tall as her, with a different flavor filling in each layer. Dancing, of course. I've never danced with her. So dancing. And a honeymoon. A real honeymoon. Not the beach. Maybe Japan or Iceland or a cruise around the world. Something daring and new.

"Boss? You awake?"

And then house-hunting. Let her choose the neighborhood. Hell, the state. She might not want to be in California. I don't need to be in California, that's for sure. She might even want to keep her job. Or find a new job. She might want to live in Denver.

Denver. Jesus.

I'd live here though. It's got an airport for my jet. Who cares where we live when we can be where we need to be in a few hours? It doesn't matter.

"Boss!"

"Shit, Ray. What the fuck do you want?" I drag myself out of my dreams and look up at my head of security. "What?"

"She didn't go to work today. The other tenants have all left, but she's still inside her apartment."

"Well…" I sit up and rub my hands down my face. I need to shave. "She had a rough few days, Ray. She deserves some time off."

"I'm just telling you. It's a workday, and she didn't go."

"OK. Well, I'm gonna go grab some coffee and see if she's ready to talk to me yet." I stand up and clap him on the back. "Thanks, man. Appreciate your help."

I almost crash into Bigmy, Grace's personal security guard, as I make my way towards the front door. "Do you need something, Bigmy?"

"I think she's asleep," he says in his thick Eastern European accent.

I nod. "OK."

"There's no noise in there. Like nothing. Silence."

"Is that bothering you?" I ask, unsure of what he's getting at.

"Most people get up, go to bathroom. Make coffee. Turn on TV. She's not doing that."

"Well, I guess she's sleeping."

"Right," he says. But he's not convinced.

"Look, Bigmy, if you think there's a problem, just say so."

He stares at me for a few seconds and then shrugs. "No problem."

I grab my sunglasses off the coffee table and place them on my head. "OK, well, then, I'm heading over to the Starbucks—"

"You should stay inside," Ray says. "The media is out there."

"Ray, the media is everywhere. They're not gonna go away until we resolve all this shit. And I refuse to be stuck inside because of them. Ray, you come with me. Bigmy—"

"Yes."

"You stay here with Grace. I'll be right back and we'll see if we can't coax her out with a muffin and some coffee."

"She likes blueberry," Bigmy says.

"I know that, thank you." Fuck.

Ray and I walk to the front door and the frenzy starts before it even opens. Ray's a tall guy. Not massive, like Bigmy. But tall. And he's got a look about him that says, *I will kill you with my bare hands.*

The shouting starts as I exit, but I just flip my sunglasses down and push right through them. I've been doing this for twenty-seven years. Some encounters have been more stressful than others, but I'm not the kind of movie star who punches out photographers. They are making a living. Yeah, they are parasites who make a living off *me*, but fuck it. I really have no beef with them. In fact, most of them are nice when they're not stalking you.

But then I see that bitch from *Buzz Hollywood*. She steps right in front of me and sticks that microphone in my face. "What will Jasinda think when she finds out you're cheating on her?"

I actually stop to laugh. Ray grabs my forearm and tugs, trying to get me moving again. But I shrug him off. "I hope," I tell the reporter as I look her in the eye, "she feels ashamed of herself. Jasinda"—I am facing the camera now, so I address her directly—"you're a lying bitch. If you're even pregnant, I'm up for a DNA test any time you are. I have a wife now and her name is Grace Kinsella-Asher." And then I turn back to look at all of them as they hover close behind me. "And now if you'll excuse me, I'm going to get her a coffee and a muffin. Blueberry," I add. "Grace likes blueberry. And she likes iced tall sugar-free caramel, nonfat, light ice, Starbucks double shot on ice. At least"—I stop to have a chuckle—"when she has money on her Starbucks app, she does."

"Does she have money on her app, Vaughn?" a reporter from an internet blog asks me.

He's nice, and funny. And never too serious about what he prints. "Her coffee worries are over, yes."

Now they chuckle with me and I turn away and start walking down the street to the Starbucks. Half of them follow, but they stay behind me. Like a little train of leeches—annoying, but harmless.

See, this is how you handle the media. You don't have to give them what they want, you just have to give them something they can *use*. Now they have two factoids about Grace to run with. Tomorrow everyone will be drinking that coffee concoction and the blueberry muffins will be sold out.

The day after tomorrow, they will be after the personal details of someone else and no one will give a shit about us until the next movie comes out, or I get nominated for an award, or Grace gets pregnant.

God, that makes me smile like an idiot and when I look over at Ray, he's shaking his head. "What?" I ask him.

He holds up a hand. "Nothing."

We turn right at 16th Street and head down towards the Starbucks.

"But," he continues, "you have a stupid grin on your face. And if I didn't know better, I'd say you are in love."

"I am in love." I let out a breath. "I love this girl. I'm gonna marry her again and get her pregnant, and spend the rest of my life bossing her ass around and pissing her off." I glance back at Ray. "She likes it. But she also likes to fight it."

"Mmm-hmm. If you say so, boss."

We walk the rest of the way to Starbucks in silence. The reporters stay outside as I go in to order. Ray blocks them and they don't put up a fight. They figure if they're nice, I'll give them something else before I go back inside our building. And I probably will.

Life is a give and take. I've always known this. You can't always get what you want, so you have to just try to get what you need. And right now, I need for the media to leave us alone. Or at the very least, not be out to destroy us.

I sign autographs while I wait for Grace's drink. Cups mostly. I sign the apron of each employee and some napkins. And thirty minutes later—yeah, it's a long time to be stuck in a Starbucks signing autographs when all I want is to think about the woman I love, but it only benefits both of us in the end—Ray and I walk back to wake Grace up with a nice iced coffee and her favorite pastry.

I turn back to the media before going inside her apartment building. "I need a little advice."

"Sure, Vaughn!" I hear from the crowd. "Ask us anything!"

"What kind of ring should I get her? We didn't have time to get rings."

They start calling out suggestions. I nod for each and make a small comment like, "'Yes," or "Oh, I like that idea." That kind of thing.

They eat that shit up. They're happy now. I gave them two factoids and I asked them for help. They feel needed and necessary and none of what I actually said makes any difference to Grace, or me, or the world.

But it matters. The media is a part of my life. The media is the reason Kristi's brother called that hotline and let me know where she'd run off to.

Sometimes I need them, sometimes they need me. And I never forget that, because that's the secret to navigating this absurd world where what my wife eats for breakfast is print-worthy news.

I scan their faces and come back satisfied with my performance… until I see that bitch from *Buzz Hollywood*. She's not happy at all. She wanted to ambush me and she failed.

I give her a wink to let her know I won, and turn to go inside. Smiling all the way upstairs. I pass Bigmy, who is standing guard at the top, and then I knock.

Chapter Eighteen - Grace

#HashtagSurvival

THERE'S a knock on the door and I twist my head to try and see where it's coming from, but the pain in my neck is sharp. And penetrating. It shoots down my arm like white-hot lightning and I moan.

"Shut up."

My mind almost shuts down, that's how badly that voice shocks me. It can't...

The knocking stops me again.

"You know the rules."

"No," I say. Or at least I try to say, but I can't say anything. I realize I'm gagged and my heart starts to beat wildly. Erratic thumps inside my chest overtake all my coherent thoughts. I imagine all the ways in which this can kill me. I imagine my heart exploding and my breaths come faster, deeper, like I can't suck up enough oxygen to save my life.

I'm pulled up into a sitting position and he whacks me on the back like I'm choking instead of suffocating. "See," he says. "You'd die without me. I saved you again. How many times have I saved you?"

The knocking continues.

I try to open my eyes but my head is swimming. This is not happening. This is *not* happening. I fall forward and hit my head on the floor in front of my feet. The tendons on the back side of my leg scream in pain, the stretch too much for me. I wiggle, realize I'm bound too, and then thrash around so I can change position and relieve the stress.

"Sit up, Daisy." I'm pulled into an even more uncomfortable sitting position and that's when I know this is all real. That's what makes it set in.

Daisy.

I've been running from this man for ten years. I've been trying to force myself to come to terms with what he is, what he did, what he wanted… and now that I've moved on and let it all go… he's back.

"No!" I say it a lot louder this time, and even through the gag, it comes out clear enough.

I get a closed fist against my head for my trouble and teeter over, almost in slow motion, until I'm lying on my side.

The knocking continues and even as I'm wondering why he's not answering the door, I know.

It's not knocking. It's a tree branch. Slapping against the side of the house.

I'm back.

I'm back in my closet. I'm back in the prison he built for me when I was thirteen. I can smell it now. The cedar lining of the closet mixed with mice and old carpet. Bile stirs up in my stomach and I know I'm going to vomit.

But I also know doing that with a gag in my mouth might kill me. *Daisy, you can cope.* No! Grace! Grace can cope. *You are Grace!*

"I know you're a good girl, right, Daisy?"

I breathe evenly, trying to calm my pounding heart. I know what to do. I know what he wants. I know what happens if I don't comply. Because I've been here before. I've been bound and gagged inside this closet so many times I'll never be able to forget it.

"Daisy?" he asks, squeezing my cheeks so my chin is cupped in his hand. "Tell me you're good."

I know what he's doing. Even though I never talked to them, I did see therapists for years after I was returned. He's conditioning me. Or, since I was already conditioned, he's re-conditioning me.

Grace, as long as you know that, you're OK. Just don't lose sight of what's happening. Agree, give him what he wants. You know what happens if you don't.

"Yes," I mumble through my gag. "I'm good."

"Excellent," he says, removing the gag.

I swallow down the pooled saliva and take in deep breaths.

"Come here." He pulls me by the elbow, making it bend and stretch unnaturally until I stand. A new pain shoots up my shoulder and I hold in a whimper and scurry closer to him to relieve the pain. That's two injuries in the first few minutes. I need to pay better attention or he might break something.

My eyes finally open, though they are so heavy from the drugs I can only see a sliver of my surroundings. He tugs me along, making me stumble, but I recover fast because he will not slow down if I fall. He will drag me, and if I get hurt in the process, that's my own damn fault.

I've played this game many times.

So I keep up and try to pay attention. I listen for sounds—birds mostly. But I can hear the whine of a small airplane engine too. Smells—now that I'm out of the closet, the mice and mildew have been replaced with the smell of a farm. Sight. The furniture is not the same. It's all different. Gone are the tattered couches and scuffed wood tables and chairs. The floor out here is tile. New. The windows have curtains and aren't covered in boards.

I can see the sun.

"They're electrified," he says. "If you try to go out the window, you'll be shocked."

I say nothing. I'm not allowed to talk until I'm asked a question. At least that's how it was last time.

And even though this asshole is not going to get me to agree to his sick fantasy again, I look up at his masked face, gasp in surprise because it's the Invisible Man and not some kid I knew from archery camp, but catch myself and nod in agreement.

This is not good. He knows about Vaughn. That's the only reason he's wearing that mask.

"Sit." He points to a chair at the kitchen table, which is not the old chipped Formica with rusty metal chairs, but a new one made of glass. The chairs are trendy molded plastic. Something you might find in a high-end retro store.

"I have a good job," he says, noticing me notice the furniture. "I told you I'd be back and we'd live happily ever after."

No. That's not what he said.

I take a seat in the chair. He didn't say that.

"You didn't want to go, remember?"

"I was sick."

He slaps me in the head, this time not quite as hard. "You were not sick. You agreed to all of it."

"I was sick," I repeat, and he smacks me across the mouth this time. I taste blood, but I don't care. I spit it out and the red stains the pristine white tiled floor. "You brainwashed me." Another smack. More blood. "Go ahead," I tell him, all the inner warnings now absent. "Kill me if you want." And then I look him in the eyes. He's not wearing the Invisible Man goggles so I can see past the mask enough to discern that his eyes are dark brown. I see a part of an eyebrow, and that too is brown. That's more than I ever saw with that other mask he wore years ago. That one was tight against his face. This one is looser.

Eyes brown. Hair, probably brown. Maybe six feet tall. Less than two hundred pounds. Skinny, actually. Birds are singing, a small plane can fly overhead, and we're on a farm.

I make my checklist.

This is how I got through the years after I came home. Checklists. I organized everything around me. Took notice of everything. I practiced closing my eyes so I could remember the way a place sounds. I noticed the little things. I saw the details.

And I planned.

Because even though I don't remember him saying he'd come back for me, I must've known it all along. A man does not kidnap you, keep you prisoner for eight months, and then let you go with no intention of returning.

I knew he was coming.

And I'm ready.

I took self-defense. I learned how to shoot a handgun. I took yoga to help me stay calm. I studied the geography of the Midwest, because even though I never knew where I was, I knew I was on a farm. One that had both cattle and crops. He came in smelling like them both at times. Sweat and soil. That's what he used to smell like.

He smelled like it when he stole me, and he smells like it now.

He might not have changed much, but I'm as different as the furniture in this house and there's no way I'm going down without a fight. It took me years to reclaim my mind after he warped it with his talk of a demented future where I'd be his wife and we'd live out our lives together in marital bliss. And if he thinks—

I'm smacked to the floor with a hard fist across my mouth. More blood.

"I know what you're thinking, Daisy. And I don't like it. Get up."

I can't get up, my fucking hands are bound behind my back. He knows this, but he rolls me a little with his boot. "I said get the fuck up."

I wiggle around until I can roll over and get to my knees, then I rock forward and stand, my leg muscles straining to lift me up without the use of my hands.

"Sit," he barks.

I sit again. And then he plops a laptop down in front of me.

"You are a disgusting whore, Daisy." He points to my Twitter account. "Password."

Is this a battle I need to fight? I'm not sure, but the blood is still dripping down my face, so I decide that's a big no. If he wants to play around on my Twitter, more power to him. "My friends will all know it's not me."

"Oh, don't worry about that. It's you. Password."

I turn my head up so I can meet his half-hidden eyes again. "My password is 'I heart Vaughn Asher.'" He grits his teeth, clenches his jaw. I'll probably be hit again for that, but I don't care. "The heart is a less-than sign and a three."

He types it in and pulls up my profile, then gives me a sidelong glance. "We're gonna cure that affliction right now. Break up with him."

What?

"Give me a Filthy Blue Bird-worthy tweet that will let him, and the police, know that you left of your own volition and don't want to be bothered. One. Tweet. And it better do the job, because if the police come here, I'll kill both of us. I will never let you leave again. I told you back when I let you go, you are mine. I always mean what I say."

And then he stares at me so hard and for so long without blinking, I have to turn my head away.

"You have one minute."

I drop my head and stretch my neck. God, that feels good. I do it again and I can almost feel his anger. A clock is ticking on the wall, and I count those seconds as I imagine the thin hand sweeping around the center, counting down to my captor's next act of violence.

I wait until the minute he straightens up. I imagine his hand drawing back as he plans where he will strike me. And then my mouth opens and I feed him the words he thinks he wants.

"'Hashtag time to delete. I'm over it. Have a nice life, bitches.'"

I look up at the masked man to see what he thinks.

"Delete?"

I nod. "Yes, I've been meaning to do it since I left Saint Thomas. I want to stop all this. So type that and delete the account."

I know he's got a mask on, but I swear to God, I see him smile.

Asshole. He's just another asshole who thinks with his dick.

"You're done with Vaughn Asher?"

"So done."

"He married you."

That's right, let's play, you psycho. I keep my edge hard, I make myself stare him in the eyes. And then I tell him what he wants to hear. "Vaughn can't marry me. I'm already married. To you."

Chapter Nineteen - Vaughn

#Not #Walking #Away

I KNOCK again. "Gra-aaace." I blow out a breath of air and look over my shoulder at Bigmy. "She's still here, right? I mean, she never left last night."

"She never left, boss. Someone was here all night."

"What time did you leave?"

"Hmmm." He hums as he thinks. "The guard from Ray's team relieved me around midnight, I think? I got called back after a few hours. You were already asleep on the couch. The doorman saw me."

I knock again, but the feeling in the pit of my stomach can't be denied.

Something is wrong.

"Grace," I call out, pressing my forehead to the wooden door. "Answer me or I'm coming in."

I press my ear up against the door and listen.

Nothing.

"Here." I thrust the coffee and muffin at Bigmy and fish through my pocket for the key to Grace's apartment. I push it into the lock and twist the handle. "Grace?" Maybe she's sleeping. I walk into the entryway and then turn down the hallway where her bedroom is. The cat comes out of the door, meowing. "Hey, kitty. Where's Grace?" The cat rubs up against my leg and I peek into the room.

Nothing.

"Fuck. Bigmy, what the fuck? She's not here!"

"Let me check the rest of the apartment."

He goes off to do that while I call Ray. He picks up on the first ring. "Yup."

"Ray, she's gone. Did you see her leave last night?"

"No. She never left. We had guys outside, both front and back. And the paparazzi was here all night too. They'd have seen her."

"Not here," Bigmy says as he comes back into her bedroom. "No signs of a struggle."

"Did she get any calls last night, Ray?"

"Let me log in and see. I'm on my way up."

I end the call with Ray and take my attention back to Bigmy. "Who was the guard last night?"

"I'm new, Mr. Asher. I don't know your men. He had a security badge. Ray sent him up. He came up from downstairs."

"You said you left around midnight, so why were you called back?"

"He said his wife needed him and could I fill in his shift. I said OK."

Ray comes down the hallway, breathless from running up three flights of stairs. "She got a text, Vaughn. Two, last night."

"Who from?"

He throws up his hands. "Unknown number. The first one told her to come up on the roof."

A shooting pain runs across my shoulders as I tense up.

"She must've hesitated, because she didn't text back. So the next message asked if she was coming. That's it. That's all there was."

"What time?"

"Twelve twenty-five."

I push past them and run down the hallway. I exit the apartment and take the stars up to the roof three at a time. The door is not even closed all the way.

"Fuck. You didn't secure the roof? The buildings next door are all connected. This is a huge fail!" I look at Ray like he's an incompetent asshole and he goes still.

"Boss, look—"

"She's been fucking kidnapped! That freak came and got her. Took her right out of her apartment and you assholes never even saw him!"

"Vaughn," Ray says, his hands up, palms out, like he's warding me off. "We have cameras in all the hallways like you requested. We can look at the footage—"

"Then go look at it, Ray! For fuck's sake! She's been missing all goddamned night! Go check the fucking footage!"

"You think the guard was the kidnapper?" Bigmy asks.

I watch Ray as he disappears down the stairs and then turn back to Bigmy. "Do you?"

"We should call the police."

A ping distracts me from any thoughts of the police. It's coming from Grace's desktop. I walk over to her desk and stare at the screen.

"Twitter," Bigmy says.

"Yes, thank you. I can see it's Twitter." But the part I'm having trouble with is that Grace just posted an update.

Grace @FilthyBlueBird
#TimeToDelete. I'm over it. Have a nice life, bitches.

I take out my phone and press Grace's number. Is it possible she just left? She walked out on me? She walked away from her whole life?

No.

No, she'd never do that.

Except she already did once. She got herself a new identity and walked into the sunset, leaving behind everything she ever knew.

I bend over the desktop and grab the mouse, then click refresh on her profile page.

Sorry, that page doesn't exist!

She did it. She deleted her account.

My phone buzzes in my hand. I press accept and put it to my ear. "Yeah."

"We got the footage. She leaves her apartment at twelve thirty-five and never comes back."

"How the fuck does that happen, Ray?"

"Vaughn, I was here for eighteen hours yesterday. I have to sleep sometimes. This guy on camera, he's legit. He's my guy."

"So where is he? Bring him in. I want to talk to him."

"I already called him. He's on his way."

"Good. You let me know where he gets here."

"Should I call the police? Or should we wait and see?"

I scrub a hand down my face as I try to work through the consequences. "Yeah. Call them. Tell them Grace has been kidnapped and we need to bring in the FBI." I end the call and look back at Bigmy. "Do you think she just deleted that account?"

"Well… you did piss her off. She was pretty hot last night when she kicked you out."

"It almost doesn't matter, does it? I mean, we can call in the police and FBI all we want, but the truth is, that last Twitter message is the only thing they're gonna care about. Couple that with the fact that she's already pulled a disappearing act when her life spun out of control, and I already know where this is going."

"What do you want to do, Asher?"

God, that hurts too. No one calls me Asher but Grace. I find a contact in my phone and press send. Three rings later and the call is picked up. "Conner. She's gone."

"What?" He sounds asleep.

"Grace. She's been taken again."

"Vaughn, fuck. How do you know?"

"She's missing and she got a text last night to go up on the roof. She never came back. And... and she just deleted her Twitter account. She's being erased. That sick freak is erasing her as I stand here. I need you to check all her accounts. Her bank, her credit cards, her Starbucks. All of it."

"Yeah, sure, V. I'm on it. I'll call you back as soon as I know anything."

I thank him and end the call and then immediately place another one. This time I get Grace's voicemail.

"You've reached Daisy Bryndle."

I put it on speaker.

"I'm deleting this number and moving on. I can't live in the public eye. I need my privacy. Thank you and goodbye."

"That's wrong."

"What?" Bigmy asks.

"She would never call herself Daisy Bryndle."

He huffs out a long gust of air. "We need to call the police, Asher. And the FBI. Every minute that passes, she gets farther away."

"Yeah, but they're not gonna believe me." I turn to face the giant man. "She's leaving breadcrumbs that will make the police and FBI ignore this. Call her a runaway wife. They're gonna tell me to give her space or some bullshit like that. She'll come back on her own." Bigmy frowns at me. "She's setting me up to let go. But I'm not gonna let go. She's crazy if she thinks I'll let go. Whatever the reason for this disappearance, I'm not going anywhere. I'll never stop looking for her. Not until I find her. I'll never accept that she ran away until I hear it from her own mouth."

I told her I'd never leave, and I meant it. I refuse to walk away, even if she wants me to.

Chapter Twenty - Grace

#MyGameMyTurn

I'M walked back to the closet after he finishes deleting my Twitter account.

"Get in."

I do as I'm told because I have no choice at the moment. But I know how he works. At least, I know how he used to work. I test it out by stopping just past the threshold and lifting my arms a little in the hope that he will untie me. Like he used to.

He laughs. "We are back to day one, Daisy. You earn privileges, child. You don't expect them."

I sink to my knees. The mattress is thicker than the one that used to be in here, so at least it doesn't hurt. And then I lie down and roll over on my side. The door closes. I can't see through the crack between the floor and bottom of the door. But I don't really need to, so I just lie still.

We are back to day one, he said.

Just the thought makes my stomach cramp and my heart beat fast.

A foot kicks the door in front of my face and I squeal past my gag. "Shut up!" the man who is wearing a mask of Danny Penning shouts from the other side of the door.

But I can't shut up. I can't stop crying. I can't stop breathing hard, or choking, or shaking. And this makes the man angry. This makes him kick the door harder, and every time he kicks the door, it starts all over again. "Please," I mumble through my gag. "Just stop kicking the door."

But he can't hear me. I can barely hear me. My sobs are too loud. I'm lying face down on a rotten-smelling mattress, and the blood is pounding in my ears.

"I saw you at the dance, Daisy."

What dance? What dance? I want to scream this at the man. What dance? I didn't go to the dance!

"He was holding you close."

I have no idea what he's talking about.

"That boy was holding you close. I should've been the one to hold you close."

I'm in seventh grade. I've never been to a dance. Danny Penning lives four hours away. I only know him from 4-H camp. He was my archery partner and he hated my guts because I was distracted last summer. I kept screwing up our chances for prizes. I've never been to a dance, I have no idea why he thinks I have, and I don't know what Danny has to do with any of this.

"He kissed you, didn't he?" Another kick to the door makes me jump again, and this time, I've reached my limit. I cry hard. I don't try

to stop it. I start hyperventilating and then I squirm around until my feet are close enough to the door to kick it back. I kick hard. Two feet at once. I kick and kick and this time the door flies open.

And I'd give anything for that mask to not be on the man's face. Anything. Because even though I can barely see any skin at all past the eyeholes, I see his shock.

Asshole. The word forms in my mind. I don't swear, but I've heard the words enough to use them appropriately. Asshole. Take that, you ass—

He kicks me this time, not the door.

And now I'm too busy trying to breathe past my gag and the blood to think about what an asshole he is.

"You little bitch!" he roars. "If you broke my door—"

His door? "You broke my nose," I try to say, but it's just a jumble of words. I'm dying. I'm choking, the blood is running down my throat. My chest is heaving in and out so bad with fear and lack of oxygen, trying to draw in more, and more, and more.

I start writhing again. The panic is setting in. I'm going to die, I realize. I'm going to suffocate right now, right here in this closet. And this man who thinks I love Danny Penning is going to watch me die.

The blood covers my eyes a few seconds later and then I lose my sight. I can't talk, I can't breathe. I can't see. I can't move.

It hits me then.

I am his prisoner.

He controls my fate.

He decides if I live or die.

I thrash around as this sinks in. He killed my parents. I watched him. He came to my bed and gagged and bound me. Tight. With duct tape so there was no chance of me making any coherent noise. And he shot them both, right there in their bed.

My brother was next. He had his .22 rifle, he even got off a shot. But he missed.

And this man who thinks he's Danny Penning didn't.

He killed them and he'll kill me because he's in charge.

My body goes still. I stop trying to cough up the blood and I let it pool inside my mouth. I close my eyes and tip my head back to make it rush down my throat.

He took away all my choices. He took away all my freedom. But he can't make me want to live.

So I choose to die.

The next breath comes automatically. A survival reflex. An instinct, like I'm an animal. But I draw in blood instead of air and now I'm drowning. I feel it enter my lungs and it burns, makes me cough. But each time I cough I take in more.

And then the tape is gone, my mouth is open. Something is sucking out the blood. I'm tipped over on my side and I can't stop myself from coughing. The liquid comes back up, out of my lungs, and my mouth is filled with the taste of copper and iron.

I don't know how long I stay like that. Maybe minutes. Maybe hours. But some time later I realize the man is sitting next to me. Not touching me, but very close.

"You're OK," he says.

But I'm not OK. Because I'm still alive and all I want right now is for it to end.

"I won't have to gag you if you don't scream. In fact, I think silence is best for you. So you can recover."

Right. Because that makes sense.

"If you don't talk you don't need the gag."
I'm A-OK with no talking so I just stay silent.
"Good girl. You're a good girl."

I drag myself up from the memory and roll it around in my head. "Good girl," I whisper. Did I realize this was what he used to call me when Vaughn came up with that nickname?

I don't think so. I haven't thought about this stuff in years. I really didn't suffer any long-term effects from my hostage abduction. I put it behind me. I moved on. I forgot.

The man's heavy footsteps approach and I'm regretting not moving the mattress so I can see his feet through the crack under the door. But he's here now. It makes no difference.

He unlocks the door and opens it. "We have to run some tests. I need you to get up."

I roll onto my knees again, and then rock back and forth until I can stand with my bound hands.

"I'm going to untie you, but if you try anything funny, if you hurt yourself, or try to run, I will be forced to take matters seriously."

God, that phrase. I haven't heard that phrase since…

"Do you understand?"

I nod and look him in the face. The Invisible Man mask looks high-quality. It doesn't look fake at all. It doesn't look like it's made out of rubber. It looks like it's a face with bandages wrapped around it.

"I do understand," I tell him back in an even voice.

And I do. I understand completely. If he thinks I'm some weak little girl who'd rather off herself than live, he's got a surprise coming.

I'm not interested in dying to erase my pain and I'm not interested in playing his game.

This time, he's going to play mine.

Chapter Twenty-One - Vaughn

#NotRunning

"MR. Asher, tell me again. The last time you saw Miss Kinsella was…"

I know I should have a lawyer, because they are treating me like a suspect. But I just don't have time for that. "I told you."

"Tell me again."

"Vaughn," Conner calls out from the doorway.

"Let him in, that's my brother," I call back, only I'm talking to the policeman standing guard at the door. The media has gone crazy outside. The entire street is covered with reporters and cameras.

"This is a crime scene, Mr. Asher."

"This is my building, Officer…" I look down at his badge. "Torrino. And you have no warrant. So feel free to get one of those before you start ordering me around. Let him through," I say again, only this time my frustration comes off as anger.

"It's *Detective* Torrino, Mr. Asher. And I can get a warrant if you'd like to be difficult. One phone call."

"OK, we're done here. You go make that call, asshole." I place my fingers on my tongue and let off a shrill whistle to break up the chatter. "Everyone out unless you work for me. Thank you. Goodbye. Come back with the paperwork and I'll get a hold of my lawyers."

"You'll compromise her safety so you can pull the movie-star card?"

"Fuck you, Torrino. I'm the one who called you, remember? I'm the one who told you what happened to her ten years ago. What she told me. What I found out."

"What you found out illegally, you mean."

"It's not illegal to ask questions. It *is* illegal to answer them when you're supposed to be silent. So you're gonna want to go talk to whomever you think told us Miss Kinsella's information and threaten them. Get out."

"Vaughn, you don't want to alienate the cops." Conner, of all people—the middle child who alienates everyone—is suddenly the voice of reason.

"If they're going to concentrate on me instead of the freak who kidnapped her ten years ago, then yes. I really do."

"Just hold on," Conner says to the detective, pushing me backwards with a hand to my chest. "Come on, let's go talk somewhere private."

Conner leads me upstairs, but I have no idea where to go. Grace's apartment is bustling with police. The roof is filled with them too. There's nowhere to go to get some privacy. I feel trapped inside this building. We settle for the second-story laundry room. I flip on the lights as I enter and Conner closes the door behind him.

"I don't want Felicity to get busted for doing your dirty work."

"What?" I'm not sure I heard that right. "What the fuck are you talking about?"

"If they start digging around, I don't want Felicity to take your fall."

I stare at him, seething from the inside out. "Who the fuck do you think you are, lecturing me about Felicity? She's *my* kid."

"She's not your kid, Vaughn. She's your partner in crime."

"We didn't hack into anything to get those records. She asked around, she paid them off. She did nothing illegal."

"But she's done plenty for you in the past. And maybe it's all pretty harmless, but you're not dragging her into this."

I stare at my brother. I give him a long, hard look. "If you're sleeping with her, I will beat the motherfucking shit out of you."

"I'm not sleeping with her, you asshole. I'm trying to do damage control."

I'm not sure I believe him, but this is not the time or the place. "Conner, are you here to help me or not?"

"I am. We looked at that computer from the other day and it's clean."

"Fuck."

"With one exception."

"What?" He hesitates and I just want to shake him until he talks. "What? Just fucking tell me."

"The IP address on that video upload comes from the free wireless network at the Hollywood Gold Theatre."

"So he's a local?" Conner hesitates again. "What, dammit?"

"He's not a local, V. He's *you*." Conner puts his hand up as I begin to object. "He's trying to make it look like you did this. The timestamp on the upload we found of the video happened during your *IM2* premiere."

"So?"

"That means he's framing you, Vaughn. He's trying to make it look like you're the one sending these messages because the security for that event was so tight, only those associated with the movie were allowed in. And furthermore, only those who had major roles got invites to the premiere because that theatre is so small. He's trying to pin this all on you. So if those guys downstairs get a hold of this info, they're really gonna think you're guilty."

"That makes no sense. How could I be the guy who took her ten years ago?"

"No one gives a fuck about ten years ago, V. They only care about last night. And you were the last one to see her alive."

"Don't you fucking dare insinuate she's dead, Conner."

He lets out a long breath. "I'm not, V. I'm just playing devil's advocate. People are going to assume you did it and they are going to assume the worst before they ever give you the benefit of the doubt. So I'm just telling you—expect questions about your involvement in her murder."

"Don't be ridiculous, I had nothing to do with this. And there's no murder. She's alive. He took her, I know it. Now I need you to find her, Conner. These assfucks are not going to do shit. Just like they didn't do shit the last time he took her."

Conner nods and shoves his hands in his pockets. "Yeah, and that Twitter stuff is bad too. They're just gonna say she ran off. They probably won't even look for her."

"She'd never do that, Conner."

"I dunno, V. She's run away from you plenty of times before."

"That was different." Wasn't it? She couldn't have run off on her own. Could she?

"It wasn't different. You married her when she was drunk. She didn't even know about it. The reporters got a hold of the girl who lives downstairs. She said she heard you guys arguing about it last night and that's why you had to sleep on the couch in the lobby."

I sigh and lean up against the washing machine.

"So, is there any possibility that she just ran off like she implied in her last tweet?"

I think about it. Like, really hard. I try to run this through in my mind, try to see it from her perspective. But I just can't picture Grace being such a coward that she'd take off like that. Yes, she ran from me on Saint Thomas, but she went *home*. And yes, she ran from me in Vegas, but she came *back once I found her*. And yes, she threw me out last night, but she'd never walk off and leave all these loose ends. She just wouldn't. Grace likes to keep thing organized. She's a planner. She'd plan the hell out of an escape like this. And nothing about what's happening feels planned.

I look Conner straight in the eye. "No, Con. She did not run off. He took her."

Conner nods his head at me. "OK then. He took her. I think you're right about the police. You're the number one suspect right now until they decide if she's missing or ran off on her own. And they don't seem to be doing a whole lot right now besides standing around feeling important. Maybe if the FBI gets involved we'll get more help. But until then, we need to proceed on our own."

"What'd you have in mind?"

"I was talking to Felicity and she thinks she can profile this guy. Narrow down who he might be by adding up all the clues. Figure out who he is and where he might take Grace through process of elimination."

A long breath escapes me and I feel myself relax for the first time all day. "OK. When can she get here?"

"She's here. She's across the street, though. She doesn't want to be seen by the media. So I'm gonna go help her and you're going to distract everyone here. You do that by cooperating. Answer every question, six times, if necessary. You are not guilty, they can't paint you into corners, but the lawyers are already at the airport, I got a message before I came in to see you. They'll be here in like ten minutes." He stares at me, waiting for an answer. "OK? You got it?"

I nod but I'm not happy about this at all. I feel like they're wasting time. Like Grace is getting farther and farther away from me with each passing minute.

Media by JA Huss

Chapter Twenty-Two - Grace

#JustAGirl

"WHY?" I growl. I know I'm risking him getting violent, but I don't care.

"To run tests. I told you." His words come out labored, like he's breathing very hard. Like he's the one who's having a panic attack instead of me.

I know that's what's about to happen. I used to get them almost daily during the eight months I spent locked in this house. But I've perfected my relaxation techniques. I might not've participated in therapy, but that's only because it was a waste of time. Who gives a shit why something happened or how I feel about it?

I only care about making sure it won't happen again. My mind is screaming at me—*But it did happen again!* Yeah, I can't control what this freak does. I can only control how I react to it. And I refuse to let him make me panic. Because I've been preparing for this. I've been mentally and physically preparing myself for round two since the day I realized I was brainwashed six years ago. So my heart calms while his beats faster. "What kind of tests?"

He leans down in my personal space, his grip on my upper arm punishingly tight. "A pregnancy test, for one."

"I'm not pregnant."

"How do you know?" He cocks his head at me. "Asher never used a condom."

I reel backwards. "What?"

"You think I don't know what kind of man Vaughn Asher is? Did he use one? Say yes and we skip the test. But I might have to medicate you and that could harm your baby. So isn't it better to know for sure?"

Hurt my baby? No!

Jesus, Grace! Stop. You're on the pill! Don't let him get to you! That's your only power right now.

But he's blackmailing me with a baby that doesn't exist and I'm falling for it.

He points to the bathroom. "I'll untie you. You go in, leaving the door open. Follow the directions on the package, and bring it back to me. We can watch for the results together."

"No."

He smacks me across the face. "That word is not in your vocabulary."

The blood is back in my mouth and I spit on the floor.

"While we're waiting, you can clean your bloody mess. There's a spot in the kitchen as well. I don't like an untidy home."

The chills run up my spine. He's a psycho. He tried to brainwash me into believing I was his wife back when I was thirteen. And it worked. I cooked and cleaned for him like I was his goddamned life partner. Like we were in this shit together. I asked him how his day was when he came home from work every day and unchained me from the closet. And by the end, I even participated in the demented dream of his. I shake my head, unwilling to even admit that part of the ordeal to myself.

Instead, I extend my shaking hand out for the box he's holding in front of me, and he places it in my palm.

"I'll wait in the living room and give you some privacy." He grips my arm again. "But leave the door open."

I walk into the tiny bathroom. It too has been remodeled. It seems like everything in this house has been remodeled except for my closet prison cell. I open the box and take out the test. Rip open the package with my teeth, then check the hallway to make sure he's really in the living room.

He waves to me from the couch. "Hurry."

I retreat back into the bathroom and unbutton my shorts. My hand shakes severely as I squat and hold the test under my stream. I place it on the wrapper on the counter, wipe quickly, and pull my pants back up.

I stare at the little window where the results will appear, my heart suddenly burdened with fear.

What if I'm pregnant?

"Is it done?" he asks from the door.

I nod and hand the test over. He can sit and watch it all he wants. I have no intention of waiting for that result with him by my side.

"I'll clean the mess," I say meekly with my head down.

"Yes." He strokes my hair and I do my best not to flinch, but don't entirely succeed. "You remember your place now, don't you?"

I force myself to look up at him and nod. "I remember."

My feet are moving, and I've never been so glad to walk away from someone in my whole life. But I do remember. And then a smile comes forth for a flash of a second. I remember what I needed to do back then to walk freely around the house.

Obey.

I cannot even count the number of nights I stayed up thinking up all the ways in which I could trick him after I was let go. I replayed every day in my mind. I imagined how it was to wake up and realize I was a prisoner. I imagined what I'd do different. I imagined I was smart enough to figure out what made him happy and what pissed him off so I could fool him into thinking I was agreeable.

In my new reality, the one I dreamed about, I wasn't brainwashed into liking the man with the mask. In my new reality, I was the smart one and he was the victim. I imagined myself one step ahead. I played all those bad things in my mind again and again. It was like a simulator for me. I planned for this. Because that's what I do. I'm a planner.

In the kitchen the layout is the same even though the cabinets and stuff are all different. So I know where he keeps the mop and bucket. In the tall slender cupboard next to the refrigerator.

I also know where to fill the bucket up. In the laundry room off to the side of the kitchen. I look at the back door for a moment, then over my shoulder. He's watching me.

"Try the handle, Daisy. Do you think I'd leave it unlocked?"

"No," I answer, then lower my head and turn the spigot on. I wait for the bucket to fill and when I turn he's still watching me.

"In my mind you're still a girl, but you're not, are you?"

Oh, shit. "I am," I insist. "I'm still a girl." He never molested me but he talked about it endlessly. He said he had to wait until I was eighteen. That was the law.

I always wanted to ask him why kidnapping was OK but sex with a minor wasn't. But I had enough sense to shut the hell up.

My hand reaches for the floor cleaner like this is my own home, and I hear him chuckle a little behind me. *Just play along, Grace. Don't feel what he wants you to feel.*

I take the bucket and mop over to the bloodstain on the floor and quickly wipe it up. This must pacify him, because he retreats to the couch once again. I steal a look as I walk past to clean up the blood in the bathroom, and he's staring at the pee stick.

I stop in my tracks when he holds up the test stick, his gaze never wandering from the results before him.

When he finally looks up, I know what that that test says. Maybe that's why I got nauseous and threw up on the plane to Vegas. Maybe that's why when I put that dress on for Kristi's rehearsal dinner it was snug. Maybe that's why the exhaustion overtook me at Kristi's parents' resort and I fell asleep, dead-assed tired.

I am pregnant.

I am pregnant with Vaughn Asher's baby and there's no way this psycho freak is going to let it live.

Chapter Twenty-Three - Vaughn

#IJustWantMySweets

I STAND at the top of the landing, watching Conner make his way through the crowd of police and witnesses, and just as he opens the door to exit the building, a familiar dark-haired girl gets up in his face.

She's one angry chick. Her manicured finger is pointing, her sensible nurse shoe is tapping, and her electric pink scrubs make her very hard to ignore. Even for Conner, the master at indifference.

He stands still for a moment as the girl says something, and then he turns and points straight at me.

And that's when I see her face.

Bebe Chambers.

She actually pushes Conner out of the way, almost mows down a uniformed police officer, and heads straight for the stairs.

I look over at that asshole detective to see if he's gonna stop her, but he's sporting a smug smile. OK. Here we go.

My very first in-person meeting with Bebe the BFF and it's not gonna be pretty.

"You," she accuses me loudly. Loud enough to make people stop talking. "You are the reason she's gone."

I walk down the stairs slowly and put on my movie-star smile. "Miss Chambers. It's unfortunate that we have to meet under these circumstances—"

"Oh, no," she says, putting her hand up as I reach the bottom of the steps. She's tall. A lot taller than Grace. And she's seething. "You do not get to pretend like we are meeting under normal circumstances, Mr. Asher." My name comes off like an insult. "My best friend was fine for ten years and you come along and rip her life apart in a matter of weeks. If something happens to her, I will—" And then her eyes well up and tears burst forth. "I'll… I'll make you pay somehow. If she's hurt. If that freak has her again. If you did something to her and dumped her body—"

"Whoa, Bebe. You can't really believe that I'd hurt her?"

"I really can, Mr. Asher. I read that spread about you in that magazine. They paint a pretty convincing picture of a sociopath."

"Socio—" I can't even say the word. "Look, Bebe. I love her. I realize we've had an unusual start to our relationship, and I understand that there are some very unique problems we have to work through. But you can't really think I'd hurt her."

"Then where is she?"

"I don't know."

"Her entire Filthy Blue Bird account is gone from Twitter! Just gone! She was on there for years! And now it's gone!"

"Miss Chambers, is it?" That asshole detective appears by her side. "We've contacted the corporate office and we're trying to retrieve her account, if that helps. We need to make sure there's no more incriminating evidence against Mr. Asher before we allow it to be deleted. Come, have a seat over here and let's try and piece together what might've happened." Bebe is led off and takes a seat on the couch I slept on last night. I follow them, but the detective stops me with a hand. "You stay there. I'd like her opinion without your interference."

Interference? Now I'm interference?

My phone buzzes in my pants and I pull it up. A text from Conner. *Are you playing nice? Just hold tight, the lawyers are outside. I'm down the street with Felicity, she's putting together a profile now.*

I text back, *OK*, and let it go with that.

When I look back up from my phone, Bigmy is coming down the stairs. He motions for me to head to the back door with a tilt of his head, and then walks right past me.

I look around, then follow him. We stop just before we get to the back door that leads to the alley and he scrubs his face with a large meaty hand. "Boss, Ray thinks the guy took her off the roof."

"Obviously, Big. Tell me something I don't know."

"We found a pair of goggles on the rooftop of the adjacent building."

"Goggles?"

He nods. "Invisible Man goggles."

Fuck. I look over my shoulder at the detective and then have a small wave of relief when the lawyers are ushered though the front door. "He really is trying to pin it on me. But—" I look back to Bigmy. "It's absurd, right? I mean, this is like Scooby-Doo villains planting clues. Right?"

"Mmmm." The big man balks. "Maybe. Or maybe it's just a lot of circumstantial evidence that adds up to only one conclusion. You did something to her."

"I was on the fucking couch all night."

"You were the last one to see her."

"She's not dead! She's been kidnapped by that freak who took her ten years ago."

He shushes me with a hand. "I know that. Ray knows that. We all know that. But I'm just telling you, he's setting you up. When a girl goes missing they always look at the boyfriend or husband first. You are their prime suspect and these clues he's dropping will make it very difficult for the police to take our suspicions seriously."

"So they're not gonna look for her?"

"They're gonna go with the most obvious choice and that's you."

"How long do you think she's been gone?"

"All night and all morning. So twelve hours, I suppose."

"Did they look for her phone?"

"We did," the detective says from behind me. "And do you want to know where we found it, Mr. Asher?"

From the tone of his voice, no. I'm pretty sure I do not want to know where they found it.

"In a car parked two blocks over."

194

"OK. So whose car is it?"

"Yours."

"It's not my car. I don't even live here."

"It's a rental, taken out in your name last night."

I'm just about to open my mouth to protest when my lawyers walk up. They are all tall, large, and menacing-looking in their black suits and briefcases. "No more questions," the oldest one says. I do not know his name. I don't have much occasion to meet with them in person. I've never been arrested in my life. I've never even been to court for a speeding ticket.

And then, before the detective can protest or make any more absurd accusations, they usher me out the back door of the building to a waiting car. "Get in, Mr. Asher. Don't talk to anyone but your family. The car will take you to your brother and then we'll regroup later."

I do as I'm told. I get into the car, alone, and then the door slams closed and the driver takes off.

Ten minutes later I'm delivered to the underground parking garage of a hotel where Conner waits for me next to an open elevator.

"I'm being set up."

"I know, V."

"Grace is really missing."

"Yes."

"Please tell me you've got something."

"I wish I could, but I don't."

This is a moment I will never forget. I thought that night in Vegas last week was my low. When my future with Grace seemed to be in the hands of a power-hungry businessman who likes to play God. But that was nothing. Li had no real power over me. It was a stupid bet.

But this. I shake my head and try and calm my nerves. This is real. He could hurt her. He could damage her psyche. He could *kill* her.

"I need to find her, Conner. I can't let him have her for another night. I need to find her *today*."

"We're doing our best, V." Conner waves me through the elevator doors and then he pushes a floor button and the doors close.

It's an ominous feeling to be inside this box right now. It makes me feel helpless. And trapped. For the first time in my life my status has little meaning. For the first time in my life my money has little meaning. For the first time in my life I realize life is meaningless without the person you want to share it with.

The car takes us up to the tenth floor and we exit into a silent hallway. "We're down here," Conner says.

I follow him down the hall, my gaze trained on the pattern in the carpet, my heart heavy with despair, and my mind racing with regrets. Regrets for leaving her alone last night. For not camping outside her door. Regrets for marrying her when I knew she was drinking. Regrets for using my power over her in Saint Thomas to conquer her sexually. Regret for not being there for the last few weeks.

I might never get to set this right. I might never get a second chance. But if I do, I will make sure Grace Kinsella understands just how perfect and precious she really is. I will spend the rest of my life making her feel loved and safe.

Chapter Twenty-Four - Grace

#IJustWantMyFantasy

"WE'LL have to take care of this."

I swallow hard, my mind racing. I need to stop him from whatever it is he's got planned. I need to stop his murderous thoughts. "I don't believe in abortion," I try first.

"I do," he says back flatly. "I do. Especially when my wife was raped. Abortion is just and righteous when a woman is raped."

I try to see the traps he's laying. He wants to insist I was raped. OK. That's his reality and I'm not sure I can change that. And I probably need him to believe that so he will not accuse me of cheating. Because I'm pretty sure cheating is an offense worthy of retaliation.

The last time I was his prisoner he let me know which acts of rebellion would earn me a beating. Sex was never discussed. But he talked a lot about what kind of clothes I could wear. He talked a lot about "asking for it" if I were to wear things that are too revealing.

If leaving dirty dishes in the sink was punishable with a slap to the face, I'm pretty sure cheating would earn me a couple black eyes.

I place the mop against the wall and step towards him. He stands up, a defensive position in case I get any crazy ideas. I have lots of crazy ideas in the plan, but I'm not about to rush ahead. I smile at him. "May I sit on the couch?"

"Who said you could talk to me?" he snarls back. "You have not earned the privilege of speech yet." His mood changes are still volatile, I sneer to myself. But I keep all that safely tucked away. I nod and take a deep breath and then stand silently.

After several minutes of me standing obediently and wordless, he says, "Come sit here," and points to the space on the couch next to him.

The thought of being so near him revolts me, but if I want any chance of saving myself from a forced home abortion, I need to win him over. So I step cautiously towards him, ease my way around the coffee table, and sit down. My heart is racing so fast I'm sure he can hear it.

His hand slips to my leg and I swallow back the bile his touch stirs in my stomach. He rubs it and I wince. "I want you to have my baby, Daisy. Not his. So it will be for the best."

Oh, God. I'm so repulsed. I nod and then chance a look up at his masked face.

"Do you like this mask?" he asks. His eyes dart back and forth, clearly nervous about the question.

I decide to be honest. "No."

"Why?" he asks quickly.

"Because I want to see your face for once. I want to know who you are."

"Does it matter?"

Does it *matter?* Jesus fucking Christ. "No," I force myself to say. "No. I'm here, I'm yours. So it doesn't matter."

"Do you wonder if I'm handsome?"

No. "Yes."

"Touch me."

No. This time I have no fake comeback answer, either. Touch him? *Please, God. Do not make me touch him.*

"Touch me," he says again, taking my hand in his. They are cold and damp. Clammy. And large enough to cover mine completely.

My breath hitches as he lifts my hand and I pull it back, but his grip is tight. He raises it to his face and places my clenched fist against his masked cheek. "Touch me."

I swallow hard, my eyes downcast. I open my fist and flatten my palm against the ragged bandages of his mask.

"This isn't you," I say, trying to keep the communication open. If I lose this battle… if I can't convince him of what I'm about to say… then I might as well be dead. Because I refuse to live if this man kills the life inside me. "This isn't you," I repeat. "I want to feel your… cheek. See your face. You have seen mine." I try to reason with him. "You've seen mine, so let me see yours."

His hand covers my hand again. His eyes stare into mine. "You won't like me if you see me."

"How do you know?"

"Because I'm ugly."

Oh, for fuck's sake. Does this man really expect me to soothe his ego as he holds me captive and threatens to kill my unborn child? "You're a good man who loves and cares for me." I recite my lines perfected a decade ago. His sick, perverted fantasy with me includes this twisted ego-stroking. "And this child… this child can be *ours*. We could start our family right now. Today. If I had an abortion"—my throat constricts just saying that word—"then…" I let out a long breath and gulp up another one. "Then it would take months for us to start again."

My trembling hand is still resting on his cheek, covered by his clammy one. I twist my palm and grasp his hand, and then bring it down. I close my eyes with revulsion as I place it over my belly. "This is your baby now," I tell him. "This is our baby now."

He sighs and I look up at his face in time to see his eyes close.

Yes, Grace. You have him now. Don't stop, keep going.

"We could raise this child together. I imagine you coming to the doctor with me to hear the heartbeat."

In my mind, in order to counteract the vision I'm feeding him, I picture Vaughn at my side. I picture his face when we hear the heartbeat together. And even though I don't know what he will think of all this if I get out of here alive and my baby is unharmed, in my fantasy, Vaughn is proud and excited.

"You would take care of me. And make sure I ate right."

I picture Vaughn and I shopping at some absurdly expensive organic food store. I see him checking labels for all-natural ingredients and vitamins.

"You would insist that I not work too hard and get enough sleep."

I see Vaughn rubbing my swollen feet and plumping up my pillows as we lounge in bed on the weekends.

And then I have a flash from that night we got drunk in Vegas. Vaughn and me, sitting in that restaurant. Him talking about stuff with me. His fantasy life as a normal father. A shitload of kids, he'd said. Cherishing painted macaroni gifts from his three-year-old. Jumping in puddles, and letting them rebel with bad grades. Watching track meets in the rain and coaching football and school plays.

A sob escapes before I can stop it.

"You're thinking about him, aren't you?" His hand jerks away from mine and grips me tightly by the upper arm.

"No!"

He shakes me hard. "Don't lie to me, you whore! You cheated on me! You got pregnant with another man's child and now you want me to raise this bastard as my own?"

"Please." I struggle to get out of his grip. I can feel the bruise forming underneath his hand.

He pulls me up and heads for the bedroom, pulling me behind him. I trip over the end of the coffee table and go down to the floor, but he never stops. He drags me the rest of the way. And when we get to the closet he kicks me in the side until I roll over and scurry into my prison. I crab-walk backwards until I'm pressed up against the back wall. He grabs my foot and reaches around the floor until he finds the shackles. It clamps down on my ankle with a tightness that tells me these are the same ones he used when I was a teenager. And they are too small. My skin rips and the warm blood pours out as he fastens the lock.

One more kick—this time it catches me in the shoulder—and then the door is slammed closed and the darkness takes over.

"You think I'm stupid," he seethes from the other side of the door. "You think I want a child you made with another man? So you can fantasize about how he fucked you? So you can replace your reality with me with your fantasy of him?" He kicks the door so hard I hear wood splinter.

It goes silent on the other side but I know he's still there. His shadow falls across the sliver of light that seeps in under the door and he waits.

My heart is pounding. The blood is rising to my head, making me dizzy. And I'm falling over when I hear his parting words as he walks off.

"That baby will be gone by tonight."

Chapter Twenty-Five - Vaughn

#ThereIsNoWay...

FELICITY is hunched over a table on the far side of the hotel room. It's set up with five computers. One is the laptop from Tray, the others are all hers from home. She looks over her shoulder at me and gives me a weak smile. "How are you holding up?"

I cross the room and take a seat on the corner of the bed near the window. "I have a really bad feeling about things, Felicity. Really bad."

Her cheeks puff out as she exhales some air, and then she turns so she can face me. "Vaughn... look... I'm really not an expert in this stuff yet. I'm still a student. But in cases like this, cases that point to a psychologically disturbed individual, there's only a few ways they ever play out. And even though he let Grace live the first time, there's no guarantee that he will follow the same course of action now."

I just stare at Felicity, angry at her for telling me this, but knowing everything she says is true. "We need to find her today. There has to be some clue, some signal that will tell us who he is."

"I've started the search with the hospital she was dropped off at in Nebraska." Felicity points to a map on one of her screens. "I think there's a high probability that he's returned to that house he first kept her at. He was never caught and it was a place he probably felt safe and comfortable taking her to. It's isolated, obviously. Since this time people would be looking for her right away. The hospital in Nebraska is not that far from here, relatively speaking. Probably within eight hours or so, because he most likely had to drug her to take her captive. Drugs wear off, so he wouldn't want to chance her waking up while they were driving."

Felicity continues and even though all of this should make me feel despair, it has the opposite effect. She knows what she's doing. She's double-majoring in psychology and criminal justice. This stuff is her life at the moment. She's been listening to the experts in this field lecture on things like this for years. If anyone can find my Grace, it will be Felicity.

"… might even be someone you know."

"What?"

"We have to consider it, V," Conner says. "Whoever took her was inside the theater for your *IM2* premiere. He might be someone you know."

"But how would he make that connection? We only just met a few weeks ago."

"Grace has been Twitter-stalking you for years, Vaughn. So it's only logical that this sicko has been Twitter-stalking *her.*"

"He deleted her account, I know he did."

"It's almost guaranteed he deleted her account," Felicity says. "But maybe we can use that to our advantage. Maybe we can use her social media connections to figure out where she is. Like Facebook, for instance. Is she on Facebook?"

"I don't know. But we have two private Twitter accounts that I set up when we first met."

Felicity grabs one of her laptops and hands it to me. "Log in and leave her a message. She might try to access that account and if she does, we need to give her instructions on what to do."

I take the laptop from Felicity and walk over to the other side of the table and take a set. *Please, God,* I say a little prayer in my head. *Please, God, let me find Grace alive.* I take a deep breath and log in, hoping that there is some message for me that will lead the way.

I practically hold my breath as the @mrinvsman account comes up.

"Nothing." I sigh and Felicity looks at me over her screen.

"We're gonna find her. Leave her a message so she knows we're looking. Give her hope."

"Right. Hope." Grace is afraid of hope because she's afraid of losing, so how do I hand her that in one hundred and forty characters?

I look to Conner for help, but he's busy on another computer. He catches my gaze and smiles.

"V, we've got a theory about this guy. He was able to get into the theatre, or at the very least, he got in before the event so he could send that message. So maybe he works there?"

"Maybe." But that doesn't give me much hope. That means she could be very far from here. She might be back in California. She might be anywhere. "What if it's not even him?"

"He's the logical person, Vaughn. He sent Tray a video of Grace."

"Yeah, but we don't know that was even real."

"Why wouldn't it be real?" Felicity isn't being argumentative, she's just asking questions but it exasperates me.

"Well, I know better than most how much you can fake with film, right? I mean, one guy could easily film a girl, pay an actress who looked like Grace as a teen. Did we get a good look at her?"

Conner types away on the computer he's using and then tilts it towards me. "It looks like her." He's got a split screen up of Grace as a teenager after she was let go and the girl on the floor.

I reluctantly admit, that girl in the movie is my Grace.

"Vaughn," Felicity says as she places a gentle hand on my shoulder. "We're gonna find her. Just write her a nice message in case she has a chance to log in. If he deleted her account, then maybe she'll have an opportunity to get to that computer."

I nod at her and take my attention back to the secret accounts we made. I pull up the pictures we traded. Naked selfies. This makes me smile at the memory. It was only a couple weeks ago, but I feel like she's been a part of my life for ages. I feel like I've known her forever. Like our souls are connected by some ethereal string that was stretched taut from our absence. But the moment our eyes met back in Saint Thomas, we reconnected. We were pulled together by the forces of a long-lost love.

I feel like I've been waiting my whole life for this girl. I feel like she is my soulmate.

My fingers find the keyboard and I try to put that into a tweet. Try to give her hope with a few words and some well-placed hashtags.

Master @mrinvsman
There's no possible way I won't find you. Our hearts are tethered by love & fate. I'm tugging on that string - feel me? #OnMyWay #Soulmates

I press send and hold my breath, hoping against hope for a reply.

But the minutes tick off and I get nothing. Just nothing.

My phone rings and jolts me out of my funk. "Vaughn Asher."

"Mr. Asher, this is Detective Torrino. We're suspending the search. Grace Kinsella just called Channel 9 and stated she's accepted a job in Singapore that was offered to her in Vegas last week in order to get away from you."

Singapore. "Well, how the hell do you know that was her?"

"She confirmed her social security number, her childhood address, and her bank account number. Her best friend Bebe Chambers confirms it was her voice."

"So? My daughter can get that information. That's not a confirmation of identity. And maybe she's being forced to say those things? How about a picture? How about a FaceTime? How about you ask her to log into her other Twitter account and read the message that's posted there?"

"The case is closed, Mr. Asher. We're satisfied she left of her own accord."

"Maybe she's being threatened?"

"I asked her—"

"You can't ask her, Torrino. If she's being told to say something, then she's going to deny it. And that wasn't the job she was offered—"

"We've shut down the case, Asher. You can appeal to my boss if you like."

I'm just about to protest again when the line goes dead.

"What just happened?" Conner asks.

"They shut down the fucking case. They say she called them and said she's taking a job in Singapore to get away from me."

Felicity's hand reaches over to cover mine. "Do you think it's true?"

"No. Grace *was* offered a job last week, but it was in Hong Kong. She's sending us a message. She's telling us she needs help. Felicity, please. Just come up with something. I feel like the clock is ticking and something very bad is going to happen if we don't get to her soon."

Chapter Twenty-Six - Grace

#Just #One #Chance

I PRESS end on the call. It's not even cloaked or rerouted or secret, that's how convinced he is that this will work. We turned on the TV, saw my face and the man-hunt. And I had an idea that might save the baby.

I'll stay with you as your friend, you don't need to be on the run. I'll stay with you willingly and even tell the police to call off the search. Just let my baby live.

He said no, of course. That's how you negotiate. Offer. Counteroffer.

His counteroffer was an annulment from Vaughn and marriage to him.

I accepted. End of negotiations.

I only hope that the police or media give my statement to Vaughn word for word. I'm starting to remember that night in Vegas. Little by little it's coming back to me. I remember being drunk and leaving the private gambling room after Vaughn came to get me. I remember being in the bar and being offered a dream job in Hong Kong by the man who was treating me like his good-luck charm.

And that is the only thing I have going for me.

"You'll call them again tomorrow if they keep running stories." He says it as a statement, not a request. I will call them every day, if necessary. Just don't hurt my baby. "Tonight we'll sleep together." Even through the mask I can see his smile and for some reason, that smile scares me more than anything else. More than the closet. More than the implied rape.

That smile implies he's a winner.

My stomach lurches and it's all I can do to force a smile back. "I'm looking forward to it."

It's four PM. Bedtime is maybe six hours away.

I have six hours to kill this asshole or he's gonna rape me and I'm not about to let that happen.

"Do you want something to eat?" I ask him politely.

"I bet you're hungry, aren't you?"

I am, but this feels like a trap. It feels like if I say yes, he might flip out because I'm pregnant and I need food. I don't want him to think about it. I need him to *stop* thinking about it.

"Take another test."

"What?"

"Take. Another. Test. I want to make sure the results are accurate."

I swallow hard and nod. So much for making him forget about it. I get up off the couch and my knee bumps into the computer he's using. It's open to my Facebook page, but it's not logged in. Yet. I'm sure he'll have me make some sort of public declaration on there too. If I could just get a message on the social sites, tell them I'm still being held against my will... but I don't even know where I am.

I slide past and walk down the hallway to the bathroom, one last glance before I round the corner, and then I stare at the second package that came in the test kit.

"Don't cheat," he says directly behind me.

I force myself not to react even though that just scared the shit out of me. "I'd never lie about a baby." I walk the few paces to the counter and rip open the second test. He's still standing in the doorway and it's freaking me out. "Can I have some privacy?"

"No."

I stiffen.

"You are my wife. You might be pregnant with my child. We're excited to find out the news."

I turn and smile. "Of course. We're so happy and excited." I smile. Big. Huge. All my teeth are showing, my eyes lift up, my cheeks stretch. "My stomach is all fluttery. I'm so nervous."

"Why?" It comes out as a genuine question. He likes when I admit I'm weak or stupid. This I do remember.

"Do you think I'd be a good mother? I'm worried about it. I didn't have the best childhood—"

I know the second it comes out it's the wrong move, but even if I didn't, the slap across my face clues me in.

"Your childhood was perfect," he growls. "I saved you from a family of abuse."

I nod as the blood trickles down my face and drips onto the floor. Just another surface I'll have to clean. My hands are shaking so bad I can't rip the test package open, and I have to use my teeth. I pull out the stick and look up at the man in the mask, hoping he will step out of the bathroom and let me have some privacy.

"Hurry up." No such luck.

I pull down my shorts and squat as I hold the test under my stream for a second time. I hand it directly to him and he turns and walks away.

The sobs inside me are threatening to break free as I pull my shorts back up and wash my hands.

Don't cry, don't cry, don't cry...

Don't cry, don't cry, don't cry... I say it over and over in my head. Just do what he says and he'll be nice. Just do what he says and he'll take care of you...

That's how it started. I went from being a carefree teenager living on a farm and fantasizing about all things thirteen-year-old girls fantasize about, to an abducted child whose only thoughts were about pleasing the man who kidnapped her.

I studied this endlessly in my late teens and even part of my first year of college. I used to go to the library and look up everything I could on the psychology of kidnappers. I was obsessed with other cases like mine. I was looking for patterns and similarities. I tried to keep track of the kids after they came home, but most of them were hiding. Like me. New names. New lives.

And then one day during my first semester of college, I ran out of things to research. Just... ran out. It was all old and there was no answer that satisfied me. That was the hardest thing to accept. There was just no good answer.

No one knew how to get over what I'd been through. Even those pretending that they did would eventually admit this is not an area that is well-studied. Too few cases. Too few willing participants.

I was tired of being Grace who used to be Daisy so I decided to create a new me. The Filthy Blue Bird. Tweeting was how I moved my obsessions into something... well, maybe not positive, but at the very least, *normal*. Everybody wants a fantasy and in today's world, it's easy to get that.

Vaughn was not difficult to research. He was everywhere I looked online. Pictures and pictures of him spanning decades. Quotes, and interviews, and pages and pages of biographical things.

And little by little, day by day, my past just slipped away. Just... evaporated.

"Come out here, Daisy."

Until now. Until it coalesced and reshaped itself in the form of round two.

But I always knew he was out there. I've been waiting for him. I've been waiting for him for ten years. He stole two hundred and twenty days. And there's no fucking way I'm going to let this sick freak claim any more.

This day is the only one he gets. It's me or him. One way or another, it will end tonight.

I dry my hands and walk back out to the living room, scanning the windows—electrified, he said—the front door—slightly ajar, but it leads to the mudroom, which I know is surely locked from the inside—the computer.

One tweet. One hashtag. One chance to shine.

It's my only hope.

Chapter Twenty-Seven - Vaughn

#NoOneIsInvisible

"WHITE male," Felicity says. "I'm pretty sure it's a white male. I think he lives up in that rural area where Grace is from. Maybe even a neighbor. Maybe even a farmer." She looks up at me, conflicted and confused. "V, I'm no good at this. These are just guesses. I have no idea what I'm talking about."

I reach across the table and take her hand. "You're the best at this, Felicity. You're an incredibly intelligent woman. You've been studying this for four years. You've been obsessed with cold-case files since I adopted you. This is your dream job and I know you can do it. Just go with your gut, because this is your purpose, Felicity. Figuring out the minds of others is your gift. You know it. I know it. And I know you're afraid to give me the wrong answer, but I'll take anything you have right now because you're the only one who cares."

She nods and looks back at her computer. "I mapped the town where Grace is from and took it out four hundred miles in every direction. That brings up a lot of possibilities, but I immediately discounted the south and anything west of the Rockies. He had to have had access to Grace and she was from a very small town. It's pretty isolated. From what I can see of the media reports when she was abducted, she rarely went out of town. The only place she went that year was to a 4-H archery camp up in the Nebraska National Forest."

"Let's start there."

"I did, there's not much up there. Only two towns."

"That's good, right? That means we don't have many places to look."

"But V," Conner says from behind his laptop. "The problem is, we've got two leads. One is in Hollywood and one is in Nebraska. We have to split up if we want to check out both."

"I just don't see the Hollywood connections though. It makes no sense."

"Well, listen," Felicity says. "In that interview Grace did the other day, she told the reporter that she never saw the guy's face. He was wearing a mask. She said it looked real, but it was of someone she knew, and not a famous person. So what if this guy who kidnapped her is involved in special effects in Hollywood? What if that's his specialty?"

I have a sick feeling in my stomach.

"What if the guy worked on the *Invisible Man* set, Vaughn?"

Conner gets up from where he's sitting and walks over to us. "Holy fucking shit, Felicity!" He leans down and kisses her on the cheek. "That's the fucking connection. This asshole worked in production. He was a special effects guy."

"And the senior team was invited to the premiere." Motherfucker might've been sitting near me that night. I might've fucking talked to him.

"Dad?" Conner says into his phone. "We've got a lead and I need your help…"

Conner steps out of the room and takes the call into the hallway. "Keep going, Felicity. You're hot, so just keep going. What else do you think?"

"Well, I think this guy saw her at that archery camp, so…" She pulls up a local 4-H website in northeastern Colorado. "We know she was in 4-H, and this is the local chapter near her town, so this was the club she was in. We should start with the leaders, I guess. See who was on that trip with her."

"So we need to travel there?"

"Yeah." Felicity shrugs. "It's footwork from here. I don't see how we can do much more online. We need to see these people. Look them in the eye and compel them to talk to us."

Conner comes back into the room. "OK, Dad's giving me access to the personnel files. I'm gonna see if we can find a connection to Colorado or Nebraska."

"This is Felicity." I look over at her and she's talking into her phone. "We're going to need a flight plan to Holyoke, Colorado. We're on our way now, please have the jet ready." She ends her call and looks up at me. "We're going to get Grace back."

Chapter Twenty-Eight - Grace

#IWillNeverBeYours

I SIT down next to him and fold my hands in my lap. "Should I call you by your name?" I ask. "Now that we're married?"

"We're not married yet," he growls. "It needs to be legal."

"Of course. But don't you want me to call you by your real name?"

He turns his head and points that stupid mask at me. "You should already *know* my name."

"You're right. But you've kept it a secret. So I don't know your name. I don't even know what you look like."

"It doesn't matter," he says quickly. "You don't get to reject me."

Right again. But I keep my mouth shut and just stare at the test in his hand. We both watch the blue plus sign appear and when it does, he throws the stick on the coffee table and gets to his feet.

"I don't want to pretend this baby is mine," he says with his back to me.

Shit.

"I might not be your average guy, but I am not crazy."

Oh, yeah, dude. Your trip to Crazytown started ten years ago.

"This is Vaughn Asher's baby and it needs to go." He whirls around and snatches my wrist so fast I gasp. "Come on."

"What—"

I'm forcefully pulled to my feet and my first reaction is to fight him. I dig my heels in and pull back, but his grip is secure and he yanks me forward until I fall face-first on the coffee table. One large hand presses on my back, keeping me pinned, while the other grabs my hair and slams my face on the hard wood. I taste blood when my lip splits. "I think you've forgotten the rules. But don't worry, little flower, I'm here to remind you." He leans down into my neck and I recoil from the heat of his breath. "You're a big girl now, aren't you, Daisy?"

A fingertip strokes along my cheek and I panic. He's never touched me like that before. Not in a way that implies he'd rape me. But I can already tell this kidnapping is nothing like the last one. Last time he was very young. Early twenties at the most. Ten years later and that boy who wanted me to like him, wanted to win my cooperation with some sick form of domestic seduction that included keeping house and taking care of him the way a wife might, is gone.

In his place is a man who wants very different things. In his place is a man who wants… a woman.

"I'm still so young," I try.

But his hand presses on my head even harder, making me whimper. "I've been patient, Daisy. I let you graduate from college. I watched you have your fun. Date a few men. Have sex. And now look, you're nothing but a whore."

Oh, God.

"You're pregnant with another man's child. If we want to be happy, that parasite inside you needs to be dealt with."

And then his hand slips between my legs and shocks me out of my compliance. I elbow him, striking something hard, like his cheek or his neck, and he grunts in surprise. I have a split second of satisfaction before the throbbing in my head takes over.

"How dare you!" he bellows, his fist connecting with the back of my head over and over. "How dare—"

I elbow him again and this time I twist out from underneath him when he recoils. He recovers and pins my shoulders to the table with both hands. "I'll kill you for that."

I spit in his face. "No, you won't. You want me. If you kill me, you can't rape me."

Besides, he's got no free hands at the moment. It's my turn to smile because he can't hit me like this. If he lets go of one of my shoulders, I will fight.

"It's not rape. You're mine."

"It is rape, you sick fuck. I will never let you rape me. Never. I hate your fucking guts. You ruined my life! You killed my parents!" I headbutt him, connecting with his nose, and blood starts to drip immediately. He recoils and one hand goes to his face.

I twist my body and draw up my leg, placing my knee between him and me, and then I kick him back. My fist connects with his ear and then automatically grabs for hair, but my fingers find the mask instead. I pull and this panics him. I pull harder, wanting to get that stupid mask off him even if I die trying. "Take it off, you coward! Take off your fucking mask."

I rip it and he lets go of my other shoulder to try and stop me from removing his shield. I reach up and punch him in the face.

"You fucking bitch! I will kill your baby right now!" He regains control and pulls me up off the coffee table, then flings me down on the couch face first. I can hear his belt being unbuckled. "I'll fuck it out of you, whore."

"If you kill this baby," I gasp through my labored breathing. "I'll never be yours. Do you understand? If you kill this baby I will fight you until you kill me. I will never be yours!" I scream the last part and his whole body presses against my back. The weight of him makes it hard to breathe. Maybe he'll suffocate me and this can all end for good right now?

"You don't want to be mine," he seethes into my ear. "You never did."

"You killed my family, you freak! Why the fuck would I want anything to do with you?"

"They sold you!"

"No! You're a lying asshole. You're not even an original one, either." I laugh this part out because it's true. He's a joke. His whole story is plagiarized from another case more famous than mine. "You're a copycat! You're nothing but a copycat. You think I never heard of the Black Hills kidnapper? How he took that little girl and kept her captive until she was grown up. Convinced her she was his wife and made her have his babies. You copied him and you didn't even do a good job because you let me go. You're weak and stupid."

He goes still on top of me. "Is that what you think? That I let you go because I'm weak?"

A trap, Grace! It's a trap. Say nothing!

"I let you go because you begged me for months."

"Then why are you back? Just leave me alone!"

"Because, dear Daisy. You made me promise."

"No!"

"Yessss," he hisses back. "Yes. You were hysterical when I said I had to take you home. You cried, my little flower. You cried big fat tears and begged me to keep you."

"No!"

"I tried my best to console you, but I had to drug you to calm you down."

"That's not how it happened! I fought you. I told you to kill me quickly, so I didn't have to suffer."

"You made me promise to come get you, Daisy. You made me promise that our love was true."

"No, no, no! That's not what happened!"

He gets up and walks across the room to the front closet. "I'll prove it." I just stare up at him. His mask is all crooked and there's blood dripping down his neck from my retaliation. "I have you on tape, flower. I have it all on tape."

He pulls out a shoebox and comes back to me. "Sit here." He points to the couch.

I obey automatically. My mind is spinning. I know I was fucked up. I know I *did* agree to some things out of fear or brainwashing or whatever. But I didn't want him to keep me. I wanted to be free. I did.

"Let's watch it together, shall we?" He sits down on the couch and pulls out a video camera and some old tapes. The kind that go inside the camera and have to be played back.

I knew he taped me. I knew this.

But for some reason I had forgotten it.

Jesus.

What else have I forgotten?

Chapter Twenty-Nine - Vaughn

#JustOneGuy

"SHE'S not close. This feels wrong."

"Well, Vaughn, we have to start somewhere. There's a reason they never caught the guy, OK? He's smart. He's calculating. He's a planner. But everyone makes mistakes. Everyone leaves a trail. He had to have contact with Grace at some point. So someone saw him. Maybe not with her, but someone knows this man. And it's our job to whittle away at the clues until we find that someone."

I look down at Felicity and realize she's in charge here. Not me. Not Conner, who is back in California sifting through records trying to make the connection Felicity is referring to.

"So come on. This is the current 4-H office. We should be able to get the names of past leaders from them."

We enter the nondescript cinderblock building on the county fairgrounds and Felicity takes over. She talks in hushed tones about Grace, only she calls her Daisy. The women in the office nod solemnly and even though they should put up a fight about handing over information, they don't. Small towns make regulations up as they go when circumstances are extraordinary.

This situation is certainly that.

We leave thirty minutes later with one name. There's only been two 4-H leaders in this county for the past twenty years, and one died last fall. So… one name to go on.

"It's better than no names, Vaughn."

I say nothing.

It takes us another thirty minutes to drive to the farm where this woman lives, and by that time my body is pumped with adrenaline and my leg is bouncing.

Felicity knocks on the door alone. My movie-star status is not helpful. It's a distraction. So I wait in the car and watch Felicity pantomime her request. I can see her in profile, so I imagine her questions as her lips move.

Can you think of anyone suspicious? Can you remember anyone taking an interest in Grace… only I'm sure Felicity calls her Daisy since that's what these people know her by.

I imagine all the ways in which this woman say no, and then Felicity is walking back towards the car.

Felicity gets in and starts the car and then turns to face me. "She gave me a lead."

My eyebrows go up in hope.

"Some guy in Alliance, Nebraska."

"Tell me exactly what she said."

"Well, she said no to the suspicious people and all that. She said yeah, she remembers that camp trip because all the

228

leaders that year were women and Grace was the only girl in archery. There was a rift in a group of friends who all hung out together and five of them took swimming instead of archery. Grace was a good archer, she won prizes at the fair every year. So she split up from them and went to the camp."

"What else? That can't be it, that's not enough."

"Well, that's it for camp. But then I asked her about the special effects stuff. Did she know anyone who was into that sort of thing. And she said yeah. A 4-H club up in Alliance, Nebraska had an excellent theatre arts program in the high school for almost a dozen years. Some stage manager from Hollywood was from there when he came home after his father died, he stayed and taught theatre in school. She said he was gifted in that sort of thing."

"Bingo. That's our guy."

"I don't think so. He's too old, V. That's not him. But we can see him. Maybe he knows someone else who fits the profile?"

Fuck. "Fuck!" I say it out loud. "It's gonna be dark soon and I swear, I just have this really bad feeling, Felicity. If it gets dark and we don't find her, she might be gone forever."

"We'll just keep moving forward then, V. That's all we can do." Felicity picks up her cell phone and calls Conner to tell him what we found, but has to leave a message.

We ride in silence back to the airport and that lingers for the hour ride up to Alliance. Conner calls back and we check our name with his list, but this old ex-theater person is not on the Invisible Man roster.

Felicity is right. He's probably not our guy. We can only hope that he gives us another clue once we talk to him.

Chapter Thirty - Grace

#JustOneNameAsshole #GetItRight

AS soon as the video begins playing on the TV, I know I can't watch it. I spring up off the couch, catching my captor off-guard, and lunge for the camcorder that's plugged into the TV by a cable. My hand clenches around the cord just as he grabs my hair and flings me backwards. I crash into the coffee table and a sharp pain shoots up my spine.

The Invisible Man leans down into my face, spittle shooting out the hole he's using as a mouth, and he seethes. "You. Will. Pay. For that."

I spit in his face and he slaps me. Once to get my attention and again to make it hurt. My lip is split open in three places now.

He yanks me to my feet by my hair and pushes me face forward into the couch, straddling my waist.

"Get off me!"

"Listen to me, Daisy. You have forgotten the rules, but I understand. It's been a long time. So I'm going to be very patient with you. I'm going to be very patient and start your training all over again. Tell me," he whispers in my ear. Chills run up my spine and the hair on the back of my neck stands on end. "Tell me the first lesson you learned."

"You need to be trained," the man tells me from behind the mask of Danny. "So you know how to behave. So you know what's acceptable and what's not."

I say nothing. I've got that part down. Silence is my friend. The first few times I tried to talk to him, he slapped me. The next few times he gagged me. When I moaned out a single complaint as I was gagged, he punched me.

Silence is my friend.

There are many other things that set him off, but I don't know what they are exactly.

This one I know.

So I give him what he wants.

Nothing.

"Tell me!" he screams.

"No talking," I croak out. The punishment is a swift smack to the back of my head. No talking means no talking. He did this to me often back when I was a girl. Make me answer a question then punish me for talking.

I can't avoid the first hit, he makes sure of it. But as long as I stay silent, I can avoid the rest.

"OK." He settles a little on top of me, his weight pressing me into the couch cushions so hard I have difficulty breathing. Maybe if I turn my head—

He yanks my face back with a firm grip on my hair. "I remember that trick."

That trick, as he calls it, was me trying to smother myself when he was pushing my face into various things. The floor. The mattress in my closet. The pillows on the couch. I almost succeeded once, early in my captivity. But he caught on.

I lived. Again.

And again, living was not all it's made out to be. It's not always better to live.

"Tonight is our night, Daisy."

He's going to rape me.

"I'm going to show you how much I love you."

After all this time, he's finally going to get what he's always wanted.

"And you're going to respond with me the way you did with Asher."

I don't react. I can't react.

"I saw you in the forest, Grace." The venom spells out with my new name. "I found you a few weeks before that trip. I found your secret whore life on Twitter. And when you told the world about your honeymoon to the Caribbean, I had to go see who your new husband was. Imagine my happiness when I realized you were not on a honeymoon."

He eases himself up off of me and then pulls me up by my elbow. It's bent at a weird angle and I twist to relive the pressure and pain he's inflicting. When I turn, we are face to face.

His mask is gone. His face exposed to me for the first time. It's not a memorable face. It's neither handsome or ugly. Brown eyes. Fair skin. Stubble that is not the least bit reminiscent of Vaughn's sexy five o'clock shadow.

My stomach turns and I have to swallow down the bile as I avert my eyes. I'm relieved when I realize I don't know him. I was always afraid I'd know him. He'd be someone I trusted. But he's not. Just a psychotic stranger.

"Look at me."

I don't want to, but he grips my chin hard and yanks my head up. I force myself to meet his gaze.

"I was so happy when I figured out you were single. But then… all that died when I saw you with him. I'm going to kill him too—"

Too? He's going to kill me first, then Asher?

"And I'm going to make him suffer. Even more than you."

I chop him in the side of the neck, hammer-fist style, then follow it up with another one to the back of his head. He sways, but does not go down. Fuck! That shit's supposed to work! I kick his feet so he loses his balance and he goes down, but he grabs my calf and takes me with him. I fling my fists wildly, but he's so much bigger. So much stronger. I'm overpowered within seconds and a closed fist crashes against my temple.

I see stars. But I don't give up. My hand reaches out, feeling the carpet for something, anything that I can use as a weapon. I've taken years of self-defense, I can do this! I can save myself!

A cord. I dig my fingers into his eyes. My other hand grips the plastic cord and yanks.

Another blow to the head and more stars. A lamp comes crashing down on the floor next to me.

He grips the hand that's digging into his eyes and squeezes. I scream in pain, but my free hand grabs a shard of glass and stabs.

Blood is everywhere in an instant. It's on my hand, on my clothes, splashing on my face.

"You fucking bitch! I'll kill you now!"

I stab again and this time I hit him in the eye. He roars in pain, letting go of my crushed hand so he can manage the blood pouring out of his face.

I scramble up, crab-walk backwards a few paces and then get to my feet and grab an umbrella from a rack near the door.

He's got one eye open, watching me stalk towards him. "What do you think you'll do with that, Daisy?"

"It's Grace, you asshole!" I stab him in the leg. Hard. Hard enough to puncture his jeans and his skin because blood shoots out from there too. He looks up and growls at me like an animal.

I grasp the pointed end of the umbrella and swing the handle at his face. It hits with a whack and he falls back to the floor.

"Asshole!" I scream again as the adrenaline races through my body. "I hate you! I hate you!" I kick him in the stomach with my bare foot and then I step back, terrified that he'll get back up, terrified that I won't be able to get out of the house. Terrified that I'm still not safe.

I'm still not safe.

I lunge for the computer and pull up the only lifeline I have.

Twitter.

Chapter Thirty-One - Vaughn

#Profile

THE farmhouse looks cold and desolate. "Does someone live here?" Felicity asks.

I pull the rental car up to the dilapidated structure and turn the engine off. There's cows in a pasture not too far off and the corn is tall and turning brown, indicating it's almost ready to harvest, so apparently, that's a yes.

My phone buzzes and I press Conner's face. "Anything?"

"OK," he starts, a little bit out of breath. "Here's where we're at. There's a guy from Nebraska who did in fact work for Asher Productions a long time ago. Like back before the kidnapping took place. But he left and went to work—"

"In a high-school theatre department in the middle of Nebraska?"

"Yeah. How'd you know that?"

"We're at his house right now."

"This isn't our guy. He's too old. Maybe he's got more info, so check that out. But the main thing I wanted to tell you is that he had a student who got a summer internship at Asher Productions after the old man left."

"What's his name?"

"Derek Hauser. And he fits the profile. Right age. Born and raised in Chadron, Nebraska—just north of the national forest. And I think if we dig deeper, we'll find a record of him being at camp at the same time Grace was at archery camp. I've got the FBI looking into it."

"So where's he live? In California?"

"No. He quit his job a few weeks ago. Right before *IM2* came out."

"Tell me he wasn't on the set."

"He's not on our roster. At least not under this name. But we think he was a guest of someone else in the effects department the night of your premiere. That's how he got inside the theatre to make that call. We're going house to house with all the effects people to try and get a confirmation. What'd you guys find out?"

"We're at the old theatre teacher's house right now. It's not looking promising."

"What's that mean?"

"I mean, there's nothing here but cows. It looks…" I hesitate to say the word. I hate to say the word But it's the only one that fits. "Dead."

"Well, this Hauser guy doesn't own any property in the area anymore. His family died way back and he sold the farm the same year. So I'm not sure where we'd even look for him. Try to get it out of the old man. He's our best lead right now. Because this guy could be anywhere."

We hang up and I look over at Felicity. "I guess we go ask this guy."

"Don't you think it's weird," she says, her eyes never leaving mine, "that we've been sitting in this guy's driveway for ten minutes and no one's come out to ask us what the hell we're doing? I mean, this area strikes me as being filled with shoot-first kinda people."

I stare at her. "You think they're in there?"

She shrugs. "I dunno. But we don't even have a gun. Maybe we should call the police?"

Just then my phone buzzes in my pocket.

@MrsInvsman has logged on to Twitter, my third-party app tells me. "Grace!" I say. "That's Grace!"

Girl @mrsinvsman
@mrinvsman help me help me help me

Oh, fuck. I almost throw up.

"Answer her, V! Quick!" Felicity grabs the phone from my hand and begins to type.

Master @mrinvsman
@mrsinvsman where are you I'm looking for you in Alliance, Nebraska

Girl @mrsinvsman
@mrinvsman I don't know! I smell cows and I see corn. I can't get outside! It's locked. I can't get outside! He's not dead!

I snatch the phone from Felicity and start typing.

Chapter Thirty-Two - Grace

Master @mrinvsman

@mrsinvsman kill him! Now. Kill him and break a window

I'm barely done reading the message when I hear a groan behind me. I whirl around and he's already on his feet. I reach for the nearest object but I'm not fast enough. He lunges for my legs and tackles me to the floor.

"No!" I scream. I'm so fucking close! I kick and squirm, but he drapes his heavy body over mine and I'm helpless. He's too big. He's too heavy. I'm too weak, and tired.

I'm caught.

Again.

Chapter Thirty-Three - Vaughn

"GODDAMN" it! She's gone! She's logged off!"

"We should check the house, V. Maybe she's in there? Maybe she's right in there?"

We both get out of the car and slam our doors closed, running to the front door as quick as we can.

We have no weapons. We might be walking into something we won't be able to walk out of. But in moments like this, I work on instinct.

I hear the knocking before I realize that's what I'm doing.

Chapter Thirty-Four - Grace

A CAR door slams outside and both of us go still. I am just about to scream for help when his bloodied hand wraps around my face so tight, it cuts off my mouth and nose at the same time. I flail my arms as I try to find a breath, but it's no use. He's smothering me.

A few seconds later there's a knock at the door.

Chapter Thirty-Five - Vaughn

WE wait. We place our ears up against the door and listen. We shuffle our feet and knock again and again and again. But no one comes.

"Let's break in."

"Felicity, if this isn't the place, we'll go to jail. We're not breaking in."

"And if this *is* the place and Grace is being murdered right now because we're standing out here on the doorstep like idiots?"

She breaks the window next to the front door and reaches inside to unlock the latch. I twist the handle as soon as I hear the click and slowly open the door.

Chapter Thirty-Six - Grace

THE door unlocks as we lie on the floor, him panting, me smothering. Both of us bleeding.

The door opens with a creak.

"Derek?"

My captor relaxes for a moment and I twist my body. His hand slips off my mouth and I gasp for air. My chest fills up, the burning in my lungs almost taking my mind off my dizziness.

And then hands are pulling me to my feet.

"Jesus! Derek! You've got blood everywhere!"

I stare at the old man in the doorway. He's got long, greasy gray hair and soiled jeans. His boots are covered in mud and his shirt is stained with food. He smells.

I recoil with too much momentum and when Derek lets me go, I crash to the floor once more.

This time I stay down. I can't see right. My vision is suddenly black and blurry and I feel like I'm going to faint.

"She tried to escape," Derek says to the old man as he walks forward to meet him. "She stabbed me in the fucking face with a piece of glass!"

"I told you, son, children and grown women are not the same thing. You waited too long. She's never going to be what you want her to be."

"I don't want to kill her. I want to keep her. You said I could keep her."

Derek sounds more like a child than a kidnapper right now and I force myself to take deep breaths, hoping the dizziness will subside. These men are discussing my life. They are discussing whether or not they will kill me.

I know Vaughn got that message. I know he's in Nebraska and I think that's where I am right now. But I'm not sure. I'm on a farm, but it could be any farm. Farms are everywhere.

"She needs to go, son. People are looking for her."

My eyes dart up but when I find the old man's face, I immediately cast them downward again.

Those eyes tell me the decision has been made.

"I just got a call from Brenda over at the extension office. She said some out-of-towners were on their way over to my place. I came over right away to help you get rid of her."

"I don't want to get rid of her, goddammit! I told you, I want to keep her!"

"Now listen, boy—"

"I'm not your fucking boy anymore!" Derek pushes the old man hard enough to send him backwards. The old man's arms flail and then he trips over the rug and goes down.

A gunshot blasts through the room and I have to cover my ears to stop the ringing.

Chapter Thirty-Seven - Vaughn

"WAS that a gunshot?" Felicity and I stand still, our heads tilted as we strain to hear. Another pop comes from outside and we bolt through the door of the house and stop on the porch.

Another shot.

"That way!" Felicity says, pointing across the field. She takes off running but I grab her arm and point down to the muddy driveway. "Look. Tracks. And boot prints."

The foot prints end near four deep depressions. Tires.

"He left in a car. Come on, we follow the tracks and I bet we'll find out where those gunshots are coming from."

We scramble back inside the car and I start the engine. "Hurry!" Felicity says. "The shooting is still going on! He could be killing her right now!"

Chapter Thirty-Eight - Grace

I'M crab-walking again, only this time I'm not the one being hunted. I'm just trying to get away from crazy Derek with the gun.

The old man is dead. His brains have been splashed all over the front door. I get to my feet, stumble, and then bolt for the kitchen. I grab the biggest knife out of the block and wield it like a woman who is about to be raped or murdered or both. "Don't come near me."

He aims the gun at my head.

"I'm warning you."

"Bang, bang, little flower. I have a gun, Daisy. Now put the knife down and be a good girl and get back in your closet."

"Fuck you!" I slash out at him, missing by feet, but it makes me feel like I'm putting up a fight. I know I can't win, but I can put up a fight.

I dart around the kitchen island and another shot goes off. This time it shatters the granite countertop and sharp slivers of stone shrapnel make their way into my skin.

I feel nothing. Nothing but fear. I duck and crawl, desperately trying to find a way to save my life.

"Daisy," Derek says from the other side of the island. "If you give up and be good, I'll only wound you."

Oh, fuck!

"If you run, I'll shoot you in the back on your way out the door."

I glance over at the door. It's open from when the old man came in.

"Now be good, child. I'm going to come around the island and take you back to your closet. We can settle up your punishment tomorrow—"

I see his feet under the cupboards, making their way towards me, one step at a time.

"—and I won't hurt you at all tonight. How's that?"

Another step. I glance at the door again. Can I make it?

Probably not, but I have to try. This time I will not let this asshole corrupt my mind and hold me prisoner. I refuse to give him permission to keep me as his prisoner. I refuse to live through it. I refuse. I'd rather die escaping with a bullet in my back than live this life again.

Another step and I raise my knife.

"Dai-sy," he calls out in a sing-song voice. "I'm coming to get you…"

He takes that final step and I thrust the knife through his shoe with all my strength. I feel it stick in the floor boards and then I run.

A shot goes off and I duck, but it misses me. I leap over the dead man's body and fly through the door. I slip on a wet patch on the porch and slide, but another shot goes off and somehow, some way, my body recovers. My heart is beating so fast as I jump down the porch steps I think I might have a heart attack.

I race for the cornfield and my hands part the tall stalks as I enter.

He can't shoot me in here. He can't shoot me in here. He can't shoot me in here.

A shot rings out behind me and I run fast.

He *can* shoot me in here. He might not be able to see me, but that bullet will find my body if he points it in the right direction.

I zig-zag. I go left for a few rows, then right, then left again. I'm a lot smaller than him, and the corn is tall and thick, almost ready for harvest. So he can't see me.

But I can't see him either.

"I know this cornfield, flower," he calls out. "I know where you're go-ing..." That sing-song voice will haunt me for the rest of my life.

Oh, God! Please don't know where I'm going. I don't even know where I'm going.

But a few seconds later I see what he meant. I stop at the edge of the cornfield, my bare feet covered in soil.

It's an opening. A very large opening. Why the fuck is there an opening in the middle of a fucking cornfield?

I want to scream it, but of course I can't, because psycho kidnapper is right behind me.

"I know you've stopped running, flower. I know right where you are. I've been watching the corn as you ran. I told you. You can't get away."

My breathing becomes so loud I'm afraid it will lead him right to me.

"Stay put now," he calls out, a lot closer than he was before.

I only have one chance. I have to cross the clearing.

I bolt for the other side, but the gunshot rings out as soon as I step into the opening. My leg is on fire and I stumble. He fucking shot me!

I fall face first next to a pipe coming out of the ground. My hands grasp for something—grass, soil, something—to hold on to as the pain rockets up my thigh. My heart is so jacked up I can't breathe. *Please, God,* I pray. *Do not let me have a panic attack right now. Please!* My hand grasps nothing but soil and my arms both reach around the pipe for something to keep hold of. It's wet here. A puddle of water is pooled up against the pipe and I realize what this clearing is.

An irrigation well.

My arms collapse as the corn parts on the other side of the circle with a crackle of dry husks. He comes out into the area bare of crops and my hand rests on a large steel tool.

A plumber's wrench. A weapon.

If he's gonna take me down, I'm bringing him with me.

I wait. I lie very still. Play dead. And wait.

And when he finally stumbles up to me, I take my last chance. My body twists. I grab that heavy wrench with both hands, and I hurl it. Straight at his face.

Time slows down for me as I watch. My vision is blurred with blood. My hands are sticky with it. The fertile ground beneath me is stained crimson with it. I should not be able to hurl a plumber's wrench with such force, but there it is.

My miracle.

My win.

It smashes against his forehead before he can block it with his forearm and then stumbles backwards, still so very, very slowly. His eyes widen for a moment, and then they roll back in his head as he crashes to the ground.

I put the pain away somewhere else and force myself to get up.

I see only one thing. The gun.

I grab it and shoot. His head splatters into a bazillion pieces.

I shoot again, this time in his chest. Large pools of blood bubble up, but it's not enough. I shoot again, and again, and again.

And then there's someone else in the clearing with me. And I shoot him too.

Chapter Thirty-Nine - Vaughn

SHE points the gun at me and pulls the trigger.

Click, click, click. Over and over again, she pulls the trigger.

The magazine is empty.

"Vaughn," she screams, dropping the gun. "Vaughn," she wails, dropping to her knees where blood is pooling. She presses her head into the soil and sobs.

"Grace!" I cover the distance between us in seconds. I kneel next to her and pull her up off the ground. "You're OK now. It's OK." Felicity talks on her phone, trying to tell the FBI where we are. "I've got you, Grace."

Grace shakes. Her body trembles in my arms and I press my lips to her head. Her blood soaks us both now. "We need a fucking ambulance!"

Felicity is still talking on her phone.

I rock Grace in my arms. "Shhh," I say to quiet her sobs. "It's over now. He's dead."

"I shot you."

"No, the gun was empty. You didn't shoot me."

"But I would've!" Her words come out hitched from her crying. "I would've killed you."

"It doesn't count, Grace. You didn't. So it doesn't count. Now be still so you don't lose any more blood."

I sit back on the ground and just hold her. The sobs ebb and then her breathing slows. "Grace?" I ask, trying to figure out if she's losing consciousness or calming down.

"I'm pregnant."

I'm stunned. "What?"

But when I tip her head up to get more information, she really is unconscious.

A few minutes later I hear the wail of an ambulance. I don't know how we will get her to the driveway, but then the ambulance drives straight through the corn on what appears to be a narrow access road.

From there life becomes blurred.

They remove her from my arms and carry her away.

"I'm her husband," I tell them when they try to prevent me from entering the ambulance with her. Those are the magic words for the next several hours. Whenever they throw up a roadblock, I say "I'm her husband," and it gets me past the waiting room after she's been treated. It gets me a one-on-one update on her bullet wound—which is bloody and grazed her femur, requiring surgery and stiches—but more importantly, it gets me answers about the pregnancy.

The test is positive, but the ultrasound conducted on her sedated body says something different.

I don't know how I will tell her. I have no idea how I'll tell her.

There will be no baby.

Chapter Forty - Grace

#NotInTheMoodToHashtag

"HOW are you doing today, Grace?" the doctor asks me as she walks into my room, closes the door, and takes a seat. This is the third time today she's been in here. Vaughn said they need me to say something before they let me leave, but I'm not a prisoner. I'm wheeling myself out of this place in twenty minutes no matter what. "Do you want to talk about it yet?"

I ignore her. No one—and I do mean no one—is getting into my head. Not this shrink. Not Bebe. Not Kristi. Not Vaughn. All of whom have come to see me since I was transferred to Denver for surgery on my leg. In fact, I think Vaughn is living here in the waiting room. I can't see him right now. I can't. I'm just too upset. He told me that the pregnancy test came back positive but the ultrasound showed an empty sac.

I wasn't pregnant. Or maybe I was, but it never developed. Either way, I'm not pregnant now.

And that just… I don't know. Makes me so fucking sad.

They keep asking me about Derek, that's what this lady wants me to talk about, but who gives a shit about that guy? He had me less than a day. I got myself out. I killed him. It's over. End of story.

I just want to go home.

"Grace?" Vaughn asks, peeking from the doorway. "Just say no if you don't want to talk about it."

But no feels like a trick. If I say no, the next question will be, why?

"Just say fuck off, Asher. I'm sure every nurse in this place wants to say that to me right now. Did you know," he says, coming fully into the room now, "that I personally talked to the guy they call a chef down in the cafeteria and had him make you those special chicken nuggets last night?"

I lower my head so I can make a face about the gross nuggets and not be seen. Fucking Asher. That was not some special request.

"And I had them put special sheets on your bed. Nothing but eight hundred percale for my wife."

Oh, God. My hand involuntarily reaches down to scratch my leg. The sheets are threadbare, which makes you think they'd be soft, but they're not. They have all those little pebbles on them. They're terrible.

"And I even requested the Mercedes of wheelchairs. I stood in line all night in the supply room to get this baby."

I have to turn to see what he's talking about. There's a nondescript folded-up wheelchair in his hands. He flops it open and waves his hand over it.

"Your chariot is here." And then he winks at me. "OK, fuck them, huh? You don't need to say shit, right?" He wheels it over to me and parks it parallel to my bed so I can ease into it. "But sweets…" He leans down to whisper in my ear and I get that familiar tingle, a chill of excitement that races down my spine from the tickle of his breath. "You'd make me so happy if you'd say *something*." His fingertips reach under my chin and gently lift my head. "Anything."

I look him in the eyes for the first time since I woke up from surgery. He looks tired. And sad. He's smiling. Every time he comes in here, he's smiling. He's putting on a front though, I can tell. I feel like I know him better than anyone in my whole life. Even though we've only known each other a few weeks, I feel… connected to him. And I realize that I don't want to push him away. I don't want to be alone and silent. I can't go through that again. I can't

So I speak.

"OK," I croak out. My voice cracks a little and Vaughn rushes to offer me a cup of water off the bedside table. I take a sip and try again. "OK." It's just two letters. Hardly my best work—not even one hashtag—but definitely my most pithy when it comes to getting Vaughn Asher's attention.

His face lights up immediately and that makes my stomach flutter. He's in *like* with me. And I'm in *like* with him. We're married. He is, in fact, my husband.

"What kind of fairytale is this?" I say it out loud, but I really didn't mean to.

"It's real, sweets," he says back, as he plants a kiss on my cheek. "It's real. Now tell me how to make you happy right now."

I drop my head and cry. I hate to cry. Crying is the weakest thing in the world because it does nothing except make you feel worse.

Vaughn sits down on the bed next to me and I hear the click, click, click of the doctor's shoes as she exits the room.

"Grace," he says as he pulls me into an embrace. "You can tell me anything. I'm your own personal secret-keeper. Nothing you tell me can hurt you."

"I'm sad," I whisper, trying to pull myself together.

"I'm sorry. I'm sorry he took you and my security wasn't good enough—"

"No," I cut him off. "That's not why." I look up at the great Vaughn Asher. His eyes are glassy and his smile is gone. "I'm sad about…" But I can't say it. It wasn't even a baby. The nurses all told me that when they came in that first night. Not even a baby. Just an empty sac of nothing.

So why do I feel like crying just thinking about it?

"You know what I'm sad about?" he asks as he lays me back on the bed and then joins me.

"What?" I turn to look at him and the tears stream down my cheeks. I bite my lip to stop the sobs, but they break through anyway. "What?" I ask again, because he looks shell-shocked.

He manages a tight smile and then blinks a few times. "I'm sad…" He stops to take a deep breath. "I'm sad that I imagined a whole life with you and that life included a baby.

I mean, back before they told me it wasn't going to be. I imagined the doctor visits. The shopping. You slapping me and cursing my name during natural childbirth." I laugh at that and he smiles. "Just kidding. I'd never be able to watch you in pain. So good God, please. Take the drugs when they ask you, OK?"

"*When* they ask me?"

"Yeah, sweets. When. There's babies in our future, Mrs. Invisible Man. Lots of them. We just got married. We're just hitting our stride. Bad things have happened over the last few weeks. But the good things will outweigh them soon enough. So don't be too sad, Grace. Don't let the sad take over your life or make you afraid. Don't let it stop the words." I look up at him and I know he's been talking to Bebe or my parents. They must've told him how I clammed up last time. "Don't let those bad things steal away your future. Or make you hide behind a Twitter handle. Or force you into a fantasy life because reality sucks. Because I'm gonna be here with you. From now on, when life comes at us, we're gonna fight it back together. We're gonna grab it by the horns and ride the fuck out of it. So please, Grace. Please. I'm begging you. Don't be afraid. And don't be too sad."

I lean up and kiss him. His hand cups my face and pulls me close. This is the first kiss we've had in forever and it feels different somehow. It feels special. Passionate. Real. "Please take me home, Asher."

He smiles at my use of his last name. It's not an insult. It's... familiar. When I look closely, I can see the tears in his eyes. "Where's home, Grace? Just tell me where home is and I'll take you there."

"Home is…" I look up at Vaughn. He's not the man I dreamed about. He's disappointed me plenty of times. He's as far away from my imaginary prince in the Land of Far, Far Away as they come.

But I'm not complaining. Because he's better. He's better than anything I could ever have hoped for. He's romantic and tender. Commanding and kind. He's protective and loving and generous and… *mine*.

He's all mine.

"With you," I tell him. "As long as I'm with you, I'm home."

Chapter Forty-One - Vaughn

#Just #What #The #Fuck

I CLOSE the limo door after helping Grace get in the back seat and walk around to my side. My phone buzzes in my pants and I grab it from my pocket, thumbing the accept tab as I bring it to my ear. "Yes."

"Vaughn Asher?"

I stop walking. "Who is this?"

"Is this Mr. Asher? Because what I have to say can only be said to him."

"Who. Is. This?"

The woman on the other end of the phone huffs out a breath of air. "Carey Keefe. And I'm going to assume you are, in fact, Mr. Asher?"

Keefe? Why does that sound so familiar?

"I'm the editor-in-chief at *Buzz Hollywood?*"

Oh, fuck.

"You still there, Mr. Asher?"

"I don't have time for this, so what do you want?"

"You *do* have time for this, Mr. Asher. Take my word on that. Because I've got pictures of you here on my desk. Actually, pictures of your wife, as well. Pictures my head gossip reporter got off Twitter."

Fuck again. "I'm going to ask you once more, and then I'm hanging up. What do you want?"

I can almost hear the smile on the other end of the phone. "No denial, huh?"

"What's to deny? You say you have pictures. Three seconds and you get the beeps."

"OK, wait. I'm wavering between allowing my reporter to publish these and making her bury the story. In fact, we had a huge fight over it. She really has it in for you."

"What's new? That bitch has been after me for years."

"Right. I've noticed that it seems a little... how should I say it... personal with her? Do you know each other?"

Do I know her? I ponder this question for a moment and then Grace knocks on the back window and silently asks me if everything is OK from inside the car.

"I just don't have time right now."

"Mr. Asher, if I don't get the story behind this, I'm going to let my reporter go to print with whatever she wants. And believe me, this spreadeagle selfie of your wife is not even news-worthy compared to what she's got on you. So I'll give you twenty-four hours to get your poor wife settled back home. And then I need a phone call and a personal meeting. Twenty-four hours."

She gives *me* the three beeps.

I let out a long breath of air and continue my walk around the car. I open the door and slide in next to Grace with a huge smile.

I'm an actor. It's what I do.

"Everything OK?" Grace asks.

"Perfect, sweets." I lean over and kiss her, then drag her up to my chest until she scoots down to lay her head in my lap. "Perfect." I play with her hair as we make the trip south to the airport where the jet is, and by the time we get there, she's asleep again.

I carry her to the plane, set her down gently on one of the couches, and then help myself to a beverage as the pilot performs the pre-flight check.

Do I know her, Keefe asked.

Fuck, I wish I could *forget* her.

I'd do anything to fucking forget that night.

SOCIAL MEDIA SERIES BOOK SIX

HOME

NEW YORK TIMES BESTSELLING AUTHOR

HUSS

Chapter Forty-Two - Grace

#TakeThePlunge

THREE days in the hospital. Three hours on the plane. And with LA traffic, three hours to get back to Vaughn's house in the hills.

Three is my unlucky number.

The limo pulls into the driveway and comes to a stop at an angle, trying to cut the distance from the car to the front door. But it doesn't matter. Standing makes me dizzy. Walking is out of the question. I have to wait for Vaughn and the driver to get the wheelchair out of the trunk.

"Here, sweets," Vaughn says as he positions the chair up to the car.

"I hate this."

"I know, baby. Later you can try to put some pressure on it. There's no broken bones, so it's just a matter of good old-fashioned healing."

But I don't want to try to walk, either. I stepped on it accidentally when I got in the chair earlier and the pain was sharp and immediate. "I don't want to," I say.

Vaughn ignores me. I've been doing nothing but bitching since I started talking earlier today and I'm sure everyone around me is wishing I'd go back to my self-imposed silence.

I scoot myself to the edge of the car, then brace all my weight on my good leg and flop down in the wheelchair.

"See," Vaughn says cheerfully. "Not so bad."

Not so bad if you're the one pushing. There are only three steps leading up to the front porch of the rambling one-story house, but even so, the effort required to get me up those three steps makes me want to curl up in a corner and die.

I'm so high-maintenance.

"Where to first, huh? Movie room? You can relax on the couch and I'll wait on you. Delivery service is complimentary."

He's still smiling when I look up at him but it falters. That makes me feel bad. "Bed," I say. "I'm so tired." It's not a lie, but I was tired on the plane too. And on the way home. In fact, tired is starting to be my new favorite phrase, because when you're injured and you say you're tired, people say you need to get some rest. And that means they leave you alone.

"You just woke up, Grace. You're not going back to sleep. In fact, let's go outside. How about a trip down the lazy river?"

"Hmmm."

He chuckles as he pushes me through the messy living room where Felicity has hoodies and shoes lying all over the place, and then stops at the wall of glass that leads out to the pool area. The doors are swept open and the heat rolls over me like a blanket.

Yeah. Maybe that feels good.

"Put your arms around me, Grace. And hold tight."

I do as I'm told and he lifts me out of the chair and cradles me in his arms as he walks over to the little foliage-covered archway that leads to the part of the backyard where the lazy river is. He turns sideways so we can fit through and then stands on the edge of the plunge pool. The lazy river is only about four and a half feet deep, but the plunge pool is exactly what it sounds like. A place to drop straight in, kick off, and shoot back up. "Trust me?"

I tilt my head up as my heart races. "It might—"

"Do you trust me, Grace? Never mind the rest."

I look him in the eye as I nod. "Yes."

He squeezes me harder and then steps off the edge.

We drop together. My mouth opens to scream, but then the cold water rushes in and shocks me silent. We drop swiftly. My wound stings from the impact or the chlorine or both and I'm just about to start flailing in protest when the soothing coolness takes over. Vaughn's feet touch bottom and there's a moment where we feel weightless. His knees bend and he laughs underwater. His joy fills my heart as we spring up and burst through the water.

We bob there. Vaughn's feet are treading water trying to keep us afloat, and I start to wiggle again.

"Shhh," he chastises me with a whisper in my ear. "Be still, sweets. I've got you. Relax. I will never let anything happen to you again. Never."

I spit some water out of my mouth and do as I'm told for once. I relax. I rest my head against his chest and the second I do that, the arm supporting the weight of my legs drops away and they float downward. He adjusts me, slipping his hands under my ass so he can pull me close.

I adjust as well, wrapping my arms around his neck and resting my head on his shoulder. "I love you," I say.

He squeezes me hard and places his mouth against my ear. "It's about time you remembered, sweets."

"I've loved you for years."

"But that was the fantasy me. The good guy. This is the reality me."

"Still a good guy," I cut him off before he can say the rest. "You're my prince. Thank you for coming to find me."

He holds me one-handed now so he can swim us a few feet over to the edge of the pool where the steps are, and then sits down so we're still immersed in water. "I was too late."

"It was the perfect time."

"You could've been killed."

"Yeah," I say softly. "I could've. But I think there was more of a chance of me getting killed if you showed up sooner. It happened the way it did because…"

He turns me around in his lap. My leg feels weightless in the water. I'm not in pain. The cold rush is still there, numbing it. Soothing it. "Because why, Grace?" He looks me in the eyes for that question and I know one thing about us right now.

Things have changed.

Yes, we're married and there's a whole lot of new things that come with that territory. But his expectations of me have changed as well.

He expects the truth.

"Tell me why it needed to happen that way."

I know why, but it's private stuff I've been holding in for a decade.

"Just say it, sweets. It's only a few words. And once you say it, you can accept it. And once you accept it, we can move forward."

I take in a deep breath. "Because…" This is therapy stuff. I know that. It's a trick. That thought almost makes me laugh. *It's not a trick, Grace. It's a technique to wrap your head around things.* "Because… I needed to save myself."

He hugs me so tight I think I might suffocate. "Yes," he whispers in my ear. "That's it. That's all you need to say about it."

"Why am I not affected by this, Vaughn? Why doesn't it bother me that three days ago I shot a man? I killed a man. I think that makes me sick. I'm a sick, sick person."

"That doesn't make you sick, Grace. That makes you strong." He kisses me again and then stands up and walks out of the plunge pool. My body gets heavy and I immediately want nothing more than to get back in the water and hide underneath its soothing surface.

Vaughn walks us over to the edge of the river, grabbing a towel from the little cabana as he goes. He tosses it down on the concrete edge and then places me on top of it. My leg hurts a little now and my clothes are sticking to me. "Lift up your arms."

I do as I'm told and he peels off the man-sized white t-shirt. My nipples are erect and hard, my breasts firm and taut. I look up at my husband and he's shirtless too. I watch his fingers as he unbuttons his jeans, kicks off his shoes, and then drops his pants. It takes both hands to get the heavy wet denim to cooperate and when he's finally standing there naked, he puts his arms out and says, "This is me."

And then he reaches down for my hand, like he wants to pull me to my feet. I hesitate because of the pain it will take to stand up. But then I decide to trust him and place my hand in his.

He pulls me up and I manage to keep the weight off my bad leg and just balance on the good one. Vaughn holds me steady for a second, and then he takes my hand and places it on his thickly muscled bicep. "Hold tight," he says.

I do.

And then his fingers unbutton my shorts and he tugs on them for several seconds, rocking the sopping wet fabric over my hips until they plop to the ground.

He steps back a little and I let go of his arm.

I put my arms out like he did and say, "This is me."

I'm pulled back into an embrace and I notice everything about this moment.

The sun is warm. The wind floats past my wet body, making it cool. There's a bird singing a sweet song on a branch above our heads.

His heart beats fast. Mine beats faster.

His lips touch my ear so softly I shudder.

"This," he says, "is us."

Chapter Forty-Three - Vaughn

#MyVersion

"I KNOW you don't remember the wedding, Grace. But it was pretty special."

"How special could it have been?" she murmurs against my chest. "We were drunk."

"We weren't that drunk, I swear." I scoop her up in my arms. She draws in a breath and I know the leg is bothering her, so I lean down and kiss her head. "Let me tell you all about it. How's that? Do you want to hear what happened?"

"Yes," she says softly.

I carry her over to the river and set her back down on the towel. "I'll tell you the whole story as we float down the river naked. Deal?"

I get a smile from her at that suggestion. It starts small, just a slight lift, but then her eyes dart to the river and I can almost see her picturing it. Her smile grows.

I walk over to the pool shed and search around until I find a floating cabana with a sun shade on it. I pump it up since it's probably been years since I've used this thing, and then take it outside and set it down in the loading area of the lazy river.

"Ready to hear all about your fairytale wedding?"

She's shielding her eyes from the sun as she looks up at me. "Oh God, I'm not sure. Was I really drunk and stupid?"

I carry her over to the river and walk down the steps. "Baby," I say, placing her on the raft, "I get that you were drunk. But please believe me—what I saw that night was nothing but perfection. I didn't take any pictures. Not because I didn't want to, but because you were so stunning in that dress, all rational thought just left the building."

"What dress? I didn't have a dress."

"You did," I insist as I climb next to her. "I swear. Now settle, sweets. And let me tell you all about it." She squirms around a little, wincing from the pain in her leg, and then she places her hand over my heart and exhales.

That exhale says everything.

It says she trusts me. It says she loves me. It says she's ready. She might not know it yet, but I do. She's ready to move on. Those eight months Daisy spent as a captive changed her. And while I'm certainly not looking to change her back, I would like to change her forward.

"Ready?"

"Mm-hmm."

"OK, this is exactly how it happened…"

"I'm yours," Grace says as she wraps her legs around my middle. "I'm yours."

I ease into her and I can feel her thighs as they grip me. Begging for me. Begging for me to fuck her harder. But I don't want it to be hard tonight. I've had her hard and rough but I haven't had her slow and sweet. And that's what I'm craving right now.

She moans in my ear, so low it's almost undetectable. Her hands are on my head, fingers threading through my hair. Her breath brushes my neck, sweeping across my skin in short bursts that match the heaving of her breasts against my chest.

"Come for me, sweets. Come for me."

Her grip tightens.

"Come," I encourage her again. "And I'll come with you." I flip over on my back and position her on top of me. My hands grip her hips, moving her back and forth as I thrust upwards. She moans louder. Her hands are on my chest, propping herself up, but with each thrust her resolve weakens until finally she is pressed against me. Our bodies are sweating from the sex, and the heat of our desire, and the strength of our emotion.

My fingers find her asshole and her upper body awakens once more, shooting up. Her head falls back. her mouth open. Her soft moans turn to screams.

We come together.

I come inside her, my hot semen spilling out in waves as her pussy clamps against my cock, and I grab her hair and yank her back down on top of me so I can bite her shoulder. "Mine," is all I can manage. It's primitive, but I don't give a fuck. This girl is mine.

"Yours," she moans back. "Make me yours."

Fuck. Fuck. I pull her hair harder, wrapping my hands around her head in a way that leaves no doubt that I want to possess her. Completely.

Our hearts race against each other and we stay this way. Still. Silent. Satiated.

I trace my fingertips up and down her spine and every time I get to the small of her back, she bucks. That makes me smile so big. It makes me happy in a way I'm not sure I can describe. "Do you like it like this, Grace?"

"Yes," she whispers and then bites my neck. "Yes. Like that, please. More."

"More, and more, and more."

"Forever. Happily ever after."

"Baby, don't tease me. I'll give you forever if you want it."

"I need forever so bad."

"Then marry me—"

"Wait." Grace stops me with a hand on my chest. "That's it? You asked me post-coital and I just said yes?"

"Shhhh." I hush her with a finger to her lips. "Just listen."

"—Grace. I have never felt this sure of something in my whole life. Ever. You, baby. You are the secret to life. You are my reason for being. You are my soulmate. We are tethered by a string. Some mystical string that connects us and has connected us since our inception. And the day I saw your sandaled foot step out of that dingy airport shuttle, I knew. You were my other half. It's the only explanation for how I feel about you. And I tried to deny it. Tried to prove to myself that this arrangement with you was… ordinary."

I flip us over one more time so I can be on top again. I prop myself up on my forearms and let my hands fall gently along each of her cheeks. I stroke her softly, my thumb arcing back and forth across her soft skin.

I devour her with my eyes. "What we have is so far from ordinary, Grace. It's not a connection. It's a reconnection. I need you to understand that and I really don't have the words to describe what you mean to me right now. But even though my expression is inadequate, please believe me. You're mine. That's all there is to it. And if you need me to make that declaration permanent, then marry me."

She stares up at me and her breath hitches like she might start crying at any moment.

"Just marry me."

"And that makes it... forever?" Her brows knit together in confusion.

I can see her point. Why would marriage change things? "No, baby. That's not what makes it forever. The forever between us? It just is." I lean down and kiss her on the lips. Our tongues tangle for a second and then they do more than that. Her fingers push through my hair and she flattens her palm against my head in her own version of possessiveness. "There's no paper or vow in this world that can surpass what the universe has declared to be true."

She swallows hard and that makes me smile, because it proves that she's taking me seriously. I'm spewing all this metaphysical bullshit about fate and souls and ties that bind.

And she's in.

"We just are. And that's the end of it. We don't need a marriage to make that true. It's the laws of physics, baby. It's under God and there's no death do us part in any of this, Grace. Because we defy—"

"Oh my God," she laughs. "You did not say all that shit!"

"Shit? I'm offended."

But we both laugh.

"It's pretty good though, huh? I mean, most of that is true. I was just a little too drunk that night to gather all those words into the same speech. But that's what I meant."

Chapter Forty-Four - Grace

#NextStep

I HAVE this stupid grin on my face and no matter how hard I try, I can't make it go away. Vaughn Asher is such a bullshitter. But it's so fucking adorable I almost die. Fate and souls and ties that tether us through eternity. That's what he meant. I giggle and he pokes me in the ribs, making me squirm. "Stop," I laugh. "You're so full of it."

"I'm not," he says. "I really mean all that shit. And even though I didn't really say it that night, I'm saying it now."

"OK, whatever. All I want to hear about is the dress. And did I at least eat cake?"

"Sweets, we were invited down to the Bellagio bakery. You got to taste everything. You dipped your newly wedded fingers into frosted cupcakes that were so pretty and perfect they looked fake."

"Stop. How do I know what's true if you keep lying?"

He sighs. I know what that means. He's disappointed that I don't remember. "You will remember, Grace. I have faith.

You had a dress, but I'm not gonna tell you about it because it was so beautiful and perfect you won't believe me." He sighs again and then he turns his head so he can gaze at me sidelong. "I can't do it justice. You need to see it in your own memories."

"But where is it? I was wearing a little white cotton nightie when I woke up. Did I get married in that?"

"No," he says sadly.

God, it hurts me that my memory lapse is affecting him so hard.

"No, we picked that out from the lingerie shop. Carl was with us." He laughs at that and so do I. I'm not sure why. "Poor Carl. I bet he gets a fat raise for putting up with me that night. I made him open the pool—"

"The pool?"

"I'm not saying another word. If you don't remember, you don't deserve to hear it from me. But you did demand a hundred underwater candles."

"What?"

"One hundred. And you wanted to count them." He laughs a little harder at that one.

"I don't even know what an underwater candle is."

"Well"—he kisses me, still laughing into my mouth—"that wish was not granted. But your list was long, baby. So I hope you're not too disappointed."

"I had a wish list? That doesn't sound like me at all."

"I know. I loved that drunk Grace had grabby hands for so many things."

"So the dress?"

His fingertips touch my lips and I open my mouth, my tongue darting out automatically. "Nah," he says under his breath. "Nah. I don't want to spoil it. I want you to remember all on your own."

I think I make him sad. And it kills me. I want to remember so bad.

"It's OK, sweets. It's OK. I'll wait. Now close your eyes. Enjoy the sunshine. Enjoy the peace. Let's just float."

And we do. We float down River Asher and my whole body just sighs with satisfaction. I think I relax. Really relax, for the first time in... well, ten years.

The masked man is dead. And yeah, I get that I'm fucked up. I understand now. Vaughn was right about that. I need help.

But not today. Today all I need is Vaughn. That's it. One man who knows me. Who loves me. "I'm glad we're married, Mr. Asher."

"Mmm. Me too, Mrs. Asher. Me too."

I fall asleep after that. And I dream. I dream of Bellagio fountains and underwater candles, and wedding dresses. Blue wedding dresses. I dream of cotton eyelet lace nighties with pink bows and bottles of champagne. I dream of the white sheepskin rug and making love to Vaughn, the soft fur against my back, under my knees, pressing against my stomach. In my dream, we have sex so many times on that rug, I lose count.

Sometime later, after the sun goes down because the trance-inducing warmth evaporates, I wake. Cooled and refreshed, but in pain. After all this, Vaughn carries me to his bedroom. I wince from the throbbing in my leg, my pain pills forgotten as we were floating.

Vaughn feeds me the little white tablets with a bottle of cold frappuccino and that drags me back to dreamland. The sheets are cool and the air-conditioning gives me enough of a chill to make me reach for the fluffy down comforter.

I'm growing used to the heat of a man next to me at night.

I never want this to end. I want to keep Vaughn Asher forever. I want more than anything to remember the night he promised to be mine.

But tonight is not my night for that. Tonight is just the first step towards healing.

Chapter Forty-Five - Vaughn

#GoingDownTogether

GRACE sleeps, but I don't. I lie there with her for about thirty minutes, my mind on the time.

Twenty-four hours was all I had before my deadline expires. Twenty-four hours of perfection. I have my wife in my house. She's safe. She's even happy. Still denying herself memories of our wedding night, but I have a feeling they will come back soon. I have a feeling that the reality she twisted to help her cope with her abduction as a teen is somehow mixed up with giving herself to me.

I'm patient. With Grace, at least.

I throw the covers off and get out of bed. I dress quietly in the closet before walking into the living room. I press Ray's number in my contacts and wait for him to answer.

"Looks good, boss," he says as he picks up. "No action outside at all."

"OK, you stand by and Bigmy stays in the house."

I end the call and go out to the back yard. Bigmy and I cross paths as we exchange places, him taking up watch in the house while I go down to the security building. There's a path on the other side of the pool that leads down the hill. It's banked on both sides by thick green foliage. I never showed Grace this side of the property. Not because I want it to be secret that I own so many lots on this hill. I just never had the chance.

I make my way down the winding path until I come to a small stucco building. I open the door and the cool air washes over me. "Hey," I say to Ray. He looks like shit. But he won't go home until this is settled, even if I tell him to. He's my number one guy. He takes care of the number one priority and he always takes care of it himself. He'll sleep here if he has to. And the overnight bag on the floor near the door tells me he has to.

"I'm ready for you. You have thirty-two minutes until your twenty-four hours are up. Should we wait till the last one?"

"Why bother? I just want to go back to sleep. So let's get this over with."

"Yes, sir," he says, handing me a phone. "Just press send."

I press the tab and the phone starts ringing. She picks up on the third ring sounding incoherent. "Hello?"

The bitch has the audacity to be asleep? "Carey Keefe? I hope I'm not waking you."

She clears her throat. "Mr. Asher. Why"—she chuckles sleepily—"I had assumed you'd forgotten about me."

"Nope."

"Do you have a time to meet that's good for you?"

"Now. My house. My security man will pick you up one street over. Here he is. He'll give you directions."

I don't wait for an answer, just hand the phone to Ray. He rattles off the street and tells her twenty minutes. I'm not sure if twenty minutes is reasonable or not, considering I'm up in the hills. But who cares. I'll be here if she's late.

After Ray hangs up he leaves to go wait it out. We have a path that goes down to the street below. I own four lots on the street just below my home. Most people don't know that. I'm a paranoid fucker when it comes to my privacy at home.

Public sex on Saint Thomas is one thing. Stalkers on my property in LA is something else entirely. I used to get stalkers often, photographers hanging out by the end of my gate when I lived in Trousdale, but ever since I moved here, things have settled down.

Part of that was my obsession with never being seen in public with girlfriends. Only dates. And dates were business deals. Negotiated with contracts and signatures.

The sex came from other places. The subs. But they had contracts too. I tried to leave them satisfied, if unhappy. Money does that.

When Felicity and I first moved here, I had some paparazzi hanging out in front of the gate. Mostly it was the *Buzz* assholes. But I never did anything interesting. I never brought girls home. I never got drunk and made scenes. I grew up the son of Adam Asher and he taught me well.

Keep your head down and work. That should be our family motto.

Of course, not all child stars have such guidance and power behind them. I knew there was stuff going on behind the scenes—hell, I saw it at the release parties from a very young age. But every time a star fucked up, my father was there to point out how they get what they deserve. *You want to party, Vaughn?* he'd ask me. *You want to go out and have fun? Just know, nothing you do is private.*

That was the lesson drilled into my head. And I heeded it. I never got into any trouble as a teen. But like most kids who go off to college, you get that first taste of real freedom. Couple that with the money I had in the bank, and well, I did a few things I regret.

But money… it might not fix everything, but it fixes most of it.

I go back up to the main backyard and walk over to the pool, then wade in up to my knees. God. I love this backyard. Felicity thought it was an extravagant luxury to put in the river and spend so much. But I love it. And Grace loves it. And even though we technically met in a bar, we met properly on that lazy river in Saint Thomas.

Just thinking about that day makes me smile like an idiot. I stunned her, throwing her dirty words back in her face. All I wanted at that moment was to possess her. Like a thing.

But even then I had this feeling about her. Like she was different. Denying my drink offer in the bar. I shake my head and smile as I recall that morning. Mr. Buttinski, she called me. Silly girl.

I sigh as I picture her back then. So carefree and happy. So sure of herself. So feisty.

And now? I've been in her life a matter of weeks—not even a month has passed—and I almost can't find the old Grace anymore.

Did I do that? Did I force that change? Do I still make her sad?

I like the old Grace. No, I *love* the old Grace. I love her dirty mouth and her sassy self-assurance. I never wanted to tear that down.

You lie, Asher. You lie. That's all you thought about. Taking her in the way that pleased you. Making her submit to your contract and your fetishes. Corrupting her sense of wellbeing to knock her down and keep her wanting.

I'm a sick fuck.

My phone buzzes a message in my pocket. *Coming up the path*, the text says.

Well, the bitch must live close, because that was only fifteen minutes.

I make my way back to the security building and then keep going right past it, down the hill a little ways.

The plan was to take her through the backyard of one of the houses below, and then leave her waiting next to an empty pool. So that's where I'm heading. I'm quiet until I enter the gate that separates this path from that yard, and then I make a lot of noise on purpose as I wind my way through the overgrown tropical trees until I find the pool area.

She's standing and on high alert when I enter the open space. There's no light back here so I imagine she's all sorts of freaked out.

Good. Bitch.

She lets out an audible breath of relief once she recognizes me and I take a lot of satisfaction in that.

"Ms. Keefe, I presume?"

"Yes, Mr. Asher." She stretches out her hand but I ignore that gesture and take a seat in the old webbed lawn chair across from her.

"Hmm. Well," she says as she sits back down. "This is some place you have here."

"Yup. I love it. It's the perfect place to have midnight meetings."

"It's three AM, Asher."

"Discretion, Keefe. It's all about discretion."

"Perfect. Then I assume we're going to make a deal here?" She fishes through her bag and comes out with a small digital recorder. "Mind if I tape this?"

"Tape away."

She turns the little machine on until the red light blinks and then mutters some words into it and checks to make sure it's working. "OK, we're ready. Why don't you start by—"

"Why don't I start by telling you what's gonna happen now?"

"Excuse me?" She looks up with fake doe-eyes. Like she's stunned. Like she expected this to go her way.

She cannot be that stupid.

"How. This. Will. Go," I repeat slowly. "It's simple really. You can fuck off. You can print whatever the hell you want. Photos of my wife? Fine. Stories about me? Go for it. But before you do that, Keefe… just make sure you tell your star reporter that I've got pictures too. And that shit will hit the public the minute I see my wife in your magazine. Or on your stupid little cable TV network. Or anywhere else for that matter. If my wife's private photos exchanged on Twitter appear anywhere, her past goes public too."

Keefe clicks the little recorder off and shakes her head. "I thought you'd take the easy way out, Asher. I really did. But you're gonna regret this. I can't control her, I can only appease her. This was your only chance. I'm gonna let Amy go tomorrow. So whatever she does, it has nothing to do with me. And I could care less if you release things about her past. It's not my problem."

"Oh, it *is* your problem, Keefe. Because whether you know it or not, that secret she thinks I'm hiding is not about me." I wait for her smug look before I deliver the last line. "It's about you."

"Ha," she laughs. "Right. I have no idea what you two are talking about. I have no idea how you know each other so well. But I do know this. Your threats are as fake as your on-screen alter-ego. You having a superhero complex, Asher? Newsflash, asshole. The Invisible Man isn't real."

"Oh, he's real. Keefe. He's real. He might take the form of well-concealed video equipment these days. But he's one hundred percent real."

"What the fuck are you talking about? You don't know me."

"I know more than you think, Keefe. A lot more. You want to know what this is about?" I stand and she stares up at me. "You want to know what Amy has against me?"

"That's why I'm here, Mr. Movie Star."

"November, 14, 2005. Issue one of *Buzz Hollywood*. A press-printed paper circulates through the Hollywood clubs. Given out at the door while people wait in line."

She narrows her eyes but the anger is replaced with confusion. She doesn't see it yet.

"You ran a story that changed your life."

"So?"

"It was a lie."

"It was not," she bellows, standing up like she's gonna take the control back. I smile and nod as I stare her down. "I had proof of that shit. Frankie Miller did not kill DeeDee Cisco, it was a suicide. We proved it. Not to mention I knew him personally from my time at UCLA. He was my graduate school advisor. And if it was false, believe me, he and I would both be in jail right now."

I stand up to take her down a notch as she is forced to admit how small she is compared to me. "He's guilty as fuck, Keefe. And so are you."

She's shaking her head, like that will make it right. "You don't know anything. You're bluffing, to make us back off."

"Honey," I say, taking advantage of her confusion, "who the fuck do you think runs this town? You and the media whores like you? Really?" I laugh under my breath at her stupidity. "Come on, Carey. Step down off your pedestal. Take off the rose-colored glasses and see this shithole for what it is."

She stares up like a befuddled child.

"*Mine.*"

"Liar," she screams at my back when I turn away. "You're a fucking liar. I'm telling Amy to go to print with those photos. They'll be all over the internet in two hours!"

I stop so I can give her a sidelong glance over my shoulder. "And your precious tabloid will be bankrupt before the week is out. So choose wisely, Keefe. There *will* be consequences."

I walk back onto the thick tree-covered path and climb back up the hill to the security building and wait for Ray. He comes through the door laughing less than five minutes later.

"Don't get cocky, Ray. I have the means to take her down, but I'll go down with her if it comes to that."

Chapter Forty-Six - Vaughn

#WelcomeToMyWorld

NINE WEEKS LATER

"GRACE?" I whisper in her ear. "You awake, sweets?"

"Mmm."

At five AM, I take that as a no. "I'm leaving for work. I have to go in early for makeup." Nine weeks have passed since I brought her home from the hospital and my Grace is still moping. It's making me crazy. "You want me to send a car, Grace? So you can have lunch with me later?"

"Mm-hmm," she mumbles.

That was a yes? I don't want to ask her again in case I'm mistaken. I'll take whatever I can get. "OK. Be ready at one."

I kiss her on the head and pull away, glancing down at the long scar running down her thigh. It's still red and raw, but it's healed. Her limp is gone. She's been working hard at physical therapy. Bebe saw to that. God, I owe Bebe hard. Grace actually listens to her. Me? She's still a little rebel with me, but Bebe snaps her fingers and Grace falls in line. Reluctantly, but she does. So I have Bebe to thank for Grace's quick recovery.

I stand up and grab my bag so I can head out to the studio.

First day of actual filming for *IM3*. Not that I haven't been working my ass off for more than a month already, since I'm co-directing this time around. I let out a sigh as I walk into the garage and climb into the 911. When I took the *IM1* deal I was hoping there'd be a part two. But part three? That's pretty cool.

I start the car and rev the engine, backing out slowly so I can turn around in the driveway and head down into the city.

The drive into the studio is quick, since five AM traffic on Saturday is light. I'm waved through the front gate and two more after that. I drive slowly on the lot until I find my parking spot.

After the success of part one, we all figured there was a good possibility we'd make it all the way to a trilogy. But after the success of part two, it was a done deal. Three weeks after release, they sent me the script. I signed off on it that same day. The writing was phenomenal. The budget was out of this world. We were all set.

And then my co-star, Scarlett, had to pull out. She got a better offer that conflicted with our schedule.

We could wait for her or—

"Vaughn, baby! Oh God! It's so good to see you again."

We could hire someone else and change the script around a little. "Valencia." My ex-Disney co-star. My ex-girlfriend.

She jogs over to me from the door of her trailer and greets me as I get out of my car.

"Oh my God, this is so great! I'm so happy we are working together again!" She wraps herself around me like an octopus. Valencia has always been one of those touchy-feely people. "I was so excited when they called to offer me the part. Did they tell you how excited I was?"

Who? But I just smile as I pry her hands off me. "Of course they did. That was the first thing they said." I smile warmly at her and give her a little push to get her walking as I contemplate how thick I have to lay it on to keep her happy.

This is the game in showbusiness. Everyone wants to feel special. Everyone has a huge ego that needs to be stroked. Everyone requires personal attention.

I figure it's no skin off my back to give people these things. And that's why I'm so successful. I'm a compliment whore.

"Oh, please, Vaughn. I know better." She leans up on her tiptoes and plants a kiss on my cheek. "But thank you."

And then she grabs onto my hand and follows me into my trailer, talking a mile a minute. I barely have time to throw my keys down before my set assistant is thrusting a cup of coffee at my face and insisting I head to makeup.

"Valencia," I say again. "Gotta run, hun. Catch you later."

Probably not. We're not scheduled to even be on set together until tomorrow. But what does it hurt to be polite and excited to see her? Nothing. Why save it up for another day? That's stupid. And goes against the first lesson in Hollywood.

Attitude is everything.

I check my watch as I walk over to the set and enter a tan metal door that leads to makeup. I wonder what time Grace will get out of bed. She spends entire days there sometimes. She has therapists but I don't think they are doing her much good. They're not really allowed to discuss her care, but one did say Grace mostly sits in silence when she goes. A few words muttered about her day are considered progress. I don't know what more I need to do to help her recover.

As soon as the door closes behind me, the sights and sounds of work fill my ears. Work invades my worries about my wife and it's a relief.

I'm not the Invisible Man for these opening scenes. I'm just Griffin. We've deviated from the original story considerably after the first movie. And so far the Invisible Man hasn't had much luck in the love department. But I have a feeling that will change in this movie. Valencia only does sexy these days, so I'm sure they added some scenes to show off her amazing body.

She looks great, I will give her that. At twenty-nine, she's more beautiful now than she was at sixteen when we dated.

But beauty was never her downfall. She's just too bossy for my taste.

I endure the hour-plus of makeup time and then wander over to the set, reading my script before we start. It doesn't take much to get into this character. Movie three should be ridiculously easy in that regard.

I spend the next seven hours waiting, acting, waiting, waiting, acting, and eating. In that order.

But every minute that passes is one that I'm not spending with Grace. Every minute that passes I miss her more. While I'm waiting, when most of the others in this scene with me are looking over their scripts, I think of Grace.

I think of her lips. And the way her pillow smells like her shampoo. And the way her eyes turn this amazing blue when we're in the pool at night. It's surreal. Sometimes I make her swim with me at night just so I can see her eyes turn that color.

I picture babies. Baby girls, mostly. Little tow-headed princesses with those same turquoise eyes. I picture holidays together. And buying a new home. Soon. I want that to happen soon. I picture all these things whenever I have a free moment.

When lunchtime approaches, I can't stop looking at the door. This will be the first time she's ever been here to see me at work. I might be nervous.

A flash of light as the doors open, letting in the outside world. And there she is.

I want to be on this set when she comes in to find me for lunch. I want to be here, in front of all my co-workers, when she enters this life with me. I want to introduce her and show her off and be proud and happy that she is mine. And I want everyone here to see that.

"Grace!" I call out as she looks around, uncertain.

The whole place goes quiet.

Daisy Bryndle seems like a phantom. She disappeared after Grace was airlifted off that dreary Nebraska farm and never came back. I know Grace still struggles. She accepted

Bebe's advice about physical therapy. She's done a good job putting it behind her.

I wave at her as I get up off my chair and walk over with long strides. I take her in my arms and kiss her on the lips. "God, I missed you," I say into her mouth.

"It's only been a few hours."

"Too many. Now come on, I'll introduce you to the crew." I take her around and give her dozens of names she will never in a million years remember. And then I call the lunch break and lead her outside towards my trailer.

"Slow down," she laughs as I pull her along. "What's the hurry?"

I open the door to the trailer and wave her in. "You're the hurry, Kinsella. Now up." She climbs the stairs and I smack her ass as we enter the trailer.

"Don't be a caveman, Asher," she throws back.

That Asher shit used to bother me. But ever since she called me that back in the hospital, I take it as a term of endearment.

I scoop her up in my arms and walk her back to the bedroom. I look down at her face before I do it. I want to see the thrill in her eyes, the smile on her face. "Don't do it," she warns me.

I throw her down and turn her over so fast the idea of struggle never enters her mind. "I owe you so many spankings, Mrs. Asher."

"No!" she protests, laughing.

"Oh, yes." I pull down her shorts and my dick gets hard just looking at her bare ass. Fuck. I smack it good and hard and she yelps out as her cheek turns pink.

"You can't spank me here."

I smack her again and this time I let my fingers slip between her ass cheeks so I can find her slick pussy. "Goddamn, Grace. I must not be fucking you enough at home if you're this turned on with two spankings in my trailer."

She's pressed into the thick comforter on the bed, so she turns her head and gives me a wink. "I've been waiting for these spankings for months, but you look like someone else right now. It's weirdly erotic."

Mmmm. Fuck. I forgot about the makeup. "It's too weird to let me fuck you?"

She shakes her head slowly. "No, Master."

Oh, fucking hell. I yank her shorts all the way down to her ankles and unbuckle my belt as fast as I can. She moans, still watching me with her head turned to the side, when my cock is finally in my hands.

I lean over her back and bite her shoulder. "I'm gonna fuck you."

"Please," she begs. "Do it hard. Fuck me hard."

We haven't had rough sex since *before*. But that doesn't mean I haven't been craving it. I was gonna fuck her hard anyway, but her invitation takes away all my doubts. My hand slides back between her ass cheeks and I stick my fingers inside her pussy. She groans and wiggles enough to make me feel like she's resisting. Like she wants me to take her, whether she wants it or not. This makes me crazy with desire.

I position the tip of my dick until it's pressing against her warm, soft folds and then I stop.

"Tell me what you want, Grace."

"You," she whispers immediately. "Just you."

I ease into her slowly. Not pushing hard enough for her, because her pussy clenches around my dick and she rams her ass backwards until I fill her up.

"Harder," she begs. "Fuck me harder."

I don't, of course. "Don't boss me, woman," I tell her instead. "I decide how hard you need to be fucked."

I decide she needs to be fucked very hard right now. But I'd rather save that for tonight. So I ease back out of her, just as slowly.

She moans with disapproval, but before she even has a chance to whine about it, I ram back into her, my thighs smacking against the back of her legs.

"Like that, you filthy bird?"

"Yessss," she whispers. "Yessss."

Her voice alone is enough to make my cock throb with want. I thrust a little harder this time and another. "Yes, please, more," is whispered into the blankets on the bed.

"I think you should come to work with me every day. Let me make you my trailer whore. Keep you tied up on this bed, your legs spread open for me, your pussy dripping wet as you think of all the ways I will fuck you wild when I come for lunch."

Goddamn, I might come from my own dirty talking.

"Do it, Master. I'm yours to use as you please."

I pound her for that remark and she starts to moan a little too loud for a back lot trailer. So I pull out, flip her over, and place my hand over her mouth as my cock slides back inside her pussy. "Shhh, you wild thing." She breathes hard through her nose as I continue to pump. Her legs wrap around my waist, her thighs pressed against my hips, squeezing as she tries to keep me close when I pull too far away.

I thrust one more time, pushing as deep as I can get. She stiffens a little with the force, her pussy gripping my cock so tight it can only mean one thing. Her reaction fuels my desire to have her. To spill my come inside her. My head falls back automatically and I feel the release and it's over.

I growl out my satisfaction as her legs, weak and trembling, unwind from my hips. I fall on top of her, my pants still mostly on, her shorts still around her knees. And I pull her over so her face is resting on my chest. She breathes hard and heavy, panting as she tries to calm her racing heart. And then things slow… the rhythm, the pulse in her neck as I kiss it tenderly, my own heart… slows.

"I love you," she says quietly.

"I love you back."

Someone pounds on my trailer door and breaks the moment. "Yeah," I call out.

"Five minutes, Mr. Asher," they yell back.

"I'm bored at home," Grace says.

"I'm sorry, sweets. You can come here every day if you want. You can come all day. I'd love for you to be here. But it's boring here too."

"Maybe it's better to be bored together?"

"It is," I say, kissing her neck one more time. She's calm now, the wild ride behind us. "It is. Stay here in my trailer and rest if you want. Or go for a walk on the lot. I can get someone to take you around?"

"No," she sighs. "I'm gonna go home and cook, I think."

"Yeah?" I'm surprised. She's never cooked for me before. In fact, she doesn't do much of anything for me. So this is a good sign. I smile and play with her hair. "What will you make?"

"What do you like that I can make at home?" She turns a little so she can look me in the eye.

"Steaks?" I don't give a fuck what she makes. She can serve me peanut butter and jelly for all I care. I just want her to be happy.

I don't think she's happy.

I'm not enough to make her happy.

"I can do steaks."

"Good." I get up and shove my dick back in my pants, then reach for her hand and bring her to her feet and then pull her shorts back up. "I can't wait to come home."

"What time will you be?" She looks up at me and her eyes have that lost look in them I've become used to.

God, she's so vulnerable right now. Her request is almost a plea. I hate leaving her home alone. "Eight? Maybe?"

"Oh." She's disappointed. I can tell. But we work long hours when we're filming. It costs money to pack things up and quit for the day. "OK. I'll see you at eight."

I hold her hand as we walk outside and then she gives me a little wave as she heads in the direction of the attendant responsible for her while she's on the lot. She gets in the golf cart and pulls a pair of sunglasses on. But I catch it.

A fingertip slides up under her glasses to wipe her eye. Like she's crying.

The golf cart takes off and I'm just about to go after her when I hear them calling for me.

She just needs time. That's what everyone keeps telling me. Time heals things.

I guess that's true. Time healed her after the first incident. But it's different now. She was a child. Children are resilient. That's what they say, anyway. Children bounce back.

"Mr. Asher?"

My assistant is right up next to me now. "Yeah, coming."

I know Grace is still sad about how things ended back in Nebraska and it makes me feel helpless. Because there's no dollar amount that can fix this for her. There's no gift, no vacation, no promise that can fix this.

It's up to her now. All I can do is make sure no one else interferes with her recovery. And so far, that's going great. *Buzz* backed off. No other new sources have turned up.

So why do I feel so sure that something's coming?

"Mr. Asher?" my assistant asks again as I stare at the disappearing golf cart.

"Right." I turn away and follow him back inside.

Chapter Forty-Seven - Grace

#NotGoodEnoughToBeAStupidWhore

"GRACE?" he whispers in my ear. "You awake, sweets?"

This must be our new thing.

"Grace? You want to come have lunch with me again today? Only this time we'll really eat?"

"No," I mumble from under the covers.

"Are you sure? I'd love it if you came to the set today."

"No," I say again with more conviction.

"OK. Well, dinner last night was delicious. Will you cook tonight? Or should I bring something home?"

"God, I don't know. It's not even time for breakfast yet."

He's silent for a few moments. I'm being a bitch, I know this. I want him to call me on it. To tell me to stop my moping. But they didn't do that back when I was a teen and no one is going to do that now.

They tiptoe around me. Even Vaughn. No one knows what to do with me, so they figure I should be allowed to do whatever I want, I guess.

Well, I want to be a bitch. Because I'm angry about something. I'm not even sure what it is. I'm just angry.

Asher is still talking but I tune him out.

I'm trying to figure out what's got me so pissed off and I just can't seem to get a hold of it. I get another kiss and I make an effort and throw the covers back. "Sorry," I say as he walks away. "I'm grumpy."

He stops and takes a deep breath. But he doesn't turn back. "I'll see you tonight, OK?"

I nod but say nothing.

And he leaves.

Good going, Grace. I guess you got what you wanted. I throw the covers back over my head and try to go back to sleep. I lie there for thirty minutes until I give up and reach under my pillow for my phone to find Bebe's face. I press it and wait for it to ring.

"*Hola*, bitch," she says in her chirpy Bebe tone. "What's shakin' bacon?"

This makes me smile immediately. She's so stupid. "Your tits, as usual. Those giant knockers are gonna take your eye out one of these days."

"Totally. But I got them strapped in at the moment."

"You at work?"

"Yup. Did you know that sweaty guys in a gym, who beat each other up for a living in a ring they call a cage, are hot as fucking hell?"

I smile wider. "So, Steve's two-hour parking limit is up, I take it?"

"So up. Dude, he was talking about kids. Do you believe that shit? I am not mother material. I mean, seriously. Anyone who knows me knows I am not mother material. I'm fun party material. I want no ties for at least ten more years. I'm all about enjoying your youth while you have it."

"Did he cry?" I laugh. Bebe has been known to make men cry. Hell, Vaughn is even afraid of her.

"Almost. Pffft. Wimp. So what's up with you, *chica*? Living *la vida loca*?"

Fucking Bebe. I miss her so damn much. "Eh. I'm at home in bed. Vaughn is working. So... eh. I'm at home in bed."

"What's wrong?"

I hesitate. Because even though a few minutes ago I was trying to pretend that I didn't know what was wrong, I know what's wrong. "I feel like... going home."

"You are home."

I take a deep breath. "No. *My* home."

The silence hurts. It really does. But I suppose my words hurt Bebe even more.

"Why?" she finally asks. "I mean, after all these years. Why now?"

"I don't know. It's a bad idea?"

"Such a bad idea."

I knew it.

"But," she adds after a few seconds, "if you need to go, Grace, then you should go."

"I have a private jet. Well, I mean, I have one available to me. As Mrs. Asher. I'm coming right now."

"Now? But I'm at work."

God, I love my adopted sister. She just naturally assumes we'd do this together. "That's OK, Bebe. I can go alone. Really. It's not a big deal. In fact, I want to go alone."

"You sure?"

"Yeah, yeah. I'll be fine. How about I call you later and maybe we can have dinner?"

"OK."

She sounds hesitant, so I say goodbye and quickly hang up before she can ask any more questions. I don't want to be alone. But I don't want her to feel obligated.

I stare at my phone for a few seconds to get up my nerve. When Vaughn gave me this phone the day after we came home from the hospital, it had all his contacts in it already. His agent. Big Hollywood producers and movie stars. Restaurants he frequents. And the flight coordinator.

I press that tab now and tell them I want to go to Denver. It's a three-hour drive up to the town I grew up in from Denver, but I can use the thinking time. Plus, I don't want those people to know I'm coming. I don't know why, but I don't want them to know I'm coming. And if I take a jet up to that little airstrip, they will know.

Once the arrangements are made, I get up and take a shower and get dressed. I skip breakfast—they always serve food on the jet—and then I climb into the Audi Vaughn says is mine, and drive out to the airport.

By the time I get there, it's fueled, the captain is on board, and the only thing missing is me. Vaughn didn't call and ask me what the hell I'm doing, so I can only assume they didn't inform him of my plans.

I breathe a huge sigh of relief at that because he'd have all kinds of questions. And I'm not ready to answer those questions.

I really just want some space. I need some space to put things together.

I spend the next few hours staring off into said space. Just thinking.

Thinking about too many things, if I'm honest. About the kidnapping. Both times. About Vaughn. About my leg. It's better, almost one hundred percent better, but it was very painful. You know, in movies and books they always make it look like getting shot in the leg is no big deal. Well, it was a big fucking deal. My scar is four inches long. It took me three weeks before I could walk without a crutch, and then it took weeks more of physical therapy to get rid of the limp.

The first time I was taken, I came back with no injuries. I mean, he injured me plenty during those eight months. But there was no medical attention required. I didn't need fixing. I was fine.

This time it's different. This time everyone knew I was damaged and that I needed attention. And believe me, I got a lot of attention. I almost prefer no attention. In fact, I know I'd prefer no attention.

I like to blend in.

I like to lie low.

I like to be still, and quiet and—

Wait. No, that's not right.

Grace—or the old Grace, at least—likes to talk. She likes to tweet, and Facebook, and chat. That was my whole social life before... before *this* happened.

How did I get so confused?

The captain comes on over the intercom and announces that we'll be landing in ten minutes. I never took my seatbelt off, so his spiel is wasted on me.

I don't even know why I want to go home to see those people. I guess it's just killing me to know that I have real blood relatives but I have no connection to them at all.

I sigh and push all those melancholy thoughts away as we descend. And when the wheels touch down, I'm resolved to see this through. No matter what.

"We have a car ready for you, Mrs. Asher. It will pull up into arrivals in ten minutes and should be waiting for you by the time you get outside."

I nod absently as I chew on my fingernail. Why am I doing this?

I wish I knew. I'm not myself these days. I know that. But it's like I have this momentum and I don't know how to stop... whatever direction it is I'm heading.

The plane taxis for another minute and then we stop. I sit quietly as the staff opens things up and then the attendant turns and smiles at me. She has very red lipstick and a tight bun. "You're all set, Mrs. Asher."

I hate that they call me that, but I use it myself when I need to get things done. Like taking my husband's jet for the day.

"Thank you," I sing back in a cheerful voice. She beams a smile at me like maybe I'm not the damaged freak everyone thinks I am.

You know, it's funny—I take a few steps off the plane and the wind and cold overtake my thoughts for a second. It's November in Colorado and I forgot my coat—it's so easy for me to smile and be fake. I did it so much back when I was a teen. It's like acting. And that's what's funny. Because I married an actor.

Is it this easy for him to hide his true feelings?

I continue with my smile as I walk across the tarmac and go inside the small, but bustling, terminal. The place is abuzz with people. Mostly rich business travelers. None of them pay me any attention as I walk straight across and out the doors to the pickup line.

And stop dead. So I can smile for real. "What are you doing here, bitch?"

Bebe is wrapped up in a stylish red wool coat with a black belt that makes her waist look tiny and her boobs look enormous. She's got on dark sunglasses and her long, almost-black hair is waving gently around her face in the wind. Bebe looks like a movie star. She slips her sunglasses down her nose and gives me a smirk. "Do you really think I'm going to let you go see those awful people alone?"

I cross the distance between us and she pulls me in for a tight hug. "Thank you," I whisper. "Thank you so much. I just need to take one more look at them, y know?"

"I know, *chica*." And then she pushes me back. "You don't even limp!"

"I know, thanks to you. I hear you called in for a progress report twice a week."

"Well," she says as she puts her arm around me and leads me towards a black car, "it was the least I could do. I wanted to be with you for every second of your recovery."

"You were, Bebe. You were. I saw your face everywhere as I struggled. I love your fucking face."

"Right back at you, bitch. Now get in," she says, opening the passenger side of her black Porsche Macan. "I'll drive and you talk. Oh," she says just as my door closes. She jogs around the front of the car and gets in before she picks up her sentence again. "I mapped out all the Starbucks from here to Holyoke!"

"They don't have Starbucks in eastern Colorado, Bebes."

"I know," she pouts. "It's like the apocalypse already happened out there."

People make fun of small towns. And I guess they deserve it for being so backwards and slow. But I never minded them. It was nice to be in a place with no traffic and no crime.

Well, I guess that's not true. My whole family was murdered in our home, so obviously every town has crime.

I still wonder why that freak fixated on me. Why me? I'm not ugly by any means. I'm cute. I have my beautiful moments. But why me?

Bebe chats all the way into Parker to pick up coffee, we use the drive-through, and then we get back on the freeway that will take us out into no-man's-land. It's a long drive up. Probably boring for most people. But it's been a while since I saw hay baled up neat and lining fields. And the farther away from Denver we go, the more I feel the tug of home. Whole flocks of turkeys wander around the side of the roads. Herds of antelope stare at us as we pass. Snow begins to fall as we make our way north. And before I know it, Bebe stops talking and we drive into town.

It's quaint, I'll give it that. It's well-kept and colorful with the fall decorations. The downtown is small, just a block really. But it's bustling with busy people.

No one looks at us and yet… everyone looks at us. I mean, a Porsche SUV is not something you see every day in Holyoke. Luckily it only takes us about thirty seconds to drive through town and then we turn east. I look over at Bebe.

"You want to see the farm, right?"

I nod. She knows me so well. And the fact that she knows how to get there without asking me for directions… well, that's something too. It's a maze of dirt roads and dead ends. And every field of winter wheat or fallow ground looks like the next. But sure as shit, she finds the house.

Bebe pulls her e-brake as soon as we stop but she doesn't turn off the engine. "I'm not going inside."

I look over at her and she turns her head to meet my gaze.

"I don't want to go inside," she repeats.

I swallow down my fear and open my door. I step out into the muddy driveway and close the door quietly behind me and then take a few tentative steps towards my home.

I still own it. Which is why it's still standing, I suppose. No one farms this land. The barns are all empty and the only sound is the slight hum from Bebe's car and the wind whistling through the trees.

My courage builds as I take a few more steps and then I'm just walking up to the front stoop. The windows aren't broken. There's no graffiti on the white siding that covers the exterior. The curtains are all closed.

It almost looks like someone lives here.

I reach for the door handle and...

"Don't do it, Grace," Bebe calls out. "Don't go in. It's locked, I bet. We'll have to break a window. And that will open it all up again. Just leave it alone."

I turn back to her. She's half in and half out of the car. One foot on the ground. The wind is blowing her hair sideways and a chill runs up my spine.

I rub my arms and hug myself to stave off the cold. "I need a coat," I call back.

"There's no coats in there, Grace. We had it cleaned out, remember? There's nothing in there."

I look back at the door, at my hand still reaching for the handle. "What if... I open that door and they're still in there?"

"They're not in there, Grace." She's right up beside me now. "They're not in there."

"I know that. But can't a girl hold onto a little hope?"

"That's not hope, Kinsella. That's denial." I look over at her and she shrugs. "Truth." And then she hops down off the stoop and picks up a rock and climbs back up. "But if you really want to go inside, I'll help you. I don't think it's a good idea, but I'll—"

Her words are cut off as a car comes slowly down the gravel driveway. A maroon sedan covered in a layer of dust and dirt.

"Who's that?" I ask. But I already know. "Aunt Rachel."

The car parks next to Bebe's and idles there. I stare into the eyes of a living blood relative for the first time in ten years and my heart goes wild with fear. Her hair is hidden by a wool hat, but even through the window I can see a few straggly strands of gray peeking out. She was pretty when I was a kid. At least, that's how I remember her. She and my mom used to look alike, but the woman I see through the glass does not look like the mother I have in my memories.

Maybe it's the frown?

I only let myself remember my mother as happy. Because my last memory of her was the horror that took place the night she was killed.

Aunt Rachel leaves the engine running and then opens the door of the car and places a hesitant foot outside. Just like Bebe did a few moments earlier. It's like this place makes everyone pause before getting out. "What're you doing here?" she yells over the wind.

I look at Bebe and she's squinting her eyes at my aunt, but she stays silent.

"Visiting," I call back from the stoop.

"You have no right to come back here and disrupt the quiet. No right."

My eyebrows go up. "I own this farm."

"*I* own this farm. This is *my* farm. I grew up on this farm. Your mama got it in the will and that's how you got it. But this farm is mine."

"Wow," Bebe says. "She wants to talk about property rights."

"No one wants you here, Daisy."

"Grace," Bebe says with a snarl. "Her name is Grace."

"I don't care what her name is. Nobody wants her here."

Bebe hurls the rock at Aunt Rachel and it hits the hood of her car with a thunk. "Fuck off, you bitch."

Aunt Rachel is screaming at her, but Bebe provoked is a force of nature. She storms down the front stoop, yelling right back. They get up in each other's faces and start pushing. Jesus Christ, we're going to jail today.

"Bebe!" I run after her. "Bebe, please." I grab hold of her coat and pull her back. "Stop, please."

"No, Grace." She turns her anger towards me now. "No. This is over. This life is over. It's been over for a decade. And this bitch thinks she can come out here to *your* farm"—she seethes that part in the direction of my aunt—"and talk shit to you? No."

He eyes are wild with anger as she waits for me to say something, but as usual, I stay silent.

"That's right," Aunt Rachel says. "She knows her place. She know she's guilty—"

"Guilty of what, you stupid whore?"

"Bebe, please!"

"Guilty of ruining this family. Guilty of ruining this farm. Guilty of ruining this town. We are forever known as the place where Daisy Bryndle's family was murdered so some sick freak could have his way with her—"

"Oh, you cunt! You did not—" Bebe lunges at my aunt and hits her full on in the chest, sending her reeling backwards until they are both on the ground.

"Jesus, Bebe! Stop!" I pull on her coat until she gets up off the ground.

My aunt stands, brushing off the dirt. And then she turns back to me, breathing heavy from the altercation. "You did this, Daisy. You led that boy on somehow—"

I slap her across the face. Hard. Harder than I ever did Vaughn.

"Shut up," I say in the wake of her stunned silence. "Just shut the fuck up."

Her hand goes to the red mark on her cheek and she shakes her head. "Get out of here. Now. Or I will press charges for assault. And don't think for a moment"—she looks over at Bebe—"that you will get out of this by declaring me a trespasser. Everyone knows this is *my* land."

Bebe opens her mouth to say something but I put my hand on her arm to make her stop. "Never mind, Bebe. You were right. There's nothing here for me. Let's just go."

Aunt Rachel stares us down as we climb back into Bebe's idling Porsche and pull the doors closed with a dull thump.

"They're all crazy."

I agree. "Let's just go." Bebe puts the car in gear and does a u-turn in the dead grass, flipping off my aunt as she passes. I rest my head back as we bump along the winding driveway and when we make it back onto the paved highway, I laugh.

"What's so funny?"

"You. 'You stupid whore.'" I look over at her and she's smiling.

"God. She *is* a stupid whore."

"Shit. She's not even good enough to be a stupid whore."

"Yeah." Bebe laughs with me now. "Stupid whores all over the world are pissed off that I insulted them back there."

"Thank you."

She gives me a sideways glance and tilts her chin up. "I got your back, bitch. Always have. Always will."

Chapter Forty-Eight - Vaughn

#IMightRatherBeSquare

"SO," the reporter says with a conspiratorial wink. "Do you want the good news or the bad news?"

Marjorie has been an acquaintance of mine for a while now—more than seven years—and in that time, she's hardly aged a bit. Looks younger than ever, in fact. Her short bobbed hair is blonde with streaks of hot pink. Her clothes are minuscule, and her shoes could be mistaken for stilts, that's how high they are. In other words, she fits right in with all the other businesswomen I have close ties with.

"Bad."

"Hmmm," she says, taunting me with her straw. I get a little distracted by her glittery lipstick before I look back up to her eyes.

"Just spill it, Marj."

"They have a lot of dirt on you, babe."

"Like what?" I know what. I just want to see if she knows what.

She shrugs. "I'm not one hundred percent sure, V. But if I had to wager a guess, I'd say it's more of the kinky fuckery type stuff."

"Bullshit. If they had *that*, they'd run it."

"And," she says, ignoring my defense, "that Jasinda bitch is still making the rounds with her baby bump."

"Damn. I really thought she was lying about that. But I guess not, huh?"

Marjorie puts her hands up. "You tell me."

I eye her. Just because I've known her for a long time and just because we're having lunch together doesn't put us on the same side. "I already told you. It's not mine. I'm one hundred percent sure because I wasn't fucking her when she got pregnant."

"Well, this is what I'm telling you, hon. None of that has gone away. Now, there are rumors that you threatened Keefe over at *Buzz*. And if that's true, well, that might explain why they are still gunning for you. I mean, come on, Vaughn. You don't threaten the annoying fly on the wall. You crush it."

"I did."

"You didn't." She's smug in the wake of her words. "Threatening with a fly swatter does not a crushing make."

I close my eyes for an exaggerated pause to collect my thoughts. I knew it went too quiet. "What's the good news?"

"Well, see… now that's gonna cost you."

"Cost me what? I already fucking pay you."

"A date."

"No way."

"Yes way," she counters quickly. "I need you to take me to a party."

"What party? Larry never even gives me those invites because I never go."

"The Black Bash."

"Well"—I laugh—"I'll have Larry check to see if I was invited, but I'm pretty sure that's a no fucking way. I'd probably be arrested if I hit that one."

"I need you to get two invitations and I need you to come with me, Vaughn. For real."

"They're not going to let us in, Marj. They hate you almost as much as they hate me."

"It's a masquerade, Vaughn. And the theme is iconic movie stars. We'll dress up."

"Just tell me the good news and I'll pay you whatever."

"No, the good news will be delivered next Friday at the Black Bash. So be there or be square, mister."

And with that, she scoots out of the booth, grabs her sunglasses off the table, and walks off.

Do I care about her good news?

I don't know. I'll have to think about it.

My phone buzzes across the table and I reach for it, palming the answer tab as I bring it to my ear. "Yeah."

"Mr. Asher, this is Josey, your aviation coordinator."

"Sure, yeah. What's up?"

"I just wanted to make sure you knew that your wife went to Colorado today."

"What?" Jesus fuck. My heart begins to jackhammer in my chest.

"Yes, sir. She scheduled the plane to Denver. And I provided a car for her, but she never showed up at the car."

"She disappeared?" I can't breathe.

"No, sir. We went through the security footage and she left with…" There's a little pause as Josey consults her notes or something. "Bebe Chambers. Do you know her?"

"Yes. Thank you." I end the call and take a moment to steady my heartbeat. Fucking Grace. I'm about to speed-dial her, but I stop myself.

Why do I have to keep tabs on this woman? Just why? Why can't she call me for a fucking change?

Goddammit.

I tuck my phone away, stand up, throw a fifty down on the table, and walk out of the cafe lowering my sunglasses. There's no paparazzi out here right now. And maybe that's normal. I mean, if I think about it, nine weeks after the release of a movie, they taper off. They find someone else. They move along. Right?

But no. It's not right. They usually chase me three or four days of the week. And now, nothing?

Something is not right.

But I don't have time for it because I have a scene with Valencia this afternoon and I'm needed back on set in twenty minutes. I jump in my 911 and pull out onto Ventura so I can make it back in time.

My mind is racing all the way there. Grace. Marjorie. A party no movie star in Hollywood wants to be invited to. The absence of paparazzi. The past.

That's what this is adding up to. The past. My past this time. Not Grace's.

God, just thinking about Grace makes me agitated. I check my messages as I pull into the studio and navigate my way through the lot. Maybe she called to let me know where she was going while I was driving through the hills? Like a dead zone. We have a few of those on the way to and from the studio.

But no. There's a few missed calls on there, but I purposefully ignored those.

Grace never called. She took off to Colorado and never called.

What the hell?

I pull into my parking spot and shut the car off so I can sit in silence for a few moments. A knock on the window startles me out of my funk and Valencia laughs at me from the other side of the window.

"What are you doing?" she yells through the glass. "Let's go, hot stuff. We've got a love scene to practice for."

I open the door and get out. "Are you excited about that?"

"Hell, yes. Do you know," she says, looping her arm in mine as we walk to the studio doors, "it's been fifteen years since I really kissed you?"

"I kiss you all the time, V." Suddenly calling her V surprises me. Her too, from the look on her face. But then that shock is gone and happiness replaces it. That's who we were back in our teens. She was my first girlfriend. They called us V Squared.

"Air kisses. Cheek kisses. Those are not kisses, V. And those kisses back when holding hands was considered a love scene... well, that's not what this is and you know it."

I hold the door open for her and wave her forward. "It's acting, Valencia. I've kissed dozens of actresses for movies. Don't get too excited."

She stops and turns her head a little, just enough to give me a wink and a smirk. "I won't be acting."

And then she walks off towards her people who receive her and hustle her deeper into the darkness of the studio set.

Chapter Forty-Nine - Grace

#ThisIsNotTheSpankingYoureLookingFor

IT was hard to say goodbye to Bebe after our day trip into the past. Bebe knew coming out here to see my ex-family would be a mistake, but she came with me anyway. She took off work, showed up at the airport, and drove hundreds of miles with me just so I could see it for myself.

And maybe not all my family out in eastern Colorado hates me. I mean, I have cousins and shit. But whatever. They're done with me and I'm done with them. You can't choose your family.

Well, some of us can.

I smile big at that. I chose Bebe's family. And I got to choose my name and remake myself at the age of fifteen. If I look at it that way, maybe I was lucky.

I mean, obviously, having your family murdered is not lucky. But everything that came after... that was good luck.

I should feel grateful. And I am grateful. There's just a lot of unanswered questions rolling around in my head.

"We're about to land, Mrs. Asher. Please put your seat belt on."

I nod at the flight attendant. She looks as exhausted as I feel. It's almost nine o'clock California time. And the drive home will probably take me an hour. Going anywhere in LA seems to take an hour. So I definitely missed dinner with Vaughn.

But he never called. He has to know where I am. Otherwise he'd be crazy with worry. Maybe he just wanted to give me space to do this on my own?

I watch the lights out my window as we land, taxi, and then finally come to a stop.

"I hope you enjoyed your flight, Mrs. Asher," the attendant says as I exit the plane.

I give her a small thank you back. She looks pissed off, actually. I kept them waiting all day. I'm not sure what the protocol is for that kind of thing. Maybe I was supposed to call?

I walk quickly to my car, buckle myself in, start it up, and press home on my GPS so it can guide me.

Home.

Sorta.

I mean, Denver feels like home. When I'm in Colorado, I know where I am. I don't need the GPS system to get me from place to place. But here, I dunno. LA is so big. So many freeways. So many neighborhoods. It just seems to go on forever.

I head out and weave my way through traffic. Even at ten at night, there's congestion. An accident clogging up the flow of traffic. When I finally make it back up into the hills, it's nearly ten thirty.

The house is dark. Not a light on in the place. Not even the porch light.

I press the button for the garage and pull in alongside Vaughn's 911. He's here. But why is it so dark?

I get out of the car and look around the garage, my heart beating like crazy. "Vaughn?" Nothing. Do I really expect him to be hanging out in the garage?

"Vaughn?" I call again, because it's freaking me out. What if someone broke in? What if he's hurt inside?

I walk quickly towards the door that leads inside and turn the handle. It opens without sound. "Vaughn," I say again. But this time I whisper. I step inside and close the door behind me, and then tiptoe as quietly as I can towards the living room.

The moon is shining through the back window, illuminating the fact that the place is a complete mess. We don't have a maid and I've been sorta useless as a wife since I moved in. And it shows. Even in the dark I can make out shadows of dirty dishes and papers.

"Vaughn," I whisper again.

He must be asleep.

I walk to the kitchen so I can turn some lights on and that's when I see him. A dark figure sitting in a chair, backlit by the moonlight. "Vaughn?" I ask. "What are you doing?"

He leans forward and the shadow that was covering his face disappears. He's still wearing his suit, but the top buttons of his white shirt are undone, leaving his chest exposed. A dark tie is draped around his neck like he was thinking of taking it off and then changed his mind.

"Did you have a nice day?" he asks in a low voice.

I just stare at him. His blue eyes are piercing me, even through the shadows of night. "No, not exactly. I mean, parts of it were."

"Which parts? The part where you took off in the plane? The part where you ditched the car that was set up for you? The part where you didn't think to call me?"

I swallow hard. Because he's pissed off.

"Come here," he commands in a low, do-not-fuck-with-me voice.

I swallow again and my heart is beating so fast it might explode.

"I said, come the fuck over here." He stands up and I step back.

"I'm sorry," I say. "Are you mad?"

"Am I mad?" he asks me back, taking a few steps closer to me. "Am I *mad*?" He continues walking until he's one step away and I have to tip my head up to look him in the face.

I never realized how big he actually is. He towers over me.

"Do I have a reason to be mad, Grace?"

"I should've called," I say meekly.

"Called? You think I'm angry because you didn't call?"

"So you *are* angry?"

He smiles at me, but it's not a happy smile. It's an I-can't-fucking-believe-you're-so-clueless smile. "What the fuck is wrong with you, Grace?"

"What?"

"Wrong with you," he repeats.

"I'm not sure how to answer that."

HIs smile is tight as he stares at me. Not really a smile, but a grimace. "Do you love me?"

"Of course I love you."

"Good. You keep that in mind." And then, before I can even understand what's happening, he whips his tie off and grabs my wrist. I start to pull away, but he yanks me back. "Hold still."

"What are you doing?"

"You owe me."

"I owe you what?" I snap at him. But he doesn't answer. He just ties the length of silk around my wrist and reaches for the other one. "What are you doing?"

He glares down at me as he pulls the knot tight. Tight enough to make me wince. "I'm tying you up."

"You want to get off on your sexual fantasies? Now?"

"Turn around." He doesn't wait for me to even do that. He just twirls me until I'm no longer facing him. "Walk over to the couch."

He gives my back a push to get me started and I do as I'm told. I start to sit down, but Vaughn grabs my hair and pulls me hard enough to stop that from happening.

"Ow. Goddammit! What are you doing?"

He yanks my hair harder and leads me around to the back of the couch. "Bend over." He pushes me again and I fall forward. My hands try to brace myself, but he swipes them forward so they drape over the cushion and then bumps his cock against my ass. My face rests on something very plush and soft and I realize it's a sheepskin rug.

"What are—"

"Shut up."

What? "Who the fuck—" A hard smack lands on my ass and I jump. It stings all the way through my jeans. "Vaughn!" Another, this one even harder. I yelp and try to wiggle away from his grip. "Stop!"

"Stop? You want me to stop, Grace? We don't have a safe word, so if you tell me to stop, I'm fucking stopping. But let me tell you this, sweets. You fucking owe me."

"What is wrong with you?" I whimper.

"Wrong with *me*? Am I the one sleeping all damn day? Am I the one walking around here feeling sorry for myself? Am I the one flying a thousand miles away without telling you where I'm fucking at?"

"I'm sorry for not calling."

"This isn't about calling me. I'm not your babysitter. I'm your goddamned husband. I'm not interested in tracking your every move, Grace. I have security for that. And you *know* I have security for that. This is about your lack of commitment. Your lack of enthusiasm. Your lack of respect. And most of all, your lack of... being Grace."

I huff out a breath. "I'm sorry, OK? And that last part doesn't even make sense."

"No?" He huffs out his own breath. "Well, let me make it clear." Something rattles behind me and then he lets go of my hair. I turn my head a little to try to get a better look at what he's doing when he kneels down. But it's no use.

"This," he says as he clamps something around my ankle, "is a spreader bar. To hold your legs"—he slaps the inside of my thigh to make me open wider—"open."

"So we're back to your sexual domination?"

He hesitates, like he's thinking hard about that. A few seconds go by in silence as he attaches the other cuff to my ankle. "The girl I met in the bar a few months ago. You're not her."

My heart, which was actually calming down, starts to pick up the pace again. Because I think Vaughn Asher might be done with me. I think Vaughn Asher might want one last kink before he throws me aside.

"That Grace out on the beach was wild and confident. She talked back and had opinions. My Grace was funny and dirty." He finishes up with the spreader bar and then stands, leaning over the couch alongside of me, and whispers in my ear. "You are not my Grace."

What's that even mean? But I don't want to ask. Because I'm afraid to hear the answer.

"I owe you punishments, sweets. And I'm here to collect. So if you want me to stop—if you want this relationship… this marriage… this everything… to stop—just say the word, babe. And we'll call it good and move on."

He's breaking up with me. I close my eyes to stop the tears.

"Stop? Or go?" he asks. "You choose, Grace. But I'm warning you. If you say go, you'll get what you deserve."

Do I want to say stop?

He walks off, not waiting for my answer, and for a few seconds I'm petrified that he took my silence as a no. But then I hear him in the kitchen pulling open a drawer. When he comes back I'm so relieved to have his hands on me again a tear slips out and rolls down my cheek.

He lifts up my shirt, pulls it taut, and begins cutting it in half. I wiggle away out of fear before I can stop myself, but he shoves me back into position and continues until the two sides fall apart. He cuts my bra too. And then he cuts the fabric away from my body completely and tosses it aside.

He moves on to my jeans, slipping the cold scissors inside my waistband and slitting it right down my ass until the denim opens up and exposes my skin, still stinging from the smacks, to the cool night air. The next snip destroys my panties.

He rubs a hand down one cheek and then his palm comes down so hard, the smack echoes off the high ceilings in the living room.

I don't move this time.

"That's it, sweets, that's what I want," he whispers. His hand rubs the spot he smacked, soothing it. The cutting continues. The scissors slip between my legs and the cold metal shocks me for a moment, making me draw in a gasping breath of air.

"Shhh," he chastises me as he slits my pant legs open from thigh to ankle on each side. He tosses the ruined fabric aside once again and then takes a few steps back. "I'm gonna make your ass so red you won't be able to sit tomorrow."

I start breathing faster. My chest does not have a lot of room since I'm still bent over the couch back, and it takes a lot of effort to draw in air.

Vaughn grabs my hair and pulls me up. "Breathe, Grace. No hyperventilating on my time."

Asshole. I fight him a little to let him know I'm annoyed but he just laughs.

He presses his mouth up to my ear and whispers, "I'm waiting."

"For what?" I growl back at him.

"Go. Or stop."

His hand dips between my legs and strokes the slit of my pussy. I moan, I can't help it. We've had plenty of sex lately. More and more as the weeks go by. But there's not been any rough play since… well, the night I signed the NDA.

"You like to submit, Grace. You know you do."

I take a deep breath and try to turn my head, but he yanks on my hair again.

"You like this. And it has nothing to do with the past. You like this because I'm your fucking prince, remember? You like this because I'll make you scream with pleasure."

He leans down in my ear. His breath comes slowly. Totally in control. "Grace," he says softly. "You like this because you want to be controlled and fucked hard, but you know you're safe with me. So…" He pulls my hair so hard this time, I squeeze my eyes closed and have to arch my back to try to relieve the tension. When I open my eyes, I'm looking straight up at his face.

"I want what you owe me, sweets. I told you back on the beach I was adding them up. Your list is long. Your penance will be difficult. But…" He sweeps his fingers along my slit again and this time even I feel the wetness because it drips down my leg. One finger dips inside me and he chuckles. Because he knows I want this as much as he does. "But if you're very good," he continues, "you won't care." He whispers the last part, alternating between the cold, dominating man I want and the soft, tender man I need. "You won't care because your screams will not be from the pain. They'll be from the pleasure. So which is it, Mrs. Asher? Stop? Or go?"

Chapter Fifty - Vaughn

#MomentsOfTruth

SHE needs to trust me. Fuck, she trusted me more out on that beach than she does now. And I'm sick of it. I've done nothing but support her. I've been there for everything. I held her hand and made her feel loved and welcome.

And maybe that was the wrong way to go. Because that's what everyone else did the first time she came home. Maybe what my Grace needs is unwavering dominance.

So that's what I'm giving her tonight.

She wants to waste her life away in bed feeling sad? Or mope around this house oblivious to the decay? I mean, holy fuck. Felicity was a pig. She made a mess just walking through a room. But eventually she picked up after herself.

Grace has disappeared. I'm not sure if it was the injury, the kidnapping, or the baby that pushed her over, but that hardly matters now. She's there. She's crossed the line of sad and moved right into depressed.

And I'm not gonna let this happen to us. I might not be able to make her get better, but I can make her choose. Either she wants us or she doesn't.

"I'm gonna ask you one more time, Grace. Say stop and we stop. You can go back to Denver and do whatever it is that will make you happy. Because clearly, I do not make you happy.

"Or say go, and I take over from here on out. You submit to me and do as you're told until I say otherwise. Because you have no idea what's good for you right now, Grace. You're in give-up mode. And for the record, I didn't put myself through twenty-seven years of Hollywood bullshit to give up. I'm not a goddamned quitter."

She struggles hard against my hold, but I keep her pressed into the couch cushion. "I'm not a quitter, either. Your life is stupid."

I laugh. "So what? I'm the first to admit my life is stupid. I didn't choose to be born to this family. It was my birthright."

"Your birthright is stupid too. You think you've had it hard, Vaughn? You have no idea what hard is."

"Boo-fucking-hoo. I do realize your tragedy trumps anything I can come up with. No, my life is not one long string of fear like yours, but it's had its challenges."

"You don't even know the meaning of the word survive."

"Apparently, neither do you."

"Fuck you. I'm here because I survived."

"You're not here, Grace." I lean down and pull her hair at the same time, making her head tilt back. "You're still there, sweets." She doesn't say anything to that. But that's her MO, right? Silence. "You refuse to go to therapy. You refuse to talk to people. You refuse to accept help. And whatever. That's your choice. But marriage is a partnership, Grace. If you want to be married, then you owe me. So what's it going to be? Stop or go?"

"Go," she snarls. "If that will make you feel better, then just do it."

"It will," I assure her. "It will."

She opens her mouth to spout off something sarcastic, but my hand comes down on her ass cheek so hard she jumps. "Holy fuck, Asher! What the—"

I smack her again, five times in a row without stopping. Five hard, flat smacks across her bare ass.

"Ow! That fucking hurts!"

I kiss her neck and then turn my mouth to her ear and whisper, "It's supposed to, Kinsella. I told you, you're gonna cry..."

"Why does this make you happy?" she asks. Her voice is already betraying her. She's losing control very fast right now. "Why does hurting me make you happy?"

"I don't like hurting you, Grace. I told you back on the island that none of this is about violence."

"Well, it sure feels like violence to me."

"That's because you're unable or unwilling to give in. Did it ever occur to you to ask me what I wanted?"

She stiffens but says nothing.

"No." I answer for her. "You have never once asked me what I want."

"So you're punishing me for being a selfish cunt?"

"No again. I'm punishing you for not trusting me."

"Why should I trust you?"

"Why *shouldn't* you trust me? I think that's a far better question."

She stays silent again. Only this time I'm not going to answer for her. The negotiations are over. "I'm going to let go of your hair and you're going to stay right where you are. Do you understand?"

More silence.

I smack her hard again and she whimpers, but stays put. "When I ask you a question, Grace, the polite thing to do is answer it. And if you don't want to answer, then you get punished. I'm going to punish you and the only way this is not going to happen is if you tell me to stop."

"But if I don't let you do this to me, then we're over."

"Yes."

"That's not fair."

"Then say no."

She sniffles before answering this time. "But I don't want you to walk out. I don't want you to leave."

"So you think you should be allowed to continue on with the way you've been acting?"

"No, but—"

"Tell me right now, Grace. If I let go of your hair will you stay where I put you?"

"Yes," she says into the cushion.

"Ah. Finally you have to give in to something." I let go of her hair and step away from her naked body. "Now I'd like to know how you want to do this. I'm going to spank you for all indiscretions, past and present. Ready?"

"Yes."

"Yes, what?" She turns her head a little so she can see me. Like she can't believe I'm going there. But I am. I'm so fucking going there. "Grace? I asked you a question. Yes, what?"

"Yes, *Master*," she spits. She looks me in the eye for it too. So score one for Asher.

I look away from her before I lose my nerve and instead look down at the bright red skin. Both cheeks are flaming. I hover my hand over them and feel the heat. "Wait here," I tell her. "Don't move."

I don't wait for an answer, just walk down the hallway to our bedroom and then turn into the bathroom. Grace has stuff all over the counters. Just shit everywhere. I flip the light on and start looking at the various bottles. I choose the one that says it soothes chapped skin, and head back to the living room.

Grace is right where I left her. Her eyes are even closed. "Don't fall asleep on me, sweets."

She open her eyes and whispers, "Yes, Master."

I don't like it. I hope she doesn't think that's what this is about. It's not. I don't want to crush her. I just need her to know I'm a man of my word. I told her when I knew her well enough I'd punish her for all her misbehaving. And even though I like the kind of misbehaving she did back on the beach, I'm less than thrilled about the way she's been misbehaving since she came home.

351

It needs to stop.

I smack her ass one more time and she sucks in a gasp of air, but says nothing. "I know it hurts. You're allowed to moan or cry."

"I'm *not* going to cry."

"OK." I uncap the bottle of soothing lotion and drip it across the bright pink handprint left over from the last slap. This makes Grace sigh and relax. "You like that?"

"Yes, Master," she says obediently.

I rub it in a little harder, squeezing the round globes of her ass. And after a few minutes of this seemingly innocuous rubbing, when she is good and relaxed, when she's breathing deep and even, almost content, I give her five more quick, hard slaps to wake her back up.

She shoots up off the back of the couch for this, but my hand is there on her back, gently pushing her down. "Be still," I tell her softly.

She relaxes again and my punishment repeats.

"Goddammit!" she squeals. This time she doesn't take my direction, and instead of relaxing, she struggles against me.

"Tell me to stop if you want it to stop, Grace."

"No," she says defiantly. "I'm not gonna tell you to stop so you can blame this on me. But I'm sure as fuck not going to let you hit me for no good reason!"

"OK, that's fair. How about I tell you why you're being punished."

"That would be a good start," she hisses up at me.

I smack her hard again, this time across the back of her thighs. She squirms and twists, but the spreader bar prevents her from taking a necessary step to balance herself, and she falls right into my arms. "Don't struggle, sweets. It's a losing battle." She growls out her protest, but since she can't walk and her hands are bound, she is forced to lean into my chest.

Her soft hot breath travels across my skin and brings my cock to life. "That last slap was for being sarcastic."

"And the others?" she asks, risking more punishment.

"Those were owed to you from our fun first night on the beach. Satisfied?" I grab her by the elbows and lift so she can regain her balance, and then I scoop her up in my arms. Her legs are still spread open as I carry her around to the front side of the couch and take a seat. "For the rest of your punishment, you have two choices because I'd like to sit down and enjoy my view of your beautiful pussy. Would you like to bend over the coffee table or lie across my lap?"

"Your lap, please." She hesitates for a moment and then adds, "Master," to the end of her sentence.

I urge her to flip over so her stomach is across my thighs and then I lean down and whisper, "I love you, Grace."

"I hope so."

"Don't doubt me."

"Why do you want me to cry?"

"Because you need to let it out."

"I did let it out. Back at the hospital."

"Grace, five minutes of tears is not crying. You refuse to give in to therapy, fine. I'm not going to insist on anything."

"But you insist that I cry here tonight. Because you're hitting me."

"I'm spanking you, Grace. Something that turns you on. It's erotic. It's not about hurting you. And this is not about making you cry. You will cry because it's natural."

She stills. Perhaps to think about this. "Do you want to know what I did in Colorado?"

"No."

She stays silent for almost a minute after that answer. "Why not?"

"Because if you wanted me to know, you'd have told me before I left for work." I trace a fingertip down the backside of her thigh, into the soft cavity behind her knee—this makes her stifle a giggle—and then continue down her calf where I squeeze and knead the muscles there until she moans. "Feel good?"

"Yes. So good."

I smack the back of her thigh. A quick downward motion, barely touching her skin, and then a retreat.

It stings my hand so I know it stings her thigh worse. She wails a complaint, but I immediately slip my fingers between the open folds of her pussy and stroke her gently there. "Better?"

She makes a sound that is halfway between a moan and a growl and I smile because she has no idea whether she should cry or come.

But then she sniffles and I know I'm on the right track.

My fingers leave the warmth of her pussy and trace a wet trail up her spine. She bucks a little, but tries her best to be still. "You're perfect, Mrs. Asher. And if you only take one thing away from tonight, let it be this. The spankings are about trust."

She takes a breath like she wants to say something, but then she stops.

"Tell me, Grace. If you have something to say, tell me."

"I'm not very good at this."

"Neither am I."

Her head turns and she relaxes. Her face pressed into the cushions of the couch. "That's funny. You're the one with all the experience."

"Yeah, but I've never done this with a woman I cared about before. It's new for me too. Before you, Grace, this domination stuff was about sexual release and satisfaction."

She lifts her head from the cushions and tries to look at me. "And now?"

"I told you. Trust. You don't trust me. And to be quite honest, I don't trust you either. I feel like you're perpetually on the verge of walking out. I can't live like this, Grace. I can't. I need to know if you're in or not."

"I'm your wife. I'm in."

"You're my wife on paper, that's it. I want you to *be* my wife, Grace."

"Will spanking me make me your wife?"

"Do you hate it?"

"No. It's just demoralizing."

"But effective. I have you here, face down in my lap, talking to me about things you'd rather not. That's not demoralizing, that's progress. This relationship is a give and take. I hate to say this, sweets, but you've been doing a lot of taking."

She balks and tries to lift her upper body, but my hand is swift on her bottom. The crack sounds off simultaneously with her yelp. "Stay put," I order her. "I'm not fucking around. You earned this spanking. Now it can be pleasant and sexual, or it can be harsh and demoralizing. It's your choice."

"How is it my choice? You're the one who gets to dole out the punishments."

"And you're the one who gets to decide when you get punished and what form that takes. Do you want to be punished like this?" My hand smacks down on the back of her legs, right where they meet the upward curve of her ass. But before she can cry out, I'm rubbing her and slipping my fingers inside her pussy. "That feels good, Grace. It's not about pain, it's about control. You resist my control because you don't trust me. And I'm telling you right now, you're making both of us unhappy by doing that."

"You want to leave me."

"I don't want to leave you. I love you. I married you. I want to fuck you and boss you around and make you have my babies. I want to keep you forever. You're the one who's got one foot out the door. I want you to *commit*, Grace. And the first step is to *submit*."

She's silent for a few moments as my words sink in. I don't want to say this. In fact, I'm terrified to continue. But it needs to be out in the open. It needs to be done. "Are you willing to do that? Or do you want to end this marriage?"

Chapter Fifty-One - Grace

#EpicQuestionsCount

DO I want to end this marriage?

My instant response is no.

But... I stop myself from saying the word. Because he's asking me an honest question and that deserves some introspection. I became his wife under less than ideal circumstances. I don't even remember it. As far as I'm concerned, this is the first time I've had a say in this marriage at all.

"Grace?" he prods.

Maybe I did say 'I do' in Vegas. But that was hardly my choice. Because honestly, if he had asked me in the morning if I wanted to marry him, my answer would've been no.

My answer has always been no. For as long as I can remember, I have never wanted to marry anyone. Not even Vaughn Asher, movie star. In fact, I have no idea what marriage looks like. I never prepared for it.

"Grace, you're making me nervous."

All this is new to me. I'm at a loss on how to answer.

He unhooks the spreader bar from my ankles and throws it across the room and then he pulls my upper body up off his lap and then stands, leaving me on the couch. He walks out of the living room and I'm too shocked to stop him.

He doesn't go to our bedroom, I know that because a few minutes later I see light flickering down the hallway. Lights coming from the home theatre.

A few minutes go by and then I hear sounds coming from the theatre room.

I'm making a huge mistake, I know this. But it feels wrong to say I feel the same as he does. I don't.

I get up and walk down the hallway until I reach the theatre room and then I prop myself up against the doorjamb. He's watching a George Clooney movie that I love about some escaped convicts during the Great Depression who become famous for a song they sing.

"I love this movie."

"Me too," he answers without turning his head to look at me.

"You never asked me."

"I did ask you. You said yes."

"I was drunk. I don't remember."

"Well, I remember."

"You're only one half of this team, Asher. You never asked *me*. Me. Sober Grace was never consulted. I can't be held responsible for drunk Grace's actions. I was beyond drunk. I blacked out. It's not fair that I found out about our marriage from the TV. It's not fair that it all happened in the same moment that I was taken again. It's not fair that—" I stop talking because he never turns. Does he even want to know? Is he even interested? He says he wants me to trust him, but he scares me when he walks away. "I want you to ask me."

"I want you to remember."

"How do I make myself remember?"

Finally he turns his head. "Grace, you talked for hours on end that night. It's impossible that you just don't remember. It makes no sense. Yes, you were drinking. But you said so many things that night. Thoughtful, well-articulated things."

"I don't remember."

He turns away again. "I'm not telling you. I refuse to paraphrase what happened that night. I won't do it. I refuse to reduce it to a *retelling*."

I sigh and walk around to the front of the massive square sectional couch. I crawl across it, my bound hands keeping me off balance a little, and nestle as close to him as I can, laying my head on his shoulder. "I want you. Is that enough?"

He doesn't embrace me. He makes no move to cuddle me and make me feel loved. He doesn't offer to untie my wrists.

"I'm past wanting you, Grace. I have you. Or at least I thought I did. And now everything is up in the air. I just want to settle. I'm tired of juggling life. I'm tired of coming home to an empty house."

"You've been coming home to me for almost three months. That's not empty."

"No," he says sharply. "How do you not see that you're not here? This place is a fucking mess. You don't do anything but mope. It's a goddamned miracle that you came to see me at the studio this week. And to be perfectly honest, after the flight coordinator called to let me know you scheduled the jet, the more I thought about it, the better I felt. I was happy that you took an interest in something. But you went about your life. All fucking day. And never once thought about me. I don't matter to you."

"That's not true. I…" I what? What am I trying to say?

"You can't even say it. You can't even admit you love me. You chased me for three years online, telling the whole world your feelings and your desires. You've fucked me in public. You married me. And right now, you can't even say you love me."

"I love you, Vaughn. I do. That's not why I'm hesitating."

"Then what is it?" His voice booms through the movie room and I startle backwards a few inches. "Why are you not here? Why are you unsure? What the fuck do you want from me?"

"Untie me." I hold out my wrists. He looks down at them, then up at my eyes. I can see the pain in there. The uncertainty I'm causing him. I hate that I'm making him feel this way. "Untie me," I say again.

He shakes his head, sighing a long breath of air that lets me know he's beyond pissed. And then swiftly releases the knots that bind my hands. "There. You're free." He balls up the silk tie and throws it across the room.

I lay my chest across his lap and place my face alongside the cushions. My back is slightly arched and my ass is in the air like an invitation.

"What are you doing?" he asks, still very irritated.

"Making a decision," I reply. "I want to be yours. Spank me."

"Oh my God. You drive me insane, woman." I chance a peek up at him and he's rubbing his hand down his face, like he really is exasperated.

"Spank me for being bad."

"Jesus, Grace. Why? Why are you doing this?"

I turn on my side so I can really look at him. And for the first time in years, maybe ten or more years... I'm honest. "Because I want to cry."

He just stares at me, a wave of horror flashing across his face.

"I want you to spank me so I can cry. And then I want you to fuck me and make it better."

His first smack is loud and hard. It stings. I lower my head back to the cushions and prepare for the next one. It comes swiftly. Then the next and the next. The stings become burns and then there's no distinguishing one from the next. The sharp pain from each smack runs together until I begin to sob. They are soft at first. When they are just from the pain of his hands on my bottom, they are soft.

But then I forget where I am and the memories take over. I feel the guilt of living. I feel the pain of knowing I am alone. That my family is dead. That my brother never got a chance to be there for me when I needed him. For my parents, who were as nonexistent at my own wedding as I was. For all the family members who turned their backs on me.

I feel the shame. Shame for allowing that monster to take me and keep me and make me into someone I didn't even recognize.

It's not the pain or the fear that undoes me.

It's the shame.

I cry hard. I gasp for air and sob uncontrollably. And I have no idea how long I do this before I realize Vaughn has stopped spanking me and he's holding me to his chest. His hands sweeping down my back as he whispers in my ear. "It's OK, Grace. It's OK."

Aside from that small breakdown in the hospital when I told Vaughn I was sad about the baby, this is the first time I've really felt anything in over ten years. "It's not OK." I tell him back. "It's not OK. He took everything from me. I have nothing left. Not even myself." For a second I fear that Vaughn will be offended at that statement, but he holds me tighter.

"I know," he says. So unpredictable, this man. "I know. He killed your parents. He killed your brother. He took you away from your life and twisted your mind. He fucked up your whole life, Grace. You're allowed to be pissed off and sad."

My crying becomes ugly as the feelings flood in. But my gratitude is so overwhelming. Vaughn gets it. Of all the people who have tried to help me, this man—this self-centered, egotistical asshole—gets it.

None of this has anything to do with him.

It's about me.

Chapter Fifty-Two - Grace

#DayOneDoOver

"SWEETS," Vaughn says in my ear. "It's morning, babe. I have to go to work, will you be OK?"

I stir in his arms and realize I'm still naked and we are still in the movie room. "Yes," I say automatically. I know he has to work. I want to throw a tantrum and tell him to call in sick, but I can't. Not after he held me all night long and let me get it out of my system. Not after he was so patient with me.

"I'll be home at eight. We only have three days of filming this week. I can't wait for the long weekend." And then he kisses me and he's off.

What long weekend?

I lie on the movie couch, snuggling up with the soft blankets, and ponder this. What day is it?

I sit upright and gasp. "It's Thanksgiving week!"

Oh my God. How does a person not know the holidays are upon them? It feels like I was just getting off that plane from Saint Thomas over Labor Day and now it's Thanksgiving week.

I count up the weeks in my mind and realize I've been in this funk for almost three months. "Grace," I begin to chastise. "This is not good. You are not allowed to wallow."

I crawl to the edge of the couch, drop the blanket, and make my way to the living room. In the bright California sunshine, the filth we are living in is painfully obvious. There's dishes and trash everywhere. Clothes, shoes, mud on the tiles near the doorway. Even outside, our movie-star backyard is littered with palm fronds and leaves from a storm last week and the various flotation rafts I've used in the pool since moving in here with Vaughn.

And then a sour smell reaches out and taps me on the shoulder. I look over at the dishes on the island countertop and wrinkle my nose. Spoiled milk in numerous cereal bowls.

I'm a terrible wife.

How has Vaughn put up with me?

A ringing startles me out of my introspection and I look around for the source. "We have a phone?" I ask myself out loud. I had no idea we had a home phone. I thought everyone just used cells these days. I follow the source just as the message machine—who has a message machine?—clicks on.

"Vaughn, baby. It's me. I just wanted to double-check and make sure we're still on for this Friday for the Black Bash. Call me."

"What the hell is a Black Bash?" I ask out loud again.

I have no idea, but I'm sure it's some sort of Hollywood party and Vaughn just didn't want me to worry about it, or was going to decline. So I drop it and go back out to the living room.

This will not do.

I really need to start making an effort. I open the folding wall of glass doors and let the sunshine and cool air in. It's not cold. I mean, it's like sixty-five. But that's nothing like Colorado is in November. The fresh air feels good. And it will make the smell of spoiled milk disappear.

I walk around the living room picking up dishes and take them all to the sink to rinse them out before loading up the dishwasher. Then I go to work picking up trash and clothes. I start a load of laundry. There's still a load in both the washer and the dryer and since I have not done laundry once since I've moved in, I can only suspect that this was Vaughn's attempt to keep the house running while I was in my funk.

Funk, Grace?

Fine. It was a depression. But I feel like a new person today. I feel like I got it all out last night. He was so perfect. He listened to me cry and held me close. I have never felt such love and support in all my life.

But now I need to move on. I need to put all that bad stuff behind me and look to the future. And even though I've lived here for almost three months, I feel like this is the first day of my new life as Mrs. Asher.

Now if only I could remember my wedding.

I just don't understand why it's such a problem. I mean, either Vaughn is lying about how aware I was of what was going on, or I'm just... blocking it out for some reason. But why? Why would I do that?

I continue to clean as I ponder this. I make a list in my head.

I'm psycho.

The idea of being married was just too much for me after all that brainwashing

I really don't want to be married to Vaughn Asher.

But none of those seem right. I'm not psycho. I might be damaged, but I'm not crazy. And yes, the whole kidnapper-trying-to-convince-me-I'm-his-wife thing did put a damper on all my future thoughts of getting married. But it's fucking Vaughn Asher. And that makes number three ridiculous. I really do love him. Maybe it's leftover infatuation kinda love from my Twitter stalking days. But it's still authentic.

So why can't I remember?

I almost wish I could go to Vegas and retrace my steps. But after my day jaunt to Colorado, I think it's probably a bad idea to take off again. Besides, it's almost Thanksgiving.

So instead of calling the flight coordinator and booking a flight to Sin City, I call my parents. My mom answers on the first ring and her unexpected happiness at my call makes me warm.

"Mom," I say, after she's got her hellos out of the way. "I don't think we're coming for Thanksgiving. Is that OK?" I'm nervous about this call. I've never spent a holiday away from home since they adopted me.

"Oh, Grace, of course. You have a new family now. We were just talking about this last night. Don't worry about us. We're going out of town this year, anyway."

"Oh." Well, shit. "Where're you going?"

"San Francisco. Your father has decided to take us to San Francisco."

"Well, that sounds fantastic." *Weird,* I don't add. "Fantastic!" We chat a little more and then say goodbye with promises to call on Thursday.

When I end the call I realize I've been cleaning the kitchen the entire time. I think this is the first time I've seen it void of dishes. Vaughn is not the best housekeeper. He and Felicity lived like bachelors.

I laugh at that and hang up the dish towel after wiping things down, and then I go get started on the laundry.

After the laundry is in progress, I find some sort of wood-floor cleaning contraption in the utility closet and get to work on those too. Layla the cat's litter box is tidy, so obviously Vaughn has been taking care of that. But the fish tank is a mess of algae. There's a sticker on the side of it with a number to call for cleaning. The man on the other end of the phone says he's in the neighborhood and can stop by in a couple hours.

Now the pool and river are something else. I know we have a pool person. That guy has been coming regularly. But the storm the other day has left the outside looking unkempt. So I spend the rest of the day putting the outside back in order. And by five o'clock the place is spotless.

"Maybe I'll cook?"

I surprise myself with that notion. I hardly ever cook for Vaughn. I've thrown meat on the grill a few times, but that's about it. But it will be good. Very domestic.

I wrangle up enough ingredients for spaghetti and meatballs, find some frozen garlic bread in the garage freezer, and by the time eight o'clock rolls around, I don't even recognize this place.

I sit on the edge of the pool next to the small waterfall, with my feet dangling into the water, sipping wine as I wait for my movie star to come home.

A flash hits me. A memory.

Vaughn and I are standing outside the Bellagio near the fountain. The heat is suffocating, but the water is shooting upward, dancing as they do, night after night, and the spray is bathing us with a refreshing rain.

Did we get married at the fountain?

God, I wish I knew.

I hear the door alarm and then the familiar punching of keypad numbers and my heart beats faster.

"Grace?" he calls out.

"Out here," I call back.

He walks through the dimly lit living room, looking around like he might be in the wrong house. And then he appears in the opening where the glass walls would be if they were not folded away. "What's going on here?" he asks with a smile. "I don't think this is my house. Am I dreaming or is that real food I smell?"

I pat the cement next to me. "Come sit here. Put your feet in and have a beer." I reach over the champagne bucket and pull out his favorite micro-brew. "It's cold," I tempt him.

He steps forward, loosening his tie as he walks, and a few moments later, the shirt is coming off. "Mrs. Asher," he says with a mischievous grin.

"Mr. Asher," I say back, trying very hard to stifle my smile. Everything about him makes me want to smile.

He drops the shirt on the concrete, his pace never slowing as he kicks off his black Versace oxfords. I have to tilt my head up when he stops in front of me. It's hard not to notice that my mouth is in the perfect position to make him relax after a long day's work. I feel the wetness between my legs just thinking about it.

But instead of guiding my hands to his zipper, he slips off his socks and bends down to look me in the eyes. "I've missed you."

"I'm back now."

"Are you ready?"

I'm confused for a moment, but then he unleashes that hidden dimple on me and places both hands on my shoulders.

"Ready for—"

And then he pushes me into the pool.

Chapter Fifty-Three - Vaughn

#WhatPills

I ALMOST feel bad as she tumbles over the side. But not quite. She goes under, her slip of a dress clinging to her body for a moment before it balloons out, exposing her legs.

God, I fucking love this woman.

She comes up sputtering and thrashing, but also laughing.

It's been a long time since my Grace has been here. A long time. She's just about to yell when I cannonball in next to her, making waves that spill gallons of water over the turquoise tiled edge.

When I open my eyes underwater, she's right there. Her long blonde hair flows out behind her like some siren's. Her pretty summer dress looks like it's caught in the midst of a breeze. Before I can surface, she grabs me by the shoulders and wraps her legs around my waist. My hands automatically cup her ass and we kiss underwater like teenagers. Her fingers weave through my hair, mine slipping up her dress, my thumb caressing her stomach as my fingers grip her back.

She's buckling from that move when we spring out of the water, the tickle too much for her.

"Ahh!" she squeals as I hug her tight. "What are you doing, Mr. Asher?"

"I've missed you. I've missed you so much."

Her smile drops a little. "I'm sorry. I've been selfish and moody. I'm so, so sorry."

"Just tell me you're back to stay. Because, Grace, I can't watch you be so unhappy. It's killing me. I need you. I love you. And if I made you sad last night, I'm sorry."

Her pout grows, but she keeps eye contact. "I needed to hear that stuff, Vaughn. I think you're a saint for putting up with me. Not many men would stick by a girl they hardly know as she works through problems that are more than a decade old."

I take a deep breath and touch my forehead to hers. The water drips down her face in small streams. I watch as they curve around her lips and her tongue darts out to swipe them away. "You're not a girl, Grace. You're my wife. I meant every word I said when I married you."

She looks away and I know it's because she can't remember our vows. But I'm not going to tell her. I want her to remember on her own. And when she's ready, she will.

"I love you, Vaughn." She meets my gaze again and nods a little. "I'm sorry I was so out of it and I'm sorry I left you out of my decisions yesterday. You had every right to be angry last night. I was only thinking of myself, the place was a mess, and you work so hard. Thank you for taking care of things. I know it must've been difficult to take care of me, work, and keep up with the household chores."

I kiss her on the nose. "It was my pleasure, princess. I can do laundry and dishes. Believe me, Felicity was the worst housekeeper ever. And you're not the maid, so don't think this house is your job. It's not."

She rests her head on my shoulder and sighs. "I don't have a job, so taking care of things here at home might as well be it."

"Grace, please. We can hire a cleaning service. Go get a job if you want one."

"I wouldn't even know where to start."

"Mrs. Asher, say the word and I will have you gainfully employed as an event planner next week."

"No." She balks. "I don't want something handed to me. I want to be part of something real. And big."

I grab her small hand and force it down to feel my bulging cock underneath my pants. "I'll show you something big." I walk us towards the small waterfall. "Close your eyes and hold tight." She grips my cock as I dip us under the falling water and step into the secret grotto hot tub. "I haven't been in here in… well, since the builder showed it to me a few years ago."

She looks around with wide eyes. "You have a secret hot tub?" And then she kisses me sweetly on the cheek. "And you've never even been in here to"—she squeezes my dick and I close my eyes for a second to enjoy it—"christen it?"

"Mmm," I reply as my hands lift up her dress. "Now is as good a time as any." She lets go of my shoulders and lifts up her arms. I sweep the dress up and over her head, ball it up, and throw it through the waterfall and into the pool. "Mrs. Asher. You're commando again." I twist her perky nipples and she squirms and unlatches her legs from my hips.

"Yes," she purrs next to my ear. "I wanted to keep you focused."

"You've got my attention."

"Oh, not yet, Mr. Asher." And then her hands are unbuttoning my suit pants.

My dick is so hard I'm ready to bend her over. Once the zipper comes down, her hands are greedily searching under the water. I help her out by climbing up onto a step. Her mouth comes dangerously close to my cock, her warm breath sweeping across it as her fingers deftly pull down my suit trousers.

She unpacks my throbbing thickness and licks the tip. My hands go to the back of her neck and I encourage her to take more of me as I sit on the edge of the hot tub.

"Mmmm," she hums, making the tip of my dick vibrate. I lean back a little, one hand on the concrete behind me, propping me up, the other fisting handfuls of hair and urging her on.

"I want to come down your throat, Grace. I want to bury my whole dick in your throat."

She responds with her hands on my shaft. Not quite up and down, not quite twisting, but a combination of both.

I almost fucking lose it right there. But instead, I pull her hair, forcing her head back so I can lean down and kiss her on the lips. "I want to fucking devour you. I want to lick your pussy until you scream. I want to fuck your ass until you beg me to stop."

"I'll never beg you to stop. Ever."

I shoot her a coy grin. "Never say never, princess. I'll take that as a challenge."

And with that I grip her hair once more and thrust deep into her throat. She gags, tries to pull back, then looks up at me with trust in her eyes, and takes a breath from her nose as her tongue flattens along my shaft. "Mrs. Asher, you are perfect."

She sucks in response to my praise. I hold steady at the depth I'm at and let her do her thing.

Her petite hands reach under to cup my balls and that's when I know it's over. She sweeps a finger back, touches my ass, applies some pressure, and I'm gone. I come down her throat, her muscles tightening, her mouth open so wide she's sucking air in around my pulsating shaft.

"Holy fuck, Grace. Holy fuck." That's the extent of my vocabulary. I pull back and saliva drips down her chin. I fist her hair to tip her face up to me and then I lean down and kiss her. "I fucking love you. I love you so much. Switch places with me and lie back, baby." My breath is coming out in long draws and she's panting so hard she looks lightheaded. "Lie back so I can lick your pussy and make you come."

She moans just from my words and sits on the side of the hot tub while I climb into the water.

"Open your legs, princess."

She opens her legs and closes her eyes at the same time, but when my tongue teases the tip of her little bundle of nerves, her eyes shoot open and she moans. Her hands reach for my head now, but I grab a wrist and guide her fingers to her pussy. "Play," I command.

She begins moving in slow circles, clashing with my tongue as I stimulate her. I ease two fingers inside her swollen folds and curve them up to find her spot. Her whole back arches up off the ground as the moans turn into stifled screams. She bites her lip to stop the release, but I suck on her clit to keep it going. My fingers begin a stronger rhythm inside her pussy and when I nip her, she lets loose. Her squeals echo off the grotto walls, the sound of pounding water adding to the symphony we are creating.

My dick is hard again so I stand up, making her whine from the interruption of her release. But when I plunge my cock inside her and finger her ass at the same time, she gasps for air. "Come, Grace. Come for me, sweets."

She comes hard.

She comes all over my dick.

And even though she's been adamant about taking her pill so she can't get pregnant, I know this is the night we start over again. This is the night when those pills go in the trash.

Chapter Fifty-Four - Grace

#TheThingsYouLearnWhenYouSnoop

WAKING up the next morning is like… damn. I'm not even excited enough to come up with some kind of metaphor. It just sucks. Asher is gone, I'm alone—again—and the house is empty and quiet.

I hate this.

Yesterday was so good. I kept myself busy all day. But today… now what do I do? I need a job.

I force myself to get out of bed and wash up, then pad my way into the kitchen. Which is still clean because after our mind-blowing secret backyard grotto sex last night, we ate my spaghetti and meatballs and cleaned the kitchen together.

I think that was the first domestic thing we've really done as a couple. And it's wrong. I mean, almost three months after I move in, we're not on our own schedule yet. We're not settled. We're not… *meshing.*

Oh, the sex is meshing. The sleep time is also wonderful. I think the best part of my day is climbing into bed with

Vaughn and having him scoop me up next to him so my face is nestled on his chest. Definitely the best part of my day.

But good God, looking forward to bed, that can't be *all* my life is about.

I really need a job.

I stick my cup under the one-cup instabrewer that Vaughn sets up for me before he leaves for work, and wait for the coffee to drip as I look around for things to clean. I really did most of it yesterday.

The only places I didn't clean are the garage and the pool shed. So I guess that's on the agenda for today.

And then that little devil on my shoulder whispers in my ear. *Vegas, Grace. You could go to Vegas and see if you can jog your memory.*

Yeah, Asher would love that. After my jaunt to Colorado, I'm pretty sure the next time I do that shit, the spanking will be more punishment than pleasure.

I chuckle a little at that. I do love me a spanking. But not when he's really mad. I don't want to piss him off. I want to make him happy.

So no. No memory-lane Vegas trips for me. I sigh and grab my coffee. It's all about cleaning the garage and pool shed for me today.

I head out back first. Might as well take advantage of the morning shade. Once the day gets older, the sun will beat down on that shed and it will be very hot inside.

And that's where I spend the next couple hours. I inflate all the rafts just so they are available for us if we want to float.

I sweep out the cobwebs and the put all the various pool toys in a large mesh bag. I even wash the two windows.

The garage is even quicker. Vaughn's garage is spotless. Not even a drop of oil on the gray painted floor. Everything is either organized in some elaborate wall shelving system complete with giant plastic tubs, or hanging on a hook over his well-equipped tool bench.

So I sweep it out and call it good. I consider washing the car he says is mine now. But it's clean. I'm not sure who cleans it, but I've never seen one of his cars get dirty. That must be someone's job.

So I go back in the house and catch the tail end of a message playing on the house phone in his office.

Damn, two days in a row there's a call on that phone that has not gotten a call in almost three months. What the hell is going on?

I walk into Vaughn's office, but the message is over.

Should I listen?

I mean, it's my house too now. He says so, at least. I'm not restricted from looking at anything. Maybe Felicity's room, because most of her stuff is still here. I would never go in there anyway, but no one ever said it was off limits.

My feet are already walking towards the machine before I can make a decision and so it's a simple press of a button to make it play.

"V," the man's voice on the machine says. "Got that Black Bash ticket you wanted. It wasn't easy, asshole, and there's no plus one. So you owe me big. I'm gonna email it now, just sent it to your phone. All the invites have a barcode on them, so they'll scan the email when you enter. I told you I think this is a bad idea, but whatever, dude. You're in. And don't forget the theme this year is classic movie stars. Later."

The Black Bash. That's what the girl was talking about yesterday too. I check the machine for yesterday's message, but it's already been erased.

Hmmm.

Vaughn never mentioned a party to me. Is he hiding something? I mean, it's pretty clear he wanted a ticket to this party and that message also made it crystal clear I'm not going with him. No plus one.

I sit down at his desk and turn on his computer. We have computers all over the place in this house. Laptops just appear. There's always one or two in the kitchen. Vaughn said that he and Felicity used to work online while they ate dinner on the couch. There's a desktop in our bedroom—that's the one I took over. And there's even a tablet that migrates around as well. It's got everyone's email on it. Even mine is on there now. He and Felicity, for all their sophisticated hacking skillz, do not seem to give a fuck about the security of whatever accounts are on these machines.

They must have private ones too. Because that's the only thing that makes sense.

I look over at Vaughn's desktop computer.

I could look on that one. Just check to see if the emails are the same. You know, to familiarize myself with our blended household.

My hand jiggles the mouse, just to check and see if it's shut down or sleeping, when it comes to life.

No password required, all his files are right there on the home screen, so I guess that should make me feel special. He trusts me implicitly. No information is off limits.

Or, that little angel on my shoulder pipes in, *he trusts you not to snoop through his stuff.*

I navigate down to the mail icon on the bottom of the screen and click.

Up comes Gmail. And nope, this is not the email he uses in the living room.

There are five messages. That's it. Nothing in his send folder. Nothing in his spam folder. Nothing in his draft folder. Five messages and all of them say unread.

Until I click on them. I start with the oldest, which is from just a few hours ago. Right after he left for work. It's some kind of production schedule from Larry, his agent. And once I check, they are all from Larry, only from different accounts. The newest one—subject line: *Invitation that you will regret, so don't blame me*—is from another Larry account.

I don't get it. Why is this Black Bash thing so strange? It's setting off alarm bells for me. I just can't put the pieces together to understand why.

I open it, of course, and I'm staring at something that looks like an online plane ticket. The kind where you just flash your phone at the scanner to board, and it reads the code.

This party that seems to be a huge deal, but for all the wrong reasons, has a barcode embedded into the invitation.

Why?

The phone rings again, and I jump up so fast I knock the phone over and it answers.

"Hello?" the woman's voice says on the other end of the line. "V?"

I do not move. I do not say a word.

"Well, that's weird," she says under her breath. "If this is the message, V, I'm telling you this as a friend, stay away from the Black Bash. OK? Just stay away. Later."

What the hell is going on?

I wait a few seconds to make absolutely sure she's hung up the line, and then I pick up the phone, mark all his emails as unread, and then turn the monitor off.

I'm just about to walk out and mind my own damn business when I have an idea.

It's not an idea I'm proud of, but I have one and once it's in my mind, I can't not do it.

I go back to the computer and access that email with the ticket. I forward it to my own email account and erase the message. Then I erase the phone messages too.

It's wrong, I know it. But I have a bad feeling about this party. And if people are coming out of the woodwork to warn him off, it's my duty as his wife to help keep him away.

If he asks for it, I still have it. I'll give it to him after we discuss.

But only if he asks.

I leave his office and go back out to the living room and have a seat. Put my feet up. Turn on the TV. Change channels for like five minutes. Turn the TV off.

I check the clock. It's only three. I have five hours until Vaughn comes home.

I get up and check the fridge. Close it up after staring for two minutes. Sit back down at the bar. Flip through old mail—hey, there's a letter from my bank in Denver. Open it and understand like two words on that statement aside from the bank balance, which has to be wrong, because it says ninety thousand dollars. Tuck that statement back into the envelope and put a sticky note on it with the letters WTF. Vaughn can deal with that. I have no clue.

Check the clock again. Three fifteen.

Scream.

Not really. It's a sigh. But I feel like screaming, that's for sure. What the hell am I supposed to be doing all day?

I list my possibilities. I have a car. I can go shopping. But seriously, I'm not a shopper. I don't need anything. And I don't like to drive in LA. It scares me. The people are crazy. The freeways are crazy. And they have so many roads. Like, in Colorado, you got two choices for freeways. The one going east and west and the one going north and south. Sure, there's a few smaller ones, but basically, you've got two choices.

LA, you've got five ways to get somewhere, and all five ways are clogged with cars going the same way. I'm just not comfortable driving alone yet.

I could call someone. But everyone I know has a job.

I ponder things for a few moments, my eyes sweeping the room. I get up and feed the fish. Now that the tank is clean, I realize there's a turtle in there. He's soaking up some UV rays under the sun lamp. That makes me smile for ten seconds.

It's hot out today, so the wall of windows is closed and I have the air-conditioning on. I could go swimming. But that's about all I've done for the past few months.

I plop back down on the couch and grab the tablet from the coffee table. I could go on Twitter. Jesus, I haven't been on Twitter since the kidnapping. I haven't even thought about Twitter. My account was deleted, but the police made them put it back up so they could monitor it. I just never bothered to delete it again.

I navigate to the web and type in my profile link and then log in.

I have so many messages, it says 99+ in the message tab. Same thing for the notifications. I check the messages first, because those are probably all from the Filthy Blue Birds. I scroll all the way down my list and start reading chronologically. Mostly it's a bunch of messages asking if I'm OK. Those are all timestamped the morning they found out I was missing. Then they get weird. Like some of them thought I was dead and were saying their goodbyes.

Creepy.

I click out of messages and go to notifications, and glance at the first one on top. A blue link appears above that notification, indicating that I have five new ones. What the hell? People are talking to me right now?

The first one makes little sense to me. It's part of a conversation tagged with my @FilthyBlueBird handle. All it says is—*You're so right*. It's from someone I have never heard of.

I click the conversation link to see what they are talking about.

Editor @Realreporter00 - 15 min

@GrapevineHW You're wrong. Asher is about done with his @FilthyBlueBird.

I hate reading Twitter conversations because you get the last message first, so you never know what the fuck is going on until you hunt down the original message. Which doesn't seem to be included in this set of tweets.

I close out of that one and go down further, to tweets more than fifteen minutes old. I swear. I must look through a hundred messages before I find the one that sparked this convo. It was five hours ago and it came from @Buzz1Hollywood. That right there should tell me to leave it alone, but I'm human. If people are talking about me, I need to see it.

Editor @Realreporter00 - 5 hrs

Who wants to see @FilthyBlueBird doing the dirty solo for her man? We got the goods. Twitter pics are not private, Blue Bird.

Holy fuck. I want to stop myself, but I can't. I have to know for sure. I scroll through every single notification looking for the "goods" but after hours of searching—like seriously, it's after eight and the only reason I stop is because I hear the garage door open—I don't find anything.

I do find several dozen references in the *Buzz Hollywood* feed to the Black Bash, which is happening this Friday.

Were they lying? Do they have these pictures or not? I'd forgotten all about that night we were phone- and Twitter-sexing back in Denver. It feels like years ago. How could I have known back then what my life would become in a few short months?

"Grace!" Vaughn calls out as he enters from the garage. I slap the cover closed on the tablet and stick it behind a cushion. He rounds the corner just as I cross my legs and look guilty. "What're ya doing, Princess?"

"Waiting for you to get home."

He grins widely at me and then joins me on the couch. "I missed you so much today," he says, drawing me into his arms and nuzzling my neck.

Aww.

And before I can even tell him I missed him more, he's got his hand up my shirt.

I should tell him about the pictures, but hell, I just want to soak up his attention. I'm so ready for company.

"Wanna go out to eat tonight? I got us reservations at Mastro's." He kisses me, his tongue doing a twisty little dance inside my mouth.

"Please, get me out of this house."

He scoops me up and carries me to the garage door, then bends down. "Grab those flip flops."

"I can't go like this!"

"Hell, yes, you can. I'm starving for steak. And you, sweets. I need nourishment and girly conversation right now, or I might die. Grab them and let's go."

I grab the flops and he sweeps me into the garage and places me in his 911, dragging the seatbelt across my lap as he kisses me.

When he closes my door I sigh. He's so perfect.

And I don't want to ruin our night with talk of the media, so I'll tell him about the tweets tomorrow.

I just want to enjoy my fairytale life for now.

Chapter Fifty-Five - Grace

#ThisCastleIsMine

"YOU'RE nervous?" Vaughn asks as we drive through the gates of his parents'—my in-laws'—palatial Beverly Hills estate.

"Of course I'm nervous. Your entire family is here." Thanksgiving at the Chambers house was a low-key affair. It was buffet-style. We ate on the couch some years. They didn't have a lot of family, and what they did have lived on the East Coast. It was not extravagant.

"Yeah, but they are pretty cool, Grace. We're all close. And besides, you saw most of them at the wedding."

"Oh, God. Please tell me all those people won't be here." My stomach twists from my nerves.

"Of course not, sweets. Only about a hundred or so."

"What?"

"I'm kidding." He reaches over to squeeze my leg as he pulls in the circular driveway and waits for the valet to come.

Vaughn exits the car while my door is opened for me. I'm just about to take the offered hand of the valet when Vaughn sneaks his hand in. "Princess," he says with a grin as he helps me out of the low-riding sports car. "Welcome back to the castle. No film crews are here this time."

I roll my eyes at him and we walk towards the front door. It's already open, there's a butler-looking man in formal attire standing guard, and his mother. He says she meets him at the door whenever he comes over, and he was not kidding. Who knew Vaughn Asher was a mama's boy?

She kisses him on the cheek, then me, chatting about food and family. I swallow hard and cling to Vaughn's hand as I'm led into the expansive living room. It's got a huge cathedral ceiling with dozens of windows covered in elegant draperies. The back yard is not a water park like ours. It has a pool, but it also has manicured gardens, and of course, the pool house where Felicity is staying.

There are children running everywhere and double the amount of grown-ups.

"How are you feeling, Grace?" Vaughn's mother asks. He calls her Mom. I know her name is Dana, but somehow I can't bring myself to call her either of those things.

"I'm much better, thank you." That's about all I can manage.

"Well, we're ready to eat now that you're here. So let's go get settled in the dining room."

"We're late?" I ask in Vaughn's ear.

"On time for food and conversation, darling. I didn't want you to be overwhelmed, so I said we'd only come for dinner."

Well, that was thoughtful.

Mrs. Asher takes my arm and leads me forward. "The children are all eating outside, it's a tradition, so don't worry. It will be a nice calm experience for you."

Vaughn snorts behind me.

She drops me off at the table set for a bazillion people and points to the little cards with everyone's name on them. "I do arranged seating to liven things up. You're here, sweetie."

Mr. Asher—Adam, for some reason I feel OK calling him that. Maybe because he's a movie star and I've heard it so often—is talking in a booming voice as he leads an entourage of relatives towards the table.

Vaughn's calming hand is on my back as he pulls out my chair. "Sit, princess. I'm right across from you, so don't worry."

I look up at his concerned expression and give him a smile. "I'm OK." I sit as he pushes my chair in, and then I arrange my napkin on my lap.

"Yo, Grace!" Felicity calls as she enters. "I'm next to you, sister." We are in the middle of the table, with Adam at the head to my right, and Mrs. Asher at the head to my left. Thankfully, Samantha is sitting on the other side of me, so I'm flanked by the only two people I really know here.

I love Mrs. Asher and her seating chart.

"Conner?" Vaughn says as his brother takes a seat across from Felicity. I watch my husband assess that situation. He's in denial about this and I have to stifle a small chuckle. I'm not sure if Conner and Felicity are dating, per se, but they are definitely up to something. Vaughn's eyes shift back and forth between the two as a waiter reaches behind him to take a crystal flute and fill it with champagne. "Is there something you'd like to tell me?"

"About what?" Conner is swiping his fingers across his smartphone, not even paying attention.

Vaughn opens his mouth to add something snide when Tray appears to his right. "What the fuck—"

"Vaughn," his mother chastises.

"We're dating, V," Samantha says as she eyes her husband with a strained smile. Or maybe he is her ex-husband and they are going for a do-over? I'm not sure. But it's none of my business. I heard Tray was the first link in the chain to getting me back, so I'm not upset with him at all.

The whole room is filled with talking and laughter as everyone settles into their places and then Adam taps his spoon on his water glass. "It's been a blessed year for the Asher family. We've had two marriages, no deaths, and two new babies."

The room goes quiet and everyone looks at me. No deaths and two new babies. I'm not sure that's accurate, so I just sigh.

Adam clears his throat to ease the uncomfortable moment and bring everyone's attention back to him. And then he smiles at the two women cuddling newborns. The men across from them beam proudly. I can only assume they are cousins of Vaughn's.

I look away quickly and adjust the linen napkin on my lap one more time.

"And Grace," Adam says, directing everyone's attention back to me. My face gets hot and my nose starts to tingle. I don't want to cry here. I seem to be extra sensitive to crying these days and I really don't want to cry here.

"You are the perfect wife for my son. So strong and sweet. Intelligent and beautiful. We're sorry we missed your wedding. Perhaps you will let us have a party for you when you're feeling up to it?"

There's a chorus of yeses from around the table and my eyes get teary. But then I look across the table at Vaughn and his smile gives me strength. "Thank you," I manage. "I feel so lucky to be part of this…" And then it hits me what I've got here. "Family." They all go quiet to see if I'll say anything else. And I'm about to just shut up and let the moment pass when Vaughn seizes control.

"That's what we are, Grace. And you're part of it now. I know we're crazy and we're far from typical, but you're stuck with us, sweets. Forever." He raises his glass and waits for everyone to catch up with his toast. I raise mine too, as I stare into his blue eyes. "I love you, Mrs. Asher."

Everyone cheers and clinks glasses at that and I raise my glass to my husband and mouth, "Thank you."

The blessing is said and then the servers enter with plates of covered food. Conversation begins and we all settle in for the feast. Sam and Felicity chat with me. Vaughn is attentive and happy. Various aunts and uncles and cousins pepper me with tidbits of information about one another, trying for embarrassment.

And it all hits home.

I have a new family.

I will never forget my real parents or my brother. I will always be grateful and love the Chamberses for taking me in when I needed them most.

But it's time to start my own family. And this is where it begins.

Chapter Fifty-Six - Vaughn

#ImInDenialAndIDontCare

"SO, Felicity," I ask, once we are all settled in with dinner. "How's school? I never see you anymore."

"Oh, Felicity," Grace says, putting a tentative hand on her shoulder. "You should just come home. I hate that you're not there."

Felicity gives her a tight smile, then looks at... Conner.

I look at Conner and catch him in a shrug.

What the fuck?

I'm about to open my mouth when Felicity beats me to it. "I'm good, ya know? Living here in the pool house. Working for Conner."

"Wait, what? How did I not know you're working for Conner?"

"Don't be silly, V," she laughs. "You know I'm working with Conner. We did Grace's case together."

"Yeah, but that was months ago."

"She's a good worker, V," Conner says as he stuffs his face with turkey. "I loooove"—and he drags that word out for an unnecessarily long time—"having her around." And then that asshole actually clicks his tongue and winks at her. At my Felicity!

I look over at her and… "Oh my God. Are you blushing, Felicity?"

She giggles nervously as she plays with her mashed potatoes. "No."

Grace kicks me under the table, but when I look down, I can see Conner's foot touching Felicity's leg.

I turn my head to glare and he grins across the table at my *daughter.*

"That is so wrong. Conner, I fucking warned you," I seethe into his ear to avoid a scene. "I asked you specifically if you were—"

"We're not," he says back, still keeping his voice low.

I breathe a sigh of relief.

"But we're considering it."

I drop my fork on my plate with a clang. "You are not. She's your niece."

Conner snorts. "She's not my niece, you perv. She's not even related by marriage."

"Um," Felicity says from across the table. "I'm right here."

"Well," Tray says next to me, "I think they are perfect together."

"How the hell would you know?" I turn to ask him.

"We double-date all the time."

"What? Since when? You're not even part of this family."

"Vaughn." Sam's foot finds my shin under the table as well. "Knock it off, you ass. He's still my husband. Felicity and Conner have been dating for weeks. We go out every weekend. You're the only one who doesn't know."

I look around and everyone is nodding. "I'm stunned. I'm at a loss for words. I'm—"

"In denial," Grace says with a smug smile.

Everyone laughs and then they go back to eating.

"I'm glad you all think this is acceptable."

"V, I'm almost twenty-one—"

"And he's twenty-seven, Felicity!" Dear God, I might have to strangle my brother at Thanksgiving dinner.

"We're just hanging out, anyway. No big deal."

"No big—"

"Hey," Samantha says loudly. "I've been hearing lots of rumors about the Black Bash this year. What's going on there? Do you know?"

Fucking hell. I can't get a break. "Don't believe everything you hear." I look over at Grace and she's way too attentive.

"What's the Black Bash?" she asks before I can think of some lifesaving interjection.

"Oh, you don't want to know," Sam laughs. "It's a horrible tradition. Every Black Friday the tabloids throw a masquerade party. Everyone dresses in the theme and wears a mask so no one knows who shows up for this repulsive invasion of privacy."

"What do they do?" my sweet princess asks with horror.

"It's nothing, Grace." I shoot Sam a glare that says shut the fuck up. But then Conner is talking on the other side of me.

"I hear they've got Sam's video in one room."

"I don't care," Sam says bravely. "Tray and I have talked about it. We're making another video this Christmas Eve. To finish what we started last year. Let them show it to whoever they want. My secret is out and I've come to accept my condition for what it is. A challenge to be overcome, not a disability to be afraid of. They have no power over me now."

I love my sister.

"Were you invited, Vaughn?" Felicity asks.

I shake my head no. "I would never go see that filth. Even in disguise."

I look over at Grace, but her gaze is difficult to read. I take that as disinterest and quickly move the conversation into neutral territory so everyone will drop the talk of the Black Bash. But my mind is not at ease. That party is tomorrow night. And I've already been warned several times that there's something big brewing.

I swallow down the guilt for my actions all those years ago and put on my stage smile.

I'm an actor. It's what I do.

So I act happy.

We finish dinner and take dessert outside in the children's tent so we can watch the annual family talent show. Grace sits in my lap, her head on my chest as countless nieces and nephews play instruments, sing songs, act out parts of their favorite TV shows, and generally act silly.

The servers come around with more coffee and I lean into Grace's ear to ask if she'd like more, but her breathing is deep and even. She fell asleep.

I scoop her up in my arms, say goodbye to my mother and aunts as I pass, and then get her in the car before she ever wakes up.

"What's happening?" she asks as I pull the seatbelt across her lap.

"Time for bed, princess." I shut her door and walk around to my side and get in.

"But I never said thank you."

"You don't have to, Grace." I stroke my hand down her cheek and she closes her eyes automatically. "It's Thanksgiving. Everyone is thankful."

She falls back asleep before we make it out of the driveway and when we get home, it is my pleasure to strip off all her clothes and tuck her into bed next to me.

She stirs a little when I pull her close so she can rest her head on my chest. "You know what I'm really thankful for, Asher?"

God, I love when she calls me Asher these days. I used to think she said it to be mean, but that's not why. She calls me Asher because she can. No one else, anywhere, calls me Asher. To my face, at least. Only Grace knows me well enough to use that moniker.

"Me, of course." I play with her.

"Yes, you," she says in her I'm-almost-asleep voice. "And I'm thankful for second chances."

"Yeah." I laugh under my breath. "I've certainly needed my share of those."

She sits up a little and she's more awake now. "I've learned something very important since all this crazy stuff happened."

"What's that, babe?"

"You don't always get it right the first time."

I stare at her eyes as they pool with tears and my heart feels like it might crack in half, that's how much it hurts me to see her sadness. So many things went wrong this year for her. The kidnapping. The miscarriage. The media discovering her alias. Which one is she thinking of now?

I scoot down under the covers with her and hold her closer. "If I had known he would take you that night, Grace—"

"That's not it, Vaughn. I actually think that do-over was... cathartic. In a way," she adds hastily. "I mean, I don't want to ever repeat it again. But it helped me confront so many things that I was hiding from all these years. No, the do-over I need is our marriage."

I stop breathing. What does that mean? She stays quiet, like I'm expected to say something. I think it through for a few moments and then give it my best shot. "I can't tell you what happened, Grace."

"Can't or won't?"

"Won't. I explained the other night. It was perfect. It can't be explained with words. Maybe if we had a video, but not with words."

"But you still want to get married again?"

"Do you?"

"I asked you first."

I huff out some air because I want to be truthful with her. But how will she take it? "I wouldn't mind a party, like my father offered. That would be nice. And I was thinking that a new ceremony would be nice. Make it a huge affair. With hundreds of guests and a new dress. The works. But I've changed my mind." I look over at her and she's stunned. Her eyes are wide and her mouth is open. "I'm sorry, sweets. I don't want a new ceremony. It was perfect the first time and I'm sorry you missed it."

Chapter Fifty-Seven - Grace

#ANewHope

WHEN I wake up I'm still reeling from Vaughn's admission last night. He does not want to marry me again. He has not even given me a ring. After all these months, I have no ring. What does this mean?

I roll over, ready to wake his ass up so I can ask him, but the bed is empty.

I sit up. "Vaughn?"

"In here, babe." He comes out of his closet buttoning up his shirtsleeves.

"Where are you going?"

He walks over and leans down to kiss my cheek. "Work. We have a few scenes to get done today. We're behind schedule, so we have to make it up. But after today, I'm all yours for two days." He grins at me like this is acceptable.

"But it's a holiday."

"Yeah, Black Friday doesn't really count, sweets. I'll probably be very late, so don't wait up."

And then he grabs his watch and wallet off his dresser and walks out.

Black Friday is the day of the Black Bash. And he said don't wait up? He's never said that to me before. I wait until I hear his Porsche roar to life in the garage and then get up and run down the hallway to check and make sure he's gone.

I open the door that leads to the garage and peek in.

Yup. Gone. Just like that I'm left at home alone all day.

I slam the door closed. Asshole. I should get my credit card and go shopping on Rodeo Drive, that's what I should do. Spend all his money.

I walk back to the living room and spy the door to Asher's office cracked open with the light on. I push it open all the way and realize he was in here this morning. What time did he get up? I didn't even hear him, I was dead-ass tired.

I walk around to his desk and take a seat, then flick the mouse until the monitor comes on.

His calendar. Hmm. Attached to a Gmail account I don't recognize. Double hmmm.

I knew that account with five messages from Larry was not his real email. But why is he hiding this one?

Grace, the gracious inner-me scolds. *Since when does he have to declare email accounts?* I mean, I have several email accounts. That's just what happens as you grow up. You make one, then another, then another. And pretty soon, you've got a collection of them.

This one references his years as the Disney sitcom star.

Triple hmmmm. In fact, red flags are going up all over the place. I scroll through the *from* column and it does not take me long to realize this email is pretty much a private one he only shares with Valencia. His co-star from back in the day and his co-star right now for *IM3*.

I open up the most recent one.

"Your wish is my command," is all it says. There's two attachments. One is a picture of the two of them as teenagers dressed up as genies for… something. Halloween? A special show? I have no idea.

But the other one is a forwarded message. Subject line: *Invitation Plus One Black Bash*

She got them tickets to the Black Bash. The very party he said he'd never attend just yesterday. And the 'your wish is my command' makes it painfully obvious that he was the one who approached her about attending.

Dammit. Vaughn is hiding something from me and it definitely has to do with this party tonight.

I walk out of his office and head straight for the coffee. While it brews, I stew in my own anger. It's bubbling up around me. Why am I so angry about this? Mostly it's because I feel left out. I feel like he's got another life without me. Like when he goes to work, he forgets all about what's waiting here for him at home.

I sit at the kitchen island bar drinking cup after cup of coffee as I think about this. What should I do? Should I ignore it and let him go to the party and then confront him about it when he gets home? Should I go down to the studio and make sure everything is on the up and up with him and Valencia? Should I use his ticket that Larry sent to go to the Black Bash and figure it out for myself?

My phone rings, startling me out of my introspection, and when I look up at the stove for the time, I realize it's already past noon. I've been sitting here for hours.

The phone rings again, so I reach for it and press accept before looking at the caller. "Hello."

"Grace," Kristi says, all out of breath on the other line.

"Kristi! Oh my God, I'm so happy to hear from you! You sound like you're panting."

"Well," she says with a smile—I can totally see that smile—"I'm all out of breath because they just brought me my beautiful baby girl and I'm so excited, I can't stop my happy cry. And the minute I was able to think, I thought to myself, 'I need to tell Grace. She's the best friend I have these days and I need to tell Grace.'"

"Awww." God, I feel so selfish and awful. I haven't thought about Kristi in weeks. "I should've been there. Do you want me to come now? I can help you out at home if you want."

The baby makes a little noise and Kristi actually sighs with contentment. I get a stabbing pain of jealousy straight through my heart.

"No, no, no," she says quickly. "You just stay home and take care of yourself, Kinsella. Or should I call you Asher now?"

Well, that's the question of the day. "Better stick with Kinsella for now."

"I'd love for you to visit when you're ready, but there's no rush." The baby starts to cry for real now, and there's some voices—Johnny and someone else who might be a nurse—telling Kristi she has to hang up. "I gotta go, Grace. But I wanted you to be the first person I called."

"Wait." I stop her from hanging up. "What's her name?"

"Oh, I'm so silly! Of course. Her name is Hope. Hope Blazen."

"Beautiful," I sigh.

And then she quickly says goodbye again and ends the call.

Hope.

I think Hope is a very good reason for me to pull myself together and go shopping. So I clean up my mess and go get ready to hand over the credit card.

And an hour later I'm on Rodeo Drive just as I planned, but this time, I'm not shopping out of spite. I'm shopping for Hope.

There are a ton of shops here. And honestly, I'm sure Target would be just as good as these fancy boutiques, but they've got a Tiffany's down here and I want to look around.

I give the car to the valet and that's where I start my afternoon. I head straight to the rings. I know, I'm just punishing myself. He hasn't mentioned a ring to me, and he just said last night we're not getting remarried, so why bother?

But I'm a princess and I have a dream. And maybe a wedding was not a part of that dream originally, but it is now. And weddings come with rings.

"Good afternoon, Mrs. Asher. Can I help you find something specific today?"

Jesus Christ. They know me. I just stare at her. I'm shocked. I'm not sure why, I know my face has been on the news a lot this year, but holy fucking shit. A clerk in a Tiffany's should not recognize me when I'm in shorts and flip flops.

"I'm sorry," I say quietly, as I back away and slide my sunglasses down to cover my eyes. "You have the wrong person."

The clerk's smile never falters. "I'm so sorry, miss. My mistake. How can I help you?"

But I'm already out of there.

Fuck this.

I walk straight back to the valet and they greet me as Mrs. Asher as well. "I just need my car, thank you."

A few minutes later they bring it around and the inside is still cool from the air-conditioning, that's how short my Rodeo Drive shopping trip was.

I plug in a request for the nearest Target and start following the GPS voice and once I get there and find my way into the familiar store with the red carts, everything goes back to normal.

Maybe I'm not cut out for this life? I mean, Vaughn is so public. Everything about us in this town is news. I don't understand that. I've been hiding from the media—from everybody—for so many years, it might not be possible to change that part of me. I don't want to be famous. I don't want people to know me. I want to be… invisible.

I love our home. I do feel like I belong there. But when I step outside without Vaughn, I'm overwhelmed with the attention.

I stop pushing my cart and look behind me, at the large glass doors that open and close as people come and go.

That city out there. It scares me.

I turn back to the store, because that's not scary, and make my way to the baby stuff. I'm sure they have all these basic supplies, so I skip right to the clothes. I bet she's got a ton of clothes too. So I choose an outfit that will take some time to grow into. It's leftover from summer, so it's like five dollars. I smile so hard at that, since Kristi and I are so rich we could afford anything. But cute is cute. Besides, it has a matching sun hat. I'll send an invitation to come visit us after football season is over. Then Hope can wear it to the pool.

I grab more stuff—not all from the sale rack—and fill up my cart. It's too much, but I don't care. I'll send some of it for Christmas.

I look down the aisle and spot the Christmas stuff and my heart pounds with excitement. I do love me some Christmas. So I wheel my cart out of the baby section and head towards holidays. They still have Halloween candy on sale and I'm wondering when the last time was that I had a Snickers when I see it.

My cart comes to a halt, and then before I know what I'm doing, I've got it in my hand.

A mask. A black mask. The kind people wear to masquerade parties.

Or Black Bashes.

I put it in the cart on top of the baby stuff and hit the cashier.

One way or another I'm going to figure out what's going on there tonight.

Chapter Fifty-Eight - Vaughn

#ThatCalmWasReallyTheStorm

"HEY," Valencia calls out as she enters my trailer.

"Hey," I say back absently as I stare at the article in the Hollywood tabloid. "Did you see this shit?"

She sits down in the booth across the table from me in the area that serves as a dining room. "I saw. What are you gonna do?"

I look up at her. She's still the same girl I knew all those years ago. Being on set with her again has been fun. We're like puzzle pieces that were missing and finally someone put them back together again. She's even prettier now than she was at sixteen, if you can believe it. I guess wealth and the ability to take extended vacations between projects have that benefit. She only does one movie a year, if that. But every single one of them has been a major blockbuster. "I've got to take care of it. I need to stop this."

"Vaughn, you can't stop her story. It is what it is. There's records of her everywhere. These images are just one more reason to let it go. Don't get involved. They will tear you apart."

"She's my wife, Valencia. I can't just let them threaten this kind of exposure and let it pass."

"So what's your answer? You've already done what you could." She points to the tabloid that has a sensitive picture of my wife taken off Twitter. "And they still found a way to get it."

"Yeah, because that Amy bitch from *Buzz* sold them."

"This tabloid says specifically that's not where they came from. You can't blame her. I mean, honestly, Vaughn. Your wife took those photos and sent them over Twitter. She knew what she was doing."

"I asked her to."

"So what? You used to ask me to do plenty of stupid things if I remember correctly. A lot worse than taking naked selfies."

"We didn't have selfies back then." I grin.

"My point is, I never said yes."

She's been saying this all day, but I can't take the coward's way out and blame Grace for what's happening. For what's about to happen.

"There's more to this story than you know, Val. A lot more."

"So tell me. Maybe I can help."

I consider it. I really do. Valencia has always been on my side and I have no doubt she'd be on my side now. But the knock comes on the door, telling us to be on set in five minutes. Five minutes just isn't enough time. "Later, maybe. After the party."

"So you're going?"

"I said I was. I am. And you don't have to come because it's gonna be a mess."

She reaches across the table and takes my hand. "Normally I'd be up for anything, Vaughn. I'd stand by you for anything. And I still will. But not at that party." She shakes her head. "They tore apart my best friend a few years ago and we made the mistake of going. I know what's going to happen and I can't watch you go through that."

I squeeze her hand back, thankful that she's so loyal, that she's one of the only people in Hollywood who really does have my back. "I get it, Val. I don't expect you to be there. And thanks for the tickets. I lean over and kiss her on the cheek. "You're a good friend."

She smiles coyly. "Well, the next scene says we'll be more than friends soon. And I can't wait. So let's go."

Chapter Fifty-Nine - Grace

#SometimesGettingLostHelpsYouBeFound

I TURN out of the Target parking lot and see the sign for Beverly Boulevard. Yes! I know where that is, so I don't need the GPS.

I turn and lose myself in thought. I feel like there's so much going on behind the scenes that I don't know about, it's starting to make me nervous. Like Vaughn leaving for work today. He just said a few days ago he was looking forward to the long weekend. Well, working on Black Friday sorta interrupts the long weekend. So what he said was either a lie then, or this is a lie now.

What could they possibly have to do today? Maybe I should stop by the studio and see what he's up to? I chuckle a little at my ridiculousness… but then I figure why not? I'm allowed to go onto the set. Well, maybe not. But I'm pretty sure no one will tell me no if I show up there.

I look up at the street signs to find one that might take me over near Studio City, but none of them look familiar. In fact, I'm heading towards downtown. Which is not the direction I thought I was going.

I stop at a red light and try to figure out where I am and how to get back to where I need to be. The GPS is on, so I hit the new destination button and I'm about to program it in when the car behind me honks.

The light is green. I move forward and get into the right lane so I can pull over and turn around, and as soon as I make that turn, I know I'm in the wrong neighborhood. There's a lot of people hanging out in front of apartment buildings and they are mostly young men.

I want to just turn into the first parking lot and go back the way I came, but there's a crowd hanging out there that does not look very friendly. I continue up the street, make another right, and hope I can just go around the block to get back on Beverly Boulevard. There are fewer people out on this street, mostly because it's warehouses, but there are no more streets to turn onto.

A girl who is very pregnant drags a suitcase to an empty bus stop and I wonder if she's escaping or coming home.

Maybe my life does suck. Maybe I did have some bad breaks. And maybe my old neighborhood in Denver wasn't the safest in the city. But it was a far cry from the living conditions I imagine lurk behind these crumbling buildings.

I would be scared to death to walk anywhere here, let alone be pregnant and dragging a suitcase.

My heart is beating fast even though I realize this is irrational. "Don't be stupid, Grace," I tell myself. "You're not lost. You're one block away from Beverly and you have a help button on your rear-view mirror if you need it. Just make the next right turn and it will dump you back where you were."

I finally come to another street where I can turn right, but as soon as I make that turn, I realize it dead-ends at a large apartment building. There's a few groups of people hanging out in front of it, talking and laughing. So I just pretend like I belong and pull into the first driveway so I can turn around.

"Nice car," a young teenage boy calls out. He says it loud enough that I can hear it through my closed window. Loud enough to make every head turn to see what he's talking about.

I ignore them all, but internally I'm wondering how frightened I have to be to push that little panic button. I would be mortified if I had to use that.

Instead I just put it in reverse, do a two-point turn, and pull back out onto the road so I can backtrack my route. I really don't want to turn back onto that street where all the crowds of people were. It looked like a neighborhood you see in movies where drug dealers hang out on the corner.

I see that girl again. The pregnant one with the suitcase, only now there's a boy with her and they are fighting. She screams obscenities at him, and just my luck I get stuck at a red light in front of their bus stop.

"What the fuck you looking at, bitch?" the boy yells at me when he notices my stare.

I turn my head away quickly. *Please, please, please turn green.*

And the next thing I know the girl is screaming. She's on the ground and there's blood coming out of her mouth.

I honk my horn. The boy flips me off. I open my door. "Stop that or I'll call the police! Stop that!" He's still hitting her and she's curled up on the ground protecting her belly.

"You want some too, bitch?" the boy says, turning to me. "Get back in your car before I knock your teeth out."

I get out and close my door. "Knock my teeth out?"

"Oh, you want some, huh, bitch?"

I squint my eyes at him. He's about five foot ten. Not too tall. Skinny. Maybe one sixty. And his eyes are blazing with anger.

I look at the girl on the ground. She's still crying and bleeding, but she's trying to get up. A few people have appeared from nowhere. They stand close by, but do not try to help her. "Do you need a ride somewhere?" I ask the girl. "I can take you so you don't have to wait for the bus."

"She ain't goin' nowhere, bitch."

I look at that boy and wish I could knock *his* teeth out. "I didn't ask you. I asked her."

"I speak for her. Now get, before me and my boys take your pretty blonde ass around the building and keep you for ourselves."

My eyebrows shoot up and I take a step forward. "Oh really? You think you're gonna take me somewhere against my will? Because I've got to tell you, I've been there, done that, my friend. And I'd like to see you fucking try."

He just stares at me, then looks over to some other boys who might be his buddies. They don't say shit. He's on his own. "She ain't going. Tell this bitch you staying here, Rosa."

"You know what, Rosa?" I never take my eyes off this little punk who thinks hitting girls and threatening to kidnap them is just another day in his life. "I don't know who this guy is, but I do know he's an asshole. So if you'd like to get the hell out of this place right now, all you gotta do is say so and I'll take you."

The punk looks over his shoulder at Rosa, then back at me. "She's stayin'."

"I'm not staying," Rosa finally says. "I'm not staying." She grabs her suitcase and starts pulling it towards my car. There's a whole line of cars behind me, watching this whole scene go down. I'm surprised they aren't honking. I suppose the YouTube possibilities trump getting where they are going on time.

Rosa approaches the punk, clearly scared to walk past him, so I take a few steps forward with my hand out to encourage her. "Come on." She tries to hurry past him, but just before she gets clear, his hand darts out and cracks her in the face one more time.

I flip out. I lunge forward, covering the few paces that separate us, and hurl myself at that asshole's back. He flies forward from the momentum and crashes to the ground. And that hammerfist to the neck that was next to useless against a raging, adrenaline-pumped Derek Hauser back in Nebraska does the trick for this stupid kid who thinks the world is his to hurt.

I pound his neck three times, enough to stun him and make him stay down, and then I jump up and grab Rosa's hand and pull her towards my car.

People clap as I shove her suitcase into the backseat and she climbs into the passenger side. The light is red again, but I don't care. Everyone in all directions is stopped to watch the scene unfold, so I look both ways and take off.

"Oh my God," the girl says. "I'm shaking so bad."

I look over at her as she holds her hands out in front of her ample belly. They are indeed shaking very badly.

"Just relax, OK? Do you know how to get out of this neighborhood? Because I'm lost."

She just stares at me.

"What?"

"Lady, I'm so lucky you got lost. He said he was gonna kill me for trying to leave."

I look over at her and study her face, streaked with blood and tears.

Do people really mean that? I mean, when a teenager says he'll kill you if you leave, does he mean that? Or is it just posturing? Is she just supposed to cower and give in to him? Or is she supposed to take his threat seriously and fight back with all her might?

It's confusing. Too confusing to think about right now. "Where should I take you? Do you have a place?"

"Turn left here, then just go straight. I'm going to a place in Silver Lake. A home for abused women. They said they'd help me."

I let out a long breath and remind myself.

#IAmNotTheGirlWithTheWorldsBiggestProblems

Chapter Sixty - Grace

#HowDoYouKissTheInvisibleMan

I DROP Rosa off at the home for abused women in Silver Lake, and in repayment, she explains how not to end up in Westlake again.

I'm very grateful for that. What I did was stupid. But it's hard to feel bad about it when it feels so good to help this girl.

I give her the cash I have in my wallet, which is not much. Seventy-two dollars. But her face lights up like I just handed her a million bucks.

And then I make my way to the studio. Not to ambush Vaughn, but to hug him and say I'm sorry for being so difficult. I am not the girl with the world's biggest problems. Maybe I was that girl once. (Or twice.) But I'm not her now. I'm lucky. I'm married to a great guy. I have a large home, lots of money, a car that doesn't break down, friends, family, and good health.

I'm so, so lucky.

When I get to the gate, the security guard nods at some hanging thing on my rear-view that Vaughn must've placed in here the other day and waves me through with a, "Good evening, Mrs. Asher."

That's it. That's all it takes to get on the lot. I expected a little more resistance, but I guess being Mrs. Asher has a lot of perks. I barely remember how to get back to Vaughn's movie set, but I manage to find the parking lot and locate his trailer from a distance.

I try there first, but it's locked.

"You looking for Mr. Asher?" an attendant asks me.

"Yes, please. Do you know where he is?"

"Yes, ma'am. He's on set right now. They are almost done. Do you want to wait here or have me take you in to watch from the observation room?"

I hesitate. I'm not sure.

"No one's in there," he explains. "It's a sensitive scene today. Only required personnel allowed on set. So you'd have the place to yourself if you want to watch."

I breathe a sigh of relief. I'm not sure I can handle much more public scrutiny.

We enter the building and I'm led down a long hallway. There's no stage in sight. No people in sight, either. He points to a door and then opens it for me. "It's down the hall and to the left. They can't hear you from this far away and you won't be interfering if you just stay back."

I nod and walk through the door alone and find myself in a dimly lit hallway. I can hear a few voices further down so I follow that until I reach a black curtain. Peeking through, I can see the set. It's incredible. It looks like an actual city street alley with a side of a building, complete with a fire escape as the backdrop.

There's lots of talking at the moment. People are laughing and joking. Vaughn is not in view. I lean against the wall and consider if I'm being overly dramatic about my recent experience.

I mean, I'm fine. Yeah, it got a little dicey for a few minutes, but I'm fine. My heart is not beating fast anymore. I've calmed down from the scare, and now I'm feeling more ridiculous than anything.

I'm just about to turn around and say forget it when I hear his voice. It's booming and boisterous and a smile immediately forms on my face. God, I love him.

He walks out onto the set dressed in a suit, like he was at a party. His face, which is usually invisible in post-production, is clearly visible now. In fact, he looks a lot like the man I met on the beach the night of Samantha's wedding.

I have not thought about that night in months, but now it hits me how far we have come from those first arguments on the island.

God, I was such a bitch to him. I smile as I watch that same man on set in front of me. He was more patient than he should've been. Especially that weekend. And I was so scared of what he represented to me. The control was frightening.

And now he's more aloof than I'm comfortable with.

It's probably my fault, but that doesn't make me wish for a do-over any less. I wish I was back on that beach right now, experiencing him for the first time again.

His co-star, Valencia Cruz, joins him in the scene. She's his ex-girlfriend from his teen years.

She's very beautiful. She's wearing a gold gown. They must've just come out of some kind of a ball in this part of the script. She's very exotic, like Bebe. Long, dark hair. Striking amber eyes. Olive skin. And a body most eighteen-year-old girls would be jealous of, even though she's about the same age as Vaughn.

They talk briefly on set, and then there's a call for quiet and the stage people do their thing.

I strain to hear what's happening, I'm not really that close, but my whole world goes silent when I witness what happens next.

They are kissing.

Vaughn leans in, cupping her face, his mouth covering hers in a kiss so passionate I almost want to faint from the steam. I move a little closer to get a better look. As he kisses her, it feels familiar. It feels like he's kissing her the way he kisses me.

Then his hands are all over her body, grasping at her tits, her ass, and then he roughly grabs one of her gown straps and pulls until it breaks. He yanks her dress down, exposing her breasts, all the while his mouth never stops its assault on her lips.

I'm stunned. I'm picturing our rough sex the other night and I swear to God, I think he uses some of these moves on me!

I've watched him kiss countless women on screen, but he wasn't my husband. I turn and walk away, following the dimly lit hallway back to where I entered, then make my way outside.

It's dark now. I click the keychain and my car beeps, so I head in that direction, still trying to process what I saw and how I feel about it.

I sit in the car for a few moments trying to wrap my head around things.

This is his job. I realize that, but I can't come to terms with the idea that my husband gets to have a rough makeout session with his ex-girlfriend and call it work.

I program the GPS for home, just in case I get lost again, and then drive off the lot. Security waves to me as I leave, but I can't even pretend to be normal and wave back.

The drive home brings me no clarity. In fact I'm more confused than ever. I don't feel like going to that Black Bash, but I feel... duped for some reason. I feel like there's a whole other world that exists outside my little bubble of isolation. Like the Twitter stuff. It's a world where people are talking about me. Like the Tiffany's stuff. A world where people recognize me in a city where I know like four people with any amount of intimacy.

And what else are they saying? How much of what they are saying are things I don't know about?

I pull into the garage just as my phone dings. A text from Vaughn.

Still working late. Don't wait up.

Yeah, don't wait up, my ass. I grab my shopping bags and take them inside, passing by Vaughn's office to get to our bedroom. The phone rings in there just as I pass.

Figures. More things to make me uneasy.

I drop the bags off on the bed and head back to the office just as the message starts to play.

"Vaughn?" a woman asks on the other line—Valencia? "We're still on for tonight, right? I wasn't sure if you were still into it. So I'm gonna assume you are. Meet you at the Bash. You're still Bogart, I'm still Bacall." The message ends.

Wow. Just wow. My husband is going to this big party after denying it in front of everyone yesterday at Thanksgiving dinner, and not only that, he's going dressed up as one half of an iconic Hollywood movie couple. And I'm not the other half.

I take a deep breath.

I'm going to that party. I need to know why my husband is acting so strange. I need to know what this Black Bash is all about. And I feel like Vaughn is trying to hide it from me. Maybe it's something personal with him. Or maybe he's trying to protect me. But either way, I don't want to be left out of his life because he thinks I can't handle things.

He's been there for me, so if this is about him, then I want to return that gesture.

And if it's about me… then I want to fight my own battles.

I like the prince, but I'm not helpless and that's how I feel right now.

I rummage through my closet until I find the Halloween outfit Vaughn bought me. We went to Larry's house for a party, but ended up going home after a few hours since I was not really up for parties back then.

I pull it out. It's Cleopatra. He was dressed as Mark Antony. This is the only costume I have, so it will have to do.

I squeeze into it, crushing my girls into the bustier, and turn to look at myself in the mirror. That makes me smile. Because I look damn good in this costume. I grab the accessories—an elaborate headdress, some costume jewelry, a black wig with pretty beaded braids. And then I do the heavy eye makeup à la Elizabeth Taylor.

If Vaughn is going as one half of an iconic Hollywood couple, I'm going as Cleopatra.

I grab my phone, pull up the invitation via email, and then head to the car.

I have no idea what is happening at this party tonight, but I'm definitely going to find out.

I get in the car and program the address into the GPS and then head out. The place is in downtown, and it's actually not far from where I got lost this afternoon. But I'm not gonna let fear prevent me from going.

I need to figure out what's going on.

Chapter Sixty-One - Vaughn

#StarOfShameThatsMe

"HOW do I look?" I ask Valencia.

"Perfect, as always, Vaughn." she coos. "But"—she's frowning now—"I think it's a bad idea. I mean, what if Grace finds out?"

"Grace is at home. Where she's been for the last three months. I told her not to wait up for me."

Val nods and hits send on the email. "OK, then here it is. Two access codes to the Black Bash. But don't say I didn't warn you tomorrow when this shit hits the fan."

"Thank you so much." I check my email and when it comes in, I download both attachments and forward one directly to my date and then turn to go.

"Hey," Val calls after me.

"What?" I say, still walking towards the studio door. I'm already late since filming went on longer than expected and I just want to get to the party.

"I hope you know what you're doing."

I don't even turn back. "I do, Val. I do."

I say that with a confidence I don't feel though. Because while I know what goes on at a Black Bash, I've never been the guest of honor before. And tonight, I am.

The drive downtown is stop and go, as is typical on Friday nights, and by the time I get there, it's nearly ten o'clock.

I pull into the old building's garage entrance and flash my access code via phone at the man with the scanner. This place is about to be torn down to make room for some trendy new lofts, so I'm sure the Bash organizers figured it was the perfect place for a party.

The location is never the same from year to year. It's all very hush-hush until after Halloween and then that's all anyone in Hollywood is talking about—the stars afraid they will be the ones on display that year, and the media excited to get even with celebrities who may have treated them badly.

One person each year is the guest of honor. The epitome of bad behavior. The one person who deserves to be shamed above all others.

And this year it's me.

That *Buzz* bitch has had it in for me for more than a decade. She blames me for what happened. And no matter how many times I tried to explain myself back then, she never accepted my apology.

Threatening that editor a few months back was probably a big mistake, but it felt good to use my status and power to fuck up her plan of getting an interview out of me.

I drive up to the top level of the parking garage and park the car. Another set of headlights flashes at me from down the row, and I get out and adjust my suit.

Marjorie steps out of her car wearing the houndstooth suit Lauren Bacall made famous in *The Big Sleep*. She eyes me up and down as she approaches. "Looking good, Bogie." She slips a masquerade mask over her eyes and I do the same.

I smile down at her. "Ready?"

She takes a deep breath and lets it out slowly. "I'm not sure, but I'm going through with it."

She wraps her arm in mine and we walk into the party together.

Chapter Sixty-Two - Grace

#*NUNYA*

IT'S dark and there must be a smoke machine somewhere to add to the eerie effect, but it's not necessary because this party is creepy as hell. Everyone is dressed up and no one looks familiar. I just hope no one recognizes me until I find Vaughn.

God, I pray, *please don't let him be cheating on me. I don't think I could take it.*

With that little prayer I walk forward into the cavernous room. The party is really all six floors of the building, but only the top two have 'exhibits'.

The exhibits are partitioned off with thick white canvas sheets hanging from the ceiling to make a sort of cubicle. And even though I know that there are things inside the makeshift rooms that I don't need to see, curiosity gets the better of me and I peek inside. On three sides, each sheet is displaying a looped video of an unlucky actor.

I wander through the crowd, not taking a drink from any of the servers—who are all dressed up as the Invisible Man and that makes everything triple creepy—because I don't actually trust that the drinks aren't drugged.

I'm here for one reason only. To find my husband and ask him what the hell is going on.

A curtain opens as I walk past and I catch a glimpse of some nude photos of a famous starlet and the sounds of a sex tape playing. Jesus. So that's what this is about. The hall of shame. The pictures that couldn't be posted publicly for fear of being sued? The sex tape someone paid to have scrubbed? Because while I might've been depressed for a few weeks this year, I was certainly on top of my celebrity gossip until very recently. I never saw or heard of that sex tape.

I follow the person who came out of the tent-like room right into the next one.

This time it's a picture of a famous singer with two black eyes and her assailant's mug shot. So he was arrested? That was never in the news either.

The singer's music is playing in the background, but her frantic call to 911 is superimposed over it.

I leave the tent, repulsed at how they are invading her privacy. Why is that anyone's business? Why do people think just because you're famous that they get to know every detail of your life?

I mean, I get it. It's wrong for him to hurt her and he deserves to be held accountable. She needs help. But how is this helping her? How is exposing her most private moments helping her?

Suddenly there's a hum of murmurs circulating through the party. People are leaning in to whisper, all looking at the elevator. I watch with them as the outdated counter over the top of the doors calls out which floor it's on.

It dings that it's arrived on six, and then the doors open. A collective gasp goes up from the crowd as Vaughn appears dressed as Humphrey Bogart. On his arm, and clinging far too tightly to my husband, is a blonde woman dressed as Lauren Bacall.

People start muttering *Grace*, around me.

"Grace!" someone calls out. "Why did you let your husband bring you to this?"

I look over to find the voice, but the crowd is far too thick now. People are pouring out of the stairwell, desperately trying to get a glimpse of Vaughn and the woman they think is me.

Vaughn ignores them, as does the woman, and he steps forward. People move aside as he enters the vast room and then he leans down and asks a question of a girl standing close.

She raises her arm and points to a tent behind me.

The whole room looks in that direction.

That tent is made up of thick black curtains. I'm only a few feet away, in fact, so I start walking towards the entrance. An arm darts out to block my way and a large man dressed as a Stormtrooper stops me from entering. "Guests of honor first, bitch. You know the rules."

OK. I stand my ground, waiting to see what they've got behind the curtains about Vaughn.

He steps forward, only a few feet in front of me, his eyes straight ahead.

And then the curtain is pulled back.

Chapter Sixty-Three - Vaughn

#JustReturningTheFavor

HER whimpering fills the room. They've got the sound on every speaker. Her sniffles boom out from every corner. But it's the images onscreen that stop me dead and make my heart want to crack.

Grace. On the floor. Trying her best not to cry as Derek Hauser kicks her in the back. I knew it would be bad, but I honestly never thought they'd show those videos of when she was kidnapped as a teen.

My heart speeds up. My face goes hot. The rage I feel at this moment builds, but then the image shifts and it's another girl lying on the floor. This one is covered in blood too, but this one is dead.

"He killed her."

Everyone goes silent as the words echo from the speakers.

"He killed my sister."

The image switches back to Grace, her nude Twitter pictures up for all to see.

I'm mortified that these scumbags should see my wife in this way.

"He uses women," the speaker system booms. "All of them. See what he made that poor Daisy Bryndle do?"

The tweets on that account are private. They require a password and no one has ever gotten our passwords. I changed them the day Grace was found to some incomprehensible string of numbers. But the pictures are not protected. If you know the link, you can get the pictures.

The scene flashes to Grace in a Nebraska cornfield, being loaded onto the Life Flight helicopter, bound for Denver.

"It was your fault she was taken again, Vaughn Asher. Your fault she was shot. Your fault she lost that baby."

How dare that bitch mention my wife's pregnancy. I turn and face the crowd. "Show your face, you bitch. Show your fucking face!"

Amy Stratton steps out of the mass of people and they part for her, just as they parted for me. "Here's my face. The one you've been trying to forget for more than a decade. You killed her and you got away with it because you're famous. You celebrities all feel entitled. You all live by your own rules. You flash your money and use your status so you don't have to be accountable. You make me sick." She walks straight up to me and spits in my face.

I say nothing.

"What, no denial?" she snarls at me.

"You know I didn't do it. You know that every word you're saying is a complete fabrication. You're the sick one. Your sister did not commit suicide—"

"You made her kill herself!"

"She was on drugs, Amy. She was doing some very questionable things."

"She hired you to be in her movie, and you fucked her over. You ruined her career. You made her kill herself."

"That's not what happened and you know it. I told you back then, that's not what happened."

"Yeah, you tried to blame her boyfriend—"

"Her boyfriend, are you fucking kidding me? Frankie Miller was thirty years older than her. He was a scumbag who was taking advantage of her."

"No. He loved her. You're just mad because he tricked you. And then you threatened him. You threatened to send him to jail."

I shake my head and look at the crowd, trying to decide if I need to make my case or not. But then I remember who my date is for tonight, and I realize I have no choice. This is it. I have to come clean and whatever happens afterward, so be it.

"Frankie Miller killed DeeDee Cisco ten years ago."

"You're a liar," Amy screams. "He was found not guilty."

"He was *not* found not guilty, Amy. The charges were dropped. There's a big difference. And the charges were dropped because…" I look over and find Carey Keefe in the crowd. She's not dressed up and she's in front to see my reaction. "Because… Because I—"

I stop talking.

But Carey steps forward. "Because what?" Her face is strained. She's breathing a little faster than normal, so her heart must be beating fast. She's nervous.

And I realize that she's as nervous about the truth as I am. She might have set me up tonight, but it's only because she never believed me. She's been trying to convince herself for months that I was lying.

But now that we're both here, she knows I'm not lying. And she wants me to shut the fuck up.

Because I am almost positive that Frankie Miller did kill DeeDee Cisco, aka Danielle Stratton. The sister of Amy Stratton, star gossip reporter for *Buzz Hollywood*.

I know this because I have video that I never turned over to the police.

DeeDee was just a film-school student in one of his classes. I met her on my eighteenth birthday. They set me up. Drugged me. Had me sign a non-disclosure agreement. And then proceeded to film me doing things I never imagined myself doing.

When I woke up in my car on the UCLA campus, there was a note congratulating me on my next blockbuster film. That was before I was a megastar. Before I made that crucial transition from the world of child actors into the world of the professionals.

So I went to my father. The great Adam Asher. And the whole thing disappeared.

Until DeeDee was found dead and I received a package in the mail a few days after her death that had the original footage of the movie they made with me, plus more. Plus *a lot* more. The NDA I signed and dozens of videos of Frankie Miller beating the shit out of her, demanding to know where she was hiding the film they made of me. It felt like a call to action. Like I should avenge DeeDee's death for her because she held out. She played ball with my father's offer and refused to give Miller the film.

But I didn't give her the same respect back. I never showed those films to anyone. I didn't want to be involved in this tragedy in any way. I was hopeful that the tide was changing with my career. I had been called in to read for three very big films, all of which fell through, but at the time it all seems so promising.

I didn't want to fuck it up. I didn't want to care about her. And I certainly didn't want to *help* her. She got what she deserved. I couldn't even fathom why she'd sent that package to me, of all people. Why me?

I figured she was setting me up again. I mean, that's a legitimate reaction. That incident changed my whole outlook on life. And not in a good way. I stopped looking for girlfriends and started looking for sex. I ran with that nondisclosure idea I was introduced to, and made every girl I fucked sign one.

Carey Keefe picked up the story of poor, ousted Frankie Miller and became his champion. After a long wait for trial and with the help of a top-notch legal team, the charges were eventually dropped. Six weeks later, DeeDee's death was ruled a suicide.

Carey is suddenly right up in my face. "Because why, Vaughn?"

I only have one out at this point. The truth. "You need to believe me, Carey. That I'm not doing this to ruin you. I'm doing this because it's the right thing to do."

She snorts. "How would you have the ability to ruin *me*? I think it's the other way around."

I lean down in her ear and whisper, "Because you're in those films too."

Her face goes white. "What films?"

"The ones DeeDee sent to me before she died."

"What's going on here?" Amy asks a stone-faced Carey.

Carey puts up a hand to silence Amy, and then proceeds. "You ruin lives, Vaughn Asher. You stomp all over women like they are things. Just watch everyone."

And then she throws her arms out in a flourish and the screen changes. There's a line of women.

"My name is Jasinda Gonzales and I'm a victim of Vaughn Asher."

"My name is Sandy Delaney and I'm a victim of Vaughn Asher."

Chapter Sixty-Four - Grace

#AndAPrincessShallLeadThem

THEY go on and on like that. Dozens of them. And as much as I love my husband, this does make me pause. Because this is who he was before we were married. Everything they're saying about him is true.

I know this because he used the same words on me. He asked me to do the very same things. It was *Yes, Master.* It was sitting at his feet. It was being hand-fed tiny morsels of meat. It was signing a non-disclosure agreement. All of that is true.

Vaughn stands quietly as the film ends and then two more curtains are raised to reveal all the women who just spoke out.

Vaughn walks up to one of the girls and looks her in the eyes. "Did you get anything out of our relationship, Terry?"

She shrugs.

"Money? I recall giving you about seventy-five thousand dollars before we called it quits. You wanted a condo in Miami with a beach view. Done, correct?"

She stands perfectly still.

He moves on to the next girl and repeats his questions. "How about you, Lisa? You wanted your student loans paid off? I did that." He moves on to the next girl. "And this one, she was a one-night stand. There was no agreement. There was no Master. There was none of this that they are claiming."

"So I don't count?" the girl asks him.

"Do you want me to lie?"

She turns and walks away.

"They're not people to you, Vaughn Asher. They are things to be used and thrown away," that editor for *Buzz Hollywood* tells my husband.

"You're wrong," he says with conviction. "They were possessions, but only in the sense that I felt obligated to care for them while they were in this specific arrangement with me."

"You make me sick," the reporter seethes. "You killed my sister. You made her so depressed she took her own life. And then you accused her boyfriend of abuse and murder."

Vaughn says nothing to that.

"Grace!" the girl calls out. And everyone turns to find the blonde woman Vaughn came in with. "Where did she go?"

I look around along with everyone else, but the girl in the houndstooth suit is nowhere to be found.

"Put her movie back on," the editor woman shouts.

The film of me as a teenager is back up for all to see. I can't believe they are showing this. As much as I hate the fact that my husband was that person this woman describes, and as confused as I am about this other stuff with this DeeDee person, there is no good reason to have this disgusting footage of my kidnapping on display.

"Take it down right now, Carey," Vaughn says calmly.

"Or what?"

"You'll see." The ice in his voice is so clear it sends chills up my arms.

"I want everyone to know what your type is, Vaughn. Broken. That's what you like. You want victims. You want girls who can't get up off the floor and stand up to you. You want to tie them up and stick them in a closet and—"

I slap her across the face so hard my palm is stinging.

I have no idea how I got so close, but I slap the shit out of that bitch. The whole place gasps as I remove my mask and my wig.

"What the fuck?" the Carey woman says as she palms her red cheek.

"That's enough." I say it with confidence, one hundred percent in control.

"Grace," Vaughn whispers. I smile up at him and he gives me a small one back. And then I step forward until I'm right in front of him, so close that I have to tip my head back to look him in the eye. I nod my head to the line of women. "I've seen that man they describe, but that's not the man I married."

"Grace," he says again. But the screams from the movie cut him off. We both look up at the scene to see teenage Daisy get smacked across the face and fall to the floor. "Let's go."

He takes my hand and starts to lead me away, but I plant my feet firm and pull him back. "No. I'm not leaving." I turn to look up at that film and I watch. I make the whole room watch as I am hit and kicked, and they really chose an Oscar-winning segment for this teaser, because just before it ends, I piss myself from fear.

"Please, Grace," Vaughn pleads. "Let's go."

I turn to face the crowd instead. "Did you all enjoy that?" I ask them. "Is that what you came to see? Are you satisfied now?"

Vaughn takes my hand and leads me away. But when I pass the Carey person responsible for this, I stop again. "You got that film from him, didn't you? My kidnapper contacted you before he took me and offered you that film."

"I don't reveal sources," she says flatly.

"Well," I say, turning to the crowd, "I'm so glad you were all so entertained by the images of me being abused as a little girl. You must all feel mighty superior right now."

This time when Vaughn tugs on my hand, I let him lead me away.

We take the elevator to the roof and the blonde girl Vaughn came with, who is no longer wearing the houndstooth suit, but a slinky 40's looking flapper dress, is waiting by his car.

"Did you get all that?" Vaughn asks her.

She smiles widely. "I got every second."

"Grace, this is Marjorie. She's a reporter for *Everyday Celebrity Magazine*."

"Holy shit. I love *Everyday Celebrity*. When I lived in Denver I had a weekly subscription. I read you guys every week."

"We like to call ourselves the 'Real Celebrity Magazine' because we deal in truth, not rumors," the pretty blonde reporter says. "People trust that our stories are accurate. And this tonight, what Vaughn did... what you did... well, let's just say, most of these people won't have jobs this time next week, let alone be putting on this kind of show next year. Some of them might even go to jail." She winks at Vaughn. "That's your good news I promised, Vaughn. I have a detective friend with LAPD who's been looking into some hacking cases and this footage I got tonight will certainly give him leverage with a judge when he starts asking for warrants."

"Thank you. You're a good friend, Marjorie. I know we haven't always seen eye to eye, but you're fair with me. And that's all I can ask for." She smiles in response but his attention is already back to me. "Where's your car, Grace?" Vaughn asks. "We need to get out of here."

"Level three."

"We'll leave it here and pick it up tomorrow."

And then I am ushered into the Porsche and I buckle myself in as Vaughn makes his way around to his side. He gets in and starts the engine as he drags his own belt across his shoulder.

"I just want to say—"

"No." I stop him with a hand on his leg. "Please, don't apologize. I love you, and that's all there is to it. My love is not conditional on how you acted in the past. Just like your love is not conditional on what happened to me in the past. This is us, Vaughn. Like it or not. This is us. I am that little girl who watched her parents murdered in front of her and was brutalized for eight months by a crazy man. And you are that asshole who used women for sex and treated them like possessions. But that's not who we are right now. People grow and learn. I don't see you as the controlling asshole I met on the beach. I love you for the man you are today."

He puts his hand over mine and squeezes, picking it up in the process. He raises it up to his mouth and presses his lips on my palm, ever so softly. "I love all parts of you, Grace. There is nothing about you I'd change. I love all the parts."

Chapter Sixty-Five - Grace

#LifeIsTooShortToBeMiserableLikeYou

THREE WEEKS LATER

OF all the words Vaughn Asher has given me over the course of our relationship, it's the ones back in his Porsche when we were leaving the Black Bash that stick with me. He loves all my parts.

I love all his parts too.

I know it was wrong for him to keep that video of DeeDee Cisco being abused from the police. But Marjorie and *Everyday Celebrity Magazine* took possession of it and used it to reopen the case of her death. Frankie Miller and Carey Keefe were both arrested last week.

Buzz Hollywood filed for bankruptcy.

The article Marjorie wrote for her magazine went to print two weeks ago and boy, you could almost hear the cheer coming from every Hollywood star who's ever been hounded by the media.

That's not to say they are all bad. Marjorie, for instance, is not bad. And Amy Stratton, the woman who hated Vaughn so much and who went to extraordinary lengths to ambush him with those ex-girlfriends at the Black Bash… she's not evil either. She was looking for justice.

I hope she gets it with a new trial.

As for me?

I'm still looking for my purpose, but I'm getting closer. Rosa, that pregnant girl I picked up when I was lost in LA, inspired me. She made me think of all the times when I felt desperate as a teen. I was never pregnant and single at eighteen. And I got really lucky with a new family and a new life.

But it was a struggle. And there were many times when I just needed a little extra help. Bebe, of course, was that help most of the time. But I got other help too. Scholarships, for one. Obviously I never sold our farm to pay for college. I told that lie about selling a house to shut people up.

The truth is, I got a scholarship from the Colorado Sibling Fund. They are a non-profit organization who provide support for people whose siblings have been lost due to violent crime. They came to see me in the hospital that first year I was back. Before I ever got adopted, even. In fact, they were the ones responsible for bringing me out of my funk. People came to see me and talked about how they lost their siblings too. I wasn't very nice to them, but they came anyway. And looking back, that was a turning point for me. They kept in contact with me, offering me that college scholarship when I was doing my senior year of homeschool.

I had a lot of help. So now it's my turn to pay it back. I took all that money that Vaughn was putting in my bank account and gave it to the charity that was helping Rosa.

And then I decided to start a new non-profit. One that will teach inner-city girls to defend themselves if they are ever attacked. No one should have to go through what I did. No girl should ever feel helpless. They may not be able to win all the battles they will fight, but they need to have a fair chance.

That's the mark I want to make on this world. To help people have a fair chance.

I think I'm over the past now. I think it's time to let it go. And that's why I'm sitting outside my Aunt Rachel's house in northeastern Colorado.

I turn the car off and wait. It doesn't take long before the curtain is parted and I see her sour face peering out at me. I don't want to go inside. I want her to come to me. And if I have to sit here all day, I will.

It takes her twelve minutes, but she finally emerges from the front door.

I get out of the car and clutch my winter coat tightly around me as the cruel prairie wind whips past my face.

"What do you want?" she calls out as she steps down off the front stoop. "I told you to stay away from us."

I reach into my pocket and pull out the envelope. "I just wanted to give this to you."

She takes a few steps forward. "What is it? Court papers?"

"No." I shake my head at her. "Open it."

She eyes me suspiciously, but she stretches out her hand and I place it in her palm. Her wary look never falters, even as she opens the envelope, removes the papers, and reads them.

"Why?" she finally asks.

"Because…" I take a deep breath. "Because I'm not Daisy Bryndle. I'm Grace Kinsella Asher. And that farm does not belong to me."

She stares at me, but her frown never wavers. "You want me to say thank you?"

"No." I shake my head again. "I just want to give that to you and say goodbye." And then I turn and walk the few paces to my rental car and get back inside.

She watches me back out of the driveway, but she never lifts her hand to wave.

I'm not sure why she blames me for what happened. I was a child and did the best I could. But it's not worth my time to even worry about it anymore.

Let her have the farm. I don't want it and hopefully this gesture will help her move on as well.

No one should spend so many years being so miserable.

Epilogue - Grace

#PerfectionComesInManyPackages

ONE WEEK LATER

"I'M home!" I call out as I enter the house. "Vaughn?" His car is in the garage. I know he's here, but the house is almost dark. And too quiet for someone to be here. It feels… empty. I make my way to the kitchen and set down the bags of groceries. "Vaughn?" I try again.

That's when I notice the note on the fridge. Only the light over the oven is on, so I can't make out what it says from here.

I sigh. "It's Christmas Eve, for fuck's sake." The movie was supposed to wrap last week, but they're behind schedule. I didn't figure they'd be this behind though. I've kept myself busy with work all week to keep my mind off our upcoming vacation to Saint Thomas, but the truth is, I'm so excited I can't stand it.

I put the groceries away and then grab the note and turn on the overhead light.

Good evening, sweets!

I smile so hard at that. God, I love him.

I got home early, so I decided to go on ahead and start our vacation without you. Don't worry, there's a driver waiting for you outside.

I run over to the front door and peek out. Sure enough, there's headlights shining in at me. I look back down at the note, biting my lip to stop the smile. What is he up to?

He will take you to the plane and I'll see you in a few hours.

Love, Asher

Fucking Asher.

P.S. I have picked out your clothes. They're in a box on the bed.

Hmmm. I run to the bedroom and see the box. It's just like the one he sent me on Saint Thomas. I'm so excited to go back there and relive our first date. I chuckle a little at that.

I want to do all of it. The beach. The forest. The restaurant—minus the parents, of course. They won't be there. And the fun spanking I never got. I'm so excited!

I pull on the black ribbon wrapped around the shiny white box and it dissolves into a puddle of satin. I lift off the lid and the paper inside makes a little whooshing sound.

Inside is… not what I expected. It's the blue dress I wore to Kristi's rehearsal dinner in Vegas. I lift up another layer of paper and find my crappy Target shoes. What the hell?

My cell phone rings in the other room, so I get up and race into the kitchen to catch the call. Vaughn. "My prince?" I ask the phone.

"The one and only," he says back. "Did you find my gift?"

"I did. But it was not what I was expecting."

"Hmmm. You need to trust me. Don't pack anything, it's all taken care of. I'll see you in a couple hours."

And then he hangs up.

"More like a shitload of hours," I tell the silent phone. I pout a little, unhappy that I have to travel all the way to Saint Thomas alone. But I don't want to spoil his preparations, so I put the dress on and manage to drag the zipper up after contorting myself into a pretzel.

I slip into my heels and grab my purse.

The driver takes me to the jet and I wonder, if I'm on the jet, how did Vaughn get to the island? But I don't ponder too much. I'm tired from work, and there's champagne chilling in the bucket next to the seat I like to sit in when we travel.

The staff pours me a drink and offers me food once we take flight.

I accept it gladly. Because I'm starved. And then, after about thirty minutes, I kick my shoes off and settle under a blanket to sleep away the long flight.

"MRS. Asher," the attendant says, shaking my shoulder gently. "We're here, ma'am."

"What?" I ask, sitting up. "But we just took off."

"Yes, ma'am. Las Vegas is a very short flight."

"Las Vegas? But I thought we were going to Saint Thomas?"

"No, ma'am. That's tomorrow night. Tonight you're staying at the Bellagio with Mr. Asher. He's already there. Your concierge is waiting for you in the limo outside."

I realize the door to the plane is already open and the cool desert air is flowing into the plane. "OK." I can go with the flow.

I get in the car and there's Carl. I remember him from our last Vegas disaster. He was very helpful when we wanted to change Kristi's wedding.

"Carl?" I ask him.

"Mrs. Asher," he says back with a smile. "I'm to escort you to the hotel and lead you to your first clue."

"Clue?"

"Yes, ma'am. Mr. Asher left me specific instructions to give you clues as to where you will find him tonight."

I have to turn away so I can process this. What is he doing? I spend the next thirty minutes wondering, going out of my mind with curiosity, and declaring my love to my husband internally over and over again.

I have a feeling…

"We're here," Carl finally says. The driver gets out and opens my door and Carl meets me, and then offers his arm so he can escort me inside. We walk between the large Asian lion statues and into the lobby of the very festive Bellagio Hotel.

I allow Carl to lead me and after a few minutes we end up on the terrace that overlooks the fountains. It's empty and when I look around for other people, Carl says, "Mr. Asher made sure this night would be completely private months ago."

My mind is spinning with possibilities. "You said I get a clue?"

"Yes, ma'am." He pulls a sealed envelope out of his pocket and hands it to me with a smile.

"Thank you." My hands are shaking with anticipation as I take it from him and tear it open.

Princess,

    This was where we came first. Do you remember what you said?
Love,
Your prince

I stare out at the view. At the people gathered around to watch the nightly show. "There's too many people, that's what I said." I look over at Carl, just to make sure he doesn't think I'm crazy. "I told him this wasn't private enough. We needed a place that was just for us."

Carl smiles and nods. "Yes, ma'am, that's what you said."

"Were you there?" I ask, surprised.

"Yes. I'm a wedding officiator as well as a concierge."

"You married us?"

He nods again and his genuine smile eases my nerves a little. "I did. Mr. Asher is waiting for you in the exact spot where you were married. I'm to accompany you, but you have to remember where you got married to find him."

"Where did we go?" I tap my finger on the ledge of the balcony and wait, but he doesn't answer me.

After more than a full minute of silence he prods me. "You're a wedding planner. Where would one have a wedding here?"

"The gardens are a pretty place." But that feels too generic. I mean, flowers? Really? Is that all I could come up with? "The pools?" But no. How stupid to have a wedding at a pool, even a Bellagio pool. "I don't know. Our room?"

When I look over at Carl, he's smiling.

"We got married in our room?" It makes me laugh a little as I end my sentence. "Please, don't tell me I was naked."

He clears his throat.

"Oh my God, was I naked?"

"No, ma'am. You were not."

"So Vaughn is in our room?" I start walking across the terrace, but Carl's hand reaches out and stops me.

"Do you remember anything else? Your dress?"

I stare at him and then look down at my clothes. "I got married in this, didn't I?"

He nods. "Minus the shoes. You said your dogs were barking."

I turn away and chuckle. "I wish I had a picture."

"Mr. Asher was afraid the media would get a hold of them. But he said, if you want, he can arrange it for tonight." Carl pauses to see if I'll answer him. "Would you like pictures of tonight?"

"Are we getting married?"

"I think that's up to you."

"Is he waiting in the room?"

"Yes, he is. But he wanted me to ask if you'd like a real dress this time. I've got the shops open for you and a selection of dresses waiting for your choosing."

Do I want a dress? "No. I don't want a dress. Like it or not, this was my wedding dress."

"I understand." And then he offers me his arm again. "Shall we go upstairs?"

I only vaguely remember nodding my head and letting him lead me away. My stomach flutters inside and I feel a little lightheaded.

Vaughn Asher is waiting for me. He's waiting to marry me. He flew me here on his private jet and he's trying to recreate our wedding night. Good God, he is the perfect man.

When we get off the elevator on our floor, Carl leans into my ear. "I'm going to wait here until you're ready. Do you remember your vows?"

"Vows?"

He smiles at me and urges me to walk forward to the Grand Lakeview Suite that we were in back in September. "Don't worry, ma'am. It will come back to you."

I walk forward, trying to put that last question out of my head. And when I reach the door, I notice that it's propped open with the swing-latch. I push the heavy door open, step inside, and then let it fall closed behind me.

I can see him standing at the end of the long hallway, backlit by the spectacular Bellagio fountains. He's got on a black tux. Maybe even the one he was wearing that night because it was the premiere for *Invisible Man 2*. His hands are folded in front of him, and he's smiling so wide I can't help but smile back.

"Mrs. Asher."

"Mr. Asher."

He steps forward and meets me halfway, then takes my hand and leads me over to the dining table where there's a spectacular array of fruits and bite-sized morsels. "You liked this part, right?"

I nod as I stare up at his blue eyes. "I did."

And then he points down to the sheepskin rug. "And that as well, correct?"

I sigh as I think about lying on the rug with him that night. I was drunk. The room was spinning a bit. But this fur felt so damn good I did not care about anything else but lying down on it. "The sheepskin rug makes everything better."

"I love that you love it."

I bend my knee to lower myself down on the rug, but he pulls me back up. "No, sweets. You misunderstand." And then he guides me to the chair. "It's your turn to sit and my turn to kneel."

I think I might cry as he urges me to sit and then I cover my mouth with my hand as he gets down on one knee and presents me with a turquoise blue box.

"Grace Kinsella. I didn't do this right the first time. I never asked you properly."

He's spinning me around the terrace and I'm laughing. Partly because I'm drunk and partly because it feels so good to be happy. He makes me so damn happy.

"Why are you smiling?" he asks, stopping the twirl to pull me towards him. My hands go to his hard chest, pressing up against his muscles like they want to ward him off. But I don't want to ward him off at all. I want him to hold me close.

"Because I'm happy."

"I love to make you happy. I could make you happy forever, you know. I could be your prince."

"I think you could too."

He unleashes a dimpled smile that stuns me silent. "I think you should make me legally required to make you happy, Kinsella."

"How does one go about doing that, Asher?"

"One makes it legally binding though a very special happiness ceremony. I promise to make you happy and you promise to let me."

"Hmmm." I laugh. "I like that promise."

"So say yes."

"Yes."

"No," he says frowning a little. "I mean, really say yes."

"Yes, Mr. Asher, I will marry you. That is what you meant, right?"

"That's what I meant. I'm in more than like with you, Grace. I'm in love. I'm so fucking in love with you. I want you more than anything.

I want to keep you forever and never let you go. I might want to make you have my babies and be my best friend, too."

My shoulders relax. Like every bit of stress in my life evaporates in that instant as I listen to him. The fountains are still putting on their show behind him. The horns are honking on the Strip. And the wind is gently blowing my hair so it drags across my face.

He gently swipes a finger and catches my blowing hair and tucks it behind my ear. "Please mean it. Do you mean it?"

His shirt is open in the front, his bow tie, just a hanging bit of cloth around his collar now. I touch his stomach. His perfect stomach. "You're built like a god, do you know that"

He cups my face with his hands. "Grace, I'm fucking dying here, sweets. Be my wife. I can't leave here without you. I can't. I've never wanted a woman so much in all my life. And I don't want you just for sex, Grace. I want you for that and more. I want you for lying in bed naked on a Sunday afternoon. I want to cook dinners with you. I want to buy a puppy together and give him a ridiculous name, like Boris or Dave. Please, be mine, Grace."

"Jesus Christ, Kinsella, you're gonna give me a heart attack. I asked you if you'd marry me. Are you gonna say yes?"

I watch his eyes as they search mine, so filled with anxiety over my decision. "No," I say softly.

His smile fades. "What?"

I shake my head. "I won't marry you again, Vaughn. Because... because we don't need a do-over."

He drops his head to his chest and waits me out.

"I don't want to marry you again, Vaughn. I remember that night now."

He looks up quickly. "You do?"

"You said…"

"Grace, I know you've had a hard life. I know some of your secrets—" My panic must be evident, because he lays both palms flat against my cheeks and kisses me softly. "Not everything, princess. Not everything. But some."

"I don't want to talk about it. Not now. I only want to talk about happy things. But tomorrow, maybe. Just give me one happy night and I'll tell you tomorrow. Be my prince, Vaughn. Be my prince and make me your princess and then I can deal with reality. But tonight, I just want the fairytale."

"And then I called in Carl," Vaughn says as he opens the Tiffany's box and presents me with the rings. There's three in there. One giant engagement ring, platinum. Easily a three-carat diamond, big, but not too big. And two platinum wedding bands. "They have inscriptions," he says as he takes his out of the velvet cushion. "Read mine."

He holds it out and I take it from him, tilting it in the light just so, until the writing becomes clear. "The Prince." I laugh. And then I look him in the eye and slip it on his finger.

"Read yours now," he sighs.

I take it and hold it under the light. "The Princess." And then he holds up the engagement ring so we can read it together.

"The Fairytale."

He slips the band on my finger, then adds the rock.

He kisses me, whispering in my mouth, "You're mine."

"I'm yours," I say back.

"No do-overs for us?"

"Never. It was perfect the first time."

THE END

END OF BOOK SHIT

Welcome to the End of Book Shit where JA Huss gets to say anything she wants about the books and you are free to either read it or not. ;)

In the Social EOBS I mostly talked about Vaughn (and my day, which BTW – It's still going… lol it's STILL THE SAME DAY FOR ME!) So in this EOBS I'm gonna talk about Grace.

I think Grace is severely underrated as a heroine. And that's mostly because this series just doesn't get the attention that other books do. Like… Rook. People love Rook. And Chella, from Taking Turns series. She's one of my favorites. But the thing that's different about Rook, Chella, and Grace, is that Rook and Chella are in a LOT of books. Granted, Grace is in these six, but that's it. Grace appears nowhere else but in this Social Media Series. Rook is in all the Rook & Ronin Books (Which is like… 8 I think?) Plus she's mentioned in a whole bunch of other ones. Even in Wasted Lust and Five. Rook has a legacy. And Chella is much the same way. Chella appears or is mentioned in Taking Turns, Turning Back, His Turn, Total Exposure, The Pleasure of

Panic, The Boyfriend Experience, and she will be in Play Dirty, even though I won't start that book until tomorrow.

I love both Rook and Chella and their worlds are big and broad. So I bring them back whenever I can.

I love Grace just as much. I think Grace is a true fighter. She never let anyone save her. Never. And she picked herself up and brought it, man. She bought it. But her world is much smaller. So people get the two books and then… that's it. That's all there is of Grace. I had originally planned to keep this world going with Conner, but other ideas got in the way and it's always better to start a new series if you get that itch. Gives new readers an entry point into my books and just makes more sense. Spin-off series are mostly for fans who want more. New series are mostly for new readers.

Grace was an unexpected surprise when I wrote her. I had the dirty tweeting thing when I started but I didn't know this series would get so damn twisty. It was my number one goal when I started it to MAKE IT AN EASY, FUN, NON-TWISTY READ. Like seriously, that was my goal.

As you can see, I completely failed at that!

Lol

Because this really is a stressful plot in the second half of the series.

Back when I wrote this I didn't mention who my real-life inspiration was, but I'll tell you now that this Grace character was loosely based on Elizabeth Smart and the horrible ordeal she went through when she was kidnapped out of her house in the middle of the night. So there's a few similarities with that case, but there was also a case in a town where I used to work of a kid who killed his parents and siblings. So it was kind of a combination of those two real-life cases.

If you've read my Mister Series then you know I got that twisted plot from another real-life case. But if you think I plan this stuff out ahead of time, you're wrong. When I started Social Media Grace was somewhat shy, had a secret in her past (but I didn't know what it was) and loved to talk dirty on Twitter. That's all I knew. All the other stuff comes as I write. I call myself a plotter but in reality I'm more of a seat-of-my-pants writer than I like to admit.

In the author world we call a person who doesn't plot every detail, but instead lets the story come to them as they go, a "Pantster" from the seat-of-my-pants expression.

I am not a true punster because I follow a very organized plot line – meaning I know how many words each book will be before I start so I know exactly where to put all the major moments.

When you plot a continuing series (as opposed to a standalone series) you have to plot the entire series just like you plot one book. All the critical points have to be in each book, but over the course of the series you also have to have all those plot points across the entire story from Book One to Book Six.

I love writing this way, but sadly lots of readers hate a cliffy. I think if you release quick and often like I do, then cliffies are OK. (By the way, Johnathan McClain and I just wrote a continuing series called Original Sin, so if you like a long series with a cliffy at the end of each book, all four of those books have been released and you can binge it just like you do Netflix!)

So writing and releasing the Social Media series in short two-week intervals met all those requirements for a continuing series. It was a lot of fun, the fans enjoyed the wait (because it was short!) and when it was all over I had...

A REALLY GREAT STORY.

That's my main takeaway from this series. I loved the progression of both Grace and Vaughn as they came to terms with themselves and each other, found common ground and equality, and then left the past behind where it belongs.

Maybe one day I will return to this Social Media world. Never say never. And if I do, I'll probably write it the same way as I did in 2014.

No regerts. (lol – regerts!)

WANT TO TRY ANOTHER SERIES?
CHOOSE ONE
THE MISTERS
(5-Book Standalone Series & 2 Spin-Offs)
ROOK & RONIN
(First Book Free!)
THE TURNING SERIES
(If You Like Menage, This One's For You!)

If you'd like to chat about this story I have a private spoiler group just for all the Filthy Blue Birds on Facebook. Just search for it and ask to join and one of us will add you when we see the request.

Thank you for reading, thank you for reviewing, and I'll see you in the next book!

Julie
JA Huss

About the Author

JA Huss is the New York Times Bestselling author of 321 and has been on the USA Today Bestseller's list 21 times in the past four years. She writes characters with heart, plots with twists, and perfect endings.

Her books have sold millions of copies all over the world, the audio version of her semi-autobiographical book, Eighteen, was nominated for a Voice Arts Award and an Audie Award in 2016 and 2017 respectively, her audiobook, Mr. Perfect, was nominated for a Voice Arts Award in 2017, and her audiobook, Taking Turns, was nominated for an Audie Award in 2018.

She lives on a ranch in Central Colorado with her family.